THE SPIES OF
HARTLAKE HALL

THE SPIES OF HARTLAKE HALL

R. L. Graham

MACMILLAN

First published 2025 by Macmillan
an imprint of Pan Macmillan
The Smithson, 6 Briset Street, London EC1M 5NR
EU representative: Macmillan Publishers Ireland Ltd, 1st Floor,
The Liffey Trust Centre, 117–126 Sheriff Street Upper,
Dublin 1 D01 YC43
Associated companies throughout the world

ISBN 978-1-0350-2195-6 HB
ISBN 978-1-0350-6402-1 TPB

1 3 5 7 9 8 6 4 2

A CIP catalogue record for this book is available from the British Library.

Typeset in Janson Text by Six Red Marbles UK, Thetford, Norfolk
Printed and bound in the UK using 100% Renewable Electricity by CPI Group (UK) Ltd

Visit **www.panmacmillan.com** to read more about all our books
and to buy them.

*To the friends, family and colleagues who
have helped me through the darkness,
and to Marilyn, who is always there.*

Hartlake Hall
Tudeley
Kent

1

'GOOD MORNING, MRS Vane. I say, it's rather chilly in here. You should light a fire.'

Jonquil Vane looked up from the keys of her typewriter. An unremarkable-looking woman in her mid-thirties, she wore a shapeless overcoat, fingerless gloves and a scarf around her neck. 'There is a fire,' she said, nodding towards the tiny, inadequate fireplace where lumps of coal smouldered feebly. 'There are also gaps around the windows that you could drive a cart through, and a thirty-knot wind from the east. What can I do for you, Mr Kingston?'

Kingston, a balding man in a badly fitting blue uniform with a single wavy gold stripe on each sleeve, consulted the note in his hand. 'When you've a moment, Mrs Vane, we need a few things from the stationery cupboard. Five reams of foolscap, if we may, and twenty bound notebooks. Oh, and a couple of boxes of pencils. If it's not too much bother,' he added apologetically.

'It's no bother,' said Mrs Vane. 'I'll fetch them now.'

The officer hesitated for a moment. 'You know, Mrs Vane, I'm sure it's jolly boring for you to have to keep hopping up and down whenever we need anything. If the stationery cupboard was left unlocked, we could just help ourselves whenever we wanted. We wouldn't have to keep disturbing you.'

Mrs Vane opened her desk and took out a set of keys. 'It is precisely because you fellows have a habit of helping yourselves whenever you want, to whatever you want, that the stationery cupboard *is* locked. It may have escaped your notice, but there is a war on.'

Kingston looked hurt. 'It's only a few bits of paper,' he said defensively.

'All for the want of a horseshoe nail,' said Mrs Vane. 'Shoo. I'll bring your paper and pencils along directly.'

Obediently, Kingston departed. Mrs Vane went out of her office, closing the door and locking it behind her. The corridor was bare, with distempered white walls and harsh electric lighting that made her eyes ache. Cigarette smoke drifted like haze in the air. Descending the stairs to the first floor, she walked along another corridor to the stationery cupboard, where she inserted her key in the lock and turned the knob.

The door refused to open.

Frowning, she tried again, and then a third time, leaning her weight on the door. Still it did not budge.

'For heaven's sake,' she muttered to herself.

On her feet were a pair of strong leather boots, unladylike but practical in the harsh winter weather. She raised one foot and stamped against the door. Nothing happened. She kicked it again, harder. Another man in uniform looked out from the office across the corridor. 'What the devil is going on?' he demanded.

'The door is jammed,' said Mrs Vane. 'Can you give me a hand?'

The officer, who was strongly built and looked like he might have played rugby for his school, approached the door and kicked it very hard. This time it moved, by perhaps half an inch. A few more heavy blows and the gap widened to a couple of feet. Mrs Vane tapped the officer on the arm. 'That's good enough. I can squeeze in now.'

'You want to call a fitter,' the officer said. 'Get him to put a drop of oil on those hinges.'

'Good idea. Thank you.'

The man went back into his own office and closed the door. Mrs Vane stepped into the stationery cupboard, turned on the electric light, and stopped abruptly. 'Sweet Jesus,' she said under her breath.

The room was large, rather larger than the name 'cupboard' might imply, perhaps twenty feet by ten, its walls lined with tall wooden shelves, with one door and no windows. The shelves were lined with boxes and cartons of stationery. All was as it should be, apart from the man in navy uniform lying face up on the linoleum floor, almost at Mrs Vane's feet. His face was blank white. Bloodshot eyes, dark and expressionless, stared up at the ceiling.

She took a deep breath. *Steady*, she told herself. *This is part of your job. You were trained for this.* The first priority was to close the door and make sure no one else saw the body; sealing off the scene, they had called it during her training course six months ago. Still tingling with shock, she turned and closed the door. As she did so, she saw that the door had been jammed from the inside with a small wedge of wood. Frowning, she put the wedge into her coat pocket.

She knelt beside the body and touched the man's neck just in case there might still be a pulse. As she expected, there was none; the waxy face and blank eyes had already told their own story. The man's skin was cold to the touch. *Dead for some time,* she thought.

Something caught her eye, a glint of silver between the fingers of the man's right hand. Lifting the dead hand carefully, she saw a small metal and glass syringe lying on the floor. She lowered the hand again, her face thoughtful.

The cuff of the man's left shirt sleeve, protruding from under the uniform coat, was unfastened. She looked more closely and saw a smear of blue ink on the smooth white cotton fabric. Carefully pulling back the cuff, she found a series of letters, *Thr. of Sat.*, followed by two sequences of numbers: *2030 2417*.

Still kneeling, she began to go through the man's pockets. She found nothing at first, and that in itself was strange; no keys, no money, no identification papers. Frowning, she reached inside the breast pocket of his uniform and found a small manila envelope. She drew it out, and felt another shock as she saw the MOST SECRET stamp on the outside. The envelope contained a single sheet of paper covered in rows of numbers.

130	13042	13401	8501	115	3528	416	17214	6491	11310
18147	18222	21560	10247	11518	23677	13605	3494	14936	
98092	5905	11311	10392	10371	0302	21290	5161	39695	
23571	17504	11269	18276	18101	0317	0228	17694	4473	
22284	22200	19452	21589	67893	5569	13918	8958	12137	
1333	4725	4458	5905	17166	13851	4458	17149	14471	6706
13850	12224	6929	14991	7382	15857	67893	14218	36477	
5870	17553	67893	5870	5454	16102	15217	22801	17183	
21001	17388	7446	23638	18222	6719	14331	15021	23845	
3156	23552	22096	21604	4797	9497	22464	20855	4377	
23610	18140	22260	5905	13347	20420	39689	13732	20677	
6929	5275	18507	52262	1340	22049	13339	11265	22295	
10439	14814	4178	6992	8784	7632	7357	6926	52262	11267
21100	21272	9346	9559	22464	15874	18502	18500	15857	
2188	5376	7381	98082	16127	13486	9350	9220	76036	14219
5144	2831	17920	11347	17142	11264	7667	7762	15099	9110
10482	97556	3569	3670						

'Dear God,' Mrs Vane said quietly.

She put the paper and envelope into her pocket, rose swiftly and went out, closing the door and locking it behind her. Back in her own office she picked up the telephone receiver and dialled a number.

The call was answered almost at once. 'Officer of the watch.'

'Commander Colson,' Mrs Vane said. 'There is something you need to see.'

Commander George Colson was a tall man in a beautifully tailored naval uniform and a carefully cultivated aura of authority. A senior officer in the naval intelligence division, he was at the moment officer of the watch, responsible for overseeing all operations within the division, including security. He looked impatient as Mrs Vane unlocked the door to the stationery room which, freed of the wedge, now opened smoothly. 'This way,' she said, motioning him inside and closing the door behind them.

Colson stood motionless for a moment, staring down at the body. Mrs Vane noticed for the first time how young the dead man was. She thought about the millions who had died over the past two and a half years, blown up, gassed, shot, drowned, and wondered at the bathos of this man dying in a stationery cupboard surrounded by paper clips and pens.

'Any idea who he is?' Colson asked finally.

'No. I've never seen him before, and he has no papers.' She handed over the manila envelope. 'The only thing in his pockets was this.'

Colson opened the envelope, and she watched the blood drain from his face. 'God's truth!' the commander said. 'This came from Admiral Hall's safe!'

'I know,' said Mrs Vane, taking the papers and returning them to the envelope. 'I put it there myself.'

Colson looked again at the body. His authority had deserted him for the moment, and he seemed dazed. 'How in hell did it end up *here*?'

'An excellent question,' said Mrs Vane, and she waited.

Colson drew a deep breath. 'Right. Well. At least we've recovered it. Return it to the safe as soon as possible, Mrs Vane, and we'll have to hope that no harm has been done.'

'I'm afraid it's too late for that,' Mrs Vane said sharply. 'Has it not occurred to you, commander, that this man may have been murdered? And if so, that whoever killed him will also have seen the telegram?'

'Jesus,' said the commander. He rubbed his forehead. 'Wait a moment. This room is always kept locked, am I right?'

'Yes.'

'Then if someone killed him, how did they get out? No, it can't have been murder, Mrs Vane. This fellow must have had some sort of accident, or . . . Who knows, perhaps he committed suicide.'

Mrs Vane looked down at the body, thinking about the syringe concealed beneath the dead hand. What had made Colson think of suicide? 'Regardless of how he died, Commander, the telegram was still taken. That means we have a security breach. Shall I inform the admiral?'

Colson hesitated. 'Was anyone with you when you found the body?'

'No,' said Mrs Vane. 'You and I are the only people who know about this.'

'Then let's keep it that way, at least for the moment. I'll inform Blinker myself, once we know the score.'

'What do you propose to do?' Mrs Vane asked.

Colson was silent for a few moments, looking around the room. Mrs Vane saw the expression on his face, hesitation bordering on panic. *This isn't just a security breach*, she thought. *For you, Commander, this is a full-scale disaster.*

'We're the naval intelligence division of the Admiralty, not Scotland Yard,' Colson said finally. 'We need a professional sleuth.'

'Bringing in an outsider will be risky,' Mrs Vane warned. 'Like you said, the fewer people who know, the better.'

'I know a man in the secret service who will be discreet. I've worked with him before, and we can trust him.'

Mrs Vane nodded. 'Shall I contact Colonel Kell?'

'Yes. Tell him I need Patrick Gallagher here, as soon as possible.'

2

THE SUN HAD just risen and an icy wind was blowing down Whitehall, stirring up dust and whirling scraps of newspaper along the street. Cold light washed across the elegant white columns and red-brick façade of the Admiralty Building.

One of the pieces of newspaper bore a headline: GERMANY ANNOUNCES UNRESTRICTED SUBMARINE WARFARE. Gallagher paused for a moment, looking at the stark black words. The news was expected, but hardly welcome. If Germany resumed its policy of sinking merchant ships without warning, vital supplies of food and oil could soon dry up. The war had been raging for two and a half years with neither side able to gain advantage, but now it felt like the tide was beginning to turn against Britain and her allies.

A messenger, a grey-haired man leaning on a stick, waited outside the Admiralty gates. 'Mr Gallagher? I'll need to see your identity card, sir.'

Gallagher handed over a printed card. The messenger nodded. 'Be pleased to follow me, sir.'

The Royal Marine sentries snapped to attention and saluted as they passed. Just for a moment, Gallagher felt nostalgic. As a boy he had joined the marines himself, and although he had handed in his uniform seventeen years ago, the memories were still there. He touched the old scar on his temple. *Once a boot-neck, always a bootneck*, he thought.

The messenger limped heavily, leaning on his stick. 'You'll have to forgive me for being slow, sir,' he said as they crossed the courtyard.

'Not at all. Were you a navy man?'

'Yes, sir. I was in the old *Hecla*, and then with the Naval Brigade in the Sudan. I got a bullet in the hip at El Teb. That was the end of my naval career.'

'Hard luck.'

'Not really, sir. Not when you think of all those poor lads who perished at Jutland. More than twelve hundred men died when the *Queen Mary* blew up.'

Something in his tone caught Gallagher's attention. 'You knew someone on the *Queen Mary*?'

'My son, sir.'

The *Queen Mary* was – had been – a battlecruiser, destroyed by a catastrophic explosion in the opening hours of the Battle of Jutland the previous year. Once, Gallagher would have offered his condolences, but no one did that any more; not now, not when everyone had lost a son, or a brother, or a father at sea, or at Gallipoli, or on the Somme. He kept his silence.

'Bad news in the papers, sir,' the messenger said after a moment. 'About the submarines, I mean. I fear we may be facing some difficult times.'

'Yes,' said Gallagher.

The messenger spoke again, echoing the thought that was already in Gallagher's mind. 'It's all or nothing now, isn't it, sir? Everything depends on two questions. Will Russia leave the war? And will the Americans join it?'

'If you can answer either of those questions, you'll be a rich man,' Gallagher said.

'Aye, sir. But I'd have nothing to spend it on.'

The porters at the door touched their caps in salute. Gallagher followed the messenger into the great hall, up the broad staircase to the first floor and along a corridor to a door with a sign saying STRICTLY NO ENTRANCE. The messenger pushed it open and led the way into the watchkeeper's office. 'Welcome to the naval intelligence division, sir. If you care to sign the entrance log, I will take you to Commander Colson.'

A young sub-lieutenant handed over the entrance log and Gallagher signed it, adding the date and time of his arrival. The messenger nodded. 'This way, sir, if you please.'

Colson was waiting in the stationery room, accompanied by a woman in a grey coat. 'Gallagher,' the commander said abruptly. 'Good of you to come. This is Mrs Vane, Admiral Hall's secretary.'

Rear-Admiral Hall, known throughout the navy by his nickname 'Blinker', was the director of the naval intelligence division. Gallagher nodded briefly; the woman said nothing.

Gallagher stood for a moment, looking around the bare little room, taking in the plain ceiling, the flickering electric light bulb, the stacked shelves obscuring the walls. Wrapping a handkerchief around his fingers, he knelt beside the dead man and studied the body for a moment. A young man, he thought, late twenties perhaps, though with crow's-feet wrinkles at the corners of his eyes; signs of hard living, perhaps, or just someone who had spent a lot of time out of doors. There was a small mole on his neck, just above the shirt collar.

'Do we know who he is?' Gallagher asked.

Colson said nothing. 'I've never seen him before,' said Mrs Vane.

'Who found the body?'

'I did,' said Mrs Vane. She related briefly what had happened.

Carefully, Gallagher lifted the corpse's head, noting the blood-shot eyes, and opened the jaws and peered into the mouth, wrinkling his nose at the smell. Lowering the head again, he lifted the dead man's right hand and saw the syringe, but did not comment. He picked up the left arm and pulled up the sleeves of both coat and shirt, pausing for a moment when he saw the writing on the shirt cuff. In the soft skin in the crook of the elbow he found what he was looking for, a small red puncture mark.

Another rush of memories flooded through his mind. I've seen this before, he thought. Cape Cod, the night of the hurricane. The code, the locked room, the syringe, the faked suicide. Only that time the victim was a woman.

'What killed him?' asked Mrs Vane.

'We'll need a post-mortem to be certain, but it looks like he was injected with an opiate. Morphine, or perhaps heroin.'

'That was my first guess,' she said. 'But the eyes didn't look right.'

Colson looked at her sharply. 'You have medical training, Mrs Vane?'

'Some,' she said. She did not elaborate.

Gallagher lifted the dead man's head once more, feeling around the skull. 'You were looking for miosis? You're right, the drug causes the pupils to contract, but after death they usually relax to their normal state. A medic would explain it more clearly with longer words, but that is fundamentally what happens. Was the door locked when you arrived?'

'Yes. It had also been wedged from the inside.'

Gallagher paused for a moment, frowning, his fingers resting behind the dead man's ear. 'Who else has a key to this room, Mrs Vane?'

'No one. Access is restricted in order to prevent the staff from pilfering. You'd be amazed at what people will steal.'

'I spent several years with the police,' Gallagher said. 'So, no, I wouldn't. Where is the key when you are off-duty?'

'Locked in my desk in my office. To save you asking, both desk and office were still locked this morning, and the locks had not been tampered with. The key was in the drawer where it always is.'

Gallagher looked around the room. 'No window, no other exits from the room,' he said, half to himself. 'Someone else could have taken the key and locked the door behind them, but they couldn't have wedged the door from the inside. Alternatively, someone else could have locked the door from the outside and our man wedged it from the inside, but . . . Why would he do that? It makes no sense.'

'I am convinced that this is suicide,' Colson said. 'If he wedged the door himself, he must have taken his own life. It's the only explanation.'

Gallagher coughed, covering his mouth with his hand. 'If someone wanted to end it all, Commander, there are easier and more convenient places to do so. Also, there is only one needle mark on his arm, meaning that this man was not a habitual user of injected drugs. Why would he choose this method of killing himself? He was an officer and a gentleman, or so his uniform would seem to indicate. Why not do the gentlemanly thing and blow his brains out with a revolver?'

The commander looked down at the body, swallowing suddenly. 'Also,' Gallagher continued, 'there is a contusion on the side of his skull, just above the right ear.'

'What does that mean?' Colson asked.

'It means he was hit with something, probably some sort of cosh. Once he had been knocked out and could make no resistance, the person who hit him injected him, emptied his pockets of anything that might identify him, and departed. He was murdered, Commander. I have no doubt of that.'

There was a moment of silence while this sank in. 'But how did the killer leave the room?' Colson asked. 'You said it yourself, he couldn't have wedged the door after he left the room. It makes absolutely no sense.'

Gallagher coughed again. 'Oh, there will be a logical explanation, of course. There always is. The more important questions are, first, who is this man, and second, what was he doing in the stationery cupboard in the first place?' He paused. 'Is there anything else, Commander? Anything you haven't told me?'

Colson hesitated. Mrs Vane took a step forward. 'You said you could trust Mr Gallagher,' she said. 'He needs to know.'

The commander took a deep breath. 'I said there was nothing in his pockets that could identify him, but there was one thing. A telegram.'

'A telegram? From whom?'

'The German foreign ministry,' Colson said.

There was a pause. 'Can you tell me anything more?' Gallagher asked.

'No. Admiral Hall has given strict orders. I'm only telling you now on condition that you keep the matter absolutely secret. No one outside of Room 40 is even supposed to know of the telegram's existence.'

Gallagher raised his eyebrows. 'Nevertheless, someone does know,' he said. 'Someone found out about it and tried to steal it. Commander, I will need you to keep everyone away from this room. Tell your staff there has been a water leak. Mrs Vane, perhaps I could trouble you to put a call through to our office? Tell them, please, that I need the plumbers at the Admiralty Building.'

'Plumbers?' Colson said sharply.

'Our specialist team who deal with these situations. They will remove the body and send it for an immediate post-mortem. We have a man in Harley Street who arranges these things.'

'Very well, but make sure they are discreet.' Colson stared at the body again. 'I can't believe it,' he said. 'I simply can't believe it. This is a bloody nightmare.'

Gallagher looked at him. 'What can't you believe, Commander?'

Colson swallowed suddenly. 'I don't—'

A sudden knock at the door interrupted him, startling them all. 'Commander Colson, sir,' called the messenger. 'There's a Captain Ryder in the watchkeeper's office. He's asking to see you, sir.'

Colson swore under his breath. 'Just when I thought this day couldn't get any worse.' He raised his voice a little. 'What does he want?'

'There's a rumour going round the building that a body has been found, sir. Captain Ryder thinks he may be able to identify him.'

Inside the room, the three of them looked at each other. 'I told no one except you, Commander,' said Mrs Vane.

'And I told no one at all,' Colson said. 'How in hell's name did Ryder get to hear of it?'

'Who is he?' Gallagher asked.

'Merrick Ryder, deputy director of the naval planning division. Thinks he's God Almighty.'

'Naval planning? What do they have to do with intelligence?'

'Nothing. They're in charge of forecasting how many ships we need, what supplies we need and where, that sort of thing. But Ryder is a protégé of Admiral Jellicoe, so he sticks his nose in everywhere. How do we get rid of him?'

'We don't,' said Gallagher. 'If he knows that a body has been found, there is no point in our trying to conceal it. And if he really can identify our dead man, it will save us a great deal of time.'

The commander hesitated again. He tries to wield an air of authority, Gallagher thought, but he can't quite hide his own weakness.

'Very well,' Colson said. 'Messenger! Escort the captain here, as soon as may be.'

CAPTAIN MERRICK RYDER was big and broad-shouldered with a shock of fair hair, and an impressive row of medal ribbons on his uniform coat. To Gallagher's not unprejudiced eye, he looked like a games master at a minor public school. He had a games master's arrogance, too. 'Colson,' he said, looking at Mrs Vane and Gallagher. 'Who are the civilians?'

'Mr Gallagher from the secret service, and Mrs Vane, Admiral Hall's secretary. She's the one who found the body.'

Ryder looked unimpressed. 'Thank you for your services, Mrs Vane. You may go.'

'She stays,' Gallagher said. 'She's one of us.'

There was a moment of silence. 'What do you mean?' Ryder demanded.

'She is an agent of the secret service,' Gallagher said. 'She is indeed Admiral Hall's secretary, but she reports to the head of our service, Colonel Kell.'

Colson found his voice. 'The secret service is running an operation inside the naval intelligence division? And I was not informed? This is scandalous!'

'Sounds like someone doesn't trust you, Colson,' Ryder said. He motioned to the body. 'Is this the man? Have you identified him yet?'

'No,' said Colson, still seething. 'Gallagher, you owe me an explanation.'

'Do you remember the clerk we caught stealing documents a few months back?' Gallagher asked. 'We're following up that case. I don't know why Admiral Hall didn't tell you, Commander, but perhaps he didn't feel it was important. Please don't take it personally. And I might remind you that we have more important things to do right now. Captain Ryder? I believe you said you might be able to identify the body.'

Colson said nothing. Ryder looked directly at the body for the first time. There was a long pause. 'This is what I feared,' he said finally, and for the first time there was a trace of emotion in his voice. 'That's the man we've been looking for. Lieutenant Paul Vasiliev, one of my aides.' He shook his head. 'Poor beggar. How the devil did he end up in here?'

Gallagher frowned. *A minute ago, the corpse was nameless and mysterious*, he thought. *Now, out of the blue, it has a name and precise identity*. In his experience, that sort of thing never happened. Aloud, he said, 'That is what we are trying to establish. If I may ask, Captain Ryder, how did you learn that a dead man had been found in the Admiralty?'

Ryder was still studying the body. 'The porters told me as soon as I arrived. One of the switchboard operators overheard someone making a call, saying that there was a corpse on the premises, or words to that effect, and started spreading it around. Colson, I'm not happy about having outsiders here, even from the secret service. We need to keep this quiet until we know what in hell is going on. Pardon my language, ma'am.'

'That is exactly what I am trying to do,' Colson snapped. 'Unless you have a trained detective on your staff, Ryder, I would think even you must realize that we need help. We can trust Mr Gallagher,' he added, not without a touch of irony in his voice.

'Gallagher.' Ryder repeated the name, and a light came on in his memory. 'Wait a moment. Are you the fellow who was on the *Lusitania*?'

'One of them,' said Gallagher.

'Ah.' Ryder's manner changed. 'Terrible business, that. I was commanding officer at Haulbowline when it happened. I remember the survivors being brought into Queenstown.'

Mrs Vane stood very still, her hands clenched at her sides. 'Yes,' Gallagher said. 'So do I.'

'Well. What happened to poor Vasiliev? Heart attack?'

Gallagher shook his head. 'He was murdered.'

Ryder stared at the body again, so hard that Gallagher wondered if he was going to ask the corpse to sit up and give an explanation. 'Are you quite certain?' he asked finally.

'Yes,' said Gallagher.

'Murdered,' Ryder repeated. 'Here in the Admiralty, of all places. What a damned strange thing to happen.' He let out his breath, like a man who has just watched his star batsman go out for a duck. 'Well, Gallagher? How will you proceed?'

'What can you tell me about Vasiliev?' Gallagher asked.

'Not a great deal. I've only been in my present post for a few months, so I don't know my staff well. He mentioned once that his grandfather was a Russian nobleman, exiled after getting involved in some coup or other.'

'Did he still have connections with Russia?'

'Not that I'm aware of. Apart from his name, Vasiliev was as English as you or I. He went to a good school, I think, can't remember which one. Exemplary officer, diligent, punctual, absolutely reliable. Which made it all the more worrying when he disappeared.'

'Disappeared!' Gallagher said. 'How long had he been missing?'

'Since yesterday. He was due to attend on myself and the director of naval planning at a meeting with Admiral Jellicoe yesterday afternoon, but he didn't show up. As soon as the meeting ended, I sent men to check his lodgings and his club, but there was no sign of him.'

Admiral Sir John Jellicoe, the victor at the Battle of Jutland, had been appointed First Sea Lord, commander-in-chief of the Royal Navy, back in November. 'And when you heard that a body had been found, you thought it might be Vasiliev,' Gallagher said. 'Why? A hunch?'

Ryder's expression suggested that he was not the sort of man who relied on hunches. 'When Vasiliev went missing, I thought that he might have suffered a heart attack. He's had a bad heart for several years, apparently. Took nitro-glycerine pills every day, carried them with him everywhere. I called at his rooms, but he wasn't at home, and no one at his club had seen him either. This morning, when I heard the rumours, I realized what must have happened.'

The captain paused. 'I wasn't expecting this, though. How was he killed?'

'Injection with a fatal dose of an opiate,' Gallagher said.

'Good God,' Ryder said softly. For a moment, his face was almost compassionate. 'When did it happen?'

'The post-mortem will tell us more precisely, but I would estimate around midnight, give or take an hour or two. You say he didn't turn up for a meeting yesterday. Could he have still been at the Admiralty?'

'He must have been,' Ryder said. 'He may have been feeling unwell. Perhaps his heart really was bothering him. Poor beggar,' he repeated. 'What a lonely way to die.'

'Do you know if he had any family, Captain?' Mrs Vane asked.
'Both of his parents are dead, I believe. I'm not sure if there
is anyone else. Who is conducting the post-mortem, Gallagher?'
'We're arranging that.'
'Good. Send me a copy of the report as soon as you have it.
Colson, who was officer of the watch last night?'
'I was,' Colson said. 'I came on duty at 2200.'
Ryder's eyebrows rose. 'Really? And yet you didn't recognize
this man?'
'I don't sign everyone in personally, Ryder, I have other
duties. One of my officers oversees the watchkeeping office. If
your man signed in, his signature will be in the log.'
Ryder looked at Colson for a long moment. The games
master was back, Gallagher thought. He could almost hear the
voice: *you've let yourself down, you've let the house down* . . . Aloud,
Gallagher said, 'We will check the log. Now, if you will excuse
me, gentlemen, I need to search the room.'
Ryder nodded. 'Keep me informed, Gallagher. Report to my
office at 1800 hours on Friday and tell me what progress you
have made.'
Colson's voice was sharp once more. 'This is naval intelligence, Ryder. You have no authority here.'
'And one of my officers is dead, Colson. I am taking control
of this investigation. That is an order.'
'Damn it, Ryder, this is outrageous! I shall inform Admiral
Hall!'
'And I shall speak to Admiral Jellicoe,' Ryder snapped. 'Who,
need I remind you, is Admiral Hall's commanding officer. Do
we understand each other?'
Colson subsided. 'I am happy to report to both of you,' Gallagher said. 'But with respect, Captain, we must also be careful
about security. Someone has committed murder in the heart of

the Admiralty, and the killer may still be in the building. They may also have accomplices working with them. Do you follow my meaning?'

Ryder frowned. He clearly wished he had thought of this himself. 'Yes, I see. What do you suggest?'

'I think we should get out of London altogether. There is a shooting party this weekend at Hartlake Hall, not far from Tonbridge. We can talk discreetly there, without drawing attention to ourselves. I'll arrange for you both to be sent an invitation. By Friday evening, I will have the results of the post-mortem and whatever we can dig up on Vasiliev's background.'

'Near Tonbridge,' Ryder repeated. 'There are good train connections, I suppose. Will there be other guests at this shooting party?'

'Of course. But there is no need for them to know who we really are, or what our purpose is. They will have plenty to talk about among themselves, I'm sure.'

'And the host? He will be discreet?'

'Sir John Borden is a prominent member of the government. We can trust him. Honestly, Captain, this is the best way.' Gallagher looked around the room. 'Walls have ears, even in the Admiralty.'

Ryder nodded. 'Very well,' he said. 'Make it so.' He turned towards the door. 'Until Friday, gentlemen.'

AFTER THE OTHERS had gone, Gallagher began to search the room. The wooden shelves that lined the room were stacked with paper and notebooks, cartons of pencils and pens, bottles of ink, staplers and boxes of staples, manila envelopes, file folders, typewriter ribbons, punch cards for calculating machines, boxes of paper clips and rolls of glossy red tape, all as he would have expected. There was absolutely nothing out of the ordinary.

The shelves were mostly free-standing, some of them on wheels. He pulled them aside and studied the walls. Running his hands over the exterior wall opposite the door, he discovered a very faint indentation. He traced its line with his fingertips and found the outline of an old window, filled in and plastered over, probably many years ago. He pushed hard against the wall, but nothing moved.

The other walls were smooth white plaster, but behind the shelves on the left-hand wall was another outline, this time of an old door which again had been plastered over. The plaster had cracked in a few places, and a few chips had fallen onto the floor. He tried pushing against the wall, but it was every bit as unyielding as the blocked-up window. The ceiling was also covered in solid plaster; the scuffed parquet floor yielded no clues.

There was a knock at the door. 'Plumbers are here, sir,' said a voice.

Gallagher opened the door to admit two men in plain dark coats and flat caps, wheeling a large box with the name TOTHILL PLUMBING SERVICES stencilled on the side. He recognized both of them as secret service men. 'We've come about the leak, sir,' one of them said solemnly.

Gallagher pointed to the body. 'You know what to do.'

'Yes, sir. Leave it with us, sir.'

THE SAME YOUNG officer was still in the watchkeeper's office. He handed over the log without demur; Gallagher wondered if he had heard the rumours. There were not many visitors to naval intelligence, and it took only a few moments to find Paul Vasiliev's signature. He had signed in at 2248 the previous evening, and had not signed out.

'Did you know Lieutenant Vasiliev?' Gallagher asked.

'No, sir, I'd never met him before. I was only posted to naval intelligence a few weeks ago.'

'Did he say what he was doing here?'

'One of the teams in Room 40 had asked him to help with Russian translation, sir. There aren't many Russian speakers on the team, so they sometimes called him down to help with translations. That's what he said.'

'Did you verify this with the teams?'

The officer looked worried. 'No, sir. I didn't think I had to. Mr Vasiliev had his identity card, sir, and all seemed in order.'

'He hasn't signed out. Did no one think to check where he was?'

'Er . . . no, sir. I assumed he was still working with the team. They work very long hours, you know. Right through the night, sometimes.'

So, Vasiliev was fluent in Russian. *As English as you or I*, Gallagher thought. Interesting that Ryder had chosen to emphasise that. But then, Ryder was probably the sort of man who cared about such things.

The sub-lieutenant was staring at him, doubtless thinking he had done something wrong and was about to be punished. No point, Gallagher thought. What was done, was done. 'Thank you,' he said. 'Can you direct me to the switchboard?'

The switchboard operators had been forewarned. They denied absolutely that they had repeated anything they had overheard, that any of them had listened in on Mrs Vane's telephone call to the secret service, and that they even knew of the existence of a body on the premises. The porters, similarly cautious, admitted that they *did* know, but could not clearly recall where they had heard the news. None of this was in any way surprising.

*

MRS VANE WAS in her office, shovelling more coal onto the grate. Smoke without heat billowed through the room. Gallagher coughed. 'This is a bloody mess,' he said.

'That's one way of putting it,' Mrs Vane agreed.

'Was it you who suggested sending for me?'

'No, the commander thought of it all by himself. You must have made a good impression when you worked with him before.'

'I tried to. Is the telegram back in the admiral's safe?'

'For the moment. I've changed the combination, too, in case anyone else gets any bright ideas.' Mrs Vane frowned. 'I don't understand what happened in the stationery cupboard. How did the killer lock the door and wedge it from the inside and still escape the room?'

'Uncle Silas,' Gallagher said.

'I beg your pardon?'

'It's a story by Sheridan Le Fanu. A murder occurs in a locked room, disguised as a suicide. The whole point of the locked room was to make everyone focus on *how* the killing was carried out, distracting them away from the more important questions, like *why* and *who*.' Gallagher paused for a moment. 'As a matter of interest, has that room always been a stationery cupboard?'

'No. A long time ago, it was the servants' pantry for the Admiralty boardroom, which is next door to the left.'

'I'd like to take a look at the boardroom.'

'You'd have to get a key,' she said, 'which is not easy. The Admiralty secretariat have the keys, and guard them like Fafnir's treasure. As it happens, I was in the boardroom a couple of weeks ago, when Admiral Hall asked me to take some papers to their lordships. What do you need to know?'

'The right-hand wall, the one that separates it from the stationery cupboard. Is there anything on it, or next to it?'

'There is a large mahogany sideboard, and above it a couple of indifferent oil portraits of old admirals. Nothing else of significance, I'm afraid. Have you any thoughts about the why and who?'

Gallagher thought for a moment. 'The first question is, who might have both the motive and the opportunity to break into the safe of the Director of Naval Intelligence?'

She hesitated. Gallagher watched her. 'You are an agent of the secret service, Mrs Vane, just as I am,' he said quietly. 'Your opinion is valuable.'

'Thank you,' she said after a moment. 'Not every man in the service would agree with you. Nor would some of the women, come to that . . . In terms of opportunity, there is one obvious person who had access to both the safe and the stationery cupboard. Me.'

Gallagher nodded. 'That had occurred to me,' he said. 'Anyone else?'

'Commander Colson had access to the safe. He also knew where I kept my keys.'

'And he was officer of the watch last night, but claims not to have seen Vasiliev. Apparently, this was not the first time Vasiliev had visited naval intelligence, and yet Colson didn't recognize him . . . What can you tell me about Captain Ryder?'

'He's Admiral Jellicoe's blue-eyed boy. He was on Jellicoe's staff at Scapa Flow, and his lordship brought him down to London when he became First Sea Lord. It remains to be seen whether he's as good as his reputation makes him out to be.'

Gallagher stood for a moment, fighting down the urge to cough again. 'Two things bother me,' he said finally.

'Only two?'

'Someone went to a great deal of trouble to hide Vasiliev's body and remove all traces of his identity and create the illusion of suicide. A few minutes later, up pops Captain Ryder, and suddenly we know exactly who he is. Why were we able to discover Vasiliev's identity so quickly?'

'Happenstance,' said Mrs Vane. 'Captain Ryder was already concerned about his man's disappearance, and was looking for him. The killer might not have reckoned with that.'

'I'm curious about Vasiliev's visit to naval intelligence,' Gallagher said. 'They said at the watchkeeper's office that he helped out with Russian translations, but I'd like to know more. See what you can find out.'

She nodded. 'What is the second thing bothering you?'

'I'm guessing that Vasiliev was killed because of the telegram. But if so, why did the murderer leave it for us to find?'

'Perhaps there was a different motive,' suggested Mrs Vane. 'Perhaps the telegram had nothing to do with the killing.'

Gallagher made no comment. 'Did you see the writing on his shirt cuff?'

'Yes.' Mrs Vane paused for a moment. 'My husband used to do that, jot things down on his cuffs when he couldn't find a piece of paper. It drove the housemaid wild . . . *Thr. of Sat. 2030 2417.* What do you make of it?'

'I assume the numbers are some sort of code,' Gallagher said.

'That was my thought too. I checked to see if there was a connection with the telegram, but the numbers don't appear in the text. What about *Thr. of Sat.*?'

'I'm betting it refers to the throne of Saturn,' Gallagher said. 'Do you know the *Rubaiyat of Omar Khayyam*, Mrs Vane?

'Up from Earth's centre, through the seventh gate
I rose, and on the throne of Saturn sate.'

'Very dramatic,' said Mrs Vane.

'But apropos,' said Gallagher. 'We live in a world full of drama, after all. The *Rubaiyat*, as it happens, is the basis for a book code used by a German spymaster, the one known as the Dreamer. Have you heard of him?'

'I know the name,' she said quietly.

'Don't repeat it', Gallagher said. 'At least not here in the Admiralty. When we reach Hartlake Hall, I will tell you more.'

A gust of wind rattled the windows. Just for a moment he heard again the scream of the hurricane, the rain crashing into the windows like rifle fire. Aquinnah, the house had been called, the place beneath the hill. The electricity had gone by then, and there was only a smoking oil lamp to illuminate the woman's body sprawled on the bed, her bare arms spotted with puncture marks.

The woman had been called Sadie Lansing, and she was the wife of an American oil baron, James Rogers Lansing. She and Paul Vasiliev had both been found dead with fatal overdoses in locked rooms, arranged to look like suicide. Sadie Lansing had a copy of the *Rubaiyat* in her house, and Vasiliev had written a phrase from the poem on his shirt cuff. *The throne of Saturn.* He had not seen that particular phrase used as a code before, but he knew the *Rubaiyat* off by heart; he had memorized Mrs Lansing's copy, looking for clues. Now, there was no doubt in his mind that the two deaths were connected.

This is the Dreamer's work, he thought. *It began at Aquinnah. And now, we must bring it to its end.*

Gallagher coughed again. 'I want you at Hartlake Hall this weekend,' he said.

The corners of her mouth turned down. 'I'm not particularly fond of shooting parties.'

'It's important, I promise. Colson and Ryder will understand, of course, and I will inform my stepfather. We'll tell everyone that you work with me at the Paymaster General's Office. You're the vice-treasurer for Irish Exchequer bills, or something, and you have been working too hard and your doctor has prescribed some fresh country air.'

'Your stepfather?' she said.

'Sir John Borden, the current tenant of Hartlake Hall and our host for the weekend.' Gallagher's voice was ironic. 'Friday will be your lucky day, Mrs Vane. You get to meet my family.'

3

TONBRIDGE STATION ON a chilly grey afternoon. Gallagher stepped out of the train onto the platform, turning up his overcoat collar against the east wind and hoisting his bag over his shoulder. A woman in a black coat trimmed with sable approached him, smiling. 'Excuse me, mister. Can you tell me where to find the Rose and Crown?'

Gallagher surveyed her for a moment. She was small, round-faced and apple-cheeked with a bun of black hair streaked with grey, and she looked like someone's favourite grandmother. Her accent was straight out of New England; Connecticut, he thought, or maybe Massachusetts.

'Turn left out of the station and follow the high street,' he said. 'It's on your right after you cross the bridge. Just opposite the castle.'

'Thanks.' She studied him in turn. 'You don't see many men out of uniform these days. Up in London, they give fellows like you the white feather.'

'I know,' Gallagher said. 'I have a small collection of them already.'

She beamed at him. 'Let me guess. Reserved occupation?'

'Sort of. I'm with the Paymaster General's Office.'

28

Her eyebrows arched. 'The Paymaster General? Is that as dull as it sounds?'

'Worse,' Gallagher said. 'Pardon me, Mrs . . . ?'

'Miss Rittenhouse, Willa Rittenhouse. Pleased to meet you, Mr . . .'

'Gallagher. I was going to ask, are you always this inquisitive?'

She smiled again, even more brilliantly. 'Sorry. I'm a journalist, so I sort of get paid to be nosy.'

Something tickled the back of Gallagher's neck. 'What brings you to Tonbridge? If I may be nosy in turn.'

'Sure.' She leaned forward a little, a conspiratorial glint in her eye. 'I'm playing hooky,' she said.

'Playing what?'

'Skipping school. Cutting class. My newspaper sent me to London to work on a story, but I got bored, so I thought I'd have a little vacation. You know, get out of that smoky old city and see some real English countryside. Somebody recommended I start in Tonbridge. What do you think?'

Gallagher smiled. 'It's as good a place as any.'

'I thought so. What brings you down here? Are you on holiday too?'

'In a manner of speaking. I've come down for a weekend's shooting, at a house near here.'

'Shooting! Golly, you Brits. There's not enough gunfire in France, so you've got to loose off a few rounds back home as well? I'm surprised shooting is still allowed during the war.'

'On the contrary, it's very much encouraged,' Gallagher said. 'The pheasants go to the convalescent hospitals. They're a cheap source of food for the wounded soldiers.'

'Oh, that explains it. Somebody has done a cost-benefit analysis and decided it's a good thing. Well, here comes the porter with my bags. Enjoy your weekend, Mr Gallagher.'

MISS RITTENHOUSE DEPARTED, followed by the porter. Gallagher watched her go, a sense of ill-defined unease creeping around his brain. He very much doubted if Miss Rittenhouse was on holiday. Journalists, in his experience, were never on holiday, especially not American ones, and it was worth checking on her background. He pulled out his watch and checked the time. It would be just after 10.30 in the morning in Washington, and Bruce Bielaski ought to be at his desk by now. A trans-Atlantic telegram would be expensive and the bean counters at the secret service would doubtless splutter about budgets, but better safe than sorry. He turned and walked towards the station telegraph office.

Ten minutes later he went out into the street, looking around in the dreary light. Tonbridge high street was full of traffic, most of it horse-drawn; fuel for domestic use was in short supply. An aeroplane buzzed low overhead, a two-seater of some sort with Royal Flying Corps roundels on its wings, sinking down towards the aerodrome at Chiddingstone Causeway a few miles to the west. Gallagher watched the machine disappear, and hailed a hansom cab. 'Hartlake Hall, please,' he told the driver.

'Very good, sir.'

Gallagher stepped in, sitting back and watching the familiar landscape pass by. The cab climbed up the road towards Southborough and Tunbridge Wells, before turning east onto a narrow lane leading to the village of Tudeley. Half a mile short of the village they came to a red-brick lodge next to a set of wrought-iron gates, which were standing open. The lodge was empty and dark;

the gatekeeper, Gallagher knew, had been called up last year, and his wife had gone away to stay with her family.

The cab drove through the gates, rattling over a cattle grid, and followed the lane past the gamekeeper's cottage through a woodland full of coppice trees interspersed with the occasional oak. After about half a mile, the woodland gave way to a park with a few more scattered oaks and chestnut trees, surrounding a big brick house. Cattle grazed among the trees, and he heard the gentle tinkle of bells.

'You here for the weekend, sir?' the driver asked.

'Yes.'

'Shooting party, is it? This used to be a big place for shooting. They'd have twenty or thirty guns every weekend, before the war, but they barely get a dozen now. Ten keepers they had too, but most of them have gone to the war. Still, better days will come again.'

'I wouldn't be too sure of that,' Gallagher said.

The cab pulled up outside the front door of the house and Gallagher stepped down, handing the driver his fare and watching as the vehicle drove away. Silence fell for a moment, broken by the raucous call of a rook flapping slowly over the trees.

Built two generations earlier as the country retreat of a wealthy industrialist, Hartlake Hall could equally have passed for a mission hospital or a house of correction. Rows of dark windows stared out from an austere red-brick façade. Two stone pilasters on either side of the oak front door were the only concessions to caprice. The gardens, on the other hand, had once been rather splendid. The centrepiece was an ornamental lake fringed with banks of rhododendrons, their leaves dark green and glossy in the grey light. A path ran around the lake and over an arched stone bridge at the far end. In summer, Gallagher recalled, the balustrades of the bridge were smothered in wisteria blossom. Now, in the dead of winter, he could see the garden plots untended, the banks heavy with dead weeds.

Around the lake lay the rest of the park, bounded by a low stone wall. On the far side of the wall, cropped stubble fields ran down to a railway line, the main line coming up from Dover. Beyond the railway was the River Medway, brown and turgid from recent rains, bordered by water meadows with glassy pools of standing water. The hills of the North Downs rose gently in the middle distance.

A train whistle sounded, and he saw a white plume of steam rising over the trees and heard the rattle of steel wheels. After a moment the train came into view, chugging up the line towards Tonbridge. He counted fourteen carriages behind the engine. All of the carriages, he knew, would be full of wounded men evacuated from field hospitals in France, several hundred of them, shot and gassed, maimed and blinded; and this was only one train of many. He remembered the height of the Somme battles last summer when the trains had come up the line every ten minutes, night and day.

Better get this over with, he thought. He rang the doorbell and waited. A footman, an older man with watery eyes, opened the door and bowed. 'Mr Gallagher, sir, welcome.'

'Thank you, Hunton. Good to see you again.'

'That's very kind of you, sir. Allow me to take your bag.'

Gallagher followed the man inside. The hall, high-ceilinged with a flagstone floor, was barren of decoration apart from two stags' heads gazing belligerently at each other from opposite walls. A log fire burned in a stone fireplace. A woman in her mid-thirties, fair and jocund in a plain grey dress, came out into the hall. She gave a little squeak of delight when she saw Gallagher, and ran to embrace him. 'Pat! Welcome back to

Wuthering Heights, darling. Do come into the drawing room, it's almost warm there. Mother will be so pleased to see you.'

'No, she won't,' Gallagher said.

The woman made a moue. 'Pat. Don't be like that. Come and see Mother, while Hunton takes your bag up to your room. I'm afraid they've given you the Cheese Room again, I hope you don't mind.'

'The mice are good company. I didn't realize you were going to be here this weekend, Penelope.'

'We were summoned only yesterday. The whole weekend has been rather thrown together, it seems. Still, as Jane Austen said, how often is happiness spoiled by preparation?'

Gallagher smiled a little. Penelope Makarian was his half-sister; they were fond of each other, though apart from the accident of parentage they had virtually nothing in common. He followed her into the cavernous drawing room, decorated in what might have been high taste forty years ago. Dark wallpaper was patterned with gilded Gothic arches; carnivorous-looking roses, blood red and white, wrapped around them. The high ceiling sucked up the heat from below and held it trapped against the plaster. Tall windows looked out across the park, monochrome grey in the afternoon light.

Maud, Lady Borden, sat facing the fire on a chinoiserie settee. She turned her head as Gallagher approached. Lines on her face pulled down the corners of her mouth. She would be fifty-eight this year, Gallagher knew, but she looked older; fair and faded, she seemed to have aged a great deal in the six months since he had last seen her.

'Patrick. You are in time for tea.'

It sounded like an accusation. Gallagher bent and brushed his lips against her cheek. 'Good afternoon, Mother. I trust you are well.'

33

'I wish people would stop asking me if I am well. Surely it is self-evident that I am not. I am constantly fatigued, my digestion is quite spoiled and my nerves are altogether ruined.'

'Have you seen a doctor?' Gallagher asked.

'I see a doctor every week. I have been prescribed a veritable cornucopia of pills, which I take every day and which do not do the slightest bit of good. I shall not be well again until this ghastly war is over, and Sir John and I are free to return to our own home. But heaven knows when that will be.'

Netley Park, her husband's ancestral home in Hampshire, had been requisitioned by the government in 1915, at about the same time as her husband, Sir John Borden, had been appointed as parliamentary secretary to the Minister of Munitions. It made sense to move nearer to London, closer to the House of Commons and the ministry, but most big houses in Kent had also been requisitioned. Hartlake Hall, as Sir John often said in a defensive tone, was the best he could get. Gallagher sometimes wondered what the other available houses had been like.

'It's cold in here,' he said. 'Shall I put another log on the fire?'

'Don't soil your hands!' she snapped. 'Penelope, ring for a servant.'

Gallagher ignored her, picking up a log and dropping it on the fire. Sparks flew upward in a red shower. Lady Maud's hands clenched, and she turned to her daughter.

'Instruct the servants to make sure the fire is properly built up at all times. Do they want us to catch our deaths?'

'Of course they don't, Mother. I'll speak to Platt.'

'And where is your husband, Penelope? Why isn't he here now, with you?'

'I told you, Mother, he is attending a board meeting in town this afternoon. He will join us for dinner.'

'A board meeting. I suppose that means he will arrive wearing a lounge suit, just like last time. Does he not understand how to dress properly, or is it wilful refusal?'

Penelope drew a deep breath. Gallagher intervened. 'Have the other guests arrived?'

'Not yet,' said Lady Maud. 'Why Sir John has chosen to invite this curious ménage of people into our house, I do not know. To the best of my knowledge he has no connection with the Royal Navy, and yet tonight no fewer than four naval officers will dine with us. I do hope that they won't bore us to death with nautical matters all evening.'

'I'm sure they won't,' Gallagher said.

'And you, Patrick? You are still with the Paymaster General's Office? I find it strange that the government cannot find some more *worthwhile* occupation for you.'

Neither Lady Maud nor her daughters knew Gallagher's real profession; Gallagher and his stepfather had agreed long ago that this was best. 'Perhaps they will one day,' he said. 'In the meantime, I am a civil servant. I go where I am told.'

'How disappointing for you,' Lady Maud said. 'Will you take tea?'

'Thank you, but no,' Gallagher said. He felt a sudden need to get away. 'There are some papers I must read before dinner.'

Penelope caught up with him in the hall. 'Don't let her get under your skin, Pat.'

'I'm trying not to,' Gallagher said.

'The war really is playing havoc with her nerves, you know. There's no getting away from it here. Aeroplanes buzzing around all day, airships swarming over us at night, the trains full of wounded. Do you remember the Somme battles, when the wind blew from the east and we could hear the guns in France? It was like thunder that never ended.'

'I know it must be terrible for her.' The conversation with Willa Rittenhouse was still fresh in his mind. 'But I don't appreciate being given the white feather by my own mother. I go where the government tells me to go. It's not my fault I'm not on active service.'

'I'm sure that's not what she meant.'

Gallagher coughed again, hard enough to make his eyes water. Penelope watched him with concern. 'Perhaps it is you who should see a doctor.'

'I already have. They say there is nothing to be done.'

'I'm sorry to hear it.' She paused. 'For my part, I'm quite glad they haven't given you anything more interesting to do. Interesting usually also means dangerous, and I should hate it if anything were to happen to you.'

'Thank you. I appreciate the thought.' Gallagher paused. 'Do you hear from Alice?'

Alice was Penelope's older sister. Gallagher, their half-brother, was the eldest of the three, a product of their mother's ill-fated first marriage. 'She is well enough. She's running a casualty clearing station somewhere in the Ancre Valley. We're not allowed to know exactly where.'

'Please give her my regards when next you write,' Gallagher said. The doorbell rang, harsh and jangling in the cold air. 'I shall leave you to welcome the other guests.'

FRIDAY, 2 FEBRUARY 1917
4.21 P.M.

Narrow stairs and creaking corridors with many steps and turns led Gallagher to the east wing of the house. The Cheese Room was the last bedroom at the end, so named because of the mousetraps baited with cheese that lay scattered around the floor. The gaps between the skirting boards and the floor were wide enough for mice to pass through with ease. In Gallagher's experience, the traps had never worked; the mice, with a cunning that would have served well on the Western Front, had learned how to remove the cheese without springing the traps. This did not deter the servants, who continued to lay the traps, apparently oblivious to the fact that they were running a buffet for the mice.

The room's single window looked out over the park towards the railway line and the water meadows beyond. Gallagher stood for a moment, wrinkling his nose a little at the smell of mouse urine and damp. Outside, the light was beginning to fade under the low clouds; the lamps of a passing train gleamed briefly and were gone. In the room itself, an electric bulb produced a wan, flickering light. A fire had been lit in the tiled fireplace, and unhappy little flames licked at the coal, clearly wishing they could give up on the attempt and be allowed to die.

Roxanne's voice, soft and full of music, spoke in his mind. *Your mother no longer has the power to hurt you, Pat. Let her be.*

But she hurts others. Alice and Penelope have done nothing. They are blameless.

They are also old enough to look after themselves. Let her be. There will be no peace for you until you do.

And what about peace for you? he asked the voice, but it did not reply.

His reflection stared back at him from the mirror on the wardrobe door. He would shortly be forty years old, but the lines on his forehead and the first flecks of grey in his dark hair made him look older. The scar on his temple, just behind his left eye, was a memorial of a day in China, seventeen years ago, when a Kansu Braves musket ball had nearly taken his head off.

That was his only external scar. The rest of his wounds, like the pain that nagged at his throat and lungs, were hidden.

He could feel the distance growing between himself and Roxanne. Once it had been easy to keep her close because he had things that reminded him of her: his brushes and paints, the book she had once given him. But now these were at the bottom of the Irish Sea, entombed in the wreck of the *Lusitania*. Increasingly, it seemed that she too was slipping away from him, borne by the currents of the cold sea.

I was unable to save you when you were alive, he said to the shadows. Now, I am losing you.

He listened for an answering voice to tell him he was wrong, but there was nothing. The silence of the house draped itself around him like the curtains of a shrine. *There will be dreams tonight*, he thought. *Bad ones.*

Enough introspection, he told himself. Time to go to work.

Behind the wall panelling, water pipes thumped like a soft drum beat; someone must be running a bath. His bag had been unpacked, his clothes placed neatly in the wardrobe, and his razor and shaving brush laid out on the side table, along with a thick manila envelope. The envelope had been delivered to his office at the secret service just before he departed; it had taken the service archivists all of the previous day to compile the reports he asked for, while Gallagher himself cleared his desk and handed over some of his other cases to another officer, and waited for Vasiliev's autopsy report. Gallagher pulled up an armchair next to the fire, opened the envelope and took out the dossiers inside, and began to read.

The first dossier was a biography of Commander George St John Colson, who did not recognize Vasiliev's body and claimed not to have seen him sign in. It was all perfectly possible, of course. As the commander said, he had other duties, and many

hundreds of people worked at the Admiralty, even at night . . .
According to the dossier, Colson's family had no previous connection with the navy. His mother came from an ancient clan
of aristocrats who had once owned much of the East Midlands
but had later fallen on hard times; his father was a self-made
man, a wealthy industrialist and factory owner. Colson had been
educated at Eton and the House, followed by a year with a bar-
rister's chambers in the Middle Temple where he had articled
but never practised. Then, for reasons that were not spelled out,
he had given up on law and joined the navy.

Family connections had ensured rapid promotion and, later,
a post as equerry to a minor member of the royal family, Prince
Maurice of Battenberg. The prince joined the King's Royal
Rifle Corps in August 1914, and when his battalion was sent
to France he requested that his friend Colson be allowed to
accompany him. After Prince Maurice was killed by a German
artillery shell at Zonnebeke Ridge in October, Colson recovered his body and arranged his funeral, for which service he
was awarded the Distinguished Service Cross and promotion to
the rank of commander.

Back in London after a spell of leave, his legal training
and education – in a service not noted for its abundance of
scholarship – made him an obvious choice for naval intelligence.
He joined the staff of the new department head, Rear-Admiral
Hall, in February of 1915.

The final paragraph of Colson's service record was already
known to Gallagher. About six months ago, Colson had discovered that a junior clerk at the Admiralty, who had lost a great
deal of money at the dogs, was recouping his losses by selling
confidential documents. Colson had called in the secret service
and a team led by Gallagher himself had set a trap for the clerk,
who was arrested with a number of stolen files in his possession.

Before he was hanged, the clerk confessed that he had been selling the documents to a German agent. He did not know the agent's identity, only their code name: der Träumer, the Dreamer. He had claimed to be working alone, communicating with the Dreamer using a book code, but the author of the dossier was not so sure of this. Three months after the clerk's execution, the thefts had resumed. So far, there were no clues as to who the new thief might be.

There was not much else. Colson was unmarried and, despite being a member of East India Club, not particularly sociable. Thanks to an inheritance from his father, he was also very wealthy; among other things, he owned a large bloc of shares in the Anglo-Persian Oil Company, enough to entitle him to a seat on the board of directors. Just before the war began he had gone to the United States as part of an Anglo-Persian delegation hoping to negotiate an agreement with an American firm, Standard Oil. They had not been successful. Standard Oil's executives had accused the Anglo-Persian team of impropriety, and the negotiations collapsed.

That was all. For someone from such a stellar background, Colson did not have much to show for his life. A brief handwritten note at the bottom of the document summed this up: *Promoted beyond his ability?*

Possibly, Gallagher thought. Possibly, too, the death of Prince Maurice had left its mark on him. It was not Colson's fault that the prince had been killed, but some people would always wonder. Perhaps Colson wondered himself. *I know that feeling . . .*

The second dossier was a summary of the career of Captain Merrick Ryder. Unlike Colson, the captain came from an old seagoing family; his ancestors had fought and shed blood at Quiberon and Boston Harbour, Aboukir and Sevastopol, but none had risen to high rank. His father had served in the navy during the Crimean War, and been invalided out of the service.

Ryder himself had attended Dartmouth naval college and been commissioned as a midshipman into the battleship *Royal Oak*. Most of his subsequent postings had been on shore duty in England or Ireland. In 1911 he was posted to the British embassy in Berlin as a naval attaché, and in 1913 he was transferred to the embassy in Washington, where he remained until the outbreak of war.

Returning to England, he was promoted to the rank of captain and attached to the staff of the Harwich Force. In January 1915 he was appointed commandant of the Royal Alexandra Yard at Haulbowline, near Queenstown in Ireland. As he himself had said, he was in command on the day that the *Lusitania* was torpedoed. From June 1915 to March 1916 he was chief of staff to Vice-Admiral Bacon, the commander of the Dover Patrol, after which he was appointed director of naval operations at the Grand Fleet's base at Scapa Flow in the Orkneys.

Ryder was awarded the Distinguished Service Order for his service during the Battle of Jutland, and was singled out for special praise by Admiral Jellicoe. In November 1916, shortly after Jellicoe became First Sea Lord, Ryder was appointed deputy director of the naval planning division at the Admiralty. This file too had a handwritten note at the bottom of the page, adding that Captain Ryder was seen as a potential high-flyer, and had influence in many places. This, Gallagher knew, was a coded warning. *Stay on Ryder's good side, don't annoy him.*

He picked up the final dossier, which contained the files on Paul Alexander Vasiliev, and read it slowly, frowning from time to time, and making notes in pencil in the margins. The dossier also contained some postcards of scenes from Saint Petersburg, with cryptic messages on the backs. Special Branch had found these when searching Vasiliev's rooms. Most of the messages meant nothing to him, but two in particular caught his eye. One read simply, *R. is respected, M.I. was there.* The second message was, *Friends in Zurich say G.Y. has bought a ticket.*

It was impossible to tell who had sent the postcards – clearly they were not a professional agent, as they had used plain language and made no attempt to use a code – but Gallagher knew what they referred to. '*R.*' was Grigori Rasputin, an important advisor and councillor to the Russian royal family. '*M.I.*' was Maxim Ivanovich Litzov, a partner in the shipping firm Makarian & Litzov, based in Saint Petersburg; Gallagher knew this because Nicholas Makarian, the other partner in the firm, was Penelope's husband.

'*G.Y.*' was Grigory Yevseyevich Zinoviev, Russian radical and close friend of the Bolshevik leader, Vladimir Ilyich Lenin. Both were currently in exile in Switzerland. But why had someone sent these cards to Vasiliev?

He rose to his feet, looking out of the dark window. Full night had fallen now; silence lay across the valley of the Medway, broken only by the distant hoot of a train whistle. Smoke from the fire tickled the back of his throat.

What he had said to Penelope was true. He had seen a doctor, several of them, including the service's own specialist in Harley Street. When the *Lusitania* sank he had nearly gone down with it, and had ingested a quantity of coal tar and dirty seawater before he was able to reach the surface. The damage, the doctors had told him, was permanent and would probably shorten his life. He had thought about this a great deal, and decided he did not really mind.

The truth, he admitted to himself, was that Willa Rittenhouse's comment had rankled, and so had his mother's. He had no burning desire to put on a uniform – he had already done so, in the Royal Marines and in the police – but he lived in a world where millions had died, and he did not know why; why they had died, why he still lived. Roxanne had been killed, and he had survived. Twelve hundred had died when the *Lusitania* sank, and he had lived. The guilt of survival hung over him like a cloud.

Forget about it, he told himself. *Stay focused on the case.* But he remembered Roxanne's body, eight years ago, cold and lifeless in the morgue on board *Lusitania*, and he remembered from much more recent times the corpses of women and children floating on the sea, bumping and rolling against him as he tried to swim for safety, and he knew he would never forget.

A faint squeaking aroused him from his reverie, and he heard the scurry of tiny feet on the floor. What he had said about the mice was true as well: they *were* good company, or at least, they didn't pass judgement. Coming to Hartlake Hall was always hard, which was why he came as seldom as possible. Penelope, at least, treated him like family, and her husband Nicholas Makarian was affable enough, although Gallagher sometimes wondered how much of it was façade. Sir John Borden, his stepfather, was stuffy and distant but at least behaved like a friend. Alice, Penelope's elder sister, had cut herself off from the entire family, himself included. And then there was his mother, the same as she had always been, ever since he could remember: cold, disapproving, rarely troubling to conceal the fact that his own existence was an error of judgement, a mistake she had regretted all of her life.

He knew that his case was not unique. Roxanne's family had made her life hell, driving her out of her own home when she was barely sixteen; he remembered her voice, soft with suffering, telling him about the pain she still felt. But somehow, knowing that other people had broken families did not help. He had spent much of his life feeling alone and unwanted; and now, he was alone once more.

'Oh, for God's sake,' he said to his reflection in the window. 'Why do you care what your mother thinks? You're a forty-year-old man. It really is time you grew up.'

Turning away from the window, he rang the bell. A few minutes later the sound of shuffling footsteps in the hallway announced the arrival of Hunton, the footman. 'How may I be of service, sir?'

'Have Captain Ryder and Commander Colson arrived? And Mrs Vane?'

'The captain is unpacking, sir. The commander and Mrs Vane have just arrived.'

'Good. Ask all three if they would join me for a drink in the billiards room at six p.m.'

'Very good, sir.'

Hunton retreated down the corridor. Gallagher turned to the window again, looking at his reflection in the glass. *It begins.*

FRIDAY, 2 FEBRUARY 1917
5.32 P.M.

Jonquil Vane's train had arrived late; points failure at Sevenoaks, someone said, in a weary voice that suggested this was by no means the first time. Night had fallen by the time she arrived at Tonbridge, and the cab that took her to Hartlake Hall passed through windswept woods haunted by flickering shadows. She was normally a level-headed woman, but by the time the lamps of the house appeared out of the gloom, her nerves were on edge.

The cab pulled up outside the house behind a motor car, a

Rolls-Royce Silver Ghost with a uniformed chauffeur unloading bags and gun cases from the boot. Servants came to take the bags and carry them into the house. Mrs Vane stepped down from the cab, carrying her own bag. 'Very nice car,' she said to the chauffeur. 'To whom does it belong?'

'This is Commander Colson's car, ma'am.' The chauffeur stepped back into the car and drove away towards the stables.

Inside the house she was greeted by an elderly manservant, who showed her into the drawing room and presented her to her hostess, Lady Maud Borden. Her ladyship took one look at Mrs Vane's tweed skirt and plain black blouse and wrote her off as a nonentity, turning her attention instead to a portly man with upturned waxed moustaches. Lady Maud's husband, Sir John Borden, pouch-eyed and balding, was on the far side of the room, deep in conversation with a serious dark-haired man in tweeds. They were talking about shooting, she judged, watching their hand gestures mime the rise of a shotgun and the fall of imaginary birds.

A footman, another elderly man with rheumy eyes, brought her a cup of tea and a slice of dry madeira cake. 'Mr Gallagher sends his compliments, ma'am, and will you join him in the billiards room at six.'

'Thank you. I am finding this room very cold. Is there somewhere warmer where I could sit until then?'

'The fire is on in the music room, ma'am. I will show you the way.'

The music room was a pleasant surprise. Unlike the drawing room, it had been decorated modestly with pale blue walls and white plaster, and a few discreet paintings hanging from the picture rail. A Broadwood grand piano stood in the centre of the room, facing a harpsichord with a polished walnut case.

Quietly, she walked to the piano and sat down on the padded

bench. A book of sheet music stood open on the stand beside her. She read the words sandwiched between the bars of music, 'Ich hab' im Traum geweinet . . .' Old memories stirred. Once upon a time she had known and loved this song, not thinking of the pain behind the words; now, that pain was her own. Her fingers touched the keys and softly, almost without thinking, she began to play.

I wept in my dream, for I dreamed you were in your grave.
I awoke, to find tears flowing down my cheeks.
I wept in my dream, for I dreamed you had abandoned me.
I awoke, and wept bitterly and long.
I wept in my dream, for I dreamed that you still cared for me.
I awoke, and my tears flowed like a flood.

'Playing the enemy's music, ma'am?' said an American voice.

Abruptly, she stopped playing. A man was standing next to her, looking down at the sheet music. She had to swallow in order to speak; she had not realized how close she was to tears herself. 'Music is music,' she said. 'Beauty should have no boundaries. We have not been introduced.'

He looked down at her, and she felt again the unease of the haunted forest. He was not a big man, but he was strongly built with dark hair and jutting eyebrows and hard planes to his face. She thought that his eyes held the promise of cruelty. 'My name's Lansing,' he said. 'James Rogers Lansing.'

He said it like he was expecting a response. 'Mrs Jonquil Vane,' she said, and waited.

Lansing's face froze for a moment, and then he smiled. 'You've never heard of me,' he said. 'Well, no reason why you should. I'm just a simple Yankee pedlar, come over to England to ply my wares. What is it you call them over here? Barrow boys? Yeah, I'm a barrow boy. Roll up, roll up! Get your Tampico crude, right here! A dollar and thirty-one cents a barrel, while stocks last! Get it while it's hot!'

'I see,' she said dryly. 'You are something in the oil business.'

He shifted from one foot to the other, and for a moment she thought she had angered him. He saw the apprehension in her face, and smiled. 'You could say that,' he said. 'What about you, Mrs Vane? Should I have heard of you?'

'I very much doubt it. I'm a civil servant.'

'A civil servant,' Lansing repeated, rolling the word on his tongue, pronouncing each syllable with malice. 'A little ci-vil ser-vant.' He picked up the book of sheet music and studied it in the lamplight. 'Say, someone has been scribbling on this book. Was that you, Mrs Vane? That's pretty rude of you, isn't it?'

Caught off guard, she stared at him. 'What are you talking about?'

'Oh, so you're trying to pretend it wasn't you? Look, see here. You've written something in pencil in the margin, and then rubbed it out again. This book might be valuable, Mrs Vane. Lady Maud won't take kindly to vandalism like this, will she? Maybe I should show it to her.'

This was nonsense, but she was already emotionally fractured and he had found a way under her skin. 'Do whatever you like,' she snapped.

'I generally do,' said Lansing. 'Most people don't reckon it's worth their while trying to stop me.' His free hand brushed the back of her neck.

'Mr Lansing,' she said sharply. '*If* you please.'

A finger caressed the line of her jaw, letting her know that he was in charge. Then his hand relaxed and he stepped back a little, replacing the book on the music stand. 'You've good taste in music, Mrs Vane,' he said. 'I'm fond of Schumann too. I still wonder about your patriotism, though.'

'I'm not sure that my patriotism is any of your business.'

'You're probably right,' he agreed. She watched his face change. Having had his moment of fun, he had now decided that she was no longer worth bothering with. 'Nice meeting you, Mrs Vane. Enjoy your weekend.'

The door closed behind him. Furious, she grabbed the book of music and held it up to the light. Lansing had been right, damn him; someone *had* written on the margin of the page. All traces of the pencil marks had been expunged, but by tilting the page she could still see the faint indentations in the paper.

Thr. of Sat. 2030 2417. The same words and numbers that had been written on the cuff of Paul Vasiliev's shirt.

Her anger faded abruptly. She sat for a long moment, staring at the page. The clock in the hall struck six.

'Pull yourself together, woman,' she said quietly. 'It's time to go.'

4

THE BILLIARDS ROOM was homely; oak wainscotting kept in the warmth, deep leather armchairs were clustered around the billiards table, and there were decanters on the sideboard. Heavy oil paintings of hunting scenes, leaden horses and stiff-backed riders, hounds dappled in splotches of black and white and liver, hung around the walls. Gallagher poured a glass of soda water from the siphon and stood for a moment, watching the bubbles fizzing to the surface.

The door opened and Mrs Vane entered quietly. 'Quite pleasant,' she said, looking around the room. 'Almost liveable, one might say. Unlike the drawing room, which is perfectly ghastly.'

'My half-sister Penelope refers to this place as Wuthering Heights.'

'Really? Emily Brontë would have sued for slander. Although I have just encountered someone who could have stepped straight out of a Brontë novel. Have you heard of an oilman named Lansing?'

'Yes,' Gallagher said.

She looked at him sharply. 'Did you know he was coming this weekend? If so, you might have warned me about him.'

'I've never met the man. Was he unpleasant?'

'If I'd been a fly, he would have pulled my wings off.' She paused. 'Is he connected to our business?'

'I don't know,' Gallagher said. 'Possibly.'

Mrs Vane sat down in one of the armchairs. 'I checked on Vasiliev's visits to naval intelligence as you asked. In December and January he visited the department four times, always during the night watch, each time staying for about three hours before signing out again. And whatever he was doing, he wasn't providing translation services.'

Gallagher's eyebrows rose. 'So what *was* he doing?'

'An excellent question. I talked to every officer who serves on the night watch, and no one recalls seeing him. Each time, after he signed in at the watchkeeper's office, he disappeared.'

Footsteps sounded outside the door. 'That will be our friends,' Gallagher said.

Captain Ryder was the first to enter the room. He had exchanged his uniform for a lounge suit, and Gallagher wondered how Lady Maud had reacted to this. Colson, coming in behind him, was dressed in a Norfolk jacket and baggy tweed trousers; every inch the gentleman visiting the country for the weekend, and looking considerably more at home in these surroundings than Ryder. The commander walked to the sideboard and picked up a decanter. 'Anyone?' he asked.

'Whisky and soda,' Ryder said. He stood by the billiards table, idly rolling the cue ball back and forth along the baize. 'Very well, we're all here. What progress have you made, Gallagher?'

Gallagher handed over one of the papers he had brought with him. 'This is Vasiliev's autopsy report. It confirms that the cause of death was an injection of a strong opiate, probably morphine. As we suspected, he had also suffered a blow to the head shortly before death, probably strong enough to render him unconscious. Time of death was about midnight, or shortly after.' He looked at Ryder. 'I believe you said he had a heart problem? That he took nitro-glycerine pills?'

'Yes. Carried them everywhere.'

'That is curious. You see, the autopsy report confirms that at the time of his death, all of Vasiliev's internal organs were in good working order. Including his heart.'

Colson could not resist. 'Sounds like he was pulling the wool over your eyes, Ryder.'

'Not necessarily,' Gallagher said, before Ryder could respond. He opened the dossier. 'Here is what we know about Vasiliev. Born in 1892, the son of Alexander Vasiliev, a Liberal M.P., and his wife Jane, née Brooke. As you suggested, Captain, his grandfather was a Russian aristocrat who backed the Decembrist revolt against Tsar Nicholas I and was forced into exile. Both parents pre-deceased him, father in a riding accident, mother of pulmonary pneumonia. No brothers, one sister who is married and living somewhere in France. We're trying to trace her.'

'Inform me when you have done so, and I will send her my condolences. Go on.'

'Vasiliev was educated at Haileybury and Trinity College, Cambridge. According to his tutor at Cambridge, he attended only a handful of lectures but was a regular at parties and galas. He left in 1912 without taking a degree. He spent the next two years in America, where he spent much of his time crewing racing yachts. During this time he formed an intimate relationship with a Boston socialite named Sadie Lansing.'

He watched their faces for any sign of reaction. There was none. 'She was married to the oil baron, James Rogers Lansing,' he said. 'She died last year at her home on Cape Cod.'

Mrs Vane's head came around, and Gallagher could almost

feel the intensity of her stare. Ryder's eyebrows rose. 'How is this relevant?'

'I don't know that it is. I mention it because Lansing is here at Hartlake Hall this weekend. I'm not sure if he was aware of her affair with Vasiliev, but we need to be discreet.'

'Understood,' Ryder said. 'What is Lansing doing here?'

'Our host invited him. They are having talks about politics, I believe. Lansing is the personal envoy of Woodrow Wilson, the American president.'

Ryder nodded slowly. Gallagher looked down at the dossier. 'Following the outbreak of war in August 1914, Vasiliev returned home and joined the Royal Navy Volunteer Reserve. He was posted to the Harwich Force.' He looked up at Ryder. 'You said you had known Vasiliev for only a few months. Yet you were with the Harwich Force at the same time as he was. Are you certain that you didn't meet him there?'

Ryder spun the cue ball across the table, watching it rebound off a cushion and roll back towards him. 'There were more than forty ships in the Harwich Force, Gallagher, and hundreds of officers. I knew only a tiny fraction of them. I was on the commodore's staff, so I had little contact with watchkeeping officers.'

Gallagher nodded. 'Now, where was I? Let me see . . . Posted to the destroyer *Matchless* . . . Saw action in the Christmas Day raid on Cuxhaven . . . Ah, here we are. Soon after Cuxhaven he reported to the doctor complaining of severe chest pains, and was diagnosed with angina. Deemed no longer fit for sea duties, he was transferred to a post at the Admiralty.' Gallagher frowned, looking again at the autopsy report. 'And yet his heart was apparently healthy. How do we explain this?'

'The original diagnosis must have been made in error,' Ryder said. 'Whatever the truth, Vasiliev certainly believed he had a heart condition.'

'Hmm. Vasiliev took a spell of leave before joining the naval intelligence division at the Admiralty in February 1915. That was almost exactly when you arrived, Commander Colson. And yet, when you saw his body, you didn't recognize him. Is it possible that *you* made a mistake?'

Colson's mouth opened, but no sound came out. Ryder tensed. 'Well?' he demanded. 'Did you know him, Colson?'

Colson ignored him, looking instead at Gallagher. He had flushed bright red. 'No,' he said. 'I never met Vasiliev.'

'I am finding this hard to believe,' Ryder said. His voice had hardened.

Colson took a deep breath. 'Gallagher, I want your word of honour that you will not repeat what I am about to tell you. You too, Ryder, and you, Mrs Vane.'

Both nodded. Colson was still looking at Gallagher. 'I presume you have seen my service record.'

'I have.'

'What you won't know, because I had it expunged from the record, was that I didn't actually take up my post at naval intelligence until after Easter that year. You see, I had been in France and Belgium the previous year, and it was . . .'

He looked down at his hands. 'It was pretty bloody,' he said finally. 'A good friend was killed, right in front of my eyes. I'm not proud to say it, but my nerves were shot to pieces. When I came home I . . . I had what they call a breakdown. I was relieved of duty just after Christmas, and spent several months in a sanatorium. I wasn't able to take up my post until April.'

'Why doesn't this appear in your record?' Gallagher asked.

'I knew someone in a position of influence. I asked for help, and he was able to have the record altered.'

'Why?'

'Because the breakdown could have ended his career,' Ryder

said, unexpectedly. 'It happens, all too often. Even the best of men will fall to pieces when placed under stress. But when it happens, instead of helping them back onto their feet, we send them to the knackers' yard. Believe it or not, Colson, I understand. I've deleted records for men in similar circumstances.'

There was a moment of silence. *Even the best of men*, Gallagher repeated to himself. Was Ryder thinking of his own father, perhaps? He had been forced to resign his commission on health grounds; what did that mean, exactly?

'Well, that clears things up,' he said. 'Vasiliev was only at naval intelligence for a few weeks before he was transferred to naval planning, so he would have been gone before you arrived.' He looked at Ryder. 'Did you know that he was transferred because he was deemed to be a security risk?'

Ryder turned sharply. 'What does that mean?'

'Our friends across the water, in the Bureau of Investigation, report that while he was in America, Vasiliev was a frequent visitor to a club in Boston connected to a Russian opposition group, the Constitutional Democrats. They are more usually known as the Kadets.'

'Never heard of them,' said Colson.

'They are a group of radicals who demand constitutional reform in Russia, including the overthrow and replacement of the Tsar.'

Colson grunted. 'You mean the Bolsheviks.'

Gallagher shook his head. 'The Bolsheviks are followers of Karl Marx. They want to overthrow the world order, abolish private property and establish what they call a dictatorship of the people. The Kadets are moderates by comparison. A lot of Russian nobles are members of the Kadets.'

'Yes, I know something of them,' said Ryder. 'How does this represent a risk to the security of Britain?'

'Vasiliev met one of the Kadet leaders in Boston, a man named Vladimir Dmitrievich Nabokov,' Gallagher said. 'The Americans think they maintained contact after Vasiliev returned to Britain, and it looks like they were right. Special Branch searched Vasiliev's flat yesterday and found a collection of post-cards from Saint Petersburg. One of these refers to the recent murder of Grigori Rasputin, the Tsarina of Russia's personal advisor.'

He laid down the dossier. 'Captain Ryder, you called Vasiliev as English as you or I. But that's not true, is it? He was in con-tact with Russian radicals, and had been for some time. The security services were aware of this, so I am somewhat sur-prised, Captain, that you didn't know as well. Did you not ask to see the service records of your officers when you took up your post?'

Ryder spun the cue ball again, watching it ricochet off the cushion and into a corner pocket. 'What are you implying, Gallagher?'

'I am not implying anything,' Gallagher said, and there was an edge to his voice now. 'I am trying to establish facts. I want to know why one of *your* officers, Captain Ryder, gained access to *your* division's offices, Commander Colson, on four separate occasions over the past two months, and on each occasion spent anything up to three hours unobserved and unsupervised before walking calmly out again. Anything that you gentlemen have to offer by way of an explanation will be most welcome.'

Colson reached into his pocket, pulled out a silver cigarette case and a matchbox, and lit a cigarette. He inhaled deeply, paused for a moment and blew out a cloud of smoke. Gallagher felt the smoke catch in his throat and forced himself not to cough.

Ryder pulled the cue ball out of the pocket and tossed it in his hand. 'I know nothing for certain,' he said finally. 'Gallagher, you seem to think that Vasiliev's political sympathies mean he might be some sort of enemy agent. That is highly unlikely. As I said, I know something about these Kadets, and their politics are no more radical than those of Mr Lloyd George, our esteemed prime minister. I have another hypothesis. What if Vasiliev really was a loyal Englishman? What if his activities in the naval intelligence offices were part of another investigation?'

'What are you talking about?' demanded Colson.

'Yes,' said Gallagher. 'I'd like to know too, Captain.'

Ryder replaced the cue ball on the table. 'Allow me to take you back to last May,' he said. 'On the morning of the Battle of Jutland, I sent a signal from Scapa Flow to London, asking if the German fleet had sailed from its base at Wilhelmshaven. I never received an answer. In fact, it turned out that the Germans *had* sailed, several hours before. If we had known the truth, we could have put the Grand Fleet into a position to trap the German navy and destroy it. In the event, we were too late and the Germans got away with only minor losses.'

Colson's voice was sharp. 'Are you blaming naval intelligence for this?'

Ryder's own voice had hardened. The moment of sympathy for Colson's breakdown had passed. 'Of course I am,' he said. 'And I am not the only one. It is no secret that Admiral Jellicoe is deeply concerned. He has said openly that he no longer has confidence in naval intelligence, and is seriously considering disbanding your division.'

'For God's sake!' Colson exploded. 'This is absurd! We have done nothing wrong.'

Gallagher intervened. 'Captain Ryder, are you suggesting that someone at a high level is conducting a clandestine investigation into the naval intelligence division? And that Vasiliev is working for them?'

'I am saying it is possible, yes.'

'And are you suggesting that someone in naval intelligence killed Vasiliev?'

'It's not impossible,' Ryder said calmly.

Colson was furious. 'Have you *met* any of our analysts? None were even in the navy before the war started. They're school-teachers, Cambridge dons, barristers, publishers, clergymen; clergymen's daughters, too. One of our people is the son of the Lord Mayor of London, another is a daughter of the secretary to the governor of the Bank of England. Most of them aren't capable of trapping a fly, let alone killing a man.'

'I can vouch for that,' said Mrs Vane. 'Also, if one of our officers caught Vasiliev snooping, their duty would be to raise the alarm, call the master-at-arms and have him arrested. Not murder him and hide his body.'

'Yes,' said Ryder. 'That would indeed be their duty. Unless naval intelligence has something to hide.'

'This is preposterous!' snapped Colson.

Ryder looked at Gallagher. 'You're the investigating officer. What do *you* think?'

'At this stage I am not prepared to speculate,' Gallagher said. He looked at Colson. 'But Captain Ryder has a point. Mrs Vane has kindly checked for me all of the names in the watchkeeper's logbook for Tuesday night. Vasiliev is the only person to log in who was not a member of the department staff. So, whoever killed him could have come from your division.'

Colson said nothing. Ryder's eyebrows rose again, the games master's face full of disapproval. 'Face the facts, Colson. Some-thing is rotten in naval intelligence, right under your nose.'

He glanced at the clock. 'Almost time to change for dinner, I think. Very well, Gallagher, that concludes our business for the moment. We'll speak again tomorrow.'

AFTER RYDER AND Colson had departed – Colson expostulating, Ryder waving him away – Mrs Vane looked at Gallagher. 'I asked earlier if you knew Lansing was coming here. You didn't answer.'

'I knew,' Gallagher said. 'Sir John told me, but he asked me to keep it quiet. Lansing is a personal friend of President Wilson. His cousin is also a senior member of the U.S. government, the equivalent to our Foreign Secretary.'

'Ah,' said Mrs Vane. 'And I have offended him.'

'I wouldn't lose any sleep over it. If he bothers you again, tell me.'

She considered this for a moment. 'What did you think of the meeting just now?'

'Ryder and Colson both know more than they are telling us. Quite a lot more.'

'But no one mentioned the elephant in the room,' said Mrs Vane.

Gallagher coughed. 'Meaning?'

'The telegram. No one said a word about it.'

'Ryder isn't supposed to know that the telegram exists. What was Colson's reaction when you showed it to him?'

'His first instinct was to hush everything up. He told me to put the telegram back in the safe and say nothing about it. How he planned to dispose of the body, I have no idea.'

'He was furious when Ryder arrived,' Gallagher mused. 'Is the Admiralty really thinking of winding up the intelligence division?'

'There is a rumour to that effect, yes. Another possibility

is that the division will be reorganized and merged into naval planning. Captain Ryder will take over as intelligence chief from Admiral Hall.'

'Ah,' said Gallagher. He coughed again, hating the dry rasping sound that came from his chest. 'That explains the edge between Ryder and Colson.'

'Ryder and Colson are like rams butting heads. Each has to be the biggest man in the room.'

'But when Colson spoke of his breakdown, Ryder showed a moment of humanity,' Gallagher mused. 'I wonder what was behind that . . . How likely is it that Vasiliev, a known security risk, would be employed on an internal investigation?'

Mrs Vane looked exasperated. 'In my time at the Admiralty, I have learned one lesson. Never underestimate the power of incompetence in the Royal Navy. If Mata Hari were to be appointed First Sea Lord tomorrow, I should not be surprised.'

Gallagher rose to his feet and walked across to the billiards table. Picking up the cue ball, he studied it for a moment. 'Anything else?'

'Yes . . . Do you remember the message on Vasiliev's cuff?'

'Yes.'

'Someone had written exactly the same message on a book of sheet music in the music room, *Thr. of Sat. 2030 2417*. Someone else had rubbed it out again. Mr Lansing spotted it and pointed it out to me.'

'Lansing!' Gallagher stared at her. 'Why did he do that?'

'Because he was trying to embarrass me,' she said caustically. 'Or was there more to it than that . . . You said *throne of Saturn* comes from the *Rubaiyat* and you think it could be part of a book cipher.'

Gallagher nodded. 'I've seen this code before, in America,

and that clerk who was stealing documents was using it too. The more I think about it, the more certain I am. This is the Dreamer's code.'

She shivered a little. 'So he is sending messages to someone here or someone is sending messages to him. That means he's here in the house, isn't he?'

'Yes,' Gallagher said.

He watched her grow calm again. It was hard to remember, he thought, that she had only been in the service for a short time. 'What is the American connection?' she asked.

'After the clerk was caught and hanged, we started hunting for the Dreamer. We found absolutely nothing at first, he has been adept at covering his tracks. But a contact in America reported that they too were looking for someone called the Dreamer, who had set up a spy ring in Boston before the war. Since then, very quietly, we have been working with the Bureau of Investigation and the American Secret Service.' Gallagher paused. 'Because America is neutral, this is a highly sensitive matter. You weren't told about this before, because it was judged that you didn't need to know.'

'I understand,' she said. 'How does the code work?'

'It's a two-part cipher, very different from the German diplomatic and naval codes which are much more complex. The Americans think the underlined phrases or words refer to individual people, but that's about as far as it goes. These people could be the senders, or the receivers, or the subjects of the message, or any combination of those. Each phrase will also have a corresponding number, which is the key to a substitution cipher. If we knew what numbers were associated with each name, the rest of the cipher could be cracked, given time. Without the numbers there's no hope.'

Mrs Vane frowned. 'So, *throne of Saturn* refers to a person?'

'Quite possibly. Which means *2030 2417* could be the key to that person's cipher.'

'What if it isn't?' she said suddenly.

Gallagher raised his eyebrows. Mrs Vane stood up abruptly. 'What if the message has already been decoded?' she asked. 'What if those numbers are a time and date?'

'Ah,' Gallagher said. He stood for a moment, thinking. '2030, eight thirty p.m. The second of April, 2 and 4. 17 refers to this year, 1917. What happens on the second of April, do you think?'

Mrs Vane shook her head. 'That's how we would write it, but an American would put the month and day the other way around. Eight thirty, yes, but on February the fourth. That's Sunday evening, a little over forty-eight hours from now.' Her voice was tense. 'Which means the clock is ticking,' she said.

'The pattern has been laid,' Gallagher said quietly. 'The pieces are being drawn together.' He paused again, frowning. 'Vasiliev wasn't an American. Why would he write the date in American fashion?'

'Perhaps he picked up the habit in America. Or someone else wrote the date for him.'

Gallagher raised his hand to his mouth and coughed. 'Very well. As you say, the clock is ticking, but not just for us. The enemy are counting down the hours too, and sooner or later they will have to show their hand.'

'So what do we do?'

'You heard the captain,' Gallagher said. 'We change for dinner.'

5

Shuffling footsteps, and a tentative knock at the door. 'Mr Gallagher, sir?'

'Come in,' Gallagher said, adjusting his bow tie in the mirror on the wardrobe door.

The door opened and Hunton entered, carrying a brown envelope on a silver salver. 'Pardon me for intruding, sir. A telegram has just arrived for you.'

'Thank you, Hunton. Please tell Lady Maud that I will be down directly.'

'Very good, sir.'

Hunton departed, and Gallagher opened the envelope and pulled out the telegram form. It was, as expected, from Bruce Bielaski, the director of the Bureau of Investigation in Washington. The text brought Gallagher's mind to full alert.

Willa Rittenhouse was indeed a journalist, and a very good one. She was, in Bielaski's words, a muck-raker, one of a particular breed of journalist who specialized in exposés of corruption in high places, both political and corporate. She was a regular correspondent for *McClure's Magazine* and the *New York World*, and her latest target was the oil tycoon, James Rogers Lansing. She had already published several articles detailing shady practices in Lansing's business empire, and was rumoured to be planning more.

Gallagher looked at his reflection in the mirror. 'I was right,' he said aloud. 'She isn't here on holiday.'

Friday, 2 February 1917
8.00 p.m.
48½ hours remaining

The dining room was not from Wuthering Heights, Jonquil Vane decided. No; the castle of Otranto, perhaps, or Elsinore, bleak and haunted by ghosts and nightmares. More dark wallpaper, densely patterned with arabesques this time, seemed to suck the light out of the room. Her husband, who had been an architect before a Turkish machine gun killed him at Cape Helles, would have described it as *William Morris, from his strychnine period*. Heavy drapes of Byzantine purple velvet had been pulled across the windows, but cold draughts were still seeping through. The ceiling was chunky white plaster stained by several decades of smoke; the chandeliers, which were French and had once been expensive, fought weakly to convert the feeble electrical current into light. The dark oak dining table lacked any kind of adornment. She thought it looked like a giant's coffin lid.

The guests were seated, the men in black evening dress with snow-white shirts, the women peacock-like in evening gowns, defiant splashes of colour against the darkness of the room. Only Mrs Vane herself was resolute in black. It was well over a year since she had lost both her husband and her mother, and she knew that according to custom she should put away her widow's weeds. *But how does one put a time limit on grief?* she

63

asked herself. *Who has the power to tell others when sorrow should cease? I shall wear black until there is light in my heart again; or else, I shall be buried in it.*

As well as Sir John Borden and his wife – she realized she could not think of the pale, brittle woman in red silk as Gallagher's mother – there were twelve guests. Ryder, Colson, Gallagher and herself made up four of them. The man with the waxed moustache, whose name was Herbert Fairbairn, sat on her left and talked to Lady Maud about cows; what interest either of them could have in cattle, she could not imagine. Fairbairn's wife Nathalie, another brittle-looking woman with red hair, stared at the wallpaper like it had personally offended her. Lansing, who did not so much as glance in her direction, sat next to a slender man in his forties who had been introduced as Nicholas Makarian, Borden's son-in-law. Makarian's wife, Gallagher's half-sister Penelope, was further up the table next to a young man named Price, who had raw scars on his cheek and a prosthetic hand protruding from the right sleeve of his coat; a common enough sight these days, she thought quietly. His wife, Edith Price, a rather sweet-looking girl, sat next to Gallagher.

Mrs Vane herself had been seated between Fairbairn and the serious dark-haired man she had noticed earlier in the drawing room, who stared straight ahead of him and did not speak. *This is going to be jolly*, she thought.

Hors d'oeuvres were served, filets of marinated herring on anchovy paste biscuits, all heavily flavoured with salt. Platt the butler began to pour wine, but Lansing waved the bottle away. 'Whisky for me,' he said. 'Water, not soda. I can't stand that fizzy muck.' He looked at the man with the waxed moustaches. 'What about you, Fairbairn? Care to join me?'

'I prefer wine,' Fairbairn said stiffly.

'Of course you do.' A footman brought a tumbler full of

whisky and water; Lansing took it out of his hands, drank about half of the contents in a single gulp, and banged the glass down on the table. 'Right,' he said. 'Let's eat.'

The young man beside Mrs Vane stirred a little. 'What a charming man,' he murmured.

'Do you know him?'

'I know of him. James Lansing. These days, he's just about the biggest thing in the oil business. He supplies at least half of our navy's oil.'

Mrs Vane searched for a topic of conversation that did not concern Lansing. 'I thought our ships were fuelled by coal.'

'Oh, we're moving to oil as quickly as we can now. The new fast battleships are all oil burners, and most of the light ships too. The older ships spray oil on the coal to make it burn faster, so it increases their speed. Oil is the future of naval warfare, no doubt about it.'

He sounded like he was rehearsing for a presentation. She surveyed him for a moment. 'You know a great deal about the subject. Are you in the navy?'

'Yes, for my sins. My name is Tovey, by the way, Charles Tovey. I'm an officer in the transport department at the Admiralty. One of my duties is scheduling shipments of bunker oil to naval bases around the British Isles. So, I end up knowing a lot about oil.'

'It sounds like fascinating work.'

Tovey sighed. 'If only it were,' he said. 'What do you do, Mrs . . . Vane, isn't it?'

'Yes. I work for the Paymaster General's Office.'

'Do you?' There was, she thought, a note of surprise in his voice, as if this was not the answer he was expecting. 'I, er . . . I don't really know what the Paymaster General does.'

'Neither does anyone else,' said Mrs Vane. 'Least of all those of us who work for him. I'm the vice-treasurer for Irish Exchequer bills, but please don't ask me what that actually means.'

The young man smiled a little. 'I know the feeling.'

He lapsed into silence again. Outside a train whistle shrieked, long and wavering in the wind.

The soup course was served, cloudy consommé with white lumps that were probably supposed to be profiteroles. Mrs Vane stirred her soup thoughtfully for a moment, and laid her spoon to one side. Fairbairn turned to her, smiling and inclining his head. 'My apologies, Mrs Vane, I fear I have been neglecting you. Our hostess and I have been engrossed in talking about sailing.'

The penny dropped. *Cowes*, she thought, *not cows. Stupid woman.* She smiled back. 'You are fond of sailing, Mr Fairbairn?'

'Very much so. I used to race my own boats before the war. Not with much success, I may add, but it was great fun.'

His voice was rich and round, of the type sometimes described as *plummy*, which Mrs Vane associated with old port and the reading rooms of gentlemen's clubs. 'At Cowes?' she asked.

'There, yes, but I also spent some time in America. I used to race out of Hyannis Port. Lovely little harbour, and superb sea conditions in the shelter of Cape Cod. I had a really fine boat there, called the *Chasseur*.' Fairbairn paused, aware that he was running on. 'Do you sail yourself, ma'am?'

'I'm afraid not,' said Mrs Vane. 'Water doesn't agree with me. I can get seasick in the bathtub.'

Fairbairn considered how to respond to this. Finally he chuckled, in a slightly uncertain way. Mrs Vane changed the subject. 'If I may ask, what took you to America?'

'Government service, ma'am. I had the honour to be His Majesty's consul in Boston for four years.'

'You're a diplomat? Where are you posted now?'

'In London. I was recalled late last year, and given a post in charge of the Russia and Middle East desk at the Foreign Office.'

'Russia and the Middle East together? That sounds an odd combination.'

'Not at all. Russia, like ourselves, is at war with Ottoman Turkey and takes a strong interest in the Middle East. Trying to second-guess Russian policy there takes up much of our time.'

'It sounds like a very demanding job,' she said.

He smiled again. The tips of his moustaches bobbed up and down. 'Perhaps. But I regard it as a privilege to hold such an important post.'

'I understand the situation in Russia is rather difficult at the moment.'

Fairbairn grew serious again. 'Indeed it is. I fear things are coming to a head. The opposition are calling for the Tsar to grant constitutional reforms or step down. Our great fear is that a new government in Russia could decide to make a unilateral peace with Germany.'

'That would be bad news,' said Mrs Vane. 'Is there anything we can do to stop them?'

'Oh, yes, there is plenty we can do. At the moment we are trying to build bridges with some of the opposition groups. There's one party in particular called the Kadets, whom we are cultivating. They're quite civilized fellows, very easy to deal with. They've agreed that if they take power, Russia will stay in the war.'

'What if they don't?'

'Ah, that's where our American friends come in, you see.' His voice sounded reassuring; she wondered if that was for her benefit, or his own. 'Our government is trying to persuade them to set aside their neutrality and join the Allied cause. Even if Russia does pull out, America's military and industrial power will more than fill the gap.'

On her other side, Tovey was listening intently. 'American friends?' she asked. 'Like Mr Lansing?'

'I wouldn't call Lansing a friend,' Fairbairn said stiffly, 'but there is no denying that he is influential. He has wealth and power, and even more importantly, he has the ear of President Wilson.'

'Oh?' She smiled. 'Where does he keep it?'

Fairbairn looked puzzled. *No sense of humour*, Mrs Vane told herself, and changed the subject again. 'Are you anything to do with oil?' she asked.

'Me? No, I own a few shares, but that's all. If you want to know about oil, talk to Commander Colson. He's a director of Anglo-Persian Oil.'

Mrs Vane glanced at Colson, who was stirring his soup in a hopeful manner and talking to the young man with the prosthetic arm. The fact that Colson should own shares in an oil company was unsurprising; she had learned a long time ago that the wealthy and powerful all knew each other and worked together. But she wondered now if Colson had another motive for coming to Hartlake Hall.

'What brings you here, Mrs Vane?' Fairbairn asked. 'I wouldn't have thought a shooting party was quite your thing.'

She smiled at him. 'My doctor told me to get out of the city for a while, and get some fresh air into my lungs. I am a colleague of Mr Gallagher at the Paymaster General's Office, and he suggested I come down for the weekend.'

She saw the look in Fairbairn's eyes before he could hide it; a momentary flash, quickly gone. 'The Paymaster General's Office?' he said politely. 'Is the work interesting?'

'Not in the slightest,' said Mrs Vane. She looked around, and saw Lady Maud in conversation with Captain Ryder. She dropped her voice to a murmur. 'It's a ghastly house, isn't it?'

'It's certainly not to my taste,' Fairbairn agreed. 'The music room is the only comfortable room in the place.'

'Yes. That's a very fine piano, and it's lovely to see a harpsichord. They're not so common these days.'

Fairbairn nodded towards the man seated beside Lansing. 'That will be Makarian, Sir John's son-in-law. When the zeppelins started bombing London, he brought his instruments down here for safe-keeping. He has a real passion for music, and plays with great skill. You should hear him.'

'I should like to,' said Mrs Vane. *I should also like to know which of the people around this table wrote the date and time on the music book, and who read it and rubbed it out. Who is passing signals to whom?*

THE FISH COURSE was cold salmon in aspic with slices of chili and beetroot, alternating blasts of heat and cold on the palate. The wine was a Chateau Langoiran, not quite as chilled as it needed to be. Nicholas Makarian held his glass up to the light. He was a rather intense man with high cheekbones and dark expressive eyes. 'What a pleasure it will be when the war ends,' he said, 'and we will once again have access to good hock and Moselle wines.'

'Ah, yes,' said Price, the young man with the prosthetic hand. '*That's* why we want the war to end.'

Everyone pretended not to hear him. 'A friend of mine acquired a case of hock the other day,' said Fairbairn. 'Smuggled out through Switzerland. Twenty shillings a bottle, it cost him. Robbery on the king's highway.'

'Not very patriotic of your friend,' said Lansing, sipping his whisky. 'You should all be drinking French wine. The French are your allies, ain't they?'

Other voices joined in. The young woman beside Gallagher turned to him. Her fair hair was carefully coiffed and her blue silk gown was a bold statement; a string of brilliants sparkled around her neck. 'We haven't been introduced,' she said. 'I'm Edith Price. That's my husband across the table.'

Her accent was American; Boston, at a guess. 'Patrick Gallagher,' said Gallagher.

Her eyes widened a little. 'Oh, you must be Mrs Makarian's half-brother! She often mentions you. You are Lady Maud's son, aren't you?'

'From her first marriage,' Gallagher said.

'Forgive me for being inquisitive, but is it permitted to ask what happened to your father?'

Overhead, the water pipes had begun to thump again. 'Nothing, so far as I know,' Gallagher said. 'My mother divorced him.'

Her blue eyes opened wide. 'Oh, dear. I'm so sorry, I didn't mean to pry.'

'Don't worry. It was a long time ago. How do you know Penelope?'

'Oh, we worked together for a little while. We were both volunteers at a Red Cross convalescent home.'

It was Gallagher's turn to stare. 'Penelope is with the Red Cross?'

The young woman glanced down the table towards Lady Maud. 'Yes, she has been for some time now. I don't think her mother knows.'

'I'm quite certain she doesn't. Never mind, the secret is safe with me. How long have you been in England, Mrs Price?'

'Oh, since before the war. I tried my hand at acting back home, but I wasn't any good. I needed something to do, so I became companion to a rather sweet old lady who decided to take up residence in London just before the war started. After she died I volunteered at the convalescent home, which is where I met my darling hero.'

'How fortunate for you both,' Gallagher said politely.

Her face grew serious. 'I'm not sure my poor Geraint describes himself as fortunate. He was at the Battle of Jutland, did you know? He was an officer on a light cruiser, and a shell hit the bridge and killed the captain and most of the other officers. Geraint was horribly wounded, but he took command of the ship and brought her and the rest of her crew safely back to port. But they had to amputate part of his arm, poor darling, and there was a time when the doctors thought he wouldn't survive at all.'

Gallagher watched Price picking apart his salmon, fork wielded in his left hand. 'He seems to have made a splendid recovery. I imagine you had something to do with that.'

'Geraint is as tough as he is brave. He has learned to do all sorts of things with only his left hand, even handle a shotgun. I think he is just marvellous. But then, I would say that.'

Gallagher smiled. 'How long have you been married?'

'Three months and fourteen days.' Her own smile was brilliant with happiness. 'Geraint can't go back to sea, but the navy gave him a shore posting and we moved to London. I just love London, don't you? The theatres especially, oh, my goodness! You could go to a different show every night for a month, and never see the same one twice.'

'Do you regret not becoming an actress yourself?'

'No. Well, not most of the time. I did go to see *Chu-Chin-Chow* the other day, and I remember thinking, I could act most of those girls off the stage . . . But no. I've seen the very best, the greats, actresses like Ellen Terry and Isadora Duncan and Roxanne Felix. I could never be anything like as good as them.'

The name startled him. 'You saw Roxanne Felix?'

'Oh, yes, dozens of times. She was *amazing*. She could do anything on stage, anything at all. Tragic heroines like Juliet and Ophelia, or comic characters like Gwendolen Fairfax and Lady Sneerwell, it was all the same to her. But who could ever forget her Juliet? *Swear not by the moon, the inconstant moon, that monthly changes in her circled orb, lest that thy love prove likewise variable.* And of course, she became a figure of tragedy herself, didn't she?'

'Yes,' Gallagher said quietly. 'She did.'

'It was just awful. She was absolutely in her prime, and to be cut off like that; oh, such a terrible waste.' She glanced at him. 'Did you ever see her on stage?'

'Many times,' he said, seeking desperately for another topic of conversation. 'I'm surprised to hear that you like London. The city is a bit dangerous at the moment.'

'Oh, you mean the zeppelin attacks? It's pretty quiet right now, not too many raids. It will get worse in the summer, they say, but we'll cross that bridge when we come to it.' She smiled, her teeth brilliant. 'And I would brave any danger to be with my darling Geraint. He is all the world to me.'

Gallagher looked around the table. Price was looking down at his plate, answering in monosyllables when Penelope tried to make conversation. Fairbairn was pontificating to Lady Maud who sat wooden-faced, staring straight ahead. Fairbairn's wife Nathalie was leaning towards Tovey, talking quietly to him; Mrs Vane was watching them with interest. Makarian and Lansing were talking about oil tankers.

'Then I wish you every happiness,' Gallagher said.

*

The white wine was followed by a red, Croizet-Bages with flecks of cork floating in the decanter. 'I must apologize,' Borden said, removing the larger chunks with a dessert spoon. 'It's not just the shortage of staff, of course, the kitchens here are tiny and very badly appointed. Escoffier himself would struggle to produce a first-class meal.'

'So unlike Netley Park, our dear house in Hampshire,' Lady Maud said. 'The kitchens there are very modern, *and* fully staffed.'

Lansing held out his whisky glass to be refilled. 'So, why did you leave Hampshire?'

'Of course, like so many other houses, Netley Park was requisitioned,' Borden said. 'It's now a convalescent hospital for Indian soldiers from the Western Front.'

'Patching them up so they can be sent back to the line again,' said Price.

There was an embarrassed pause, filled smoothly by Captain Ryder. 'If you'll forgive me, Sir John, I'm surprised this house wasn't requisitioned as well.'

'Hartlake Hall wasn't considered suitable,' Borden said. 'Steep stairs, narrow corridors with sharp bends, badly fitting doors and windows, unreliable electricity and limited hot water, none of which makes for a good hospital.' He chuckled. 'The matron who came to inspect the place said you couldn't pay her enough to spend the night here.'

'I know how she feels,' said Lady Maud. 'Platt, you may serve the entrée.'

Another train whistle sounded, and they heard once again the faint rattle of steel wheels on rails. The entrée was chicken in moulds with a rabbit farce, both dry and smothered in an aromatic bay sauce; the remove that followed was overcooked sirloin of beef with rubbery oysters. Braised carrots lay dying on the edges of each plate. Lansing speared an oyster with his fork and held it up. 'Is there a dog around here? This is the sort of food a dog would appreciate, don't you think?'

Borden was red-faced. 'Mr Lansing, I apologize again—'

'So how are you liking being back in England, Fairbairn?' Lansing said, ignoring him. 'I thought you were all set to stay in Boston.'

'I am a servant of my country,' Fairbairn said. 'I go where I am called.'

'Sure you do. Bit rough on your lady wife, though. Hey, Mrs Fairbairn? You liked Boston, didn't you?'

Nathalie Fairbairn looked up sharply. 'Yes, I was happy there,' she said. Her voice had a trace of a Scots accent, heavily ironed out. 'But the time had come to return home.'

'You left pretty suddenly, didn't you? You didn't even say goodbye to your old friends.'

'I said farewell to the ones who mattered,' she said, and there was a razor's edge in her voice.

'If you say so.' Lansing transferred his attention back to Fairbairn. 'I understand they gave you some big job in the Foreign Office. Head of a desk, which I'm guessing is something pretty important. And they made you a knight too. Sir Herbert Fairbairn, how does that feel?'

'You are mistaken,' Fairbairn said. 'I do not have a knighthood.'

'Don't you? I was sure I saw in the *Gazette* that you'd been given the Order of the Bath.'

'Yes, I was made a Companion of the Order of the Bath. CB, not KCB.'

'A Companion?' Lansing laughed a little, ignoring Lady Maud's basilisk stare. 'That's rich. A companion in the bath. But that's an odd thing, though, isn't it? You were a consul over in the USA, and you did a pretty good job, or so I heard. You come back here and get promoted to head the Russia and Middle East desk, and they still don't make you a K? Did you do something wrong over in Boston? Some skeleton in your closet, maybe?'

Fairbairn stared at him. 'What are you suggesting?' he demanded.

'I'm just surprised that a man of your obvious ability has been overlooked for honours that are conferred on lesser men as a matter of routine. Maybe you should ask Sir John here to put in a word for you with Mr Churchill. He has influence, he might be able to help you. Or I can speak to my own contacts if you like.'

'Thank you for your concern, Lansing,' Fairbairn snapped. 'I will let you know if I require your assistance.'

'Sure,' said Lansing. 'Happy to be of service, *old bean.*' He looked around the table. 'So tell me, folks, how's the war going? Not too well, from what I hear.'

'Mr Lansing,' Lady Maud said forcefully. 'We do not talk about the war at the dinner table.'

Lansing looked genuinely startled. 'Don't you? Forgive me for asking, my lady, but what *do* you talk about?'

Another awkward silence, the latest of many, descended on the table. This time Edith Price was the first to fill it. 'We went to see *Zig-Zag* at the Hippodrome yesterday,' she said eagerly. 'It has George Robey in it, and some wonderful songs. Geraint absolutely loved it, didn't you, darling?'

'It sounds very good,' Makarian said, smiling. 'Penelope, we must find some excuse to go.'

'Musical theatre,' Lansing said, draining his glass. 'Sure. Let's talk about that.'

A sour cherry sorbet, bitter pools of slush in frosted glasses, was followed by quails on toast with a sickly sweet madeira sauce. Another train rattled up the line towards Tonbridge.

Edith talked eagerly about her favourite London shows. 'Do you often go to the theatre, Mr Gallagher?' she asked.

'I used to,' he said. 'Not any more.' He had not set foot in a theatre since Roxanne died. That part of his life was broken, and could not be mended.

The meal ground to its interminable end; dessert, in the form of riz à la Nelson: rice pudding with a rum and lemon sauce. Colson held up a hand. 'Listen,' he said sharply.

Everyone fell silent. At first there was only a distant vibration, a pulse beating in the air. Slowly it resolved itself into a coherent noise, the thrum–thrum–thrum–thrum–thrum of unsynchronized engines. Lady Maud went pale, her hands clutching at her napkin in front of her.

'What is it?' asked Edith Price.

'It is a zeppelin,' Lady Maud snapped. 'Do you not recognize the sound?'

'Getting closer,' said Colson. He seemed calm, his hands clasped on the table in front of him, but his knuckles were white with strain. 'Flying low, too,' he said.

'Coming in under the clouds,' said Borden. 'They follow the railway line to London. A train went up the line just now, and this one is probably tracking it, following the glow of the engine's firebox.'

The noise was louder now, *thrum–thrum–thrum–thrum–thrum*, filling the room. Behind the drapes lightning flashed, once, twice, a long pause and then a third time. 'Searchlights,' Colson said, his voice almost a whisper. 'There's a second one too, coming behind.'

'Here they come,' Ryder murmured.

THRUM–THRUM–THRUM–THRUM–THRUM.

Everyone sat rigid, staring up at the ceiling. A single zeppelin was armed with eight machine guns and carried up to five tons of bombs, enough to obliterate the house and everyone in it. Sweat had broken out on Colson's forehead. Price sat immobile, staring up at the ceiling. Gallagher wondered what memories were passing through his mind.

THRUM–THRUM–THRUM–THRUM–THRUM. The searchlights flashed again. The first airship was directly over the house now. The room shook. Cutlery vibrated and rattled on the table. The noise faded a little, but quickly swelled in volume again as the second airship passed directly over the house, even lower than the first. After a moment its engines too began to fade, dwindling to a murmur in the distance. Slowly, the party began to relax. Colson unclasped his hands.

'They're gone,' said Borden. 'They'll turn over Tonbridge and follow the line north-west towards London.'

'How often does this happen?' asked Tovey.

'This time of year, usually about once a week. This isn't the prime raiding season, of course. Last summer, they were over most nights.'

'Where's the Royal Flying Corps?' demanded Lansing. 'Somebody told me there's an aerodrome just a few miles from here. Why aren't your pilots up trying to shoot them down?'

'The aerodrome is only a wireless training school,' Borden said. 'The aeroplanes are not equipped for night flying, let alone fighting. Some of them don't even have guns.'

Lansing looked incredulous. 'So you let German airships wander over your countryside and drop bombs on the capital, and you do nothing to stop them?'

'That's not true,' Ryder said sharply. 'We have defences, anti-aircraft guns and night fighters, but they are deployed to protect London. Out here, we're too far from the city to be covered.'

Lansing snorted and drained his glass again. 'All I can say is, it's no damn wonder you're losing the war,' he said.

6

THE DOMESTIC ROUTINES of the country house had accreted over many generations, and not even the passage of enemy airships could disturb them for long. The ladies withdrew. A decanter of port was placed on the dining room table, and some of the men lit cigars. 'Tomorrow morning there will be a driven shoot,' Borden said. 'We should be able to get four drives in before lunch. There will be time for rough shooting tomorrow afternoon, of course, and Sunday after lunch too. On Sunday morning, my wife and I will attend divine services at All Saints church in Tudeley. You are welcome to join us.'

'Thank you, sir,' said Tovey.

'Commander Colson, I believe you brought your own car and driver. Mr Lansing, did you come by car?'

Lansing shook his head. 'I don't like automobiles. Damned unreliable things, in my experience. Give me a first-class railway carriage any time.'

Borden nodded. 'Of course. If anyone else requires transport to Tonbridge station on Monday morning, speak to Platt and he will arrange it.'

'What about aeroplanes, Mr Lansing?' asked Tovey. 'Do you fancy a ride in one of those?'

Lansing blew out cigar smoke. 'Aeroplanes? Damned flying

78

coffins, if you ask me. No, what I want is one of those big airships. I'd give my right arm for one of those.'

Everyone tried not to look at Price, who glared at Lansing. The oilman looked around the room, perplexed, until his eye fell on Price's prosthetic arm. He raised his hands in apology. 'Ah, that was clumsy of me. Sorry, Mr Price. No offence.'

'Go to hell,' Price said, and he rose and left the room, banging the door behind him. Lansing shrugged, drained his port glass and refilled it. Colson cleared his throat, leaning forward. 'Mr Fairbairn, there is a rumour from Russia that Rasputin has been assassinated. Is there any truth in the matter?'

Some of the tension drained out of the atmosphere. Fairbairn touched the tips of his moustache. 'I'm afraid so,' he said. 'It's making things a bit difficult for us in Russia, I have to say.'

'Even more difficult for the Russians,' said Makarian.

Borden looked at him. 'Your business partner is in Saint Petersburg, Nicholas. What does he say?'

Makarian shook his head. 'Whenever I ask Maxim Ivanovich about the political situation, his answer is always the same: Russia is a madhouse, nothing makes sense, and however bad we imagine the outcome will be, the reality will be even worse. He is usually right, too.'

'That's not good news for you fellows,' Lansing said. 'There's fifty German divisions fighting in the east, but if Russia caves in, all of those troops will come rushing back to reinforce the Western Front. You and the French are barely clinging on now. If Russia falls, you're done for.'

He did not sound particularly troubled. Gallagher remembered the messenger at the Admiralty. *Everything depends on two questions. Will Russia leave the war? And will the Americans join it?*

He leaned towards his stepfather. 'May I have a word in private, John?'

'Of course. Come through to the library.'

The library was small and cramped, and most of its shelves were bare of books. The few volumes that were visible bore titles like *Fatigue Study, Experiments in Industrial Organization, Factory Administration and Accounts*. Water stains marked the plaster ceiling and some of the paint had begun to peel away.

The two men sat down facing each other in the firelight. They were fond of each other, in a distant sort of way; unlike his wife and daughters, Borden knew the real nature of Gallagher's work, and respected him for it.

'I'd like to know about some of the other guests,' Gallagher said. 'What is your connection with the Prices?'

Borden rubbed his eyes. He looked exhausted, Gallagher thought; his hair was thinner than it had been last summer, and he had gained weight. Gallagher wondered if he was unwell.

'I know young Price's father, of course,' said Borden. 'He's a navy man too, vice-admiral. I ran into him at my club the other day. He told me the boy has recovered physically from his wounds, but he still isn't quite himself. His father thought a day's shooting might cheer him up.'

Giving a shotgun to a man still suffering from the trauma of battle in order to cheer him up was, Gallagher thought, a uniquely English thing to do. 'I gather his wife knows Penelope.'

Borden looked at him sharply. 'They were volunteers together for a couple of months until Penelope was transferred. Not a word to Maud, of course.'

Gallagher nodded. 'And Tovey?'

'He has a post in the transport division at the Admiralty. I hadn't met him before today, but we've been corresponding for some time about shell supplies. He wrote to me on Wednesday and asked if we could meet, and I invited him to come down. He's responsible for oil shipments, too, and so of course I thought it might be useful for him to meet Nicholas.'

This, of course – *of course* – was how the British Empire was really governed; not in the houses of Parliament or the corridors of Whitehall, but in club smoking rooms and on shooting weekends. It had always been thus, Gallagher decided; Hubert Walter and Stephen Langton, Walsingham and Cecil had probably conducted their business in much the same way, minus the cigars and shotguns. 'Thank you,' he said aloud. 'I'm sorry to pry, but I'm sure you understand why I must.'

Borden sipped his port. 'Of course. Being inquisitive is all in a day's work for you fellows, isn't it?'

'Then you'll understand too if I pry a little further. Why did you invite Herbert Fairbairn?'

'Surely it's obvious,' Borden said. His jowly face was watchful. 'Fairbairn is an influential fellow, with connections in both Russia and America. This is a sensitive time, of course, and I am counting on him for advice.'

Gallagher paused for a moment, considering his words. 'So,' he said finally. 'Let me see if I have this straight. James Lansing is a personal friend of President Woodrow Wilson and the man who personally financed Wilson's last election campaign. His cousin is also Wilson's Secretary of State. He is in Britain as Wilson's secret envoy, come to assess the situation and report back to the president. Wilson's instincts are telling him to stay neutral. You hope to influence Lansing, so that he will persuade Wilson to abandon his neutrality and commit America to the war on our side. How am I doing so far?'

'Spot on,' Borden said. His jowly face was watchful.

'Where do you fit in, John? You are parliamentary secretary

to the Minister of Munitions, not a diplomat. This is a Foreign Office matter.'

'That's why I invited Fairbairn, of course.' The older man looked miffed. 'And I'm not just an ordinary parly sec, Pat. I've served on the Board of the Admiralty, and I have influence in my party and in government. Lloyd George trusts me. So does Winston.'

'Ah, I thought I detected the hand of Churchill in all of this. But he's not even in government at the moment.'

'Not yet,' said Borden. 'But the time is coming. Winston has admitted responsibility for his mistakes at Gallipoli, and people reckon he has atoned for his sins.'

'Sixty thousand men were killed at Gallipoli, in a campaign that he devised and promoted,' Gallagher said. 'Some would say that calls for quite a lot of atonement.'

'You can't blame Winston for everything that went wrong at Gallipoli. There were many other failures, of course.' Borden drank some more of his port. 'Winston has his eye on becoming the next Minister of Munitions. Can't happen too soon, in my opinion. The current chap is useless.'

The current chap was Christopher Addison, a physician and ardent social reformer; he was never likely to have much in common with Sir John Borden, for whom conservative privilege was bred in the bone. Gallagher leaned forward a little. 'And so, this is Churchill's bid for a return to power,' he said. 'Half-American himself, he is positioning himself as a bridge between America and Britain. If he can bring the two together in an alliance against Germany, his future will be assured. I'm sure he will be duly grateful to the men who helped him along the way.'

'Winston is loyal to his friends,' Borden said.

'Have you spoken to Lansing?'

'We had a brief conversation this afternoon, after he arrived. He is, as you saw, pessimistic about our prospects. And of course, America has her own worries.' Borden's irritation faded. 'I fear I am facing an uphill task.'

Gallagher nodded. 'There is something you don't know about Lansing,' he said. 'As well as being Wilson's envoy, he is in London to further his own ends. Specifically, he wants control of the Middle East oilfields.'

Borden stiffened a little. 'Anglo-Persian Oil has the concession for those fields.'

'As you know full well, that concession was granted by the British government, which is also a major shareholder in Anglo-Persian. It can easily be revoked. Ask yourself a question, John. How badly does Churchill want this American alliance? How far will he go in order to get it?'

Borden stood up. 'Be careful, Pat. Being an officer of the secret service gives you a great deal of licence, but there are limits.'

'I understand,' Gallagher said after a moment.

'Good. Now, I think it's time we joined the ladies, don't you?'

THE ARCTIC WASTES of the drawing room were filled with people so still and lifeless that they could have been cardboard cutouts; either that, Gallagher thought, or they had frozen to death. The Prices and Makarians were playing cards, each staring absorbed at their own hand. Colson stood watching them, chin cupped in his hand. Lansing and Mrs Vane sat at opposite ends of a settee, each with a cup of coffee resting in their lap, ignoring each other.

Gallagher looked around the room. 'Where are Ryder and Tovey?' he asked Mrs Vane.

'Playing billiards,' she said.

'Sounds like a dandy idea,' Lansing said. 'Think I'll join them.' He rose to his feet, bowed to Lady Maud, who was seated in an armchair next to the dying fire, and left the room. Ignoring the expression on his mother's face, Gallagher walked over to the fireplace, took two logs from the basket and dropped them onto the fire. Sparks swirled briskly and flew up the chimney. Dusting his hands on his trousers, Gallagher crossed the room to join Fairbairn, who was studying an oil painting depicting a street scene in a vaguely Mediterranean town.

'Congratulations on your new posting,' Gallagher said quietly.

Fairbairn touched the tips of his moustache. 'Bit of a poisoned chalice, if you ask me. But thank you.'

'You chose your words carefully in the dining room, but what do you really think? Will Russia blow up?'

'Of course it will, and sooner than we think. The conservative nobles murdered Rasputin in the hope of restoring the power of the Tsar, but they made a grave mistake. The people adored Rasputin, they saw him as one of them, and his death is the signal that the opposition have been waiting for. The Tsar will be off his throne by the end of the month. After that, God knows.'

'During your time in Boston, did you ever run across a man called Paul Vasiliev? English, but with Russian ancestry?'

'I never met him, but I know the name. He used to crew for some of the big yacht owners, down Rhode Island way. The Vanderbilts, Jack Morgan, people like that.'

He was talking, Gallagher knew, about some of the richest men in America, if not the world. 'He also visited Boston,' Gallagher said. He dropped his voice. 'He had an affair with Sadie Lansing.'

Fairbairn's head came around. His dark eyes were sharp. 'How do you know that?'

'The Americans told us.'

'Bielaski didn't mention it at the time.'

'Maybe he didn't know,' Gallagher said. 'Your wife was a friend of Mrs Lansing. Might she have met Vasiliev while he was in Boston?'

'I have no idea,' Fairbairn said. 'I do not enquire too closely into my wife's social life.'

Gallagher remembered Nathalie Fairbairn during dinner, talking quietly to Tovey, her head close to his. 'Where is Mrs Fairbairn now?'

'She retired early. She is indisposed.' Fairbairn hesitated for a moment. 'Did you hear any more about what happened there? At Aquinnah?'

'No. What are your instructions from the Foreign Office about Lansing?'

'I have none.' Again, a little hesitation. 'The Foreign Secretary doesn't know I am here. This is an unofficial meeting.'

Then what are you doing here? was the obvious question, but Gallagher let it pass. 'Don't let Lansing goad you. And whatever you do, don't promise him anything.'

'I have no intention of doing so. Trust me, I can handle Lansing. I am well aware of his ambitions in the Middle East and his desire to control the oilfields, and I also know how slippery he is. You have my word that he will not touch a single drop of our oil.'

'Good,' said Gallagher. 'But play your cards close to your chest.'

Fairbairn nodded. Gallagher walked to where his mother sat by the now reinvigorated fire. 'My apologies,' he said, 'but I am going to turn in. It has been a long day.'

'Of course,' Lady Maud said after a moment. 'You must do

as you wish.' Suddenly, surprisingly, she raised her eyes to his. 'Forgive me,' she said quietly.

He was startled. 'For what?'

'For showing fear, when the airships came.'

'I think everyone was a little afraid,' Gallagher said. 'I certainly was.'

She looked down at her hands. 'It is different for you. For all of you. You don't know what it is like, with nothing to do but sit here, day after day, waiting. Just waiting.'

Gallagher studied her for a moment. 'What has happened?' he asked softly.

There was a long pause. He was surprised when she finally answered. 'Do you recall Phoebe? My maid?'

'Of course.'

'We received word yesterday. Her husband was in the Royal Flying Corps, an observer in a machine called a B.E.2c. He was shot down on a reconnaissance mission over Lens. The aeroplane caught fire in mid-air, and burned all the way to the ground. They sent back his wedding ring. It was the only part of him that could still be recognized.'

There was a long silence. Instinctively, Gallagher made a motion with his hand, but his mother looked up sharply. 'No,' she said. 'It is too late.'

He nodded. Slowly, he bent and kissed her fair, greying hair, and felt the effort she made not to flinch away from his touch. 'Goodnight, Mother,' he said.

Lady Maud retired soon after, escorted by her husband. Jonquil Vane watched them go, thoughtfully.

'I'm freezing,' Price said, rising to his feet. 'I'm going to sit by the fire and get warm. Care to take my hand, Commander?'

Colson stared at Price's prosthetic arm, his face shocked. 'My hand of cards,' Price said evenly. 'You can partner Edith.'

'Oh.' The relief was clear in Colson's voice. 'Yes, of course. Don't mind if I do.' He sat down in Price's vacated chair, and Price walked to stand by the fire, holding his good hand down towards the flames. Mrs Vane smiled at him. 'Wherever Shackleton is, it must be warmer,' she said.

'Tell me about it,' Price said. 'By lunchtime tomorrow, we'll be eating the sled dogs.'

Behind them, Makarian said something and Edith laughed. Momentarily, the room seemed a little lighter. Mrs Vane smiled again. 'You're a lucky man,' she said to Price.

'Yes. I suppose I should remember that more often. There are times when I don't feel very lucky.'

'You are alive,' she said quietly. 'That's more than many can say.'

Price straightened. 'Really?' he said, and there was iron in his voice. 'Is that the best you can offer?'

'What would you like me to say?' she asked, her own voice still quiet.

'I'd *like* someone to tell me why the Royal Navy has seen fit to throw me on the scrapheap after all I have done. Look at Colson. He spent a few weeks in France, picked up some dead sprig of royalty and organized his funeral tea, and they gave him the Distinguished Service Cross. Or Ryder, who sat on his arse all through the Battle of Jutland, safe and sound at Scapa Flow. He got the DSO, for God's sake. I brought my ship back from Jutland with half of her crew dead or wounded, and what did I receive? Precisely nothing. Now I'm a penpusher in the Admiralty secretariat, and there's no bloody future in that. I've had it, Mrs Vane. I'm getting out of the navy as soon as I can.'

'What will you do?' she asked.

'I don't know. There must be something a one-armed man can do. Perhaps I'll learn to juggle, and join a circus. That would be quite an attraction, wouldn't it?'

Mrs Vane rose to her feet, gathering her skirts around her. 'I think you should stop feeling sorry for yourself,' she said.

Price stared at her. 'What do you mean by that?'

'I said earlier that you are lucky, and you are. My husband was killed on the first day of the landings at Gallipoli. I don't even know where he is buried. You are young, you have a whole life ahead of you and you have a beautiful wife who adores you. That is what I mean, Mr Price.'

Price rubbed his eyes. 'I'm sorry,' he said.

'Don't be sorry,' she said. 'Be thankful. Goodnight, Mr Price.'

LANSING DID NOT go to the billiards room. Climbing the stairs from the frigid hall, he made his way through the warren of passageways to the west wing of the house, stopping in front of a door and rapping his knuckles hard on the oak panel. 'Who is it?' a woman's voice asked.

'It's me,' Lansing said. 'Open up.'

Several seconds passed before the door finally opened. Nathalie Fairbairn stood in the doorway in a white dressing gown, red hair falling over her shoulders. 'What is it?' she demanded.

'Is your husband here?' Lansing asked.

'We have separate rooms. What do you want?'

Lansing gripped her by the shoulders and pushed her back into the room, kicking the door shut with his heel. 'Guess,' he said.

'I'm not in the mood.'

'I don't care.'

She raised her hand to slap his face, but he gripped her wrist, pushing her against the dressing table. Furious, she tore her arm free, wrenched open the drawer of the table and pulled out a small revolver, aiming it at his chest. 'Touch me and I'll kill you,' she snapped.

'No, you won't,' Lansing said.

Nathalie's finger caressed the trigger. 'Why not?'

'First of all, everybody downstairs will hear the shot. Even if you manage to get out of the house, Sir John's gamekeepers will track you down. And second, you won't kill me because you like me.'

'*Like* you? I hate your guts!'

'Yes, but that's what gets your engine running, isn't it? Bend over.'

'I'm not—'

'Yes, you are,' said Lansing, unbuttoning his flies. 'Bend over.'

Nathalie spat at him, threw the gun onto the bed, turned around and bent over the dressing table. Lansing lifted the hem of her dressing gown and pulled her drawers roughly down around her knees. Sweating, he caressed her for a moment and felt her shiver. 'Now, that is nice,' he said, squeezing hard. 'I've always said it. The rest of you ain't much to look at, but that is the finest ass north of Mexico.'

'Get on with it!'

'As my lady wishes,' he said, and he gripped her hips with hands like the jaws of a vice. Silence fell, broken only by Lansing's hard breathing and the rasp of Nathalie's fingernails clutching at the edge of the table, and then Lansing leaned forward suddenly, slapping his hands down on the table and panting. He stood in that poise for a moment, recovering his breath, and stepped back and buttoned his flies.

Nathalie turned around, leaning back against the dressing table. 'Give me a cigarette,' she said.

Lansing took his cigarette case from his pocket, extracted two cigarettes and lit them both with a silver lighter. 'That feels better,' he said. 'You know, there was a moment during dinner when I thought I was going to lose my temper. But I feel much more mellow now.'

She took one of the cigarettes and inhaled deeply. 'You, mellow?' she asked, blowing out smoke. 'Pull the other one.'

'What are you doing here?' Lansing asked. 'I know why Fairbairn is here, but why did he drag you out to this dump in the middle of nowhere?'

She blew out smoke. 'Mind your own business.'

'Ah, I see it now. You're fishing. That lad Tovey is, what? Half your age? Just how you like them. You and your pal Sadie. Always fond of the boys, weren't you?'

'Don't you dare speak ill of Sadie! She should never have married a prick like you.'

'Don't get all holier-than-thou on me, lady. She was *my* wife, remember.' Lansing paused. 'Although, maybe she was closer to you than she was to me. Is that why you're so sensitive? Did you two have a little dalliance of your own, maybe? Did you munch on a little hair pie together?'

She stubbed out the cigarette and threw it at him. 'By God,' she said. 'There will come a day when I use that gun.'

'I ain't holding my breath,' he said.

'Get out. You've had what you came for, now leave me alone.'

Lansing was halfway to the door when she spoke again. 'James.'

'Yes?' he said, turning.

'What really happened to Sadie?'

'How the hell should I know? Ask your husband, he was there the night she died. I was two thousand miles away in Mexico.'

'She didn't take an overdose, James. She used heroin, yes, but she was never careless.'

'Oh, yes? If you knew her so damned well, what's your explanation?'

She shook her head in sudden distaste. 'Never mind. Go on, get out.'

'Sure. Until next time.' Lansing bowed, mocking her. 'Good night, Mrs Fairbairn.'

It was late when Gallagher went up to bed, trying to fend off the inevitable for as long as possible. Opening the door to the Cheese Room, he saw at once that the room had been searched. The signs were slight; the searcher had been an expert, keen not to give themselves away, but the pillows on the bed were not quite as they had been, and one of the mousetraps had been moved, leaving a bare dark rectangle in the thin layer of dust on the floor. This was to be expected, he thought, and in a way welcomed.

Far away to the north-west there was an orange glow in the sky, flames reflecting off the low-hanging clouds. The zeppelins had found their way to London.

He undressed, lay down and went to sleep.

The dream came without warning, as it always did, fastening itself upon him and gripping his mind with iron claws. He struggled to wake up, but he could not tear himself away. At first he was floating in the air; then he was falling trapped in a cage of fire. That, a corner of his mind knew, was in response to the death of the maidservant's husband, burned to death in a falling aeroplane.

The fire changed, as he knew it would, into water cold and dark, surrounding him, drawing him down. The surface of the sea was high above him, a circle of light growing smaller and smaller as the water sucked him back into the bowels of the ship. The pain in his lungs grew stronger, the rest of his body numb with cold. An object slapped him in the face, a drowning rat being pulled down with him. The darkness increased and he heard Roxanne's voice, dim and full of echoes, reciting Juliet's words.

> *Shut me nightly in a charnel house*
> *O'er covered quite with dead men's rattling bones,*
> *With reeky shanks and yellow chapless skulls . . .*

The circle of light disappeared, and in its place came her face, beautiful, fair, haunted.

> *. . . or bid me go into a new-made grave*
> *And hide me with a dead man in his shroud . . .*

A hard knocking sound, repeated; the ship, rolling over and preparing to settle in her last resting place, with himself entombed inside her. The knocking came again, and with it another voice, insistent, worried. *Mr Gallagher! Mr Gallagher, are you all right?*

The face vanished. The dream shattered and fell away in fragments. He sat up quickly, listening to the wind rattle the windows. A mouse scurried across the floor, squeaking faintly. He reached for the light switch and the light bulb flickered into life. 'Mr Gallagher!' Mrs Vane's voice said sharply outside the door.

'Come in.'

The door opened and Mrs Vane slipped inside, wrapped in a heavy wool dressing gown to keep out the cold. 'I think you were having a nightmare,' she said.

'Yes.' Gallagher rubbed his eyes. 'Did I wake the entire house?'

'I don't think so. I only heard you because I was already awake.' She sat down on one end of the bed. 'Do you want to talk about it?'

'No.' The dreams in which he relived his own near death on the *Lusitania* two years ago were commonplace. What tore at his soul were the images of Roxanne that these dreams sometimes evoked. Roxanne did not die when the ship went down; her murder had taken place eight years before. Earlier, he had wondered if he was losing his memories of her. But in his nightmares, she became real again.

'Why were you awake?' he asked.

'I sleep poorly at the best of times. Tonight, something was bothering me.' She paused. 'I'm certain that both Lieutenant Tovey and Mr Fairbairn know who I really am.'

'Fairbairn does, yes, because he knows who *I* am. We have met before. I'm sorry, I should have warned you about that, but I didn't reckon with you being sat next to him at dinner. Tovey . . . What makes you say that?'

'I told him that I work for the Paymaster General's Office. His face changed, just for a moment. Perhaps he doesn't know who I *really* am, but I reckon he knows I work at naval intelligence.'

'It's possible. Tovey also has a post at the Admiralty. I didn't know he would be here at all,' Gallagher said. 'I seem to have planned this rather badly.'

'Why is he here?'

'To stitch up a deal with my brother-in-law to charter oil tankers to the navy. Nicholas is already ludicrously rich, but his appetite for money never decreases.'

'That's how the rich grow richer,' said Mrs Vane. 'Very well, forget Tovey.'

The memory of the dream was receding. Gallagher smiled a little. 'Go on. What do you make of our fellow guests?'

She rolled her eyes. 'Tovey, dull. Price, angry and dull. Colson, a man being eaten alive by his inner demons. Ryder, really should have been a Latin teacher.'

'Really? I was thinking games master.'

'If so, very second eleven. He's jealous of Colson, too . . . Edith Price is too good to be true. There must be something wrong with her.'

'She is very fond of musical theatre.'

'There we have it. Fairbairn is one of Spy's caricatures, animated and given a voice. His wife . . . I'm not sure. I haven't seen enough of her to say.'

'And Makarian and Penelope?'

'Enigmatic,' she said.

'Which one?'

'Both of them.' She paused. 'As for myself, I think the word is fusspot. The real reason I couldn't sleep is that I am worrying about everything. How did Vasiliev's killer escape from a locked room? And this connection with Lansing's late wife. What does that mean?'

'There's a few more things you need to know,' Gallagher said finally. 'First of all, Lansing and Fairbairn already know each other. Mrs Fairbairn was a close friend of Mrs Lansing. And finally, Sadie Lansing's death was very similar to Vasiliev's.'

Mrs Vane sat up straight. 'She was murdered?'

'At the time, we gave out that she had died by accident. An overdose of heroin. But yes, she was murdered.'

'I think you had better tell me about it,' said Mrs Vane.

7

THE CAR, AN Oldsmobile Limited, slowed as it descended the hill towards the sea. Bruce Bielaski, sitting beside the driver, wiped his brow with his shirt sleeve. 'It's damned hot,' he said.

In the back seat, Gallagher nodded. 'Feels like there might be a storm brewing.'

The sky overhead was clear, but a white haze was building on the southern horizon. The harbour to their left was full of choppy blue waves, and further out to sea big swells were coming in off the Atlantic. White surf piled onto the beaches of Martha's Vineyard a few miles away. The road ran down past the harbour and across a short bridge onto a little island, steep and stony with clumps of stunted pine trees. A narrow stretch of water separated them from another, larger island to the south, Nonamesset. The scene was quite beautiful, Gallagher thought.

Turning a sharp bend in the road, they looked up and saw an enormous house, three storeys high, perched on rocks fifty feet above the sea. The house was built of brick and wood, with straight, severe lines that reminded Gallagher of a factory. The second and third storeys were lined with tall glass windows facing out over the sea.

'There it is,' Bielaski said, pointing to the house. 'That's Aquinnah. It's an old Indian name, means the place under the hill.'

Gallagher shaded his eyes against the sunlight. 'House, you said? I've seen smaller palaces.'

Bielaski chuckled. 'That's what you can buy when you have all the money in the world. Charles Bonaparte, old Napoléon's great-nephew, built the place when he was attorney-general, and he later sold it on to the Warren family.'

'Lansing doesn't own the house?'

'No, Sadie Lansing, née Warren, inherited it before she was married. The gossip is that Lansing would like to get his hands on it, but Sadie won't give it up.' Bielaski chuckled again. 'When Sadie gets hold of something, she doesn't let go.'

Another car, a Buick, was pulled up outside the entrance to the house. Two men stood beside it. Gallagher recognized the first man, dressed in a pale suit with a straw boater, as Herbert Fairbairn, the British consul in Boston. The other wore an overcoat despite the heat, and a fedora tilted back on his head.

The driver pulled the car to a halt, and Bielaski and Gallagher stepped out. Fairbairn stepped forward to shake hands. 'Good to see you again, Gallagher,' he said in his rich voice. 'I trust you had an easier crossing than . . . Than last year.'

He was referring, delicately, to the final, fatal voyage of the *Lusitania*. 'At least I kept my feet dry this time,' Gallagher said.

Bielaski motioned to the man in the overcoat. 'Pat, meet Joe Flynn from our Secret Service. Joe, this is Pat Gallagher, your British counterpart.'

The man with the overcoat nodded. He had a face like a stone slab, with an old scar along the line of his jaw. 'How's things in London?' he asked. 'I hear the zeppelins are making a mess of it.'

'It's not too bad so far,' Gallagher said. He looked up at the sky. 'What's happening with the weather?'

'A hurricane is coming,' Fairbairn said. 'See the flags?'

A flag mast stood at the mouth of the harbour, a large red flag drooping in the windless air. More flags could be seen outside the lighthouse at Nobska Point, further along the coast, and across the passage on the northern tip of Nonamesset.

'Is it coming near us?' Flynn asked.

Fairbairn nodded. 'I checked with the Weather Bureau this morning. They reckon the eye will pass over Nantucket sometime before midnight. We're in for a rough night.'

Bielaski looked worried. As director of the Bureau of Investigation, he was a lawyer, not a man of his hands. 'Will we be safe here?' he asked.

'Aquinnah has been through plenty of hurricanes,' Fairbairn said. 'We're high enough to avoid the storm surge, that's the main thing.'

'You've been here before?' asked Gallagher.

Fairbairn touched the tips of his moustache, one-two, as if checking that they were still there. 'A few times. I have met our hostess socially, but I don't know her well.'

They walked to the front door. A manservant opened it and led them up an oak-panelled staircase to a hall tiled in rich swirling patterns of deep red and green, with a fireplace faced in black marble. Light poured down from a glass atrium high overhead. From there the servant guided them into a drawing room flooded with sunlight reflecting off the water outside. The view from the tall windows, across to Nonamesset and over the rolling sea towards Martha's Vineyard, was breath-taking.

'Madam will be with you shortly,' the servant said, and closed the door behind him.

Flynn looked around. 'Quite the place,' he said.

The other three walls were panelled with wood marquetry in rich geometric forms like a Moorish palace. Paintings hung from the picture rail, all painted in bold modern colours: a Cézanne still life, a group of nudes by Picasso with rose-tinted flesh against a sharp blue and black background, a Braque landscape, a blue horse which Gallagher guessed was by Franz Marc. According to intelligence reports coming out of Germany, Marc had been killed six months ago at Verdun. Slowly but surely, everything bright and colourful was being extinguished from the world.

Flynn was looking at the Picasso. 'Are those meant to be women?' he asked.

'Yes,' Gallagher said.

'Thought so.' Flynn turned away and stared out to sea.

The door opened and a woman walked in. She was barefoot, in a white satin dressing gown belted with a brilliant red and purple paisley scarf, and her hair was tucked under a bathing cap. 'Brucie!' she cried. 'How splendid to see you again, darling. Did you have a good journey up from Washington?'

'Fair to middling,' said Bielaski. The woman kissed his cheek and turned to Fairbairn. 'Herbert, my dear,' she said, and kissed him too, with somewhat less enthusiasm. 'And who have we here?'

Bielaski introduced Gallagher and Flynn. 'And this, as you may have guessed, is Sadie Lansing, our hostess,' he said. 'Thank you for letting us use the house, Sadie. It's good to have somewhere quiet and out of the way for our conference.'

'My pleasure, darling. Have you had lunch?'

'It's a little late for lunch, Sadie,' Fairbairn said.

'Late? Darling, I only got up half an hour ago. I'm going for a swim, and then we shall all lunch together.'

She walked out of the room. They heard her calling to one of the servants as she ran down a wooden stair to the sea. At the platform at the bottom she untied her scarf and slipped off the dressing gown. Flynn's jaw dropped. 'Good God, she's naked.'

Sadie Lansing turned and looked up at the windows, her body washed in sunlight. She saw the men watching her, and smiled a brilliant smile and waved. Balancing on her toes, she dived into the rolling sea and swam with quick strokes across the little harbour.

'Do you think she knows why we're really here?' Fairbairn asked.

'Sure she does,' said Flynn. 'She's testing us.'

Bielaski rubbed his chin. 'Maybe. I'm still not certain about this. You know my own investigation found absolutely nothing.'

'That doesn't mean there was nothing to see,' Gallagher said.

'I'm aware of that,' Bielaski snapped. 'All right, what do you suggest?'

'You know her best, Bruce,' Gallagher said. 'Try to reassure her that we're harmless. We don't want her trying to skip out on us.'

By the time lunch was served half an hour later, the southern horizon had been obliterated by a wall of cloud. Overhead the sun was going dim. Sadie Lansing joined them in the dining room, dressed now in a striped sailor's jersey and long white skirt. 'There's no need to be formal, darlings. We are in the country, after all.'

They took their seats at the polished maplewood table, and servants in starched white uniforms served turtle soup, cold lobster and a fresh orange jelly. The paintings on the walls of the dining room were less aggressively modern: another Cézanne, this time depicting men playing cards, one of

Gauguin's Tahiti scenes, a Seurat showing well-dressed people promenading by a river. Gallagher remembered Bielaski's words. *All the money in the world.*

'Are you alone here, Sadie?' Bielaski asked.

'For the moment, darling. A friend promised to drop by later, but don't worry, we'll be as quiet as little mice. We won't interrupt your conference.'

'Who is the friend?' Fairbairn asked. 'Do I know her?'

Sadie smiled. 'No. You wouldn't like her, darling. She's far too pretty for you.'

Fairbairn coloured a little. 'I try not to make judgements about people,' he said stiffly.

'Of course you make judgements, darling, everyone does. My brother Frank, for example, claims that I am too fat. I regard myself as pleasingly statuesque.' She watched Gallagher for a moment, following his eyes. 'Are you fond of paintings, Mr Gallagher?'

'I used to paint a little,' Gallagher said after a moment. 'When I was younger I tried to copy the pointillists, but that was a long time ago. I still admire Seurat's work.'

'Do you like that one? Take it with you when you go. No, don't be silly, I have plenty of others back in Boston. I'll never miss it. And you, Mr Flynn? What are your interests when you are off-duty?'

'Horses,' said Flynn.

'Oh? Do you ride?'

'No,' said Flynn. 'I place bets.'

Sadie Lansing whooped with laughter. Picking up her wineglass, she drained it at a gulp. 'Gentlemen, it has been lovely entertaining you, but now I shall leave you in peace. Please remain as long as you wish. My house is at your disposal.'

She departed. Gallagher looked at Flynn. 'What do you think?'

'Like I said, she knows why we're here,' Flynn said. 'She's trying to cut one of us out of the herd. The way I read it, she thinks Bielaski is already on her side. Fairbairn she's not sure about, so she's looking at you or me. If she can win one of us over, she can at least count on a split decision.'

Bielaski sighed and rose to his feet. 'Let's get this over with,' he said.

MONDAY, 25 SEPTEMBER 1916
3.44 P.M.

The clouds had sealed off the sky. Out of the south came the wind, tearing across the surface of the sea and lifting the crests of the waves in white foam, stretching out the red hurricane flags so they crackled and snapped like gunfire. They heard the sound of a car pulling up. The figure who climbed out and hurried inside was wrapped in a mackintosh, its face covered by a broad-brimmed sou'wester.

'What do we know about Sadie Lansing?' Gallagher asked.

'Well, you've read the dossier,' Bielaski said. 'Sadie Louisa Warren, born 1883, eldest of two children, father a senior judge. Both the Warrens and her mother's family, the Saltinstalls, are part of a group of families called the Boston Brahmins, who control pretty much everything in Boston and a lot of the rest of New England, too.'

'Old money,' Gallagher said.

'And lots of it. Sadie inherited a fortune from her aunt, enough to make her rich for life, along with this house. Why she married Lansing is a complete mystery. My guess is that he wanted to get his hands on her money, but she wasn't having it. They're all but separated now.'

'And in her husband's absence, Mrs Lansing enjoys the high life.'

'You can say that again. Wild parties, affairs, heavy drinking, and there's a rumour she's a drug user as well. That's not in her dossier, but it's what I hear on the gossip circuit.'

'What is your connection with her?' Gallagher asked.

'We're family, believe it or not. Her mother and my mother were first cousins. I've barely seen her since I moved to Washington, but she still makes out like we're old friends.'

'What about her brother?'

'Frank Saltinstall Warren. Black sheep of the family. Four years younger than Sadie, no fixed abode, no permanent occupation. He has a couple of convictions for burglary, and did a year inside at Concord. The rest of the family disowned him, but Sadie still looks out for him.' Bielaski looked at Fairbairn. 'I believe you know him.'

'Yes,' Fairbairn said a little stiffly. 'He is a very fine sailor. He often crews for me during races.'

Flynn raised his eyebrows. 'You're a racing man, Mr Fairbairn?'

'I have a boat at Hyannis Port, yes. The *Chasseur*.'

'And you don't mind having a convicted felon on your boat?'

'Frank has already been punished by the courts and the correctional system,' Fairbairn said. 'Everyone deserves a second chance.'

'Very laudable,' Gallagher said. 'Tell me about him.'

'He is a bit of a wastrel, yes, but in my view he has a good heart. As I said, he's an excellent sailor and also a very fine mechanic. He can take a watch apart while wearing a blindfold, and put it together again, too. He once told me that if he had his life to live over again, he would have apprenticed as a watchmaker like Henry Ford, because that way he'd be as wealthy as Ford. His great weakness is that he is obsessed with money.' Fairbairn paused. 'Frank grew up expecting to have everything handed to him. His tragedy was to be born rich.'

'We all have our crosses to bear,' said Flynn.

Bielaski looked puzzled. 'Wastrel is putting it mildly. He sponges off his sister, and anyone else who crosses his path. You must have seen that, Mr Fairbairn.'

Fairbairn touched the tips of his moustache. 'He has borrowed money from me, yes. And to save you asking, he has never repaid a penny. I don't mind.'

'What does he spend it on?' Gallagher asked. 'Gambling, drink? Drugs?'

'Drink, mostly, although he never drank when we were out on the water. Never drunk at sea, and never wholly sober on land . . . Drugs, no. He'd think nothing of downing a bottle of whisky, but heroin and that sort of thing really frightened him.'

Flynn gazed out at the roaring sea. Waves exploded against the rocks; fountains of spray soared white against the darkening clouds. 'Gallagher, you want to tell us why you're here?'

Gallagher watched the storm too. 'About eighteen months ago, we captured a German naval officer travelling from America back to Germany,' he said. 'His name is Captain Franz von Rintelen of the Nachrichten-Abteilung, German naval intelligence, and he was the leader of a highly effective German espionage operation in New York. During his interrogation he told us about another spy ring operating in the Boston area. We had heard rumours of this before, but this was the first real confirmation.'

'Did he tell you anything else?' asked Flynn.

'Rintelen didn't give much away. He was bargaining with us, hoping to extract a promise that we wouldn't return him to America. He is wanted in New York for a range of offences. The ring he had established was behind the Black Tom bombing, for example.'

The others nodded. Just over a year ago, German agents had blown up a ship loaded with artillery shells bound for Russia, killing several people and causing millions of dollars of damage in New York and New Jersey. 'Rintelen let out information in dribs and drabs,' Gallagher continued. 'He told us that the Boston ring had been established before the war, but he didn't say when. The original leader of the ring had a code name, der Träumer, the Dreamer. We passed this information to our American friends, and also to our consul in Boston, Mr Fairbairn.'

Fairbairn nodded. 'I had already heard rumours of a spy ring,' he said. 'Frank Warren let slip that his sister, Mrs Lansing, was the lover of Count von Bernstorff, the German ambassador to Washington. I began to suspect that she might be involved, and I informed our embassy in Washington.'

'Yet you continued to see Mrs Lansing socially?' Gallagher asked.

'It was difficult to do otherwise, as she and my wife had become close friends. Nathalie, my wife, confirmed that Bernstorff and Mrs Lansing continued to meet frequently, whenever Bernstorff came to Boston. They conducted their liaisons here, at Aquinnah.'

Bielaski shook his head. 'We've been over this before. Bernstorff is a ladies' man. Everywhere he goes, women fall at his feet. He took some leave in Germany before the war, and when he returned to America there was an absolute crowd of women at the pier waiting to welcome him, shouting and cheering. Some of them threw their knickers at him, for God's sake. You can't accuse every woman who slept with Bernstorff of being a spy.'

'No,' Gallagher said, 'but there is more. A few weeks ago we caught a junior clerk selling documents from the Admiralty. His contact was the same man Rintelen had mentioned. The Dreamer.'

A harder gust of wind struck, and the house shuddered a little. 'This happened in England?' Flynn asked. 'Well, your Dreamer can't be Sadie Lansing. She hasn't left Massachusetts.'

'We're not saying that she is the Dreamer,' Gallagher said. 'But she might know who is. And if she really is an agent, she is very well placed.'

'Why do you say that?' asked Bielaski, watching the storm.

'America may still be neutral, but the Allies depend on your factories and oil wells. Sadie Lansing's friends and family are industrialists, politicians, diplomats, and her husband is one of the most important figures in a vital industry. She knows a lot of things that could be very important to the Germans, and she is sleeping with the German ambassador. And also, I don't care how rich her family are, if she really does have a stack of Seurats sitting in her attic in Boston, she must be getting money from somewhere. I doubt if her husband is buying them.'

Fairbairn started to say something, and stopped. 'Bruce, I understand your reluctance,' Gallagher said, 'but we must look into this. At the very least we need to check her finances and see where her money comes from.'

Bielaski sighed. 'All right. Have it your way. Shall we call her in?'

'Not yet,' Gallagher said. 'Let her assume we are still having our conference. We'll give it until six, and then send for her.'

Flynn nodded. 'Hand of poker while we wait?' he asked.

Gallagher had no interest in playing cards. Restless, he got up and wandered around the room, listening to the roar of the wind. Outside, the fading light had a sepia tint, and for a moment he imagined he was watching a moving picture rather than a real scene. Waves hurled themselves in a frenzy at the rocks below the house. Nonamesset, close by, was half hidden by flying spray; in the distance, masses of white foam boiled against the shore of Martha's Vineyard.

A book lay on a side table; Fitzgerald's translation of the *Rubaiyat of Omar Khayyam*. Gallagher picked up the book and read the first few verses.

> *Awake! for morning in the bowl of night*
> *Has flung the stone that puts the stars to flight:*
> *And lo! The hunter of the east has caught*
> *The sultan's turret in a noose of light.*
>
> *Dreaming when dawn's left hand was in the sky*
> *I heard a voice within the tavern cry,*
> *'Awake, my little ones, and fill the cup,*
> *Before life's liquor in its cup be dry.'*

Something on the page caught his eye. Gallagher held the book up to the lamplight, looking again at the final two lines of the first verse. *And lo! The hunter of the east has caught, the sultan's turret in a noose of light.* There were faint indentations on the paper under *the hunter of the east*, as if someone had underscored those five words with a pencil and then very carefully rubbed them out again.

He looked at the next verse. *Dreaming when dawn's left hand was in the sky, I heard a voice within the tavern cry.* The words 'dawn's left hand' had the same indentation beneath them.

The house shuddered again. The wind moaned like a lost soul. Gallagher stood for a moment, remembering typhoons in the South China Sea, when even the heaviest battleships rolled drunkenly from wave crest to trough. *God help poor sailormen on a night like this*, he thought. *Bootnecks, too.*

Roxanne had loved storms, especially storms at sea. Most of the time she was gentle and ethereal, but in wild weather she almost crackled with electricity. Storms remind us that we are all savages, she had said once. They remind us that we are capable of anything.

The electric lights flickered, blinked once, came on again, and went out.

'Christ,' Bielaski muttered under his breath. 'I knew this wasn't safe.'

'Not afraid of the dark, are you?' asked Flynn.

Bielaski did not respond. A servant entered with candles and a box of matches, and within moments the yellow glow of candlelight filled the room. The light outside was a dull metallic grey. White flashes shot through the gloom, the lighthouse on Nobska Point and other more distant lights on Martha's Vineyard and Chappaquiddick. In the hall a clock struck six, mellow chimes cutting through the keening wind.

Gallagher looked at the others. 'It's time,' he said.

MONDAY, 25 SEPTEMBER 1916
6.03 P.M.

Sadie Lansing was in her white dressing gown once again, her hair dishevelled and her face flushed. She had doused herself in eau de violette, which filled the room in sweet noxious clouds. Bielaski wrinkled his nose. Flynn's expression did not change, but then, it probably never did.

'I hope this is important,' she snapped. 'I don't like being interrupted when I am resting.'

Flynn is right, Gallagher thought, she knows why we are here. This would not be as easy as they had hoped. 'I'm sorry to have disturbed you,' he said. 'Please return to your room and dress, if you wish.'

'I don't wish.' She flung herself down in an armchair. The dressing gown slipped off one shoulder. Candlelight reflected off glowing skin; her cleavage was a hollow full of shadow. The four men sat down as well. Something stuttered against the windows; the first drops of rain, propelled almost horizontally by the storm.

Gallagher studied Sadie Lansing for a long moment. He saw something he had missed before; the pupils of her eyes, dark and dilated. She had dosed herself with something, probably heroin, not long before.

'Has your guest departed?' he asked.

'Yes. She wanted to get back to Boston before the weather hit.'

'Mr Fairbairn asked earlier who she was. I don't recall your answer.'

'That's because I didn't give one. Her name is Lily Sparrow, and she is an old friend.'

Gallagher nodded. 'I hope she makes it safely back to Boston. This is a bad storm. Mrs Lansing, when Mr Bielaski asked permission to hold our conference here, did he tell you why we were here?'

'Something about diplomatic relations between Britain and America. I didn't pay much attention.' Her voice was strong and level, with no trace of slurring. 'Brucie is an old friend. I would never refuse him *anything*.'

Bielaski looked uncomfortable. 'What he said was true up to a point,' Gallagher said. 'We are here because we think that a German espionage ring is operating in Boston. You know a lot of people in high places, Mrs Lansing. Have you heard anything about this?'

She looked contemptuous. 'You woke me up to ask me *that*?'

'Have you?' Gallagher repeated.

The rain was much harder now, hammering at the glass, almost drowning the noise of the wind. 'Of course I have,' Sadie Lansing said. 'Everyone in Boston has heard about it.' She stabbed a finger at Fairbairn. '*You* have, haven't you, Herbert?'

'I have,' Fairbairn said steadily. 'Your brother told me.'

'Why didn't you tell *me*?' Bielaski demanded of Sadie.

'It must have slipped my mind.' She sat up. The dressing gown slipped down a little further. 'Give me a drink,' she ordered.

Flynn rose and walked to the sideboard and poured a glass of brandy and soda, handing it to her. She gulped the drink. 'My favourite,' she said. 'How did you know?'

'Lucky guess,' said Flynn.

Gallagher coughed, drawing her attention back to him. The wind was still rising, sending draughts shivering through the room. The candle flames wavered, and shadows jumped around the walls. 'How well do you know Johann von Bernstorff?' Gallagher asked.

'The German ambassador? Pretty well.'

'Are you lovers?'

She laughed and drank some more brandy. 'Lovers. Such a sickly little word, don't you think? Do you have a *lover*, Mr Gallagher?'

'Are you?'

'Let me put it more accurately, but in a way that won't offend Herbert's delicate sensibilities. He has carnal knowledge of me. Will that do?'

'How long has this been going on?' Bielaski asked.

'Three years or so.'

'Since before the war, then,' Gallagher said. 'How would you describe your relationship with your husband, Mrs Lansing?'

'James? He is a human pustule. Does that answer your question?'

'Not entirely. Are you still in contact with him?'

'I will spell it out for you,' she said. 'We detest each other. But we both love the smell of money.'

Gallagher smiled. 'Does Count von Bernstorff give you money?'

Bielaski flinched a little. Sadie's fingers drummed on the wooden arm of the chair. 'What business is it of yours?'

'It really would help us if you answered the question,' Gallagher said gently.

The drumming increased in tempo. 'Ask my man of affairs in Boston. I don't concern myself with such things.'

'Did you ever arrange for Count von Bernstorff to meet your husband?' Gallagher asked.

Tap-tap-tap-tap-tap her fingers went, percussive counterpoint to the shriek of the wind and harsh roar of the rain. 'No,' she said.

'But that's not true, is it?' Fairbairn said quietly. 'You attended a party hosted by my wife and myself on my boat, the *Chasseur*, a few months ago. Your husband attended too and, to my displeasure, so did Bernstorff. Your brother told me that you had invited Bernstorff specifically in order to meet Lansing.'

The drumming stopped. Sadie laughed. 'Frank told you that? Little Frankie? He'd say anything. He drinks, you know. Completely untrustworthy. But you already know that. Don't you, Herbert?'

'We know Bernstorff and your husband were both there on the same day,' Flynn said. His voice sounded like it had been mixed with gravel. 'We have other witnesses.'

'Have you been spying on me, Mr Flynn? You have, haven't you? I'm disappointed in you.' Sadie swirled the drink in her glass. 'Very well. Yes, Johann was there, and so was James. And so was Frankie.'

'Where can we find your brother now?' asked Flynn.

'I have no idea. He turns up when he turns up. I haven't a clue what he does with the rest of his life, and I don't want to know.'

'Even when he is in prison?' Gallagher asked.

'Especially when he's in prison.'

Gallagher paused, listening to the wind. 'What does *the hunter of the east* mean to you?' he asked.

The other men stared at him. Sadie gazed at him for a long moment. 'Ask Herbert,' she suggested. 'He knows. Or if he doesn't, he knows someone who does.'

'Could the east mean Russia?'

'Russia.' She paused for a moment, sipping her drink, face partly hidden behind the glass. 'Are you interested in Russia?' she asked.

'Did Bernstorff talk to you about Russia?'

'Sometimes.'

From the hill behind the house they heard the snap of pine trees breaking in the wind. 'What did he say?' Gallagher asked patiently.

'A lot of things. None of them would interest you.'

Bielaski started to speak, but Gallagher raised one finger. 'I think that's everything,' he said. 'Thank you, Mrs Lansing.'

SADIE LANSING ROSE to her feet and stalked out of the room. The door slammed behind her. They heard her voice briefly, speaking in tones of anger; to one of the servants, presumably. 'What do we think?' Flynn asked.

'She's involved, all right,' Bielaski said reluctantly. 'How deep is anyone's guess.'

'Someone has trained her,' Gallagher said. 'The aggressive responses, the drumming of the fingers to distract the interrogator, these are all professional techniques.' He looked at Fairbairn. 'The hunter of the east. Why did she say I should ask you?'

'God knows,' Fairbairn said. He shook his head in exasperation. 'Gentlemen, as I said at the beginning, I don't know Mrs Lansing all that well. To be honest, I only put up with her for the sake of my wife. Personally, I find her quite tiresome.'

'I don't understand,' Bielaski said. 'What is this "hunter of the east"?'

Gallagher glanced at Flynn, who nodded slightly. 'It's part of a book code, based on the *Rubaiyat of Omar Khayyam*. The

Dreamer uses this code. And Sadie Lansing knows about it.'
Gallagher paused for a moment. 'How well does Mrs Fairbairn
know her?'

'They play bridge together in Boston, and Nathalie
comes down to Aquinnah for the summers. I usually take
the opportunity to go sailing.' Fairbairn paused, watching
the flutter of the candle flames. 'I feel free out on the water,'
he said. 'There's something pure about the sea.'

There was a little pause. The hurricane lashed at the house,
and the building shuddered again. Gallagher turned to Bielaski.
'Bruce, can you go through her financial affairs? Something will
come up, I am sure of it. And perhaps you could start checking
on her friends and her other contacts.'

'I'll take care of that,' said Flynn.

'What do you want me to do?' asked Fairbairn.

'Nothing.'

Fairbairn looked disappointed. 'There's nothing else to
do, at least not for the moment,' Gallagher said. 'This is
intelligence work, Mr Fairbairn. There are no eureka moments,
no sudden revelations. Most of our time is spent waiting.'

'You asked about Russia,' Bielaski said. 'Does Russia have
anything do with this?'

'Russia has everything to do with it,' said Flynn. 'The
Germans and the Bolsheviks are making common cause, trying
to knock Russia out of the war. We think the plot started here
in Boston, and we think the Dreamer, or some of his agents,
were at the heart of it.'

'But where does Lansing come into the picture?'

'That's what we need to find out,' Gallagher said.

Bielaski persisted. 'America is still neutral, gentlemen. The
fact that Lansing met Bernstorff doesn't mean anything.'

'Depends on what they talked about,' said Flynn.

Someone knocked at the door. Bielaski raised his voice to be heard over the wind. 'Come in.'

One of the servants entered, bowing. 'Madam sends her compliments, gentlemen. Dinner will be a cold collation. And also, given the inclement weather, she is pleased to offer you accommodation for the night.'

Joe Flynn raised his eyebrows. 'Isn't that kind of her,' he said.

DINNER WAS COLD soup, ham, lobster and salads, eaten by candlelight while the rain lashed against the high windows. The house shivered in the wind. Bielaski looked more nervous than ever.

Servants showed them to their rooms on the third floor. Gallagher's room was comfortable, furnished in very modern fashion; it reminded him of his cabin on the *Lusitania*, except that it was about four times as large. Sleep in that roaring storm was never going to be possible. He pinched out the candle and stood in darkness, looking out at the blurry flashes from the lighthouses illuminating a raging sea. Far away to the south, lightning flashed dimly through the rain.

A deafening crack, like the sound of a gun, followed by the sound of shattering glass: the ceiling of the atrium had fractured and was caving in. He ran out into the corridor, hearing the clatter of thousands of glass fragments roaring like a waterfall in the stairwell. Joe Flynn was at his shoulder. 'The whole house could go,' he said.

'Find the servants,' Gallagher said. 'Get everyone down to the cellars.'

Flynn disappeared into the flickering darkness. A maidservant hurried past and Gallagher called to her. 'Which is Mrs Lansing's room?'

The young woman turned, her face terrified. 'At the far end of the corridor, sir. But she's locked the door.'

'Go downstairs. We'll look after her.' The woman ran towards the stairwell, and Gallagher turned to find Fairbairn, carrying a flickering oil lamp. 'Did you hear?'

'Yes. We have to get her out.'

They ran down the dark corridor. Gallagher tried the door once to confirm it was locked, and kicked the panel hard just beside the doorknob. Wood splintered and the door swung open. He saw the key still in the lock on the inside, and in the fluttering lamplight he noticed a pale smudge on the brass shank of the key. It had been years since he had picked up a paintbrush, but he still recognized it immediately: lead white paint, the kind that artists use.

The room was big. Paintings hung on the tiled and painted walls. Another painting stood on an easel by the windows, a nude woman reclining, the lower half of her body and the arms mostly finished, the torso and head just outlines on the prepared canvas. One outstretched hand held a white rose, painted with the same lead white pigment. Fine marquetry tables and wardrobes glistening with walnut and maple veneer stood around the room. The bed was enormous, with a high, painted headboard. The air reeked of eau de violette.

In a grotesque parody of the painting, Sadie Lansing lay sprawled on her back in the middle of the bed, the white dressing gown discarded on the floor. A cord had been tied around her left arm above the elbow, and a silver hypodermic syringe and empty glass phial lay on the bed beside her. Her skin was cold to the touch.

'Jesus,' said Fairbairn, his rich voice for once unsteady. 'What happened?'

'Bring the lamp closer.' Outside the room all was chaos, rain and wind roaring through the shattered atrium. Gallagher lifted Sadie's bare arm, noting the tattoo of marks from previous injections. One was new, still with a little dot of dried blood crusted on top of it. He looked at her bloodshot eyes and noted the smell coming from her mouth.

'She has taken an overdose,' he said.

Bielaski entered the room and stopped, mouth open, eyes staring. 'Go and help Flynn,' Gallagher said. 'Get the servants down to the cellars and stay with them. We'll be there as soon as we can.'

Bielaski nodded and hurried out of the room. Gallagher stood up, looking around. On the right-hand side of the room was another door, slightly ajar. Quietly, Gallagher opened it and looked inside. Lightning flashed through the windows, showing a dressing table with a mirror, more wardrobes, an enormous bathtub with gilded taps gleaming in the shadows. The smell of perfume was less strong here, and cutting through it came another odour, sharp and sweet at the same time. *Diethyl ether*, Gallagher thought. Artists sometimes used some forms of ether as a solvent for their paints, but diethyl ether was also a powerful anaesthetic. A thought formed in his mind.

A single sash window looked out from the rear of the room, locked from the inside. Gallagher opened the fastener and lifted the sash, letting a blast of wind and rain into the room. Outside, there was a long drop onto stony ground. He slammed the window shut again and secured the fastener.

Fairbairn came into the room behind him, holding a book in one hand and the lamp in another. 'You need to see this,' he said.

The book was a photograph album. The photographs were taken with a cheap camera, something like a Box Brownie;

given their uneven exposures, most had probably been developed in a private darkroom. The photographs showed people posing or talking at parties. Many were taken here at Aquinnah, others outside on the rocks or on beaches, or on the decks of boats. There were no labels, and at first Gallagher did not recognize any of the people.

'Look at the next page,' Fairbairn said quietly.

Gallagher turned the page. The first thing he noticed was that several photographs had been removed, torn from their mounts so hastily that a few scraps of photographic paper were still attached to the page. Of the remaining photographs, one showed Count von Bernstorff shaking hands with a smiling man. Gallagher had seen the man's likeness many times, and he had no difficulty in recognizing Sadie Lansing's husband, James Rogers Lansing.

Another photograph showed Lansing and Bernstorff together on the deck of a yacht, both in sailing clothes. Another man, round-faced and smiling with a short, closely-trimmed moustache, stood beside them. A third showed Fairbairn on what looked like the same yacht, also shaking hands with Bernstorff. The fourth made Gallagher close his eyes, and for a moment he almost forgot the hurricane raging around them.

In the centre of the photograph was Bernstorff, in a bathing costume this time, standing on a beach. His arms were around two women, one on either side. Both wore their bathing costumes pulled down to their waists, their breasts glistening in sepia-tinted sunlight. They rested their heads on Bernstorff's shoulders, smiling at the camera. One of the women was Sadie Lansing.

Gallagher opened his eyes again and looked at Fairbairn. 'Yes,' said the other man, and his voice shook a little. 'The other woman is my wife.'

8

'THE HOUSE DIDN'T collapse,' Gallagher said, 'although the rain and wind made quite a mess of it. By morning the hurricane had passed on, and Bielaski was able to get out and send for the police and a doctor. The post-mortem found that Sadie Lansing had died of an overdose of heroin, but did not determine whether it was suicide or an accident. Bielaski instructed the coroner to report a verdict of accidental death. I suspect this was to spare the feelings of her family.'

'Another death behind a locked door,' Mrs Vane said.

Gallagher nodded. 'Which could have pointed towards suicide, of course. She locked the door so she would not be disturbed, left the key in the lock and injected herself. That would have made perfect sense, except for the smudge on the key. It was paint, lead white to be precise, exactly the same as the rose in the portrait.'

'Might she have touched the portrait with her fingers?'

'There was no paint on her fingers, nor could I find any trace of it elsewhere in the bedroom or dressing room. Someone else was in the room. And I think the same person also removed some of the photographs from the album, possibly because they themselves were in the pictures.'

'Were there fingerprints on the key?'

'No, and none on the syringe either apart from Sadie's own. We checked for fingerprints on the syringe we found with Vasiliev, too, by the way. Exactly the same, Vasiliev's were the only prints we found. In both cases the killer must have worn gloves.'

Gallagher paused. 'And then, there was the ether. The post-mortem made it clear that Sadie had been rendered unconscious before she was injected. Someone clubbed Vasiliev over the head, but the result was the same.'

'What about Sadie's guest?' Mrs Vane asked. 'What was her name? Something Sparrow? She must have been the last person to see Sadie alive.'

'Lily Sparrow, yes. Flynn's men found her almost at once. She works for an art dealer in Boston, where Sadie Lansing was a frequent customer. She is also an art student, quite a good one, too. She studied with William Bradley, and worked for a time in Tiffany's studio. That painting of Sadie Lansing was very much in Bradley's style. I used to paint a bit,' he added, almost apologetically.

She smiled a little. 'I would never have guessed.'

'Sadie took a liking to Lily, who is a good bit younger than herself, and invited her to paint her portrait. They had a sitting that afternoon after lunch. According to Lily, she cut the sitting short when she saw how severe the storm was becoming. The house servants confirm that she left at about four thirty, not long before the electricity cut out. Sadie Lansing didn't die until at least eight p.m.'

'How did she explain the paint on the key?'

'She said she knew nothing about it. Sadie herself had locked the door, to ensure privacy during the sitting, and unlocked it again to let Lily out. Lily herself never touched the key.'

'Could one of the servants have been responsible?'

'Flynn's men interviewed them. All were well paid and well looked after, and none had any motive for killing her. We also searched the house for a pair of paint-stained gloves, but we found nothing.'

'And was Mrs Lansing really an agent?'

'Oh, yes. So was her brother, Frank Warren. Flynn and Bielaski caught a few members of the spy ring, all of them small fry who didn't know very much. Warren escaped, probably helped by his connections in the underworld.'

'And the hunter of the east? From what you said, it sounds like Sadie Lansing was pointing a finger at Fairbairn. Either that, or someone Fairbairn knows.'

'Fairbairn professed to have no idea what she was talking about.'

'Mmm. He was photographed shaking hands with an ambassador from an enemy country. That's not supposed to happen, is it?'

'No,' said Gallagher. 'In neutral countries, our diplomats and their diplomats are bound to bump into each other at social engagements, but the convention is that they politely ignore each other. In this case, Fairbairn says it was an ambush. Someone came up and offered his hand, and he took it instinctively without realizing at first that it was Bernstorff. He also didn't realize anyone was photographing them.'

'Forgive me for sounding sceptical,' said Mrs Vane, 'but how does he explain the picture of his wife twined half-naked around one of our country's enemies?'

'He doesn't. Until he saw the photograph, he had no idea the affair was taking place.'

There was a little pause. 'I assume you also questioned Mrs Fairbairn.'

'I left that to Flynn and Bielaski. Everything happened on

American soil, so it was their province. And I wanted to keep my own profile as low as possible.' A gust of wind stirred the ashes in the fireplace and Gallagher felt the air rasp in his lungs. 'She admitted to going to a private beach party with Sadie Lansing, and to posing for the photograph with a friend of Sadie's whom she didn't know. It was, she said, that kind of party. People didn't ask questions.'

'Do you believe that?' she asked.

Gallagher smiled a little. 'Do you?'

Silence fell again. 'Mrs Lansing was a German agent, Vasiliev was working for the Russian opposition,' Mrs Vane said finally. 'But they were killed in the same way. What else connects them?'

'I don't know,' Gallagher said. 'I thought I understood what was going on, until now. Sadie Lansing was killed by the Dreamer, or on his instructions, because she had come under suspicion and the Dreamer wanted to silence her. Because Vasiliev was killed in an almost identical fashion, I assumed the Dreamer had killed him as well. But now, instead of one plot, we seem to have two.'

'Or one plot with two parts,' Mrs Vane pointed out. 'Someone searched my room this evening, before I came up to bed.'

Gallagher nodded. 'Mine also.'

'Captain Ryder is convinced that there is a traitor in the naval intelligence division. But the Dreamer could be somewhere else in the Admiralty, couldn't they?'

'The Dreamer could be anywhere,' Gallagher said. 'They don't even have to be in the navy. I spent most of dinner looking around the table and trying to work out who it might be.'

'Did you come to any conclusions?'

'Price and Tovey are unknown quantities. Sir John explained

why they are here, but I want to know more about them. They're quite junior, but that doesn't mean anything; the best places to hide are the ones where no one would think to look. Fairbairn is an interesting one.'

'I assume you had him under surveillance at Aquinnah,' she said.

'Joe Flynn was quite convinced that he was involved, but there was no evidence. It's a possibility, though. He was in Boston around the time the Dreamer was establishing his spy ring, and he knew Sadie Lansing. Furthermore, Fairbairn returned to England around the same time as the thefts began again at the Admiralty. I'm also bothered by the fact that both Fairbairn and Vasiliev raced yachts, but they never met. How likely is that?'

'Perhaps their paths simply never crossed,' said Mrs Vane. 'Or, perhaps someone deliberately kept Vasiliev away from Fairbairn. I have another name for you to consider. James Rogers Lansing.'

'Why him?'

'The Bernstorff meeting, for a start. Also, his wife's activities. Their marriage may have failed, but they were still in contact. And he too arrived in London about the time the thefts resumed.'

'You don't like him,' Gallagher said.

'I don't imagine his dog likes him, but I'm trying not to let that get in the way. To complete the set, how well do you know your brother-in-law?'

Gallagher was silent for a long time. 'You referred to Nick Makarian as enigmatic,' he said finally. 'You're right, he is. There are large parts of his life that none of us know anything about. Or if Penelope does, she hasn't told the rest of us. I like Nick, but . . . do I trust him? No. And like Lansing, he has both the brains and the organization to enable them to conduct espionage.'

He paused again. 'I think they are outside chances,' he said. 'But let's not rule them out. You haven't mentioned the women.'

Mrs Vane rose to her feet. 'As you say, we can't rule them out,' she said. 'But my feeling, intuition, call it what you will, is that the Dreamer is a man. What professional intelligence agency would entrust the organization of a major spy ring to a woman, when our governments don't even trust us to have the vote?'

'It's a fair point,' Gallagher agreed. 'But again, let's keep our minds open.'

Mrs Vane looked down at him. 'You should try to get back to sleep,' she said, and paused. 'I have some chloral hydrate, if you think it would help.'

'I find it actually makes the dreams worse,' said Gallagher. 'But the offer is kind. Thank you.'

She smiled a little. 'Goodnight, Mr Gallagher,' she said.

SATURDAY, 3 FEBRUARY 1917

7.36 A.M.

The hand of Gothic madness that had decorated so many other rooms in Hartlake Hall had not reached as far as the morning room. Here was the opposite: bare distempered walls with a few pale watercolours on display, an oak floor with a faded Chinese carpet, linen drapes that would not have looked out of place in a hospital ward. Ryder and Fairbairn sat near the foot of the table, eating kippers and talking about partridge shooting in Norfolk. Colson stood by the window, gazing out over the park. Lansing sat on his own, working his way through an immense plate of breakfast and slurping coffee from his cup.

Jonquil Vane looked into the chafing dishes on the sideboard. The kedgeree smelled of burnt rice, but everything else looked more or less edible. She helped herself to toast, ham and a cup of strong tea and walked over to Edith Price and Nathalie Fairbairn. 'Do you mind if I join you?' she asked. 'The conversation at the other end of the table is a bit too masculine for me.'

'Please do.' Edith looked slightly apprehensive. 'I hope you don't mind, Mrs Vane,' she said quietly, 'but Geraint told me about your conversation yesterday. I'm so sorry for your loss.'

She is American, Mrs Vane thought, *and new to war.* If America does join in, wait until they have buried their first hundred thousand dead. Then they too will learn to keep silent. They too will learn that while most reactions to grief are bearable, kindness hurts like a knife.

'It's quite all right,' Mrs Vane said, ignoring the sudden ache around her heart. She groped for another topic of conversation. 'If you don't mind my asking, where are you from?'

'America,' said Edith. 'Oh; you mean where in America? I'm from Lexington, a little village just outside of Boston.'

'Lexington,' said Mrs Vane. 'Isn't that where the revolution began?'

'Oh, I'm a loyal Englishwoman now,' Edith said, a tinge of mischief in her voice. 'It would not be appropriate to talk of such things.'

'Why not?' asked Nathalie. 'There's nothing wrong with revolutions.'

Mrs Vane raised her eyebrows. 'Really? From what I have read, revolutions tend to start well, but most of them end very badly.'

Price entered the room, dressed like the other men in tweeds for shooting, and bent and kissed his wife's cheek. 'Good morning, darling,' Edith said brightly, and she dropped her voice a little. 'How is your arm?'

Price smiled down at her, ruffling her hair. 'Not too bad this morning. I can cope.'

'I'm so glad, darling. Are you ready for the fray?'

'As ready as I shall ever be.' Price seemed, if not exactly cheerful, somewhat less dour than he had been the night before. 'I shall bring us back a brace of pheasants.'

'Super!' said Edith. She watched Price cross to the sideboard and dropped her voice again. 'Do you know,' she murmured to Mrs Vane, 'I am the luckiest girl in the world.'

'I'm sure you deserve your good fortune,' said Mrs Vane, and she wished the pain in her chest would go away.

Gallagher came in a few minutes later and helped himself to coffee from the sideboard. On the excuse of fetching another piece of toast, Mrs Vane crossed to join him. 'How did you sleep?' she asked quietly.

'Somewhat better,' Gallagher said. 'Would you like an excuse to avoid the shooting altogether?'

Ladies did not shoot, but the sound of the gunfire would be clearly audible in the house. 'Yes, please,' said Mrs Vane.

They walked to the end of the sideboard, out of earshot of the others. 'I'd like you to go into Tonbridge and send two more telegrams,' Gallagher said. 'One to Bielaski, asking him to find Lily Sparrow. We have some more questions for her. And one to the service, asking for files on Tovey and Price.'

Tovey was sitting alone, eating bacon and eggs. Price had sat down next to his wife. Mrs Vane frowned. 'Why do I keep thinking that Lily Sparrow sounds like a made-up name?'

'I don't know,' Gallagher said slowly. 'Why *do* you keep thinking it?'

'Lily doesn't sound like a name that people called Sparrow would give to a child. But then, my parents saw fit to name me Jonquil, so what do I know?' She handed the piece of toast to Gallagher. 'Be sure to eat something,' she said. 'It's cold outside, you'll need your energy.'

Their eyes met, and she walked away. Gallagher spread marmalade on his toast and, carrying it and his coffee, crossed the room to join Colson by the window. They stood for a moment in silence, looking at the grey windswept park and the wet fields beyond.

'Bloody awful weather,' Colson said finally.

'As usual,' Gallagher said.

'I hate this time of year,' said the commander. 'The days are grey, and the nights are long. A man has too much time to think.'

'What do you think about?'

Colson roused himself, shaking his head. 'Nothing,' he said.

Gallagher finished his toast. 'What do you make of Lansing?'

Colson glanced at Lansing, who was shovelling kedgeree into his mouth. 'Complete boor,' he said.

'He doesn't seem to give much for our chances of winning the war.'

'He doesn't know anything about it. Look, he's been very successful in business, but what of it? Being rich doesn't make you clever.'

If Colson, an oil company director and the owner of a Rolls-Royce, saw the irony of this statement, he gave no sign. 'Have you ever had dealings with Lansing?' Gallagher asked. 'By you, I mean the board of Anglo-Persian.'

Colson looked a little uncomfortable. 'No. We tried doing

business with the Americans once, but never again. I don't trust them.'

'If Britain is going to win this war, we'll need America's help,' Gallagher said.

'So everyone keeps saying, but I don't agree. I think America is a greater danger to us than Germany.'

'What do you mean?'

Colson lowered his voice a little. 'America is a young, powerful nation looking to flex its muscles. They're jealous of our empire, too. They've already grabbed the Philippines and Puerto Rico from Spain, and they're looking for more territory. I recommend you read a book called *The Naval Engineer and Command of the Sea*. The author forecasts that our next war will be with America, fighting for control of the sea lanes. I happen to agree with him.'

'Does your author believe that we can win a war with America?'

'Yes, but only if we are ready for the fight. We should be preparing to face down the Americans, rather than cosying up to them.'

'It's an interesting theory,' Gallagher said. 'Allow me to change the subject, if I may. Does the phrase *the hunter of the east* mean anything to you?'

'What?' Colson was nonplussed for a moment. 'That's Omar Khayyam, isn't it? From the *Rubaiyat*?'

'Yes, the first verse. "And lo! The hunter of the east has caught, the sultan's turret in a noose of light." It's part of a code.'

'Is this to do with Vasiliev?'

'It could be. My reason for mentioning it is that I saw it paired with another phrase, *dawn's left hand*. That also comes from the *Rubaiyat*. "Dreaming when dawn's left hand was in the sky." My hunch is that *dawn's left hand* refers to the Dreamer.'

Colson looked around. Ryder had risen from the table and left the room. 'And you think the *hunter of the east* might have been Vasiliev?' he asked quietly. 'My God. If you are right, that means one of Ryder's own officers was a traitor. This looks bad for Ryder, doesn't it?'

'Let's not get ahead of ourselves,' Gallagher said. 'Ryder has only been in post for a few months, and he hasn't had time to get to know his own officers. And you have to give him credit, he's clearly aware that something is wrong.'

'But his response is to cast aspersions on my department! For God's sake, it's his own staff that are rotten!'

'We're still trying to understand what Vasiliev was really doing.' Gallagher cleared his throat. 'The fact is that *someone* killed him, and like it or not, we can't rule out that an officer from naval intelligence is responsible. There is a third code-phrase going around, *throne of Saturn*. We have no idea what that refers to, or whom.'

'Have you told Ryder about this?'

'Not yet,' Gallagher said. 'Keep this to yourself, Commander.'

A wagon had pulled up outside and men in rough clothes were climbing into it; the beaters, going out to take up their positions for the first drive. 'Right,' Gallagher said. 'Looks like we're almost ready.'

'Wait a moment.' The others were rising from breakfast and departing. Colson waited until they were alone. 'The telegram,' he said, and his voice was nervous. 'Why did Vasiliev try to steal the telegram?'

'I don't know.' Gallagher gazed at him. 'What do you think?'

'Vasiliev can't have known what was in the telegram. Only a handful of people know.'

'Including you,' Gallagher said.

'Yes . . . What are you implying?'

'Yet again, I am not *implying* anything. I am stating a fact. Another fact is this: people don't burgle private safes and steal telegrams at random. Vasiliev *did* know the importance of the telegram, or he wouldn't have taken it. The question is, who told him?'

Colson was silent. Somewhere in the distance a whistle blew. 'We must go,' Gallagher said, and he smiled a little. 'Don't worry, Commander. We'll find them, whoever it was. They can't hide for ever.'

SATURDAY, 3 FEBRUARY 1917

8.14 A.M.

Outside the east wind was bitter and raw, stinging against their cheeks and biting through heavy overcoats. Grey clouds raced low overhead and the light was dim. 'Lousy weather,' Lansing grumbled.

'You should have let us know you were coming,' Price said under his breath. 'We'd have arranged for it to be bright and sunny.'

Gallagher felt the wind bite into his chest, and coughed. 'It's not the light, it's the wind. It'll be tricky shooting.'

'If you say so,' said Price. The scars on his face were livid in the cold.

The guns came together in the turning circle in front of the house, shotguns broken open and cradled in their arms. Pale light gleamed off polished walnut stocks and the intricate patterns of Damascus steel barrels. Colson's shotgun was made by Purdey, one of the more exclusive gunmakers; Ryder's was a more workmanlike Westley Richards. Sir John Borden came out with a pair of his own shotguns, handing one to Gallagher.

Lansing glanced at Gallagher. 'Don't have your own gun?' he asked, in a tone suggesting that a man who had to borrow a shotgun might not be worth talking to.

'Shotguns were frowned upon in the marines,' Gallagher said.

'You were in the Royal Marines? How come you're not on active service now?'

Captain Ryder frowned. 'That's not a question we ask, Lansing. Every man has his reasons.'

Lansing shrugged and moved away. Ryder's eyes met Gallagher's for a moment, but he said no more.

Dogs could be heard in the distance, yelping with anticipation; after each drive finished, they would be let loose to pick up the dead birds. Borden was talking to Tompkins the head gamekeeper, a man in his sixties with a seamed face and a mane of shaggy silver hair. The other keepers stood by, waiting. There were only three of them: a couple of men too old to be called up, and a girl resting a shotgun over her shoulder and holding a bowler hat in one hand. Gallagher recalled that she was Tompkins' granddaughter. As the cab driver had said, all the rest of the keepers had gone. Gamekeepers made excellent sharpshooters; those that had not already volunteered were among the first to be called up.

Finally Borden nodded, and he and Tompkins turned to the waiting guns: Gallagher and Lansing, Fairbairn and Makarian, Price and Tovey, Colson and Ryder. 'Good morning, gentlemen,' the keeper said, bobbing his head a little. 'We'll be shooting the west woods on the first drive. That's them woods stretching away towards Tonbridge, north of the carriage drive. You'll be loading for yourselves today, cuz as you can see, we're a bit short-handed. The beaters will drive from west to east, meaning you'll have your backs to the wind for this first drive, at least. The birds will rise into the wind, and that ought to hold them up a little and give you a bit better chance. No ground game, gentlemen, and as always, respect the beaters.'

Everyone nodded. From overhead came a droning noise, an aeroplane taking off from the field at Chiddingstone Causeway, rocking a little in the wind as it climbed towards the clouds. 'That blasted kite will frighten off the pheasants,' said Tovey.

Tompkins shook his head. 'Birds are used to it.' He turned to the girl. 'Let the gentlemen draw their pegs, Maisie.'

Maisie held out the hat, and each gun drew a number, indicating the position they would take up on the shoot. Captain Ryder drew number one, on the end of the line; Makarian was next to him. Gallagher walked across and tapped Makarian on the shoulder. 'Swap with me, Nick?'

Makarian smiled. 'As you wish.'

They walked across the park, a line of heavily muffled men in tweed coats, breath steaming in the cold. Rooks cawed in the trees. Gallagher and Ryder moved out to the right towards their pegs. Gallagher said nothing at first, waiting for Ryder to speak.

'Any more thoughts about the investigation?' Ryder asked after a while.

'Can you think of any reason why Vasiliev would have been in the Admiralty at midnight? Was he on the night watch?'

'No,' said Ryder. 'But his duties sometimes required him to work late. And there is, of course, the suggestion that I made last evening, that Vasiliev was involved in an investigation of naval intelligence.'

'He claimed he provided occasional translation services for officers in the division,' Gallagher said. 'Did you know that he spoke fluent Russian?'

'No, I didn't. Have you spoken to the officers who were on duty that night?'

Gallagher nodded. 'Vasiliev signed in at the watchkeeping office, but apart from that, no one in naval intelligence claims to have seen him that night. Nevertheless, someone knew Vasiliev was there. This person lured him into the stationery cupboard, knocked him unconscious, locked the door and wedged it from the inside so they would not be disturbed, injected Vasiliev, and then somehow escaped from the room. This was a deliberate killing, planned in advance.'

They walked on in silence for a few moments. 'To me, that suggests that he was killed because he had discovered the presence of a German agent in the Admiralty,' Ryder said finally.

'Why do you say that?'

Ryder looked impatient. 'Let's stop fencing with each other. We both know that someone in the Admiralty is selling information to the Germans. Not much, and not often, but enough to worry about. The thefts most likely take place at night, when there are fewer people about. What if Vasiliev caught the thief in the act?'

'It's plausible,' Gallagher said. 'But what if Vasiliev himself was the thief?'

'*If* he was, and one of our people caught him; well, as Mrs Vane said yesterday, they wouldn't kill him and hide the body, they would detain him and send for the master-at-arms. What you are suggesting doesn't make sense.'

'It does,' Gallagher said, 'when you realize that before the war, Vasiliev was the lover of a German agent in America.'

There was a moment of silence. 'When did you learn this?' Ryder demanded.

'Yesterday.'

'Why didn't you tell me?'

'Because I'm still trying to understand what it means. The agent was Lansing's wife, who is now dead.'

Ryder glanced at Lansing, who was walking and talking with Makarian. Gallagher coughed. 'That's right,' he said. 'The man whose support we need in order to convince America to declare war on Germany. I want to dig deeper into Vasiliev, especially his time in America. He's your officer, so I need your permission.'

'You have it,' Ryder said, with a trace of reluctance. 'Changing the subject, what do you make of Colson?'

Gallagher thought for a moment. 'He lacks confidence, I'd say.'

'That's putting it mildly. I'm beginning to wonder if he's up to the job.'

'What do you mean?'

'He had a funk after his time in France,' Ryder said. 'He admitted it, and I respect him for that, but . . . he's not natural officer material. He comes from a trade background, you know. Nothing wrong with that, of course, but chaps like that often feel they have something to prove. They're prone to overstepping the line.'

Gallagher waited. 'I made enquiries after Jutland,' Ryder said. 'You'll recall that naval intelligence failed to pass the word about the movements of the German fleet. The duty officer that day, who was responsible for the failure, was Colson.'

Down the hill another train was chugging up the line towards Tonbridge, its plume of white steam blown quickly away by the wind. 'Why are you telling me this?' Gallagher asked.

'I thought at first that it was just a blunder. A serious mistake, yes, but one that anyone could make. But there have been more failures since. Half of the time, naval intelligence seems completely in the dark about German intentions. Is that just incompetence, or is it something more? And there's another thing, too.'

Gallagher heard Mrs Vane's voice in his mind. *He's jealous of Colson.* 'Is this to do with Colson's business interests?'

Ryder looked surprised. 'Yes, it is. Before the war, when I was naval attaché in Washington, Anglo-Persian Oil's board sent a team of its directors to negotiate a partnership with an American company, Standard Oil. Colson was one of them. The negotiations collapsed when Standard Oil's executives accused Colson and his people of spying on them. Someone removed papers from a Standard Oil safe that revealed the American bargaining position. There was a hell of a stink about it, and our ambassador had to intervene to smooth things over.'

'Interesting,' Gallagher said. 'But how is that relevant to the death of Vasiliev?'

'Perhaps it isn't,' Ryder admitted. 'You're the expert on these things. But you're barking up the wrong tree where Vasiliev is concerned. He's no more a German spy than I am.'

'Yesterday, you suggested that Vasiliev might have been investigating on behalf of someone at the Admiralty. Did you mean that?'

'It's quite possible, yes. Admiral Jellicoe has not forgiven or forgotten. He is quite capable of ordering a clandestine investigation. He's a subtle man, Jellicoe, and in my view, a great one.' There was a note of admiration in Ryder's voice. 'It is an honour to serve under his command. I don't expect you will know him.'

'He commanded the naval brigade when I was in China, during the Boxer affair,' Gallagher said. 'I was just a sergeant of marines, though. He wouldn't remember me.'

Memories flashed through his mind. Another grey sky with a hurrying wind, but it had been hot that day outside Peitsang, Chinese artillery shells dropping all around and exploding in bright flame and puffs of white smoke, shrapnel hissing in the air, marines and bluejackets scattering for cover, and the cry going up, *Captain Jellicoe! He's been hit, he's down!* Himself, bending over Jellicoe, the captain flat on his back with blood pouring out of his chest, face already white with approaching death. Dropping his rifle, picking up the unconscious man and running through the falling shells towards the aid station by the riverbank. The medics, helping him lay the captain on a stretcher, one of them taking his pulse; *you needn't have bothered, mate, he'll never make it* . . . Returning to his company, his men staring at him, looking down to see his own blue uniform jacket soaked with blood . . . A little later, the Japanese troops out on the right broke through the Chinese entrenchments and silenced the guns, and the battle dragged to its end. They heard that evening that Captain Jellicoe had been given the last rites; only two days later did they learn that, by some miracle, he had pulled through.

Somewhere in a drawer in Gallagher's rooms in London was a little oak leaf badge, signifying *mentioned in dispatches*. He never wore it.

They were approaching the woods. Bare trees swayed in the wind, limbs dark against the leaden clouds. A gust of wind filled Gallagher's throat with cold air, and he coughed. 'There's one other thing,' he said. 'Commander Colson asked me to keep this secret, but you need to know. We found a document in Vasiliev's pocket, a telegram that had been taken from Admiral Hall's safe.'

'A telegram!' Ryder stared at him. 'From whom?'

'From Arthur Zimmermann, the German foreign secretary, to the German ambassador in Mexico. That's all we know. The whole thing is in cipher, and we haven't been able to break the code.'

'How did naval intelligence get hold of it? Was this a wireless intercept?'

'No,' Gallagher said. 'We used the old, time-honoured methods of intelligence gathering, namely bribery, lies and theft. We're quite skilled at all three. We should be, we recruit from all the best schools.'

Ryder ignored this. 'Zimmermann, eh? I used to know him when I served in Berlin. Dined with him a few times. Jumped-up little peasant, but a clever chap all the same. Does this mean the Germans are trying to stir up trouble in Mexico again?'

'Possibly,' Gallagher said. 'We'd know a lot more if we could decrypt the telegram, but it seems a fair guess. The Mexican government is furious with the Americans for sending troops into Mexico to punish Pancho Villa and his guerrillas, and the Germans will see this as a chance to pour oil on troubled fires. The important point, however, is how did Vasiliev find out about the telegram, and who sent him to steal it? Would Admiral Jellicoe really authorise someone to burgle the safe of one of his own admirals?'

'Of course he would,' Ryder said without hesitation. 'If he thought there was a traitor in the Admiralty, he would take any measure necessary to deal with the situation. So would I. Look, I'm not saying Admiral Hall is a traitor, of course not. But Blinker needs to clean his own house. If he doesn't, Admiral Jellicoe will do it for him.'

Gallagher nodded. 'You know his lordship's mind on this.'

'I do. And I'll say it again, Gallagher, you're barking up the wrong tree. Dig into Vasiliev's background by all means, but remember he is the victim, not the killer.'

'I will,' said Gallagher.

'Good. Keep me informed.'

*

They reached their pegs and took their positions. The beaters were coming through the trees, whooping and shouting and thrashing the undergrowth with their sticks. The first pheasants began to rise, squawking with alarm, and the bark of shotguns echoed over the fields, sound wavering on the wind. The guns blew on their numbed fingers, reloaded and fired again, and a few birds turned over and plummeted to the ground. Most turned and fled downwind towards safety.

The first drive ended and they walked towards the next one. Gallagher fell in beside Nicholas Makarian, both of them a little behind the main group. 'How are you, Nick?'

'Wishing I was somewhere warm,' said Makarian. 'Do you enjoy shooting, Pat?'

'I don't mind it in peacetime,' Gallagher said. 'I know we're feeding the wounded in the hospitals, but it seems like an odd pastime in war.'

'I feel about shooting much as I do about golf. A good walk, spoiled. But Sir John enjoys it, and I strive to be a good son-in-law.'

Gallagher smiled. 'Clearly he is grateful. He brought Tovey down here in hopes that he would offer you some fat government contracts.'

'I have spoken to Tovey. I do not think much of him.'

Gallagher cleared his throat, trying not to cough. 'Oh?'

'He is in charge of oil shipments for the navy, but he knows absolutely nothing about oil or tankers. I asked him what grade of oil the *Queen Elizabeth*-class battleships use for fuel, and he didn't know what I was talking about. Still, that's the navy for you. No offence.'

'I was a marine, Nick. Don't expect me to stick up for the navy. What about your business? Is it prospering?'

Makarian shook his head. 'Unrestricted submarine warfare

will be the ruin of us. Yesterday alone we lost two ships, both sunk by U-boats. The lifeboats managed to rescue the crew of one, but sadly not the other. My heart goes out to those poor men's families.'

'I imagine oil tankers are a prime target.'

'Of course. And until the navy gets serious about protecting them and organizing proper convoys, I will continue to lose ships, and more families will lose their husbands and sons. The navy's incompetence in this matter has me absolutely steaming. I shall go to the Admiralty and demand action.'

'You might have a fight on your hands,' Gallagher said.

'I like fighting. I come from a nation of warriors.'

Gallagher smiled again. 'Talk to Captain Ryder. He has direct access to Admiral Jellicoe.'

'Oh, I intend to do so.'

They walked on. Lansing was up ahead, talking to Borden and Colson and waving his hands. 'Do you do business with Lansing?' Gallagher asked.

'Of course. We have an important contract with Lansing Oil in Mexico.'

Gallagher glanced across at Colson. 'What about Anglo-Persian Oil? Do you work with them?'

'Anglo-Persian? No. Their board is composed of nabobs and mandarins, and only does business with people who belong to the right clubs. Not with Armenian upstarts like me.'

'You know a lot about oil, Nick. Perhaps you can help me.'

'I know everything about oil. What do you want to know?'

'Explain the Middle East oilfields to me.'

Makarian's eyebrows rose. 'The secret service is taking an interest in the Middle East? How interesting. There are two major oilfields in the region. One is in Persia, where the British held a knife to the shah's throat until he agreed to give them the concession. That concession was handed over to Anglo-Persian Oil. Thanks to the demand for oil brought about by the war, Anglo-Persian's owners are now very rich.'

'So I am given to understand.'

'The real prize, though, is the much larger field in the Middle East, specifically in Mesopotamia. This is controlled by Germany's ally, the Ottoman Turks. Those same Turks who gave you a bloody nose at Gallipoli.'

'Sixty thousand dead is more than a bloody nose,' said Gallagher. 'Don't tell me that you, of all people, admire the Ottomans.'

'*Admire* them? After what their army did to our people?' Makarian paused for a moment. 'The Germans are pressing the Turks to hand over the oilfields to them, in exchange for military assistance, and are building a railway to Baghdad to exploit the oil. However, the British are also staking a claim. As everyone knows, Britain and France have a highly secret arrangement to divide up the Middle East after the war. As part of that deal Britain, and Anglo-Persian, will get the oilfields.'

'The oilfields are also adjacent to Armenia,' Gallagher said.

'Your geography is impeccable, Pat. Why is the secret service interested?'

'Lansing also wants those oilfields. That's one of the reasons he came to Britain.'

'So what if he does? It is nothing to do with me.'

But you do business with Lansing, Gallagher thought, *and Lansing's wife was a German spy.* 'Does the name Paul Vasiliev mean anything to you?'

'Absolutely nothing,' Makarian said. 'Who is he?'

'He was a navy officer. Dead now. I wondered if your partner, Maxim Litzov, might have known him.'

'I cannot imagine Maxim having anything in common with

a Royal Navy officer, but I will ask next time I write. You are asking a lot of questions, Pat.'

'It's my job,' Gallagher said. *The question I really want to ask is, why did someone mention your business partner in a postcard to Vasiliev, and why was he present when Rasputin was murdered? What connects them, and you?*

They crossed the carriage drive. Up ahead the others were moving towards their new pegs. Makarian glanced down the lane towards the lodge. 'Who is that woman? She can't be one of the beaters.'

Gallagher looked and saw a small woman in a black over-coat with a scarf around her hair, walking steadily towards the house. 'Some rambler, probably,' he said. 'Carry on, Nick. I'll warn her off.'

Willa Rittenhouse stopped when she saw Gallagher approaching. 'Hullo again,' she said. 'Surprised to see me?'

'How did you find me?' Gallagher demanded.

'It wasn't hard. You said you were shooting, and the porters at the station said there was only one shooting party in the district this weekend.' She looked at the guns walking across, and pointed to Tovey, who had also fallen behind. 'What's that fellow doing here?'

'Do you mean Lieutenant Tovey? You know him?'

She stared hard and then shook her head. 'Tovey, you say? Well, I must be mistaken. Never mind, I need to talk to you. James Lansing is here, isn't he? Yes, there he is. I see him now.'

Lansing was out on the far end of the line, standing with his back to them and talking to Captain Ryder. 'What is this about?' demanded Gallagher.

'Let's level with each other, shall we? I know who you are, Mr Gallagher, and I'm pretty sure you know who I am, too.'

'I told you who I am.'

'Paymaster General's Office? Pull the other one. I telegraphed some friends in America and called in a few favours, and they told me all about you. Are you here because of Lansing?'

'If you know who I am, you must also know that I'm not going to answer that question.'

'Lansing is a bastard,' she said. 'He treats his workers like dirt, especially the Mexicans. People get killed or hurt in his oilfields pretty much every day, and he does nothing about it. And there's something fishy about his wife's death too. Whatever happened, it wasn't an accident.'

'Lansing was in Mexico the night his wife died,' Gallagher said. 'Are you suggesting that he had something to do with Sadie's death?'

'I don't know, but I intend to find out. More importantly, did you know that Lansing has also been negotiating with the Germans?'

'Go on.'

'He's putting together a cabal of financiers and oilmen like himself. They've bought shares in the railway the Germans are building from Berlin to Baghdad. In exchange for investment, Lansing will get the concession to the oilfields that the Ottoman Turks control. That'll give him control of a big chunk of the world's oil production, and he'll have your Royal Navy by the balls. If you'll pardon the expression.'

'Why do you care?' Gallagher asked. 'America is neutral. Lansing is free to make deals with whomever he wishes.'

She looked impatient. 'I may be a muck-raker, dear, but I still know the difference between right and wrong. I know America is neutral, but damn it, we *shouldn't* be. We should be over here, fighting for peace and democracy, like you're doing. Not cosying up to the Germans to get rich.'

'Is that everything?' Gallagher asked.

'Not quite. There's also the little matter of that body they found at the Admiralty.'

Gallagher froze. 'How do you know about that?'

'Never underestimate the tongue-loosening influence of a pint of mild. Admiralty porters like to gossip just as much as the next person. I reckon I know who your dead man is, and I'll bet he isn't called Paul Vasiliev.'

Gallagher took a step towards her. 'Miss Rittenhouse, I am about to invoke the Official Secrets Act.'

'Save your breath, I already know it off by heart. You don't have to take my word for it, I'll bring you my evidence and you can decide for yourself.'

Gallagher glanced around. The others had moved on to their pegs, all except Tovey who had stopped and was re-tying his boot laces. 'When?' Gallagher asked.

'This afternoon. I won't come to the house; I don't think Lansing would be very pleased to see me.' She pointed at the ground. 'Meet me back here at three p.m.'

'Why didn't you bring the evidence with you now?'

'Because I didn't know what kind of reception I'd get. I thought you might clap me in irons, or set the dogs on me. But you seem like a reasonable young man, and I reckon we can do business together.'

A whistle blew in the distance and Gallagher heard the beaters moving through the woods. Tovey hurried away to join the other guns. 'You'd better get back to town, Miss Rittenhouse,' he said. 'For your own safety.'

'Why? Do you think someone will mistake me for a pheasant?'

'It's not a good idea to wander around in front of the guns. Accidents happen.'

'Point taken. I shall beat a hasty retreat.' She turned, pulling her overcoat more tightly around her. 'Until this afternoon, Mr Gallagher.'

The birds were coming over in greater numbers now. Price raised his shotgun and fired left and right barrels, and two pheasants plummeted out of the sky and thudded to the ground. Resting the gun against his prosthetic arm, he broke open the breech and inserted two more shells, closing the breech with a click. Tovey watched with admiration. 'Bloody good shooting,' he said. 'How long did it take you to learn to load like that?'

'Long enough,' said Price, raising the gun again.

'I must say, you've done amazingly well to recover from your wounds. I admire you.'

'That's why I did it,' Price said. He fired again, and another bird fell. 'So people would admire me.'

Tovey raised a hand in apology. 'Sorry, that was clumsy of me. I can't imagine what you have been through. The pain must have been terrible.'

'You learn to live with pain,' Price said. 'Like everything else.'

Guns barked all along the line. The stink of cordite drifted on the raw edge of the wind. Tovey watched Gallagher returning to the beat, and frowned a little. 'What do you make of that fellow?'

'Nothing,' Price said. 'I try to mind my own business.'

'He's our host's stepson, did you know that? Some past indiscretion of the old girl, no doubt. You wouldn't think it to look at her.'

Price pointed upwards. 'Your bird.'

Tovey fired and missed. 'He's not really with the Paymaster General. Gallagher, I mean. And the lady who claims to work for him, Mrs Vane. She's actually a secretary in naval intelligence.'

'Like I said, I try to mind my own business.'

Tovey persisted. 'Did you hear about the body they found at the Admiralty the other day? That was in naval intelligence too.'

More birds; Price raised his gun and squeezed the trigger, and yet another pheasant tumbled out of the sky. 'You're having all the luck today,' Tovey said. 'Look here, Price, something is going on at the Admiralty. I just wondered if you had heard anything, that's all.'

'No,' said Price.

Tovey grinned suddenly. 'And if you did know anything, and you told me, then you'd have to kill me.'

Price spun around, facing him. 'What's that supposed to mean?' he demanded.

'Calm down, old boy. It's a joke. Sherlock Holmes, you know? And, do you mind not pointing that shotgun at me? The ruddy thing's loaded, remember?'

'Sorry,' Price said curtly. He turned away. 'A man's dead, Tovey. That's nothing to laugh about.'

'I was just—'

'You haven't been in action, have you? If you had, if you'd seen your friends and fellow officers blown to pieces in front of your eyes and their guts splashed all over the bridge, you would know better. Give the dead some respect, Tovey. They deserve that much, at least.'

9

THE FINAL DRIVE ended and they walked back to the house, heads bent against a shower of freezing rain sweeping in from the east. Makarian dropped behind the main group, and Lansing fell back to join him. 'You're an intelligent man,' the American said. 'Whatever made you choose a windswept, rain-sodden heap like Britain to live in? You should go south, man. Go somewhere warm, like Mexico.'

'Britain is the place where decisions get made,' Makarian said. 'The people who matter live in London, not Mexico.'

'They may not live here much longer.' Lansing shaded his eyes against the rain. 'I meant what I said last night. The way I see it, Britain is losing the war. The country is rotten from the inside, you know. There's treason everywhere.'

'Treason?'

'Bolshevism, man. Communism, socialism, call it what you will. Britain is rife with it. There's a part of Glasgow called Red Clydeside, have you heard about this? It's mob rule in there, no law and order whatsoever. Even the police don't dare to go in.'

'I've been to Clydeside,' Makarian said. 'There was not a mob in sight. But you are right about being rotten from the inside.'

145

'How do you mean?'

'I will tell you a secret,' Makarian said. 'Patrick Gallagher is an agent of the secret service.'

'The cloak and dagger boys? Well, now, that's interesting.'

'Aren't you curious about why he is here?'

Lansing shrugged. 'He's your brother-in-law. Perhaps this is just a family reunion.'

'No,' Makarian said. 'It is not.'

'Come on, man, you can't leave it there. What do you know about him?'

'Later, perhaps. When you have told me more about the business deal you have in mind. That's why you dropped back to join me, isn't it? To talk business?'

Lansing grinned a little, wiping rainwater from his face. 'I'm putting together some projects in the Middle East,' he said. 'I'll cut you in, if you want. There'll have to be a big upfront investment, but if we pull it off, there could be some really juicy returns.'

'It is generous of you to think of me. What do you want in exchange?'

'Your support. The British government will try to fight me, and I need someone to help bring them around. You know people. Your father-in-law is a friend of Churchill.'

Makarian considered this. 'I can talk to them,' he said. 'What do I get in exchange for my upfront investment?'

'An exclusive shipping contract,' Lansing said. He leaned closer. 'No matter which side wins the war.'

'That's a big promise,' Makarian said after a moment. 'Can you keep it?'

'I can. I'll tell you how, but first I want your commitment.'

Makarian pursed his lips. 'I'll think about it,' he said.

*

STANDING IN THE hall, Gallagher watched Lansing and Makarian come in. It was not hard to guess what they had been talking about.

Everything depends on two questions, the messenger at the Admiralty had said. *Will Russia leave the war? And will the Americans join it?* It was starting to feel like both were part of the same question.

Or, as Mrs Vane had said, *one plot with two parts*.

Tompkins the head keeper took the shotguns away to be cleaned, and the guns huddled around the near-warmth of the hall fire. 'That was good shooting, young fellow,' Borden said to Price, and the others murmured agreement. 'You must come and shoot with us again, of course. It was a pleasure to watch you.'

Surprisingly, Price smiled. 'Thank you, Sir John. I must say, it is good to be out and about again.'

'How long were you in hospital?' Lansing asked.

If Price remembered Lansing's *faux pas* from last evening, he gave no sign. He was on his best behaviour now, and Gallagher wondered why. 'Two months, and two more in a convalescent home. It felt like for ever.'

The door opened and Mrs Vane came in, rain dripping from the brim of her sou'wester. 'Mr Gallagher, might I impose upon you for a moment? I have received a message from the office that you need to see.'

Gallagher looked up to see Fairbairn watching him. The other man touched the tips of his waxed moustache and turned away towards the fire.

In the music room, Mrs Vane reached into her pocket and pulled out an envelope. 'This is from headquarters. No response from America yet, but it's still early for them.'

The telegram contained two paragraphs of text, summing up

the careers of Lieutenant Charles Tovey and Lieutenant Geraint Price. Tovey had been born in Gloucestershire in 1882, the son of a landowner. His career was unremarkable: preparatory school, Dartmouth, commissioned into the navy at eighteen, a succession of postings with the Channel Fleet and the Mediterranean before moving to the transport division at the Admiralty in 1913, a year before the war broke out. He was unmarried and solitary, not known to be a member of any club.

Price was ten years younger. He had spent most of his naval career at sea, finishing as a watchkeeping officer on a light cruiser based at Scapa Flow. His war and his life changed for ever on the afternoon of the 31st of May 1916 during Beatty's run to the south, when an eleven-inch shell from a German battlecruiser exploded on the bridge of his ship, killing everyone else and badly injuring him. The rest of his story was already known except for one thing: the shore posting his wife had mentioned was at the Admiralty, on the staff of the permanent secretary of the navy, Sir Graham Greene.

'You've read these, I assume,' Gallagher said. 'What did you think?'

'I was surprised to see that Tovey is thirty-five. He looks younger, but then, some people age well. I can't see anything to connect either of them with Vasiliev.'

'No,' Gallagher said slowly. 'But something peculiar has happened.'

He told Mrs Vane about his encounter with Willa Rittenhouse. 'She thought she recognized Tovey, but then said she must be mistaken. She also thinks that the dead man at the Admiralty may not be Vasiliev.'

'But what about Captain Ryder? He identified the body straight away. Why would he do that, if it wasn't really Vasiliev?'

'An excellent question,' said Gallagher. 'Assuming, of course, that Miss Rittenhouse isn't blowing smoke in our eyes. Which is entirely possible.'

'Will you talk to Ryder?' she asked.

In his mind's eye he saw the numbers, *2030 2417*. Just over a day and a half until the throne of Saturn comes. They were juggling with time, but moving too quickly could be as dangerous as being too slow. 'Not yet,' he said. 'I want to see how this plays out.'

UP IN HIS room, Gallagher changed out of his shooting clothes and went back down to the hall. Hunton the footman was putting more logs on the fire which, as ever, was pumping heat straight up the chimney and sending almost nothing out into the room. 'Have you seen Mrs Fairbairn?' Gallagher asked.

'I believe she is in the library, sir.'

The library was warmer, the fire on the grate crackling merrily. Nathalie Fairbairn was standing by the sideboard. Her husband stood near the door, watching her with his arms folded over his chest. Neither of them spoke. The atmosphere hissed with tension.

Gallagher looked at Fairbairn. 'I'd like a word with your wife, if I may.'

Fairbairn looked as if he was about to speak, but changed his mind. Silently, he left the room, closing the door behind him.

'Are you happy to be home in England?' Gallagher asked.

Nathalie picked up the brandy decanter and poured a glass half full, banging the decanter down again. 'What do you think?'

'I'll come to the point. Has your husband told you about the photograph we found at Aquinnah, after Sadie Lansing died? The one of you, and her, and Count von Bernstorff?'

'You mean, the one where Sadie and I are showing the world

our diddies?' She gazed at him. 'There. Are you not going to rebuke me for unladylike language?'

Fairbairn had insisted on keeping the photograph and not showing it to the police. 'So, he did tell you,' Gallagher said.

'Oh, he told me *all* about it. He said I had been sleeping with the enemy, and made me promise to keep it all quiet. If word got out, it could wreck his career. That's all he really cared about, of course. His career.'

'At the time, you claimed you didn't know who Bernstorff was. It was that kind of party, you said.'

She smiled a little. 'Aye. He was just a friend of Sadie's. No names, no pack drill.'

'Who took the photograph?' Gallagher asked.

'Who took—' She checked. 'What difference does it make?'

'Was it Paul Vasiliev? Did he take the photograph?'

'*Paul?*' She looked incredulous. 'Why on earth would you think that?'

'So, you knew him,' Gallagher said. 'Did you know he was Sadie Lansing's lover?'

'For God's sake, of course I did. It was hardly a secret.'

Gallagher looked at her more closely. 'He was your lover as well, wasn't he?'

Nathalie sipped her brandy. 'Are you shocked? Darling, you really are remarkably unacquainted with the world. Bed-hopping is practically a national sport on Cape Cod. It's even worse than the Cotswolds.'

'Vasiliev is dead,' Gallagher said, watching her face. 'I'm trying to find out what happened to him.'

Her face and voice were both calm. 'Sorry to hear it, but it's nothing to do with me. I haven't seen him for years.'

'Did your husband know Vasiliev?'

'They never met, no. I took care to keep them apart.'

That at least had the ring of truth about it. 'We also found photographs of James Lansing with Bernstorff, on the deck of a yacht. Your husband was present too. Were you there as well?'

'Of course. The party was on Herbert's boat, the *Chasseur*. I was there as his hostess, to make everyone welcome.' She paused. 'Some more welcome than others, of course.'

'Did your husband invite Bernstorff? Or did he show up unannounced?'

Their eyes met. 'Herbert invited him,' she said calmly. 'That was not the first occasion they met, or the last.'

Gallagher nodded. 'You still haven't told me who took the photograph.'

'Are you sure you want to know? Your sensitive soul will be shocked.'

Gallagher said nothing. 'Frank took the photograph,' she said. 'Sadie's brother. For your information, at the time Frank was wearing even less than we were. Frank always was an exhibitionist. But then, I suppose we all were.'

Her smile was slow and malicious. 'Do you want to know what the four of us did after Frank took the photograph?'

'Not particularly,' said Gallagher.

'I'm sure you don't. That really would shock your wee soul. Is there anything else?'

'Thank you, Mrs Fairbairn,' Gallagher said. 'You have been most helpful.'

Saturday, 3 February 1917
1.48 p.m.

Lunch was lukewarm soup, boiled salmon, rabbit stew and a hazelnut tart with bone-hard pastry, accompanied by the rhythmic thump of the plumbing in the ceiling overhead. The conversation, which mostly centred around the latest rise in income tax, was as turgid as the meal itself. Edith Price tried to lift the atmosphere by talking about a show she had seen in London, called *Houp-la!*

'It's so silly that it's actually quite fun,' she said. 'A circus owner is running out of money, so he decides to put all of his savings on an accumulator at the races and every horse wins except the last one so he doesn't get a penny, and the star trapeze artist is in love with a rich polo player, only he himself is in love with one of the circus dancers, and on and on.' Edith started to giggle. 'You'll never believe it, one of the songs is actually called "How Could She Yacki Hacki Wicki Wacki Woo!" It's so ridiculous, you just have to laugh!'

Lady Maud cut through her pastry with an audible crunch. 'Musical shows are vulgar,' she pronounced.

'Mother!' Penelope said sharply, but Edith, at the other end of the table, was too far away to hear and carried on happily.

They rose at the end of the meal. 'I'm going out to do a little rough shooting,' Captain Ryder said. 'Anyone care to join me? Price?'

Price shook his head. 'I promised my wife a walk around the lake. That is, if the rain has stopped.'

'Oh, it has,' Edith said eagerly. 'And the wind has died away a little, too. I do believe the weather is improving.'

Gallagher looked out at the scudding grey clouds and the cattle huddled in the lee of wall around the park. Even for someone with Edith's optimism, this was a glass half full.

THE ROOM EMPTIED slowly. Mrs Vane and Penelope left together, talking quietly; by the looks on their faces, Gallagher thought, they were talking about him. He smothered a brief annoyance and checked his watch; he was due to meet Miss Rittenhouse in just over an hour. Strains of music drifted through from the music room, and he went in to find Makarian playing the harpsichord. Nathalie Fairbairn was sitting on the bench beside him.

'Pardon me for interrupting,' Gallagher said.

Makarian's eyes met his. 'You weren't interrupting anything,' the other man said.

Gallagher let that statement dissolve slowly in the air. 'I was looking for Lansing. Have either of you seen him?'

Makarian's gaze was challenging. 'He is in the library, talking with Sir John.'

In the library, Borden and Lansing were seated in armchairs before the fire. Neither noticed Gallagher enter at first. 'I appreciate your position,' Lansing was saying. 'But you have to appreciate mine as well, Sir John. So far as I'm concerned, this is an empty deal. If America declares war on Germany, that's going to require one hell of a commitment in terms of money and industrial output. I'll put this crudely, because I'm a crude sort of man. What's in this for us?'

'World peace,' said Borden. 'That should surely be good for business.'

'You think so? In my experience, war is a damned sight better for business. Look, Sir John, here is the situation. America has her own problems, closer to home. We have our own Bolsheviks and anarchists and other assorted rabble stirring up trouble. There's still a God-almighty ferment in Mexico, what with Pancho Villa and his bandits on the loose and our troops south of the border chasing after him. God, the bribes I've had to pay to keep my oil wells safe. And as if that wasn't enough, now we've got the Japanese sneaking around in the Pacific, looking for a chance to grab our colonies, maybe even get a foothold on our western seaboard.'

'Japan is on our side, of course,' said Borden.

Lansing stabbed a finger at him. 'On *your* side, Sir John, not ours. Japan regards America as a rival, not a friend. They're starting to interfere in Mexico, too, they've even got a secret navy base somewhere on the west coast. So you see, we have plenty of other fish to fry, without getting dragged into a war in Europe.'

'Public opinion in America doesn't agree with you,' Borden said. 'Neither do the newspapers.'

Lansing's face was full of contempt. 'President Wilson makes decisions based on reason, not the voice of the mob or the gutter press. We've been here before, when the *Lusitania* sank. Your people in Washington played the newspapers for all they were worth, pushing stories about German atrocities, and tried to bounce us into war. Well, it didn't work then, and it won't work now. Frankly, Sir John, unless I can see clearly how going to war will benefit America, I might as well head back to London. No point in wasting any more time.'

Gallagher cleared his throat. 'I hope I'm not intruding,' he said.

'Not at all,' Borden said heavily. 'Mr Lansing and I were just setting the world to rights. What can I do for you, Pat?'

'Actually, it was Mr Lansing I wanted to see.' Gallagher pulled up a chair and sat down. 'Do you mind if I ask you a couple of questions, sir?'

'Go ahead,' Lansing said.

'This is rather delicate,' Gallagher said. 'Mr Lansing, I am sorry to rake up the past, but did you ever meet a man called Paul Vasiliev? He was an associate of Vladimir Dmitrievich Nabokov, and I'm afraid he was also one of your wife's lovers.'

Lansing's response was surprisingly calm. 'No need to be

afraid. What's past is past. But no, I never met anyone called Vasiliev.'

'Thank you. I believe, however, that you have met Count von Bernstorff, the German ambassador in America. Is that correct?'

Lansing gazed at him, unblinking. 'Why does the British secret service want to know? What's it got to do with you?'

'You don't have to answer,' Gallagher said.

'You're damned right I don't. But just to set the record straight, yes, I met Bernstorff last summer. I did so at the behest of my president, Woodrow Wilson.'

Gallagher nodded. 'May I ask why?'

'Do I have to spell it out for you? Woodrow wants to put an end to the war between Britain and Germany. He reckons America can act as intermediary between you, to bring about peace. He asked me to sound out Bernstorff about the prospects.'

'How did Bernstorff react?'

'Very positively. He promised to raise the matter with his government in Berlin.'

'And did he?'

Lansing shook his head. 'I stepped back at that point. The White House and the State Department are doing the rest.'

'Who introduced you to Bernstorff?'

'My wife did. She knew him socially.'

'Biblically too, I believe,' Gallagher said.

The oilman stood up. 'God damn it, Gallagher, the woman's dead. Don't drag her reputation through the mud.'

'That's going to be a little difficult to avoid,' Gallagher said. He too rose to his feet. 'Did you know that your wife was also a German agent? That as well as sleeping with Bernstorff, she was also spying for him?'

'Bullshit. Sadie threw a lot of parties and slept with a lot of people, but a spy? Not a chance. She didn't have the brains for it.'

'We have evidence,' Gallagher said. 'I can arrange for the Bureau of Investigation to show it to you. When you met Bernstorff, did you talk about anything else?'

'What if I did? America is a neutral country. I can talk to the German ambassador about any damned thing I want.'

'A journalist named Willa Rittenhouse alleges that you are negotiating with the Germans. Is this true?'

Tiny beads of sweat had formed under Lansing's eyes. 'Rittenhouse is like all journalists,' he said. 'She peddles lies for a living.' He turned to Borden. 'Think it over, Sir John. If you're serious about an American alliance, come up with something to sweeten the pot. When you're ready, we'll talk again.'

THE DOOR BANGED shut behind Lansing. 'Do you mind telling me what that was about?' Borden said sharply.

Gallagher turned. 'Surely it was obvious,' he said.

Borden had risen too. 'Are you seriously suggesting that he is in league with Germany? For God's sake, Pat, he's President Wilson's personal envoy!'

'He is also serving his own ends, first and foremost. Didn't you hear him? Come up with something to sweeten the pot, he said. Isn't it obvious what he means? As I said yesterday, he wants the oilfields. That is his price for bringing America into the war.'

'I know,' Borden said finally. 'Thank you again for pointing it out, Pat, but we had already anticipated this.'

Gallagher regarded him for a moment. 'You're going to do it, aren't you? You and Churchill and your friends will break your word to Anglo-Persian Oil and hand over the oilfields to Lansing in exchange for American help.'

'We don't want to, of course. But if that's what it takes to get America on side, then that is what we will do.'

'Is this government policy?'

Borden made an impatient gesture. 'We're *making* policy, here and now. It's not just the war, Pat, we have to think about the future. If we join forces with America, we can crush Germany, but that's only the beginning. Think of the possibilities, man! America's industrial power, joined together with the might of our empire, will create a force that no power can withstand. We can build a hegemony that will last for centuries, longer even than Rome! We *must* get America on side!'

America is as dangerous as Germany, Colson had said that morning. Somewhere between the two delusions, his and Borden's, lay the truth. 'Fairbairn and the Foreign Office won't agree with you. And Anglo-Persian will fight you tooth and nail. Colson must know what is going on.'

'Colson on his own cannot stop us,' Borden said. 'And we can bring Fairbairn around.'

'What if he also owns shares in Anglo-Persian?'

'I own shares in the company myself,' Borden said. 'But I won't let that stand in the way of my duty.'

Something in his tone of voice caught Gallagher's attention. 'Is that why Fairbairn is here? So you can twist his arm?'

'So that we can make him see reason,' Borden said. 'Greatness comes with a price, Pat. Winston Churchill taught me that lesson. I've always remembered it.'

'Lansing's wife was a German spy. Lansing himself is doing deals with the Kaiser's representatives and investing in German railways. If my source is correct, the German government will also offer him a concession. If you give in to him now, then no matter who wins the war, Lansing gets the oilfields, and that's all he wants. Do you really think that, no matter what you promise him, he is truly serious about committing America to a war with Germany?'

Borden rubbed his forehead. 'If what you say is true, this is quite appalling.'

'You are being manipulated,' Gallagher said. 'By buying Lansing's influence, Germany is manoeuvring to keep America neutral. And at the moment, they are succeeding.'

'If the Germans can buy Lansing, so can we,' Borden said, but his voice was uncertain. 'Winston believes this is the right strategy. He is certain that it will work.'

On impulse, Gallagher reached into his pocket and pulled out the waterproof wallet with the folded letter and handed it to Borden. 'Read this,' he said.

Puzzled, Borden read the letter.

To the director of the secret service,

Know that the bearer of this letter is protected, and is acting upon my full authority. You are charged to give him whatever aid and assistance is required. This entire matter is to be considered most secret, and the bearer has been instructed to show this letter only to you. You may not disclose any details even to your closest subordinates and all written records are to be destroyed immediately, including this letter. The outcome of the war and the fate of nations are at stake.

'I don't understand,' the other man said.

Gallagher retrieved the letter. 'You recognize the hand-writing?'

'It's Winston's, of course. Where did it come from?'

'I took it from the body of a dead man on the *Lusitania*, just before she was torpedoed. His name was Harry Chalfont, and before he died, he admitted to being a German spy.'

'I don't understand,' Borden repeated. 'What does this mean?'

'I want to know how Winston Churchill's letter came into Harry Chalfont's hands,' Gallagher said. 'Any ideas?'

'I'm certain there is a plausible explanation for this.'

'Of course there is. As you said, greatness comes with a price,' Gallagher said. 'Don't trust anyone, John. And for God's sake, don't promise Lansing *anything*. String him along, keep him in play for as long as you can, but no promises. We can break his game, but it will take time.'

'Time?' Borden said sharply. 'How much time?'

'Until eight thirty tomorrow evening,' Gallagher said.

NATHALIE FAIRBAIRN WAS waiting in the hall when Tovey came in from the gun room, carrying a shotgun. 'Has he agreed yet?' he asked.

'Not yet. He's still trying to play off both ends against the middle. I don't blame him, in his place I'd do the same.' Nathalie smiled a little. 'Don't worry. He'll agree in the end, because he knows we can give him what he wants.'

Tovey leaned the gun against the wall and began pulling on his mackintosh. 'What happens if he doesn't? I'm the one running the risks here, Nathalie.'

'Have faith,' she said. 'Go on. I'll see you at dinner.'

Tovey drew a deep breath. 'Have faith,' he repeated. 'That's easy for you to say. Did you see which way Captain Ryder went?'

'Across the park.'

'I'll circle around and keep out of his way. I don't want to get shot by accident.' He clapped a sou'wester on his head. 'Are we going to get away with this?'

'Of course we are. Leave it to me. Good hunting, if that is the correct expression.'

Tovey went out, closing the door behind him. Nathalie Fairbairn stood for a moment, looking after him, an expression of contempt on her face.

EDITH PRICE STOOD on the bridge on the far side of the lake, wrapped in a heavy overcoat with a silk scarf around her hair to ward off the wind. One gloved hand rested on the gnarled grey trunk of the wisteria intertwined with the balustrade. 'It looks completely lifeless,' she said to her husband. 'Withered and dead, all of the life force gone out of it. Yet in a few months' time it will be covered in leaves and flowers. The circle of life and death . . . I feel quite spiritual in places like this, don't you?'

Price stood beside her, the collar of his overcoat turned up against the bitter wind. Around them stretched bare trees and cold dreary fields. 'This is a strange time to be talking about spirituality,' he said.

'Is it? I can't think of a better time. This old bridge will be so beautiful when the wisteria is in flower. And the park, too. Imagine it in spring, when the trees are in leaf and the candles are blooming on the chestnut trees. It will be magical.'

Price gazed at the dark water. 'Spring seems like a long way away.'

She took his arm, her voice suddenly intense. 'But it *will* come, darling. I promise you. Spring will come.'

He looked down at her, his face wry. 'Don't make promises you can't keep, Edie.'

'Oh, darling!' Her own face was a sudden picture of woe. 'Have I *ever* broken a promise to you? Please don't doubt me, I beg you. I couldn't bear it if you did.'

'I'm sorry,' he said gently. 'I don't doubt you, really I don't.

You're all the world to me, Edie. I was a wreck when you found me, but you helped me back to my feet again. I owe you more than words can ever express.'

Silence fell for a while. An aeroplane passed overhead, engine spluttering a little, descending towards the aerodrome beyond Tonbridge. A train whistle screeched and they saw another white plume of smoke and steam coming up the line.

'Are you frightened, darling?' Edith asked.

Price's voice was reflective. 'Not really, but . . . I don't like the waiting around. That was the hardest bit about Jutland, moving into contact, seeing the enemy's smoke on the horizon, not knowing what was going to happen next. Once the shells started dropping around us, it was different. There was too much to do, and no time to think or feel emotions.'

He paused, watching the train. 'All of those poor devils coming back from the front, battered and broken as I was. How much longer? How many more people have to suffer before it ends?'

'Not much longer,' she said softly.

Price smiled a little. 'You believe that, I know. I wish I could.'

She squeezed his hand. 'Be strong, my darling.'

'Don't worry. I will do my duty.'

'I know you will.' Her face, framed by the headscarf, was soft with love. She stretched up and kissed him on the lips. 'You're my hero,' she said softly.

SATURDAY, 3 FEBRUARY 1917
2.21 P.M.

Lansing stamped into the gun room and found Tompkins seated on a wooden stool, oiling the breech of a shotgun. 'Give me a gun,' Lansing snapped. 'The Parkers with the inlaid grips, those are mine.'

Tompkins rose and handed him the shotgun. 'Going out after ground game, are you, sir?'

'No, I'm going to watch a Punch and Judy show. What the hell do you think I'm doing?'

'Begging your pardon, sir. I just wanted to let you know that Captain Ryder and Mr Tovey are already shooting on the far side of the park. You might want to try the west woods, so you don't run afoul of them.'

Lansing grunted. The keeper handed him a box of shells, which he dropped into his overcoat pocket. In the hall he found Nathalie Fairbairn in boots and hat and coat, pulling on a pair of gloves. 'Are you going out?' she asked.

'Of course I'm going out, what does it look like? For Christ's sake, what's wrong with you people?'

Nathalie rolled her eyes. 'Oh, God, you're in one of your moods again.'

'Take it or leave it,' Lansing snapped. 'Are you coming with me?'

'Of course I'm coming with you,' she mimicked. 'What does it look like?'

They stepped outside, seeing the wind ripple the waters of the lake. Price and his wife stood on the bridge on the far side, leaning on the balustrade and gazing out over the fields. 'What a sweet young couple,' Nathalie said mockingly. 'Were you and Sadie ever like that?'

'Don't talk to me about Sadie. I've heard enough about her for one day.'

They started to walk towards the west woods. 'So *that's* why you're in a mood,' she said. 'What happened?'

'That fellow Gallagher is asking questions about her. It turns out he's some sort of secret service agent.'

'And you think you're so god-damned clever,' she said with contempt. 'Didn't you know? Gallagher was there at Aquinnah, the night she died.'

'He claims she was spying for Bernstorff. I've never heard such crap in all my life.'

They walked on in silence, reaching the trees and making their way through the dripping woods. 'Go on,' Lansing said finally. 'You're dying to tell me something. Spit it out.'

'Why do you think Sadie was so keen for you to meet Bernstorff? She wasn't trying to further your business interests, you fool, she didn't give a damn about you. She was following German orders. What did they want you to do? Use your influence with President Wilson to keep America neutral?'

'Something like that.'

'And what did they offer in exchange? The Middle East oil-fields? That's right, I can see it your face. Oh, James, you really are a bloody fool. If word gets out, you'll be pilloried from one end of America to another.'

'Yeah, well. Gallagher has been talking to that damned journalist, Rittenhouse. She claims she knows about my arrangement with Bernstorff, and is threatening to publish. I'm going to have do something about that bitch. She's a pain in the ass.'

'Oh, poor you,' Nathalie said, and the sneer was plain in her voice. 'I've read some of her articles, and so far as I can tell, they're all true. You really do maltreat your workers. You do pay them starvation wages. When they get killed or hurt in the oilfields, you don't do anything for their families, even though you have millions salted away in the bank. What have you got to complain about?'

'You sound like a god-damned Bolshevik.'

'Oh? What would you do if I was?'

'I'd shoot you dead, right here and now,' Lansing said venomously. 'I hate those bastards.'

'Why?'

'Because they're trying to take away what's mine. *I* built Lansing Oil, *I* made it what it is today, but those god-damned communists want to give it all to the workers! What have the workers ever done, hey? Everybody knows the lower orders are undeserving filth. They should stop whining when they get sick or sprain their little pinkies working in my oilfields, and be god-damned grateful to have jobs at all.'

Nathalie slapped him viciously across the face. He stared at her for a moment, blood rushing to his cheek, and grabbed her by the shoulders and pushed her violently back against the nearest tree. Her hand came up hard and fast, grabbing him by the groin and squeezing. Lansing dropped the shotgun, pulling her overcoat open and hauling up her skirt while she undid his fly buttons. Fabric ripped as he hauled her drawers down, lifted one bare leg with his hand and pushed roughly into her. She clung to him, biting his neck.

'How WELL DO you know Pat?' asked Penelope Makarian. 'Mr Gallagher, I should say?'

They were sitting in the dark drawing room, huddled as close to the fire as they could get. 'Not well,' Mrs Vane said. 'We have worked together for about three months.'

'I've always wondered why he isn't doing something a little more, well, you know. Active. Don't get me wrong, I'm grateful that he's not on the front lines. The last thing I want is to see him coming through my hospital, broken and hurt. Or worse. But it is surprising.'

'Perhaps he reckons he has done his bit,' said Mrs Vane.

'Yes, perhaps. He's had an interesting life, certainly. He was in the marines and then in the police. Did he tell you that?'

'He mentioned something about it.'

Penelope glanced at the ring on her hand. 'Are you married, Mrs Vane?'

'Widowed.'

There was the usual small silence. 'That must be very hard,' Penelope said softly.

She too has not yet learned the rules, Mrs Vane thought. 'It is. They say time helps, and it does, to some extent. But you never really get over a thing like this.'

Penelope reached out and squeezed her hand. 'You're very stoic, much more than I would be. If something ever happened to Nicky, I think I'd fall completely to pieces.'

'I did, for a while,' said Mrs Vane. 'It was doubly hard because I lost my mother at about the same time. But, it's true what they say. Life goes on.'

'Life goes on,' Penelope repeated. 'What a world of sadness there is in those three words. My mother sometimes says the same thing.'

'She too is sad,' said Mrs Vane.

'You saw that? Most people don't. Yes, she is very sad. She has so many regrets, about Pat, about missed opportunities, about the times in her life when she came to a fork in the road and chose the wrong way. I don't know when she last was happy. Not in my memory, anyway.'

'Have you tried to reconcile her with Mr Gallagher? It might be good for them both.'

'Mother and Pat have one thing in common,' said Penelope. 'Neither of them ever does what is good for them . . . The answer to your question is, yes, I have tried talking to both of them. Pat feels that she abandoned him as a child, and she thinks Pat ran away because of her. Both of them are right, of course.' She paused. 'I'm worried about Pat, too.'

'Why?'

'His health, for a start. He has that horrible cough that won't go away. And his mood is so . . . bleak. I think he must be lonely. There was a woman in his life, once, but she died. He never talks about her.'

'No,' said Mrs Vane.

Penelope reached out and touched her hand. 'Look after him for me. He's only my half-brother, but I'm awfully fond of him . . . Oh. Speak of the devil.'

Gallagher approached the fire. 'Mrs Vane, could I have a moment of your time?'

A COUPLE OF minutes of frantic thrusting and then Lansing was spent, gasping and shuddering. A train whistle sounded in the distance, long and mournful, echoing through the trees in a dying fall.

Lansing leaned back, exhaling slowly and buttoning his flies. Nathalie glared at him. 'Is that all I get?'

A shotgun boomed in the distance. 'Isn't that what you wanted?' Lansing asked. He rubbed his cheek where she had slapped him, and nodded in the direction of the shot. 'Young Tovey's out there. Go find him if you want another.'

'You utter shit!' she snapped. She hauled her drawers up, pulled her skirt down and stalked away through the trees, leaving Lansing standing behind her. When she reached the edge of the park, she was smiling.

The smile did not last for long. The wind was rising again, so bitter that it made her eyes water, and as she started across the park the rain came down, mingled this time with sleet. Teeth chattering, head bowed against the wind, she looked up to see

Gallagher and that mousy little woman, Mrs Vane, coming towards her, blurry figures in the rain.

She waved to them. 'Wherever you are going, it's not too late to turn back,' she called.

Gallagher waved in reply, but neither he nor Mrs Vane spoke. She had just reached the carriage drive and was turning towards the front door of the house when she heard the crash of another shotgun. This time it was much closer.

'I'm meeting Miss Rittenhouse in a few minutes,' Gallagher said. 'Will you come with me? I'd like your opinion of her.'

'Certainly.'

The rain started again almost as soon as they left the house. Mackintoshes, boots and sou'westers kept out the water, but nothing was proof against the icy knife of the wind. 'I had a nice chat with your sister,' Mrs Vane said.

'A chat about me?'

'Yes. I get the impression she thinks I might be sweet on you.'

Gallagher pulled out his handkerchief and coughed into it. 'Blasted wind. Are you?'

'Very amusing.' Mrs Vane peered into the rain. 'Who is that coming towards us?'

'I think it's Mrs Fairbairn.'

Nathalie Fairbairn called out something indistinct as she passed them heading towards the house, her voice lost in the roar of the wind in the trees. 'Where do you suppose she has been?' Gallagher asked.

'If I were guessing, I would say it involved Mr Tovey. There is something between them.'

'Yes.' Gallagher paused. 'You said last night that you weren't sure about Mrs Fairbairn. The word I would use for her is *complicated*. She is intelligent and subtle, but she is also deeply unhappy with the hand life has dealt her. She has repeatedly been unfaithful to Fairbairn.'

'If I were his wife, I would be unfaithful too. Those ghastly moustaches.'

'Steady on. Not every man with a waxed moustache is a villain.'

'Even when they fraternize with enemy diplomats behind their own government's back? What do you suppose his superiors at the Foreign Office would say if they found out?'

'That is one of the things that is bothering me. Sooner or later, they *will* find out, because if we know about his meeting with Bernstorff, we can be certain that others know too.'

'Do you believe his story about the meeting? That he didn't know Bernstorff had been invited?'

'Of course not. So, that raises another question. What is Fairbairn's game?' Gallagher thought for a moment. 'Lansing claims he met Bernstorff on secret instructions from President Wilson. Is it possible that Fairbairn was there for the same reason? To ask Bernstorff to open a channel to the German government with the knowledge of, or maybe even the instructions of, the Foreign Office?'

'Back-door peace talks,' she said after a moment. 'It's possible. But if I may ask the usual question, what does this have to do with Vasiliev?'

Gallagher frowned. 'I'm damned if I know. Vasiliev was the lover of both Sadie Lansing and Nathalie Fairbairn. Does it mean anything? Does it matter? Or is this all just a red herring?'

Mrs Vane did not answer directly. 'I've been watching Commander Colson,' she said. 'He is jumpy as a cat, and he takes great care to not be in a room alone with either Lansing or

Captain Ryder. He was bending Sir John's ear about something just before lunch. I was too far away to hear them, but Colson was clearly not happy.'

'What about Ryder?'

'He has been quite busy being Captain Ryder. I watched him and Tovey take a turn around the lake just before lunch, and it looked like Ryder was giving a lecture. Correcting Tovey's Latin declension, probably.'

Gallagher shook his head. 'Telling him to pull his socks up if he wanted to make the First Eleven. I trailed the telegram in front of Ryder this morning, but I didn't get much response.'

A woman screamed, a wordless shriek of desperation and despair echoing through the trees. A shotgun crashed once, the blast fading and dissolving in the wind.

'This way,' said Gallagher, and they both began to run. Sleet rattled off the bare branches of the oak trees overhead. Despite the wind, the air stank of cordite and the hot reek of blood. It took only a minute to find the body.

Willa Rittenhouse lay on her back among the trees, a few yards from the carriage drive. Her overcoat gaped open, and the front of her wool blouse was a pulsing mass of blood, crimson in the shadows of the woods. One of her hands moved a little before relaxing into stillness. Her dark eyes stared blankly up at the rain.

10

GALLAGHER KNELT BESIDE Miss Rittenhouse and felt for a pulse. He did not expect to find one; no one could survive being shot in the chest by a twelve-bore shotgun. He wiped his hands on the grass and rose to his feet.

'Search the area,' he said quietly.

A piece of burnt wadding lay a couple of yards from the body, confirming that Miss Rittenhouse had been shot at close range. There was nothing else to find; the ground, carpeted with rotting dead leaves, revealed no tracks.

Gallagher put the wadding into his pocket. 'Let's go,' he said.

The head gamekeeper's cottage was next to the carriage drive, about halfway to the gatehouse. The girl, Maisie, opened the door and looked at them in surprise. 'Is your grandfather here?' Gallagher asked.

She curtseyed. 'This way, sir.'

Tompkins was seated before the fire, smoking a pipe and warming his feet. He stood up as Gallagher and Mrs Vane entered, stooping a little under the low beams. 'Good afternoon, Mr Gallagher. Filthy weather, isn't it? What can I do for you?'

'I am sorry,' Gallagher said, 'but I need to call you and your men out again.'

He related what had happened, and Tompkins shook his head. 'Poachers,' he said. 'I was afraid something like this might happen one day. The beggars are getting so much bolder, now that we're short-handed on the estate.'

'Why would a poacher shoot anyone?' Mrs Vane asked. 'Taking pheasants is no longer a capital crime. They'd have no reason to kill, even if they were caught red-handed.'

'You don't know poachers, ma'am. They're a terrible, rough lot, with no respect for God nor man. Violence comes natural to them.'

'Did anyone from the house go out shooting?'

'Aye. Captain Ryder went out straight after lunch, and Mr Tovey a little after. Mr Lansing went later.'

'And Commander Colson, Pops,' Maisie said.

'The commander? I didn't see him.'

'You were in the larder, hanging up the pheasants. He came into the gun room, and I gave him his piece and some shells.'

'So, those four,' Tompkins said, knocking out his pipe.

'Keep everyone away from the scene until the police arrive,' Gallagher said. 'Put a guard on the body, and send someone to the police house in Tudeley. Ask the police to remove the body and conduct a search, but to stay away from the house. Tell them that this is on my instruction. They'll understand.'

Tompkins' expression did not change. 'Yes, sir. Anything else?'

'Find Sir John and ask him to tell everyone at the house to stay indoors until the police have finished searching. Mrs Vane will go with you.'

'Very good, sir. What will you do?'

'I'm going into Tonbridge,' Gallagher said.

He coughed, hard enough that he had to reach for a

handkerchief and wipe his eyes. Mrs Vane looked at him, concern in her face. 'Are you well enough?'

'I'll be all right. Keep a lid on things until I get back.'

ALL WAS QUIET at the house. Tompkins went to find Sir John Borden. Alone in the hall, Mrs Vane listened to the murmur in the library, first the keeper's voice, then Borden's exclamation of shock. The rain had spoiled the shooting and all of the guns had returned; several overcoats were hanging in the hall, still dripping wet from the rain. Silently she examined the coats, looking for bloodstains, and ran her hands through the pockets of each coat. The first three were empty, but in the outside pocket of the fourth she found an empty shotgun shell. Holding it carefully by the rim to avoid smudging any fingerprints, she raised it to her nose. The sharp smell of freshly burnt cordite filled her nostrils. The shell had been fired recently.

She looked at the label sewn into the inside of the neck of the overcoat and saw the owner's name. LANSING.

Tucking the shell into her pocket, she crossed to the fire to warm her hands. Something on the hearth caught her eye, a little scrap of what looked like paper with a charred edge. Nudging it out of the ash with the toe of her boot, she picked it up. It was indeed paper, but heavier and thicker than ordinary writing paper, and it had a glossy feel to it. Photographic paper, she thought.

She heard Borden calling for Platt, the butler. 'Call all of the guests into the drawing room, please.'

'Very good, sir.'

Mrs Vane went into the drawing room. The others assembled quickly: Colson looking puzzled, Tovey quiet and fairly obviously avoiding Nathalie Fairbairn – *have they quarrelled?* Mrs Vane wondered – Lansing looking disgruntled, Edith Price wide-eyed with surprise. Sir John Borden stood in front of the fireplace. Pouch-eyed and puffy-cheeked he might be, but at the moment there was an air of command about him, and Mrs Vane began to realize why he was a force in politics. His wife sat beside him, hands clasped tightly together.

Borden looked around the room. 'Where is Mr Fairbairn? And Nicholas?'

'I heard them say they were going for a walk,' said Price.

Borden's voice was sharp. 'A walk! Where to?'

'Something about going over to Tudeley, I think. Is something wrong, Sir John?'

'Yes,' Borden said. 'I'm afraid I have some bad news. A woman's body has been found in the woods. I'm sorry to say that she has been shot.'

Everyone went still. Edith Price looked perplexed, as if she could not quite take in what she was hearing. Lady Maud's hands were clenched tightly in her lap. 'Who was this woman?' she asked. 'Was she a trespasser?'

'Her identity is unknown for the moment. Tompkins believes this may be the work of poachers. I must ask you all to remain here until the police have searched the woods and made certain we are no longer in danger. If you must leave the house, remain within the park and do not go near the woods.'

Ryder took a step forward. 'Why wait for the police? We have men, we have shotguns. Let's go after them.'

'I don't advise that,' said Borden. 'If the police are hunting for poachers, they will be armed themselves. Also, dusk is falling, and if we bump into each other there could be accidents. I'm sorry, Captain Ryder, I know it's hard to sit and do nothing, but we must let the police do their work.'

'What about Fairbairn and Makarian?' Price asked.

'If they stayed on the high road to Tudeley, they should be all right.' Borden glanced at Penelope, whose hands were clenched tightly in her lap. 'I'm sure he will be safe, my dear,' he said kindly. 'As for the rest of us, so long as we remain here, we have nothing to fear.'

He looked at Lansing, who still looked dissatisfied. 'Well, Mr Lansing? As we have time on our hands, perhaps we could continue our conversation, if you are willing.'

'Do you have anything to say that I haven't already heard?' Lansing asked.

'I suggest that Captain Ryder join us,' Borden said. 'As a distinguished naval officer, perhaps he can persuade you where I have so far failed.' The three men went into the library. Commander Colson rose to his feet, his hands clenched, staring after the others. The snub could not have been more pointed.

'I need a cigarette,' Colson said, and he walked out of the room into the hall.

'We must find some occupation to pass the time,' said Lady Maud, her voice stiff. With tremendous effort, she was maintaining her self-control. 'We shall play bridge. Mrs Fairbairn, be good enough to partner me. Mrs Price, perhaps you will partner my daughter.'

Nathalie Fairbairn inclined her head. 'Apologies, my lady, but I fear I am rather tired. I shall retire for a while. Perhaps Mrs Vane could take my place.'

'Very well,' said Lady Maud, with an air of resignation. She rose and moved towards the card table. 'There should be time for a rubber before tea. Let us begin.'

TONBRIDGE WAS ONLY two miles away, but by the time Gallagher arrived at the railway station dusk was already falling under the hurrying clouds. His chest hurt and he was coughing steadily. Taking off his dripping mackintosh, he called at the telegraph office and wrote a quick telegram to the service, asking for the plumbers to be sent to Hartlake Hall. The clerk glanced at his name as he handed over the form.

'Mr Gallagher? There's a wire just come in for you, sir. Overseas service.'

Gallagher opened the envelope and read the form. WHERE-ABOUTS OF LILY SPARROW UNKNOWN. NEIGHBOURS SAY SHE MAY HAVE GONE TO NEW YORK. NYPD SEARCHING.

He paused for a moment, thinking. New York was a huge city; even if Lily Sparrow was there, it could take the police days to track her down.

'May I have the other telegram back?' he asked.

The clerk handed it over and Gallagher added another line to the bottom, *Need access to Rintelen urgent*. He handed it back. 'Top priority,' he said.

'Yes, sir.'

He walked up the high street. The ramparts of the castle stood dark against the clouds. The river was rising, dirty brown water swirling under the bridge. Much more rain and there will be flooding in the water meadows, he thought.

The lobby of the Rose and Crown glowed with lamplight and was blessedly warm. Gallagher approached the desk and took his identity card from his pocket. 'I need access to Miss Rittenhouse's room, please.'

The desk clerk read the card. 'Very good, sir. That cough sounds bad. Shall I fetch you a toddy?'

Gallagher hesitated for a moment. 'Thank you.'

The toddy, strong with rum and sweet with honey, soothed his throat and chest a little. *I really must go and see the doctor again*, he thought, but another voice in his head said, *why bother?* He finished the drink, took the key from the clerk and climbed the stairs to Willa Rittenhouse's room.

The room was tidy and neat, which came as a surprise; in his experience, most journalists lived in a state of squalor. He searched the wardrobe, rifling through her clothes and checking the pockets, and found nothing. The drawers of her dressing table were empty and her vanity case contained only a hairbrush, hairpins, some basic cosmetics and a couple of bottles of scent. There were no books or magazines of any kind, which again surprised him because most people who wrote for a living were also voracious readers. Perhaps Miss Rittenhouse had taken after Disraeli: *When I want to read a good book, I write one.*

But, of course, she had not come to Tonbridge on holiday. She was here with a purpose, and that purpose had led to her violent death. He continued to search the room, checking the writing table and looking under the mattress, thinking all the time of the lively, confident woman he had seen that morning, and the blood bubbling from the wreckage of her chest.

He found what he was looking for under the bed, a soft leather satchel not unlike a messenger's bag, locked with a small brass padlock. Taking a hairpin from the vanity case, he picked the lock quickly and opened the bag. Inside were papers, some in typescript, some in neat handwriting. All were drafts of articles or notes. There were several rather mundane pieces about life in wartime Britain, presumably destined for an American audience, but there were also drafts of two articles about Lansing.

His eyebrows rose as he read them. The articles showed, in detail, how Lansing was conniving with the German government to get the concession to the Turkish-held oilfields in the Middle East. Pencilled annotations in the margins showed where she had gathered information. There were references to the *New York Times* and other newspapers and, several times, a set of initials: *Information provided by F.W.*

F.W. Could that be Frank Warren? He would have been in a

position to know what Lansing and Bernstorff had talked about. It made sense.

Along with the papers was a sheaf of photographs. They had been taken with a hand-held camera and developed in an amateur darkroom, and he was reminded at once of the photos in the discarded album at Aquinnah; these were surely taken by the same person. Being a woman of tidy mind, Miss Rittenhouse had labelled each photograph on the back. Some of the names and locations meant nothing, but there were several photographs of two men with moustaches on the deck of a yacht. He did not need a label to tell him that these were Count von Bernstorff and Herbert Fairbairn. Both appeared to be deep in conversation. There were also several photographs of Lansing, including one of him talking with Bernstorff and the Kadet leader, Vladimir Dmitrievich Nabokov.

He looked at the next photograph, and froze.

The subject was a man in his mid-twenties, dressed in flannel trousers and a striped sailor's jersey, leaning on the rail of the same yacht. A sailor's cap was perched on his head, with a ribbon showing the name of the boat, *Chasseur*. He was facing the camera and smiling; he clearly knew he was being photographed, and judging by the look in his eyes, he probably knew the photographer as well. Gallagher turned the photograph over and saw the label on the back: FRANK SALTINSTALL WARREN.

'Jesus Christ,' he said softly, and turned the photo over again to look at the face. He saw the crow's feet wrinkles around the eyes, and the small mole on the neck. Frank Warren was Sadie Lansing's brother, the man who had crewed for Fairbairn, and spent time in prison for burglary, and disappeared into the underworld after his sister's death.

He was also, beyond any shadow of doubt, the man whose body had been found in the stationery cupboard at the Admiralty.

SATURDAY, 3 FEBRUARY 1917
4.39 P.M.

Down in the lobby, Gallagher rang the bell for the clerk. 'Miss Rittenhouse is checking out. I'll settle her bill now, and please ask your staff to pack her bags. Someone will be sent to fetch them.'

'Of course, sir.'

Next of kin would have to be notified, whoever and wherever they were; Bielaski could handle that. There would be a post-mortem too, although there was no mistaking the cause of death. None of this really mattered at the moment. What mattered was to find out who had killed her, and why, before eight thirty tomorrow evening.

He stopped at the telegraph office and wrote another wire to the service. *Find photograph of Paul Vasiliev.* A corner of his mind wondered how much he had spent on telegrams in the past twenty-four hours. The bean counters would be tearing their hair out.

By the time he left the office the rain had stopped. The wind had eased back too, and overhead the clouds had parted a little and stars could be glimpsed through the gaps. When he reached the lodge there were lights on, and police officers with rifles stood outside, barring the way. Gallagher held out his identity card, and one of the officers shone a torch on it. 'Mr Gallagher, sir? The inspector is inside. He'd like a word, if you please.'

The inspector was a young man, clean-shaven with an air of competence, wearing a long trench coat dark with rain. Gallagher wondered how he had avoided conscription, and then noticed the empty sleeve. 'Mr Gallagher,' the inspector said, saluting. 'Your men have arrived and taken away the body. More are on the way. I've been ordered to give them, and you, our full cooperation.'

'Thank you,' Gallagher said. 'For the moment, keep watch on the estate and intercept anyone who doesn't have a valid reason for being here. Either myself or my associate, Mrs Vane, will send more orders tomorrow.'

'Very good, sir. Will your men be investigating the murder of Miss Rittenhouse, or will that be handled by Scotland Yard?'

'We will do that. Keep your men away from the house, Inspector, and be discreet. I don't want to alarm the other guests.'

The inspector nodded. 'Very good, sir,' he repeated.

Walking back to the house, he heard cowbells tinkling an eerie melody in the shadows. The dark woods preyed on his nerves and he was glad to see the lights of Hartlake Hall sparkling dimly ahead. He wondered if there would be nightmares again tonight. It seemed likely.

In the hall he took off his coat and hung it on a peg. Mrs Vane was perched on a settle in front of the fire. 'Are you mad?' Gallagher asked. 'It's bloody freezing out here.'

'Believe it or not, I'm starting to get used to the cold,' said Mrs Vane. 'So, yes, probably. I endured a rubber of bridge and then came out here to wait for Mr Fairbairn and Mr Makarian. They went for a walk together before the shooting.'

Gallagher's voice was sharp. 'Have they come back?'

'Yes, about half an hour ago. Fairbairn was apologetic, Makarian couldn't see what all the fuss was about.'

'Where are the others?' Gallagher asked, suppressing the urge to cough.

'Just finishing tea in the drawing room. Did you find anything?'

Silently, he handed her the photograph. She studied it for a moment and turned it over, and he saw her eyes go wide.

'Is this genuine?' Mrs Vane asked.

'I'm pretty certain it is. There were three more, all of the same person, all with Frank Warren's name on the back. There were also photographs of Bernstorff, Fairbairn and Nabokov.'

'So, Captain Ryder lied about Vasiliev. Why?'

'I don't know,' Gallagher said, 'but I'm looking forward to asking him. He'd better have a damned good excuse for interfering with an investigation into a security breach, because if he doesn't, then Admiral Jellicoe or no, I'm going to skin him alive.'

'Do we know who took the photographs?' Mrs Vane asked.

'I reckon it was the same person who took the photos we found in Sadie Lansing's bedroom. Someone who was on friendly terms with their subjects, too, which would preclude Willa Rittenhouse herself.' He paused for a moment, thinking. 'My guess is that Sadie took most of the pictures, but some of them might have been taken by Warren.'

'How do you think Miss Rittenhouse got hold of them?'

'Frank Warren was giving her information, or more likely, selling it to her. He might well have stolen the photographs from his sister and sold them too. Given that Sadie supported him financially, he doesn't seem to have been very loyal to her.'

'Everything I hear about Frank Warren suggests that he was loyal only to himself,' said Mrs Vane. 'I have something for you, too.' She handed over the empty shotgun shell and the piece of photographic paper. 'I found the shell in Lansing's overcoat pocket,' she said. 'Here is a hypothesis for you. Miss Rittenhouse said she was bringing you evidence about the body at the Admiralty. The evidence was another photograph of Warren.

Someone intercepted her, took the photograph from her, killed her, and brought the photograph back here and burned it.'

Gallagher sniffed the shotgun shell. 'But you don't think it was Lansing.'

'Mr Lansing may be many things, but he does not strike me as a careless man. If he had shot someone, he wouldn't put the empty shell into his own pocket.'

'Unless it was a double bluff,' said Gallagher. 'He might have put the shell in his own pocket to make us think someone else was trying to frame him. Alternatively, he might not be as clever as we think he is. As someone pointed out to me this morning, just because someone has a lot of money doesn't necessarily mean they are intelligent. You look dubious.'

'I think you may be over-thinking this. But three other people also went out to shoot this afternoon.'

Gallagher nodded. 'Ryder, Tovey and Colson. We also saw Nathalie Fairbairn coming back from the woods just before the shot was fired.'

'So she can't be the killer,' said Mrs Vane.

'But she may have seen who it was.' Gallagher looked again at the shotgun shell. 'I'll talk to the guns. Will you see what you can get out of Mrs Fairbairn?'

Her eyebrows rose. 'Because you think an appeal to the sisterhood might work?'

'No, because she dislikes me intensely. She doesn't know you well enough to hate you.'

Mrs Vane considered this. 'Deep under the rubble of that statement, I suspect there may be a compliment waiting to be discovered, but I'm not sure I can be bothered to dig for it. Will you talk to Mr Fairbairn, too?'

Gallagher nodded. 'As soon as I can get him alone. That will be a difficult conversation, I think.'

The door to the drawing room opened and Penelope Makarian came into the hall, dressed in a vivid blue gown that matched her eyes. Her usual good cheer had been restored; she stopped and swirled the fabric around her legs. 'Do you like my gown?'

'Very nice,' Gallagher said.

'I saw the fabric in a shop window a few weeks ago and admired it, and Nicky went back next day and bought a length and sent it to my dressmaker. Don't tell me I'm spoiled, Pat, I already know it. Why are you two out here gossiping in the hall? Come and have some tea before you freeze to death!'

LANSING HAD NOT come to tea, nor had Fairbairn. There was no sign of the latter, but Gallagher eventually found Lansing in the billiards room, practising cannons. He looked up sharply as Gallagher entered the room, and his face changed a little. He was expecting someone else, Gallagher thought.

'Any luck shooting this afternoon?' Gallagher asked.

'No.' Lansing lined up another shot, and the cue ball clicked off the red. 'Too damned wet,' he said, straightening. 'I gave up in the end. What happened to that woman in the woods?'

'She was shot at close range with a twelve-bore.'

'Jesus.' Lansing straightened, staring at him. 'Borden said she'd been shot, but that sounds more like an execution.'

'You could be right.' Gallagher set the empty shotgun shell down on the edge of the billiards table. 'This was found in your overcoat pocket.'

Lansing glanced at the shell. 'There must be some mistake. I never fired a shot the whole time I was out. I *heard* a couple of shots, yes, but none of them came from me.'

'There's no mistake,' Gallagher said. 'The dead woman is Willa Rittenhouse.'

He had said it to shock, and he succeeded. He watched Lansing lay down the billiards cue and step back. His face did not change but his eyes blinked rapidly for a moment. 'You're sure about this?' he asked finally.

'Unquestionably.'

'What was she doing here?' Lansing answered his own question. 'Spying on me, of course. That woman has been a thorn in my god-damned side for the past year. You wouldn't believe the things she's accused me of.'

'She maintained that you are in league with Germany, and was preparing to publish the evidence,' Gallagher said. 'You had more than enough reasons to kill her, Mr Lansing. If those articles had seen the light of day, your reputation could have been destroyed.'

'Oh, bullshit. She doesn't have any real evidence, just a lot of gossip and hearsay. I reckon my reputation can stand anything that dame could throw at me. Look, Gallagher, she was a damned nuisance, but she wasn't a danger to me. And I sure as hell didn't kill her.'

'How do you explain the shotgun shell in your pocket?'

'I don't. I've no idea how it got there, but I didn't put it there.' Lansing pointed the billiard cue at Gallagher. 'And if you ever allege that I did, I'll make it my business to break you.'

Gallagher ignored this. 'How well did you know your brother-in-law, Frank Warren?'

Lansing blinked in surprise. 'Warren? What's he got to do with this?'

Gallagher said nothing. Lansing smiled suddenly, baring his teeth. 'Why don't you ask Fairbairn? He knew Warren a lot better than I did. If you take my meaning.'

'You disapprove of Warren.'

'Look. Warren screwed anything that moved, all right?

Women, men, farmyard animals, you name it. I'm a broad-minded man, or so I like to think, so I didn't care one way or the other. But I drew the line at incest.'

Gallagher paused for a moment. 'You're sure of this?'

'I caught them both, in flagrante. It was about a year after we were married. I knew Sadie was playing around, but that was way over the line. I wanted to beat the living daylights out of Warren, but Sadie stopped me. She said it was just a bit of fun, if you can believe it.'

'She liked to shock people,' Gallagher said quietly.

'Well, she sure as hell shocked me. We separated after that. So to answer your question, I don't know Frank Warren very well, but what I do know sickens me.'

'And yet, you managed to overcome your qualms,' Gallagher said. 'When Sadie invited you to meet Johann von Bernstorff, you agreed to meet on Fairbairn's yacht, the *Chasseur*. Warren was there too; we have photographs to prove it. So was Vladimir Dmitrievich Nabokov, the Kadet leader from Russia. Why did you meet with him?'

Lansing shook his head. 'I don't know any Nabokov.'

'You spoke to him.'

'I speak to a lot of people. I remember some Russian being there, but I don't know anything about him.'

Gallagher paused again. 'Did you know Warren was in London?'

'No.'

'Are you sure? You've had no contact with him in the past few weeks?'

'No, God damn it! What does this have to do with Willa Rittenhouse?'

'Warren was selling information to her,' Gallagher said. 'That's how she knew about your deal with Bernstorff. If you'll forgive my saying so, Mr Lansing, you've been a damned fool. You've let the Germans play you like a harp. They conned you into using your influence with President Wilson to keep America neutral, and if you don't comply, they can blackmail you by threatening to make your deal with Bernstorff public. If you think your reputation can survive that, you are dreaming. How long would your friendship with President Wilson last, if the news came out?'

Lansing picked up the billiards cue. 'Are you threatening me?'

'You mean, am I going to publish Miss Rittenhouse's articles? No, I'm not. But you are fishing in very murky waters, Mr Lansing. Do you really think the Royal Navy would continue to buy your oil, if it was known that you are doing deals with the Kaiser's representatives?'

Lansing smiled, baring his teeth. 'And where else are your admirals going to get their oil? Anglo-Persian can't supply the quantities they need, nor can the Dutch. And if you breathe so much as a word of this, I'll go straight back to Woodrow Wilson and tell him that in my view, America should remain neutral for ever. Woodrow will listen to *me*, not the muck-rakers, and you can kiss your American alliance goodbye.'

Gallagher said nothing. Lansing lined up another shot; billiard balls clicked and one dropped into a corner pocket. 'Actually, go ahead and publish those articles,' he said. 'Frank Warren is a criminal, a liar and a drunk. If you publish, my lawyers will tear Rittenhouse's reputation to shreds, and Warren's, and yours too. What will the world think of your secret service, if you rely on the word of men like Warren?'

'And what happens if we win the war without you?' Gallagher said. 'A defeated Germany will be in no position to fulfil whatever bargain they made with you.'

'It doesn't matter,' Lansing said, and he smiled again. 'No matter which way things turn out, I'll get what I want. I always do.'

Hunton the footman was in the kitchen, polishing brass. He rose to his feet, wiping his watery eyes as Gallagher entered. 'How may I help you, sir?'

'I'm looking for Mr Tovey. Have you seen him?'

'He retired earlier, sir. He's in the Oak Room, if you're looking for him.'

'And Mr Fairbairn?'

'I believe he went for a turn around the lake, sir. I reminded him to stay away from the woods.'

'Thank you. Is the gun room locked?'

'Yes, sir. I'll fetch you the key.'

The gun room was tidy and neat, all of the shotguns secure in their cases, clean and oiled. That was unsurprising; whoever had fired the fatal shot would have been careful to clean their gun upon returning, to wipe away any evidence.

Upstairs, Gallagher made his way to the west wing of the house and knocked at the door of Tovey's room. After a long moment Tovey opened the door, yawning and rubbing his head. 'Gallagher? What is it?'

'Sorry to disturb you,' Gallagher said. 'Might I have a word?'

'Of course, I was just catching forty winks. Do come in.'

The Oak Room, named after its mock-Gothic oak wainscotting, had a four-poster bed and an enormous oak wardrobe in one corner. A faint whiff of cigarette smoke drifted in the air. 'I assume you know who I am,' Gallagher said.

Tovey nodded. 'I'm afraid I rather guessed,' he admitted. 'Mr Lansing is an important man, so I'm not surprised the secret service has sent someone here to keep watch on things.'

'Did you have any luck shooting this afternoon?'

'None at all. I took a shot at a rabbit, but I missed. I'm not a very good shot.'

Dull, Mrs Vane had called him, and he was, but almost contrivedly so, practically a caricature of the well-educated idiot. That in itself was nothing unusual. The navy was often a dumping ground for types like him; Gallagher had once served under a captain who couldn't remember his own navigator's name, and frequently confused port with starboard. But something about Tovey suggested that he was brighter than he seemed.

'Did you see or hear anyone else out in the woods?' Gallagher asked.

'I didn't see any of the other guns, no. I just tramped along hoping I might get sight of another rabbit, but when the rain came I gave it up and started for home. I heard another shot about then, but that's all. I guess that must have been the one that . . .'

Tovey paused, uncertain of what to say next. 'The one that killed the woman,' Gallagher said. 'Her name was Rittenhouse, Miss Willa Rittenhouse. She was American.'

'Oh,' said Tovey.

'Did you know her?'

'Not at all, sorry. I don't think I've ever heard the name.'

Gallagher nodded. 'If you remember anything that might be helpful, please let me know. How are your talks progressing?'

Tovey looked blank. 'Talks?'

'Sir John invited you down here because you wrote to him and asked to talk about shell production. You deal with ammunition distribution and storage as well as oil, don't you?'

'Oh, yes, certainly.' Tovey spread his hands. 'To tell the truth, I haven't really had a moment to talk to Sir John. He seems to be spending a lot of his time closeted with Mr Lansing, and I haven't had a look-in. I'll try to bend his ear this evening, or maybe tomorrow.'

'What about Makarian? Have you had a chance to talk to him about tankers?'

'No, not yet. I went looking for him this afternoon when I came in from shooting, but he'd gone out.'

'If he proves tricky, let me know.' Gallagher smiled. 'He's family. I know how to handle him.'

'Thanks very much, I appreciate it. Look . . . I'm really sorry about the American lady. What a terrible thing to have happened. I hope Sir John and Lady Maud aren't too upset.'

'It has been a shock to my mother,' Gallagher said. 'But I expect she will deal with it. And now, I shall leave you to your rest. See you at dinner, Mr Tovey.'

After Gallagher had gone, Tovey locked the door and turned towards the wardrobe. 'You can come out now,' he said.

The door opened and Nathalie Fairbairn stepped out into the room. 'Hiding in the wardrobe,' she said. 'God, what a dreary cliché.'

'What other choice did we have? He can't find you with me.'

Nathalie opened the cigarette box and lit a cigarette, blowing out smoke. 'It hardly matters now,' she said. 'He's on to you.'

'I know.' Tovey twisted his hands in agitation. 'Damn it, it's too soon! We're not ready!'

'Keep your voice down,' Nathalie commanded.

'We took too many documents,' Tovey said in a painful whisper. 'I said as much, didn't I? A few might not have been noticed, but we got greedy, and now the secret service is involved. They hanged the last fellow, remember?'

Nathalie gripped him by the shoulders and shook him. 'Listen to me,' she said, her Scots accent suddenly strong. 'You must be patient. We're almost there. We just need to hold on for another thirty-six hours.'

'I'm not very good at this, Nathalie.'

'No,' she said cuttingly. 'You're really not, are you? Well, it's too late now. You're in up to your neck, laddie, so make the best of it. Have you arranged for a car?'

'It will be waiting for us at Tonbridge station. I've booked a room at a pub down by the coast, under a false name, of course. What are you going to do about Lansing?'

Nathalie blew out more smoke. 'I'm thinking of rat poison. Perhaps with a dose for my husband, too, while I'm at it. Good riddance to them both. The world will never miss them.'

Tovey watched her for a moment. 'What made you so bitter, Nathalie?'

'Life,' she said, stubbing out the cigarette. 'Now, let me go. Gallagher will be looking for me, too, and I must let him find me.'

Tovey unlocked the door. 'Be careful,' he said.

'You too.' Her harsh mood melted a little. She kissed him on the mouth, firmly and with promise, and went out, closing the door behind her.

11

The fire in the drawing room popped, sending sparks flying up the chimney. The roses on the wallpaper seemed to sway a little in the reflected light. Mrs Vane tried to ignore them.

'That poor woman in the woods,' said Lady Maud. 'I hope the police have contacted her family.'

They were sitting together by the fire. Tea had finished; the room was empty now apart from themselves. 'I would imagine that they are in America,' said Mrs Vane, trying not to remember the gory mess of Willa Rittenhouse's body. 'It will take some time.'

A long silence followed. The fire popped again. 'My daughter told me of your loss,' said Lady Maud. 'I hope you do not mind.'

Mrs Vane was startled. 'Not at all,' she said.

'I know we never speak of these things,' said Lady Maud, and her voice sounded suddenly weary. 'But that is wrong. There have been so many tragedies that we have let ourselves become immured by them. As a result, we are losing part of our souls.'

Mrs Vane was uncertain of how to respond to this. 'It is hard,' she agreed. 'When terrible things happen a long way away, we can read about them but not feel moved by them. But when something happens closer to us, we are brought face to face with reality.'

'And that is wrong,' Lady Maud repeated. 'Are you familiar with John Donne, Mrs Vane? *Any man's death diminishes me, because I am involved in mankind.* And now, we are all so diminished that we have grown accustomed to violent death. Did you see their faces this afternoon? Five years ago, if someone had been killed during a shooting party, everyone would have been shocked, horrified beyond words. Now, they barely notice.'

The words were so unexpected that Mrs Vane could think of no reply. 'It is the war,' Lady Maud said, but her tone hinted that something greater and infinitely sadder was at work. 'Every one of us has lost things and people that we held dear. Memories that were once as warm as the sun have become corrupted and dark.'

'Not all of them,' said Mrs Vane. 'Some of my memories are still bright and warm. They are what gives me sustenance, and keeps me alive.' She looked suddenly at the other woman. 'What is it that you fear, my lady?'

'My other daughter is a nurse at a field hospital in France, within range of German artillery. I wait daily for news of her death. When that happens, I shall truly have lost everything.'

Mrs Vane opened her mouth to say that it might *not* happen, but closed it again. She saw the grim determination in the older woman's face as she fought down her moment of weakness and rebuilt the armour around her soul. Finally Lady Maud turned to her. 'You play bridge very well,' she said. 'We must play again.'

'Thank you,' said Mrs Vane, feeling tears behind her eyes. 'I would like that very much. If you will forgive me, my lady, I must go and refresh myself before dinner.'

She managed to get out of the room before the tears came. In the hall she met Gallagher, who looked at her in concern. 'What's wrong?'

'Nothing,' said Mrs Vane. 'Everything. Don't worry about it. What is new?'

'I've spoken to Lansing and Tovey. Lansing has all the motive in the world, but denies everything. Tovey apparently thought he could conceal Mrs Fairbairn in his room by hiding her in the wardrobe. He should have opened the window to get rid of the cigarette smoke. He is up to something, but I don't know what.'

'It might be the obvious,' said Mrs Vane. 'I looked for her earlier but couldn't find her. Now we know why. I'll try to track her down now.'

'Wait a little,' Gallagher said. 'If I'm right in my thinking, she will come to us.'

IN THE DRAWING room his mother sat alone, staring silently at the fire, hands clenched in her lap. Gallagher did not disturb her.

The door to the music room was open and someone was playing Schumann's *Dichterliebe*, very well. Gallagher looked in and saw Nicholas Makarian seated at the piano, hands gliding slowly across the keys. Once again Nathalie Fairbairn was sitting on the bench beside him, turning the pages. Makarian looked up and saw Gallagher, and stopped.

'Don't stop on my account,' Gallagher said.

'I was just going,' said Nathalie, rising to her feet. She smiled down at Makarian. 'It was a pleasure to hear you play.'

Nathalie left the room, closing the door behind her. Makarian began to play again. 'I should not be playing this,' he said. '"I wept in my dream, for I dreamed you were in your grave." There is enough weeping in the world already, is there not? We should only play happy tunes.'

'You know Mrs Fairbairn is sleeping with Tovey, and very probably with Lansing,' Gallagher said.

'And you wish to remind me of the perils of venereal disease? How thoughtful of you. Rest assured, Pat. The lady and I were merely discussing a matter of mutual interest. She has no appeal for me.'

'Did you enjoy your walk to Tudeley?'

'Not in the slightest.' Makarian stopped playing and began leafing through the book of sheet music, stopping to make an annotation on one page with a small pencil. 'The weather was even more appalling than this morning, but Mr Fairbairn wished to see the brasses in the church. Actually, I was surprised to find them still there. I would have thought that by now, the brass would have been melted down for shell casings.'

'We're not that desperate, yet. You could have shown him the brasses tomorrow, when you go to church. The weather might be better.'

Makarian began to play again, a Brahms ballade. 'I no longer attend church services, Pat. I haven't for more than a year now.'

'Because of what happened to your family?'

'Not just my family, but all of my people. The notion of a kind and loving God is not consistent with a world where hundreds of thousands can be allowed to perish so barbarically. The Bolsheviks reject God as a capitalist construct. I begin to wonder if they are right.'

'I didn't know you knew any Bolsheviks.'

'Ah, but they are everywhere, Pat. Under the bed, under the table, hiding in plain sight. You just have to know where to look.'

Gallagher considered this. 'Have you seen Captain Ryder?'

'He is in the library, bending Sir John's ear about the proposed American alliance. If you wish to be bored rigid, go and join them.'

*

RYDER AND BORDEN sat by the fire in the library, leaning back in the big armchairs, each with a glass of whisky and soda in hand. Borden greeted Gallagher with a wave of the hand. 'Join us, Pat. Help yourself to a drink.'

'Any word on those poachers?' Ryder asked.

Gallagher poured a weak whisky and sat down. 'Nothing yet. The police are patrolling the woods. Captain, did you hear or see anything while you were out?'

Ryder looked surprised. 'I heard a couple of shots in the distance, nothing more. When it started to rain I gave up and came back to the house. Why do you ask?'

'I was hoping you might have noticed something,' Gallagher said.

'It's a police matter now, surely. Leave it to the coppers. This is their job, not yours.'

'I have had a wire from the chief constable,' Borden said. 'If they learn anything, they will of course inform me at once. The house is now well protected and we should be safe enough.' He sipped his whisky. 'Captain Ryder was just telling me about Admiral Jellicoe's plans for the expansion of the navy.'

'Don't we have enough ships already?' Gallagher asked.

'More than Germany, yes,' Ryder said. 'But the task of naval planning is less about fighting the present war, and more about preparing for the next one. Our forecasts envisage a situation where we might have to fight two enemy fleets at the same time. We must be strong enough to take on both enemies, and win.'

Borden shook his head. 'It's an ambitious plan, but of course we haven't the money to build ships on that scale. The war is already costing us a fortune, and our shipyards are full of Bolshevik agents agitating for peace and calling on the men to strike. The kind of war you envision, Captain, can only be fought and won with American support.'

Ryder nodded. 'Our plans are predicated in part on an American alliance. I applaud your efforts in attempting to bring this about, Sir John. You are doing your country a great service.'

How was it, Gallagher wondered, that Ryder managed to make even words of praise sound faintly condescending? *Well played, young Borden, now get out there and take another wicket.* 'Not everyone would agree,' he said. 'Commander Colson thinks the Americans are a threat to the empire.'

'Ah, yes,' said Ryder. 'Colson is very taken by that book, *The Naval Engineer and Command of the Sea*. He keeps citing the chapter where the American navy plunders and burns Belfast.'

Borden snorted. 'If the Americans want Belfast, let them have it. They can sort things about between Carson's fanatics and Sinn Féin.'

Ryder smiled. 'Colson is getting muddled, which is not unusual. I've read that book too. In fact, I know the author, Francis Burton. He's not suggesting that the Americans *will* be our next enemy, but merely giving this as an example of fighting a war on several fronts at once. We're the biggest shipbuilders in the world, but the Americans are not far behind us. That's why an alliance makes sense.'

'And, of course, the Germans will do anything to prevent that from happening,' Borden said. 'I strongly suspect that they are putting pressure on people like Lansing, to encourage President Wilson to remain neutral.'

Ryder raised his eyebrows. 'Then let us apply some pressure of our own. What does Lansing want? Find out, and give it to him.'

'It may not be quite so simple as that,' said Gallagher. Reaching into his pocket, he pulled out the photograph of Frank Warren and handed it to Ryder. 'What do you make of this, Captain?'

Ryder looked at the photograph, turned it over and read the name on the back. 'Where did you get this?'

'From the hotel room of the woman who was killed this afternoon. She was an American journalist named Willa Rittenhouse. She knew, or at least suspected, that Warren was the man we found dead at the Admiralty. The man whom *you*, Captain, identified as Paul Vasiliev.'

Ryder continued to study the photograph. He did not speak.

'Would you care to explain?' Gallagher asked.

'What is this?' Borden demanded. 'What are you talking about, Pat?'

Ryder hesitated. Gallagher retrieved the photograph. What followed was going to be tricky, but he very much wanted Borden present as a witness. 'Sir John is a member of His Majesty's government,' he said. 'We can trust him.'

'Very well,' Ryder said. 'But what I am about to tell you must never leave this room.'

Gallagher waited.

'I didn't recognize the body at the Admiralty,' Ryder said, 'and I have never heard of Frank Warren. But when I heard what had happened, I realized this was a heaven-sent chance to make Paul Vasiliev disappear. Your lot would whisk the dead man away before anyone else saw him, and Vasiliev could go underground.'

'Vasiliev is still alive?'

'Alive and well, and carrying out his duties. Gallagher, I tried to warn you this morning. Vasiliev is not a German agent, he is a loyal officer serving his king. But no one else must know. If Colson or anyone else at naval intelligence ever gets wind of this, Vasiliev's life could be in danger.'

'Vasiliev is investigating the naval intelligence division,' Gallagher said. 'On whose orders?'

'Mine,' said Ryder. 'And my own orders come directly from Admiral Jellicoe.'

Gallagher looked at the photograph again, thinking what a long journey it had been from the deck of a yacht off Cape Cod to death on the cold floor of the Admiralty stationery cupboard. 'Frank Warren was a German agent, part of a network set up in the Boston area by a German spy whose code name is the Dreamer,' he said. 'We are familiar with Warren's activities in America. The open question is, what was he doing in London, and how did he manage to penetrate the Admiralty?'

'My God!' Borden said, his face registering his shock. 'A German spy in the Admiralty!'

Ryder's voice was hard. 'This confirms what Admiral Jellicoe and myself believe. There is something deeply rotten in naval intelligence. Documents going missing. The apparent inability to crack key German codes. The failure at Jutland. The sinking of the *Lusitania*. The attempt to steal that telegram from Zimmermann, which damned nearly succeeded, and a dead German agent on the floor.'

Ryder paused. 'That telegram still bothers me. Why is naval intelligence sitting on it? And what else are they concealing? I know you said they're working on decrypting German telegrams, Gallagher, but what if they have already succeeded? They can read German messages but they're holding out on the rest of us?'

Gallagher said nothing. 'What do you mean about the *Lusitania*?' Borden asked. He looked nervous, and Gallagher knew he was thinking about Churchill's letter.

'I was in command at Haulbowline naval station on that fatal day,' said Ryder. 'We received a signal from the Admiralty indicating that U-boats were operating around Fastnet and off Cape Clear. I ordered this information passed to all of our ships in the area, with the result that they were able to steer clear of the U-boats. What the signal did *not* tell us was that more U-boats were present further east, off Kinsale and right in the *Lusitania*'s path. By the time we learned of their presence, the *Lusitania* was on the bottom of the sea and twelve hundred people were dead.'

Still Gallagher remained silent. 'What is your point?' asked Borden.

'Naval intelligence knew about the U-boats waiting in ambush,' Ryder said. His voice was shaking a little with anger. 'Why did they fail to pass the word? Was it an error? Or is there some more sinister explanation? Twenty months have passed since the sinking, and not a day goes by that I do not ask myself these questions, and wonder what the answer is.'

'You were not to blame,' Gallagher said.

'I know I am not to blame,' Ryder said. 'I am responsible, because I was in command, but I acted as best I could with the information I had to hand. The fault lies with those who failed to warn us. The twelve hundred people who died are on their consciences, not mine.' He paused. 'I checked the duty log at naval intelligence to see who was on watch when the *Lusitania* sank. You'll be unsurprised to learn that, just as with Jutland, the senior duty officer was Commander Colson.'

The captain finished his drink and rose to his feet, looking down at the other two men. 'We must get to the bottom of what is happening in naval intelligence, Gallagher,' he said. 'We can't expect the Americans to ally themselves with us when we are holed below the waterline. Lansing thinks we are losing the war. Unless we sort this mess out, very soon, he may well be right.'

THE MUSIC ROOM was silent; Makarian had finished playing and was gone. Mrs Vane approached the piano and sat down. The music book was open at Brahms's Ballade No. 2 in D major. She turned back to the beginning of the piece and saw that someone had written the word *andante* beneath the title in pencil. Below it, there were marks on the paper and a tiny smudge. Holding the page up to the light, she saw that two more words had been written and rubbed out: *7th gate.*

Up from Earth's centre, through the seventh gate, I rose, and on the throne of Saturn sate. Mrs Vane was a prosaic woman, not given to irrational fears, but she shivered a little. There was something unworldly about these almost invisible messages and how they appeared and disappeared.

Tentatively, she began to play; the piece was not one she was familiar with. She managed to work her way through a dozen bars before the door opened and Nathalie Fairbairn entered the room. The other woman closed the door and leaned against it, watching Mrs Vane play. 'You're rather good,' she said after a while.

Mrs Vane stopped. 'I'm really not,' she said.

'Better than me, at any rate. My mother tried to teach me to play, but I was hopeless.'

'Was your mother musical?'

'She taught music at a girls' school. My father was a riveter from Clydebank. God knows what they saw in each other.'

Even more curious, thought Mrs Vane, was how this hard, bitter woman had met and married an effete diplomat like Fairbairn. 'Actually, I've been looking for you,' she said.

'So Mr Gallagher said. Well, now you've found me. Ask me what questions you like.'

Mrs Vane paused. 'You know who I am?'

'My dear woman, everyone in the house knows who you and Mr Gallagher are, apart from the old lady and her idiot daughter.'

'What makes you think they don't know?'

'Mrs Makarian wouldn't recognize a fly if it landed on her nose, and Lady Maud is so deep in a state of denial that she is beginning to drown. She has no interest in anything that does not concern herself.'

State of denial was an odd phrase, Mrs Vane thought. She had read *The Psychopathology of Everyday Life* at the suggestion of her husband, who had added, *if I ever start acting like one of Freud's archetypes, you have my permission to poison my soup.* But it was not usual reading for women of her generation.

'May I ask you a question first?' said Nathalie. 'Why do you do what you do?'

Mrs Vane considered her answer. The truth was not something that she wanted to discuss. 'I'm helping the war effort,' she said finally.

'The war effort? Don't make me laugh. This war is the most futile exercise in human history. Mind you, not that peace will be any better when it comes, not so long as the lunatics remain in charge of the asylum.' Nathalie shook her head. 'I was hoping to provoke you into some intelligent conversation, but I see I am wasting my time. Ask your questions.'

You're wrong, Mrs Vane silently told Gallagher. *She does hate me. She hates all of us.*

'You walked up to the woods this afternoon,' she said. 'We saw you coming back not long before Miss Rittenhouse was killed.'

Nathalie Fairbairn was still leaning against the door, her hands behind her back. 'And you want to know if I saw or heard anything. Sorry to disappoint you.'

'May I ask why you went out in the first place?'

'I was with Lansing,' Nathalie said calmly. 'We walked into the woods together. You can guess what we did there, I'm sure.'

Mrs Vane pursed her lips. 'Not exactly the weather for it, was it?'

'I'm not particular. Neither is Lansing.'

'What happened after you finished?'

'I came straight back to the house. I was in a bad mood. Lansing isn't a particularly thoughtful or caring lover at the best of times, and this afternoon was downright disappointing.'

'Did Mr Lansing carry on shooting?'

'Yes. I saw him return to the house about half an hour later. He looked thoroughly wet and miserable. That made me quite happy.'

'While you were returning home, did you hear a shot?'

'Yes, just as I reached the house. Was that when Miss Rittenhouse was killed?'

Mrs Vane nodded. 'You know Lansing. Do you think he is capable of murdering someone?'

'All of us are capable of murdering someone. You could, if your life depended on it.'

'That doesn't answer my question,' said Mrs Vane.

'Lansing can be cruel. He enjoys violence, especially towards women.'

Mrs Vane shook her head. 'Why?' she demanded. 'Why do you go with him?'

'My dear woman, can you really be so naive? Not all of us had genteel upbringings like you. For some of us, the rough and the smooth are both part of life.'

'Did you ever meet her?' Mrs Vane asked. 'Miss Rittenhouse, I mean.'

'Yes, a few times, in Boston. She sometimes went to parties at Aquinnah, Mrs Lansing's house. I don't know how she got invited, as Sadie didn't particularly care for her, but she was one of those people who manage to worm their way in anywhere.'

'What sort of woman was she?'

Nathalie paused. 'Inquisitive, of course, but that goes without saying. Energetic, lively, usually quite cheerful. Surprisingly optimistic about life, for a journalist. Sadie disliked her, as I say, but I found her good company. I'm sorry to hear she's dead.'

Could that odd undertone in her voice be compassion? Mrs Vane wondered. 'Speaking of parties,' she said, 'do you recall an occasion on your husband's yacht? You were there, along with Mr and Mrs Lansing, and Mrs Lansing's brother Frank. The German ambassador was there too, and a Russian named Nabokov. Someone took photographs of the guests.'

Nathalie shook her head. 'That was Sadie. One of her friends had given her a Box Brownie not long before and she was on a kick, photographing everything in sight. Herbert was furious, but there wasn't much he could do about it.'

'Who was the friend?'

'She was called Lily Sparrow. Some silly little girl who worked for an art dealer in Boston that Sadie patronized. Sadie took a liking to her, God knows why.'

'Was she at the party?'

Nathalie shook her head. 'Lily didn't mingle with the rest of us. Sadie kept her to herself. Make of that what you will.'

'Some of those photographs found their way into Willa Rittenhouse's possession,' Mrs Vane said. 'That's why she was killed.'

Nathalie considered this. 'Lansing was on the yacht to make an agreement with Bernstorff,' she said, 'but he wouldn't have wanted the world to know about it. If Willa Rittenhouse had photographs of him and Bernstorff together, and he knew about it, surely that would give him motive. Don't you think?'

Mrs Vane closed the lid of the piano and stood up. 'You

made love to Lansing this afternoon, and now you're as good as accusing him of murder. Why?'

'Love had nothing to do with it,' Nathalie said, reaching for the door handle. 'Now, if you'll forgive me, I'm going to have a drink.'

AFTER RYDER LEFT the library, Gallagher and Borden sat on in silence for a while, watching the fire. Finally the older man rose to his feet, dropping another log on the hearth before picking up his glass and crossing to the sideboard to refill it. 'Can I get you one, Pat?' he asked.

Gallagher shook his head. Borden squirted soda from the siphon into his whisky and resumed his seat. The water pipes thumped overhead and he looked up in irritation. 'Your mother is not well,' he said.

'I know. She told me.'

'You should speak to her,' Borden said.

'Will it change anything?' Gallagher shook his head. 'I'm sorry. I shouldn't have said that.'

'You need to let go of the past, Pat.'

'Why?' Gallagher asked. 'It's all that I have left.'

Borden sighed. 'I understand why you are bitter. Part of it is my fault, of course. I should have made certain that you were properly looked after. We could have found you a better school, perhaps. But . . . the world has changed, Pat. The war has changed us. We're different people, now. And your mother needs forgiveness.'

'She needs first to forgive herself,' Gallagher said. 'I can do nothing until she does.'

'If she came to you and asked you to make amends — asked you for forgiveness — would you give it?'

'I don't know,' Gallagher said. 'I can't imagine that being a possibility. John, I know you mean well. But this is not something that you can repair, and right now I don't have the time or the strength to repair it myself. When the war is over, perhaps we can talk again.'

Borden sighed again. The bags under his eyes were dark with strain. 'Alice says much the same. It's a pity you and she don't get on. You have a great deal in common.'

'Do you write to her?'

'Penelope does, and gives me her news. She was awarded the Military Medal last month. I'm immensely proud of her, of course.'

And yet you don't write to her, Gallagher thought, but he kept silent. He himself was in no position to lecture anyone. As Borden had said, he and Alice did not get along. She was angry with him, and had never really forgiven him for running away to sea.

'I'd like to get Maud away from this place,' Borden said after a while. 'But she won't go without me, and of course I can't leave so long as the war lasts. Which could be a long time yet.'

Gallagher stirred a little. 'Are we losing? Or was Ryder being too pessimistic?'

Borden sighed. 'We're certainly not winning. We're spending ten million pounds a day on armaments, and we're running out of credit. The Bank of England is empty and foreign banks won't lend us any more money, so in six months' time the country will be bankrupt. And if there is treason to contend with as well, as Ryder suggests . . . I shudder to think what will happen.'

Gallagher said nothing.

'If Lansing finds out about the problems at the Admiralty, he really will walk out,' Borden continued. 'It will be the final straw for him.'

Gallagher shook his head. 'Lansing is playing both sides against the middle. Claiming that we are losing the war is a bargaining chip. He knows full well that he might be wrong, so he is counting on you to give him what he wants. Have you twisted Fairbairn's arm yet?'

'I have barely spoken to Fairbairn,' said Borden. 'I get the impression that he is avoiding me.'

'And me. So, someone else is doing the arm twisting. One way or the other, I can pretty much guarantee you that by tomorrow morning, Fairbairn will have dropped his opposition to giving Lansing the oilfields. And you, John, will have a hard choice to make.'

Another silence fell. Borden brooded, looking into his glass with weary eyes. His thinning hair was plastered to his pale head. 'What Ryder said about the *Lusitania* is quite shocking,' he said finally.

'Yes,' Gallagher said.

'That letter you showed me, the one written by Churchill. What do you think Winston intended?'

'I don't know,' Gallagher said. 'I was hoping you would.'

Borden studied him for a moment. 'Churchill was First Lord of the Admiralty at the time *Lusitania* was torpedoed. He could have issued an instruction to suppress the intelligence about the U-boats. Is that what you are thinking?'

'No,' Gallagher said. 'It would have been far too risky. If Churchill had given such an order, and it became public knowledge, it would have sunk his career far more effectively than Gallipoli. And the Americans would have screamed betrayal, and any chance of an American alliance would have disappeared over the horizon.'

'So who was responsible? These German agents of Ryder's?'

Gallagher shook his head. 'There was no plot to sink the *Lusitania*,' he said. 'There was, however, a plot to create public anger against Germany in America and increase pressure on

President Wilson to commit to the Allied cause. It was a subtle plot, well-conceived, and it very nearly worked. It probably *would* have worked, had we not sailed into the crosshairs of a U-boat's periscope.'

'But if Ryder is right, someone stopped the navy and *Lusitania* from learning of the presence of that U-boat,' Borden said. 'We are agreed that it was not Churchill. Who, then?'

'I don't know,' Gallagher said. In the hallway, the longcase clock chimed the three-quarter hour. 'With a bit of luck, it may soon no longer matter.'

THE DOOR OPENED and Commander Colson entered the library. Big, fair-haired, well-dressed in a beautifully cut dark suit, he was an imposing figure as always, but he also looked rather hesitant, as if he was not entirely certain he would be welcomed. 'Am I intruding?' he asked.

Gallagher glanced at Borden. 'Not at all,' the latter said. 'Help yourself to a drink, and join us.'

Colson poured a drink and sat down. He pulled a cigarette from his case and lit it, staring at the match flame for a moment before extinguishing it. 'Is there any word on the woman who was killed?' he asked.

'She was an American journalist, a Miss Rittenhouse,' Gallagher said. 'Does the name ring any bells?'

'No. What was she doing here?'

'She was following a story. She wasn't killed by poachers, either.'

The hesitancy disappeared. Gallagher watched the intelligence officer's mind swing into action. 'You think it was someone in this house,' Colson said. 'Any ideas about who it might be?'

'Not yet. You were out shooting this afternoon. Did you see or hear anything?'

Colson frowned. 'I heard a couple of shots. The first one was somewhere off to the south, or maybe south-west; hard to say in among the trees. I was just lining up for a shot at a dog fox, but the sound spooked him and he ran off. Several minutes later there was a second shot. That sounded like it came more from the west, the direction of the lodge.'

'That will be the shot that killed Miss Rittenhouse,' Gallagher said. 'Did you see anyone else while you were out?'

Colson shook his head. 'The light was dim and visibility was quite poor, especially under the trees. Who else was out shooting?'

'Captain Ryder, Mr Tovey and Mr Lansing.'

'Ah,' Colson said. He puffed on his cigarette and blew out smoke. 'Interesting . . . I don't know Tovey at all.'

'We've checked his background, and it is clean,' Gallagher said. 'Only one thing bothers me. One of his duties is the transport of fuel oil for ships, but according to Nick Makarian he doesn't actually know much about oil. Of course, it's not unusual for the navy to put people in charge of something they know nothing about.'

Colson looked at his whisky glass. 'I'd like to say you are wrong, but that would be a lie . . . Lansing doesn't like journalists, he said as much when we were out shooting. He equates them with Bolsheviks and rats. All three should be exterminated, he said.' He looked up. 'What happened to Miss Rittenhouse sounds like an extermination.'

'It does,' Gallagher said. 'But I have another theory about Lansing. He may be innocent, at least of this killing, but someone may have tried to implicate him. Lansing has a short fuse, to put it mildly, and the killer may have hoped that if we accused him of murder he would, in the American idiom, blow his top and walk out. Bang goes our American alliance.' He watched Colson's face. 'Which you are not in favour of,' he added.

'I've never made any secret of my views,' Colson said steadily. 'American help will come at a high price, one we may not be able to afford to pay. But if you think I killed Miss Rittenhouse, you are wrong. I have never harmed any woman in my life, and I certainly wouldn't murder one. No cause can justify that.'

'Are you certain?' Gallagher asked. 'A great deal of money and power is at stake.'

'I am not interested in power, and I already have all the money I need. My concern is that we do the right thing for our country. If you hand over the oil concession to Lansing, Sir John, he will have the largest share of the world oil industry. He can hold the entire British Empire hostage, whenever he chooses.'

'I know,' said Borden. 'But if that is the price we must pay for an American alliance, what choice do we have?'

'There is another option,' Colson said.

'Oh?' said Borden. 'If so, I would very much like to hear about it.'

Colson hesitated.

'You mean the telegram,' Gallagher said. 'Don't worry, Sir John already knows about it. Captain Ryder knows, too.'

'Oh, Christ,' Colson said, and his face was full of dismay. 'Who else knows?'

'An excellent question,' Gallagher said. He watched Colson's face again. 'Never mind the telegram for the moment. You haven't asked me about the Vasiliev investigation, Commander, but I will tell you anyway. Paul Vasiliev is alive and well. The man found in the stationery cupboard with the Zimmermann telegram in his pocket was Frank Warren, Lansing's brother-in-law.'

He paused for a moment. 'But you already knew that, Commander. Didn't you?'

Colson's face seemed to collapse. He reached for another cigarette, fumbling with the matchbox. 'Yes,' he said. 'I knew.'

Gallagher let the silence drag on for a long time before he spoke. 'When did you first meet Warren?'

Colson's hand twitched. 'About a week ago. I only met him once, and not for long.'

Borden sat quietly, watching. Once again, Gallagher was grateful for his stepfather's presence as a witness. 'Tell me what happened,' he said.

'He came to my rooms late one night. How he found out who I was or where I lived, I have no idea. He said he had intelligence about a plot being hatched in America, which he was willing to sell. I was sceptical, largely because the man was drunk. But I gave him some money, and he told me Lansing had made a deal with the Germans to get control of the oilfields. He knew this, he said, because he himself had witnessed a meeting between Lansing and the German ambassador.'

'Have you told anyone else about this?' Gallagher asked.

'Not yet. I didn't know whether to believe him, and I still don't. I asked if he had anything else. After I gave him some more money, he told me that someone was trying to break into the naval intelligence division. They were looking for a telegram, he said, sent from Germany and intended for the German ambassador in Mexico. I realized at once that he was talking about the Zimmermann telegram, and I asked how he had heard about it. A source, he said.' Colson mopped his brow. 'My God, Gallagher, you're right. How many people do know about this?'

Gallagher ignored the question. 'What happened next?' he asked.

'I demanded again to know who his source was, and he refused to say. He said that if anyone found out he had been talking to me, he would be dead. He went away. The next time I saw him, he was on the floor of the stationery cupboard.'

'I see,' Gallagher said. 'Did you report Warren's visit to Special Branch, or our service?'

'No,' Colson said. His hand was shaking again. 'And yes, before you start, I know I should have, just as I should have identified him right away, before Ryder came. But I needed time to think. The fact that he knew about the telegram really rattled me. And then, I remembered the clerk who had been stealing documents, who worked for the Dreamer. I realized Warren could be working for the Dreamer as well.' He lowered his voice. 'To be honest, given that story about meeting the German ambassador, I wondered if the Dreamer might be Lansing.'

'Why didn't you identify his body immediately?'

'Because . . . Because nothing made sense. I didn't think he had been murdered, for a start, and I still don't understand how that happened, how whoever killed him could have got out of the room. And if he was the Dreamer's agent . . . That's why I asked for you specifically to take on the investigation. I wanted to talk to you in private, without Mrs Vane present, because of course I didn't know she was working with you. I was about to send her away when Ryder arrived.'

Gallagher said nothing.

'I'm aware that you don't trust me,' Colson said. 'That's why Mrs Vane was sent to work at naval intelligence, isn't it? To keep an eye on me.'

Gallagher touched the scar on the side of his face. 'You must have been surprised when Ryder identified him as Vasiliev.'

'Surprised is one word for it. I was, and am, absolutely

bewildered. When Ryder spoke up, I suddenly realized that I didn't know who I could trust. And, Christ, if the secret service was spying on me, could I even trust you?'

'You should still have told me,' Gallagher said.

'Oh? If the positions were reversed, if you had no idea whom you could trust, would *you* have told *me*?'

'But the positions aren't reversed,' Gallagher said. 'You concealed the identity of a man responsible for a very serious security breach at the Admiralty. You also withheld the information that he is Lansing's brother-in-law, and as the director of a rival oil company you have a motive for discrediting Lansing and collapsing Sir John's attempt to win over the Americans. That is misconduct at the very least, and possibly quite a lot more. If I tell Admiral Hall what you have just told me, you could be drummed out of the service.'

'And the scandal would engulf the rest of naval intelligence, Admiral Hall would lose his job and Captain Ryder would take over,' Colson said angrily. 'That's what he has wanted all along, you know. Is that what *you* want?'

'Who is to say it wouldn't be for the best?' Gallagher said.

Out in the hall the clock struck seven. Colson drained his glass and rose to his feet. 'Forgive me,' he said curtly. 'I need some fresh air before dinner.'

THE DOOR CLOSED behind him. Borden, who had remained silent for the past few minutes, looked at Gallagher. 'Do you think he was telling the truth?'

'Some of it,' Gallagher said.

'He'd met Warren before, of course. I was watching his hands.'

'Yes.'

'Do you think Warren had some sort of hold over him? Was blackmailing him, perhaps?'

'Perhaps,' said Gallagher. 'But Warren is dead now, and Colson is free to tell the truth. Why isn't he doing so? Unless the truth is something that will discredit him.' He sighed suddenly, looking up at the water-stained ceiling. 'There are times when I truly hate this job.'

'What do you mean?'

'Sometime during the next twenty-four hours I am going to have to break a good man. Possibly more than one. It seems like a pitiful and stupid way to win a war. But what choice do I have?'

'None,' said Borden. 'No more than I do. Our role is to endure, Pat. You, Maud and myself, Penelope and Nicholas, everyone. It is all we can do.'

12

NICHOLAS MAKARIAN OPENED the door of the billiards room and stopped. 'There you are,' he said. 'I've been looking for you. Do you know it is almost time for dinner?'

Lansing bent over the table, lining up a shot. A glass of brandy sat on the edge of the table beside him. 'I'll come along when I'm ready. I'm in no rush to eat that food again.'

'I'd appreciate it if you would try to avoid offending my mother-in-law,' Makarian said. 'It's all right for you, you can leave at the end of the weekend. I have to see her again.'

Lansing grunted and played a cannon. Straightening, he took a gulp of brandy. 'What's on your mind?'

'I think I can come to an arrangement with the Russians, but you'll have to hold your nose. It involves the Bolsheviks.'

'God damn it, Makarian, I told you I hate those bastards.'

'I'm not exactly enamoured of them myself, but we need them on our side. Otherwise, they're a threat to us.'

'All right, just don't ask me to speak to them. Who's dealing with them? Your partner in Saint Petersburg?'

'No, I am. Their negotiator is someone quite close to home.' Makarian smiled. 'You'd be surprised to know who it is.'

'I don't care, so don't bother telling me.' Lansing eyed him.

'Are you sure you can get away with this? If the British find out, they'll skin you.'

'Don't worry about them,' Makarian said. 'I've made my own arrangements with the Foreign Office. No one will interfere.' He paused. 'This will cost you, Lansing. You and me both.'

Lansing lifted his brandy glass and drained. 'I don't care what it costs,' he said. 'If I can get control of those oilfields, it will be worth every penny. I'll be the biggest oil producer in the world, and I can write my own ticket. And you, my friend, will have to buy a hell of a lot more tankers to ship it all.'

Makarian smiled. 'I'd rather not count my ships until they are launched,' he said. 'See you at dinner.'

FROM HIS BEDROOM window, Tovey watched Colson step outside and walk across the park towards the lake. Light flared briefly as the commander lit another cigarette. Tovey drew a deep breath. *Here goes*, he thought. *Time for the seventh gate.*

He walked along the corridor, wincing every time the floorboards creaked, listening to the monotonous thumping of the pipes and the whistle of yet another train coming up the line. He wondered how many trains there were, how many wounded there were, at a time when the Western Front was comparatively quiet. Nathalie was right, it was time – more than time – that this came to an end. That thought steeled his resolve.

Colson had locked the door of his room, but he picked the lock with the tools Nathalie had given him, using the technique she had taught him, all the while listening nervously for the sound of footsteps approaching. The lock opened with a soft click. He slipped inside and closed the door. The curtains were closed but he didn't dare turn on the overhead light in case the glow showed through. A shaded torch, the beam carefully directed downwards, showed him the room.

Working swiftly with a handkerchief wrapped around his fingers, he searched the room, going through the wardrobe, looking under the mattress, lifting the corners of the rug. He found nothing. He frowned, looking at the polished, inlaid writing case on the side table. It seemed too obvious; no one would hide a secret document in such an obvious place. Or was it a double bluff? *Only one way to find out*, he thought, and he opened the box.

Floorboards creaked in the corridor and he froze, but it was only one of the maidservants hurrying along towards the servants' stair. Shining the torch into the writing case, he leafed quickly through the papers inside. Most of the letters were personal, to Colson's family, but at the end he found one of more interest.

Sunbury-on-Thames
31st January 1917

My dear Colson,

I note your position with regard to the potential concession for the Mesopotamian oilfields, but there are three points that deserve our consideration. First, those oilfields are at the moment in Turkish hands, so the question of who will ultimately exploit them remains moot. Second, the British government remains the majority stakeholder in Anglo-Persian Oil, so as directors we are duty-bound to take their views into account. The Foreign Office currently supports our ultimate right to that concession, but if its views should change, there is very little we can do about

*this. Third, I understand your personal views, but we must
be expedient. As a board of directors, we have worked very
hard to reach our present position. We must not jeopardize
that now.*

*Yr obedient servant,
Cargill*

Distantly he heard the front door open and close, and Colson's voice in the hall below. Cursing silently, he closed the writing case and hurried out of the door, closing it behind him and remembering to use the hairpin to lock it. The pin stuck in the lock. Colson's footsteps could be heard on the stairs. Sweat broke out on Tovey's forehead and he rattled the pin. It moved again, turning the tumblers of the lock, and he straightened and hurried along the corridor just as Colson reached the top of the stairs. 'Good evening, Commander,' he said, hoping his voice was steady.

'What's good about it?' Colson snapped. He walked away towards his room. Tovey watched him go in and close the door behind him, and hurried along to Nathalie Fairbairn's room.

Nathalie was in her dressing gown, seated in front of her dressing table and pinning up her hair. 'Did you find the telegram?' she asked.

'No. It's not there.'

'Well, it must be somewhere in the house,' she said calmly. 'If Colson doesn't have it, someone else does. That's what this weekend is all about.'

Tovey thought. 'The Dreamer might have an accomplice, of course.'

'Almost certainly. Did you find anything else?'

Still tingling with adrenaline, Tovey told her about the letter.

'John Cargill is also a director of Anglo-Persian. He's influential, too. He's close to Winston Churchill.'

'So,' Nathalie said, still calmly, 'the British government is preparing to screw Anglo-Persian and hand the oil concession over to Lansing. They must be desperate for that American alliance.'

'Can we do anything to stop them?'

'Aye, but do we want to? Think about what's in our best interests. Remember the old saying. My enemy's enemy is my friend.'

'I don't understand,' Tovey said.

'You don't need to. Leave it with me.' She turned her head to look at him. 'You're sweating up like a racehorse.'

'I nearly got caught. God, Nathalie, I'm really not cut out for this business.'

'You need something to calm your nerves.' She rose to her feet and turned to face him. He looked at her, his mouth suddenly dry. She was twenty years older than himself, but he was unable to resist her. He never had been.

'Do we have time?' he whispered.

'There's always time,' she said, and she opened her dressing gown.

THE TELEGRAM FROM the service confirming the meeting with Rintelen was economical; the bean counters had clearly had a word. *Rose and Crown tomorrow 0930 Room 6.*

'What are you hoping to learn?' Mrs Vane asked.

They were in the Cheese Room, listening to the squeaks of mice and the patter of tiny feet on the floor. Outside the wind hissed, stirring the drapes and sending cold draughts like little electric shocks through the air. Gallagher coughed. 'I'm hoping for answers to questions I should have asked a long time ago,' he said. 'Only they weren't obvious questions, then. What did you learn from Nathalie Fairbairn?'

Mrs Vane summed up the conversation in a few sentences. 'She is a strange character. Quite full of anger and bitterness, I would say. She gave away a few hints about her background. There might be something there . . . She is repulsed by Lansing, and yet she went willingly into the woods with him. Her unconscious clearly isn't constrained by her conscious.'

'What?' said Gallagher.

'Sorry. Freud. She doesn't let her rational mind get in the way of satisfying her unconscious desires. Stop rolling your eyes.'

'Can't help it. The fire is smoking.' Gallagher coughed again.

'She lied about what happened in the woods,' said Mrs Vane. 'And I think she was lying when she said she didn't know Vasiliev.'

'Of course she was,' said Gallagher. 'They're all lying. But then, why should we be surprised? Everyone lies, all the time. Governments lie to their people, people lie to their governments. Children lie to their parents, and parents most certainly lie to their children. Why should this lot be any different?'

'So,' Mrs Vane said patiently, 'who is lying about what? Let's summarize.'

'You go first. What was wrong with Nathalie's account?'

Mrs Vane paused. 'I'm still trying to decide. She returned to the house before the shot was fired, so it couldn't have been her that picked up the shotgun shell . . . Although she could have picked up another one. Two shots were fired this afternoon.'

'Yes,' said Gallagher. 'Tovey admitted to firing the other one.' Their eyes met for a moment. 'Go on,' said Gallagher.

'Her story was almost too plausible. If she had planned the whole thing to give her an alibi for killing Willa Rittenhouse, she could not have done better. But at the same time, she went out of her way to say something nice about Miss Rittenhouse, which is quite unlike her.' *You should have heard what she said about your mother,* she almost added.

'Tovey also lied about not knowing Miss Rittenhouse,' Gallagher said. 'What's more, Miss Rittenhouse thought she recognized him at the shoot this morning. Very well, they may have conspired to frame Lansing, but at the moment I can't see any reason why either of them would want to kill Willa Rittenhouse.'

'Clearly there is more to Tovey than his service record suggests,' said Mrs Vane.

'I'll ask Colonel Kell to put someone to work on that. As we know, Ryder lied about Vasiliev, but he claims he had good reason. He himself is running a parallel investigation on the orders of Admiral Jellicoe.'

Mrs Vane's eyebrows rose. 'Interesting.'

'Isn't it just.' Gallagher could not quite keep the anger out of his voice. 'However, the biggest purveyor of porky pies has to be Colson. By concealing what he knew about Warren, he has deliberately impeded our investigation. If I was his commanding officer, I would break him to the ranks.'

'Hold on,' said Mrs Vane. 'If he deliberately held back what he knew about Warren, why did he send for you in the first place? If he was concealing something, the last thing he would do is involve you. Do you see what I am getting at? Colson made a serious blunder, but that's not the same as treason. If it was, we'd have shot all of our generals a long time ago.'

Despite his mood, Gallagher smiled a little. 'That remark could itself be close to treason.'

'I'll take my chances,' said Mrs Vane. 'Let's look at some alternatives. We know Warren worked for the Germans in

Boston, but after his sister died that spy ring was broken up. Is Warren necessarily still working for the Germans now? What if someone else hired him to steal the telegram, and the Dreamer's agents found out about it and killed him, to prevent him taking it away?'

'You're right,' Gallagher said after a moment. 'We've allowed ourselves to become distracted, or else someone has deliberately distracted us . . . The Dreamer has no need to steal the telegram because, being a German agent, he already knows its contents. So, someone else must have been behind the theft. Who else might Warren have been working for?'

'We know that he sold information to Miss Rittenhouse. Might *she* have hired him?'

Gallagher looked dubious. 'A well-known and respected journalist paying someone to burgle the Admiralty? Stranger things have happened, I suppose.'

It was her turn to frown. 'I can't stop thinking about the locked room. There is something significant about that, something that we are missing.'

A gust of wind in the chimney blew smoke out into the room. Gallagher coughed again, waving away the smoke. 'Go on,' he said. 'Follow your instincts.'

'I agree with what you said earlier, that the locked room was meant as a distraction. But getting in and out of that room, however it was done, was unlikely to be simple. Would someone really go to such elaborate lengths just to kill Frank Warren? Perhaps, but it doesn't feel right to me. Something else is happening, and someone was using the stationery cupboard for another purpose. Disposing of Warren's body there feels like a bit of improvisation.'

'Who uses the stationery cupboard?'

'Only naval intelligence. Owing to the nature of the work,

Room 40 gets through a lot of paper. Other departments have their own stores.'

'And you have the only key.'

'That's right. And I'm only on duty during the day, so whoever killed Warren that night could have been confident that no one would discover his body for several hours at least. That would give them time to get well clear.'

'And leave us with an apparently unsolvable problem,' Gallagher mused. 'Good. Keep working on it, and let me know what you come up with.'

SATURDAY, 3 FEBRUARY 1917

8.00 P.M.

The gong sounded for dinner. They gathered in the dining room, the men in evening coats and white ties, the women in bright gowns, and dined on crab soup gritty with pieces of shell, trout so overcooked that the flesh was white and crumbling, rubbery chicken croquettes, boiled pork with grey potatoes, and cold rum omelette oozing with undercooked egg. The guests tried to make conversation at first, but most eventually lapsed into silence. Gallagher watched them: Colson fidgety and nervous, Price sunk in gloom, Tovey glancing at his pocket watch, Nathalie Fairbairn staring at her wine glass like she wanted to start a fight with it, Penelope Makarian lost in contemplation. Lady Maud ate slowly, chewing each mouthful with resignation; her husband picked at his food and watched grimly as Lansing drank one glass of whisky after another without showing any signs of intoxication. Makarian and Fairbairn talked quietly, almost in whispers.

Train whistles sounded, echoing mournfully up the hill. 'Like the souls of dead men weeping in the night,' said Makarian.

Edith Price gazed at him. 'That is very poetic,' she said. 'Do you think the dead really can communicate with us?'

'I hear them,' said Makarian. 'Every day, in their tens of thousands.'

Lady Maud raised her head. 'We will not speak of this at the dinner table,' she commanded.

Silence fell once more.

They escaped after dessert, the five women to the drawing room, Borden breaking with tradition and inviting the men to take port in the library where it was warmer. Ryder looked at Gallagher. 'The woman who was killed, Miss Rittenhouse. Is there any word about what happened?'

'There are several possibilities,' Gallagher said. 'I am waiting to see what develops.'

'In other words, no,' said Price, taking a seat and placing his port glass on the table beside him. 'By the way, I agree with you, Makarian. I hear the dead too.'

'What were you really talking about?' Tovey asked. He looked grateful for the change of conversation.

Makarian stared at him. 'Do you not know?'

Borden was uneasy. 'Nicholas, perhaps this is not the time . . .'

'No, I'm interested too,' Lansing said. He sat in a deep armchair, port glass in one hand and a cigar in the other. 'This is about the Armenians, right?'

'At last, a man who knows what is going on in the rest of the world. Yes, this is about the Armenians.'

Fairbairn touched the tips of his moustache. 'Don't be too hard on them, Makarian. Given the amount of slaughter that is going on, it's easy to overlook yet another massacre.'

'But this is not one massacre,' said Makarian. 'It is many. The

Ottoman Empire has persecuted my people for years, but when the war began they lost all restraint. Soldiers went into our villages, where they shot and bayonetted thousands. The rest were rounded up and marched into the desert, and left there to die of thirst and hunger and disease. Hundreds of thousands, old men, women, children, all perished. And the world stood silent, and did nothing.'

'What could we have done?' asked Colson. 'What did you expect us to do?'

Makarian laughed. He was a little drunk, Gallagher thought. 'How far the Royal Navy has declined,' he said. 'The navy of Drake and Hood, Jervis and Nelson. England expects every man to do his duty. And now the battle cry goes up: *what did you expect us to do?* No wonder you failed at Jutland.'

Colson flushed deep red. 'Did you lose family yourself?' asked Ryder.

'I lost three generations, Captain. The village of my fathers is peopled only by ghosts now. First, the Ottomans took away their shoes. Then they nailed horseshoes to their bare feet. You are not human, the Turks said, you are mules, donkeys. After that, they drove them with bleeding feet out into the wastelands to die. And the world says, *what did you expect us to do?*'

'I think you are embarrassing our guests,' Borden said sharply.

Makarian reached for the decanter and poured his glass full to the brim. 'Do not lecture me on this, Sir John. On many other matters, I will accept your criticism. Not on this.'

'Hell, I'm not embarrassed,' said Lansing. 'I'm interested, Makarian. I might even be able to help your people.'

'Can you give them freedom?' asked Makarian. 'Can you give them a homeland, an independent state they can call their own? Can you give them arms to defend themselves?'

'Personally? No,' said Lansing, refilling his own glass. 'But America might.'

'For a price,' said Colson. He was still red in the face.

'Of course,' said Lansing. 'Everything has a price.'

Fairbairn touched the tips of his moustache again. 'And I think we all know what America's price will be,' he said. 'The Armenian communities in Turkey are very close to the oil-fields. Be careful about whom you are dealing with, Makarian.'

Makarian turned on him. 'To free Armenia from the Ottoman Turks, I would make accommodation with the devil himself. The world has abandoned us. We owe the rest of you nothing.'

'I admire your spirit,' said Ryder. 'But you'd better hope Germany and Ottoman Turkey don't win the war. If they do, the Ottomans will be stronger than ever, and the future for Armenia will be bleak.'

Makarian said nothing.

'Nonsense,' Colson snapped. 'Of course Germany won't win.'

Price sat forward in his seat. 'Oh? Why do you say that, Commander? Do you have some special information from naval intelligence that you would like to share with us? If so, we would all love to hear it.'

'Don't be ridiculous, Price,' said Colson.

'Ridiculous, am I?' Suddenly agitated, Price stood up. His wooden arm knocked over his port glass. The glass itself was nearly empty; the residue sprayed across the polished oak floor, droplets gleaming like rubies in the firelight.

'How many of you have seen active service?' Price demanded. 'Tovey? No. Makarian? No. Sir John? No. Captain Ryder? No disrespect to you and your glittering career, sir, but you've never seen a shot fired in anger. Well, *I have*. I have seen things no man should ever have to see. Ships on fire, ships exploding and vaporizing a thousand men in an instant, men drowning in oil slicks, or torn in half by shrapnel. Have you seen men blown apart by shells, any of you? Do you know what it looks like? Do you know what it *smells* like?'

'I have,' said Colson, 'and I do.'

'But you haven't learned very much from the experience, have you, Commander? You've been out there, on the front line, and you still believe we can win the war? Sixty thousand dead at Gallipoli, a hundred and fifty thousand at the Somme; six thousand at Jutland, and the German fleet barely scratched. How many thousands more must die before you all get it into your thick skulls that the entire war is futile and we can never hope to win?'

'Price!' said Ryder. 'That's enough. That is an order.'

Price turned on him. 'Excuse me, *sir*, but in case it has escaped your notice, we are off-duty and you are not my commanding officer. *You* do not give orders to me.'

'No, but I can have you removed from your post,' Ryder said. 'How do you think your little wife will enjoy a transfer to the Falkland Islands? No musical shows there, I think.'

'That's a bit harsh, Ryder,' Lansing said. 'We've all had a few belts, and the boy was speaking his mind. Let him be.'

'I am not your *boy!*' snapped Price, and he walked out of the room, slamming the door behind him. They heard the front door of the house close a moment later. A long silence followed.

'Poor fellow,' Makarian said finally.

'Poor fellow, nothing,' said Fairbairn. 'He needs to get a grip. Talk like that is bad for morale.'

'Nothing wrong with my morale,' said Lansing, exhaling cigar smoke. 'But I'd say young Mr Price is suffering from shell shock. He needs a good doctor.'

'Good luck in finding one,' Colson said quietly. 'Why did you invite him here, Sir John?'

Borden wiped his forehead. 'His father thought some fresh country air might do the lad some good, but it doesn't seem to have made much difference. Perhaps Captain Ryder may be onto something. Not the Falklands, of course, but a post with a bit more activity. I don't think Price was cut out for pushing papers at the Admiralty secretariat.'

'I'll see what can be done,' Ryder said. He paused. 'Gentlemen, I continue to have absolute faith that we will win the war, but Mr Price reminds us that we must be honest with ourselves. The situation is bleak. We all know the danger posed by the U-boats, but the threat from the air is growing too. More zeppelins are coming into service, and the tempo of their attacks will increase. Even more ominously, I fear, the Germans are also preparing a fleet of fixed-wing heavy bombers to attack London. Have you heard of these bombers, Colson? They're called Gothas.'

Colson looked at him suspiciously. 'No, I haven't. How is it that *you* have heard of them?'

'Friends in Washington, who receive news from Berlin.' Ryder shook his head. 'Sometimes, Colson, I feel like we at naval planning have better sources of intelligence than you do.'

Colson opened his mouth to reply. Ryder held up a hand. 'Listen,' he said.

There was no sound at first, apart from the crackle and hiss of the fire and the murmur of women's voices from the drawing room. A train whistle sounded far away, coming up the line from the east. As the echoes died away they heard another noise, blown on the east wind: thrum–thrum–thrum–thrum–thrum . . .

13

In the drawing room, Mrs Vane had taken the closest seat to the fire she could get but her feet, in inadequate evening shoes, refused to become warm. She longed for her boots upstairs in her room, and briefly considered going to fetch them. Then she thought about Lady Maud's reaction if she appeared in an evening gown and leather walking boots, and decided against it.

Lady Maud sat playing patience at a table near the window, oblivious to the draught stirring the drapes beside her. Either she did not feel the cold, Mrs Vane thought, or she regarded it as some form of penance. Nathalie Fairbairn had retired. Edith Price and Penelope Makarian were, like herself, huddled around the fire. Edith rose to pour more coffee. 'Can I fetch anyone a liqueur?' she asked.

'That's very good of you,' said Penelope. 'I'll take a chartreuse, if I may.'

Edith poured green chartreuse into a fluted glass, and a parfait d'amour for herself. The purple colour of the parfait d'amour was an almost exact match for her gown. 'Are you certain you won't have one?' she asked Mrs Vane.

'Thank you, but I am content with coffee.'

Edith giggled, holding her glass up to the light. 'It's quite a disgusting drink, isn't it? My Geraint says it tastes like it came from the perfume counter at Selfridge's. I can't imagine why I am so fond of it.'

Lady Maud's sniff of disapproval was just on the edge of hearing. Penelope turned to her. 'Mother! Mrs Price is our guest. There is no need to be beastly.'

Lady Maud did not respond. 'But as I keep saying, I'm British now,' said Edith, taking a seat. 'I must find something proper to drink. Gin, perhaps.'

The two younger women giggled together. *They're quite sweet*, Mrs Vane thought. *I suppose I may have been quite sweet too, once upon a time, but it is so difficult to remember.*

Edith sighed suddenly. 'I'm sorry, I shouldn't be making jokes, not while poor Miss Rittenhouse is dead. It's strange, isn't it? So many people have died in the war, and yet I found her death profoundly shocking.'

'It's different when it happens on your own doorstep,' said Penelope. 'Don't you agree, Mrs Vane?'

'Yes,' Mrs Vane said quietly, seeing again in her mind's eye the dripping woods, and the blood.

'*Please* change the subject,' Lady Maud said wearily.

There was silence for a while as everyone searched for a safe topic of conversation. From the ceiling, the water pipes thumped and gurgled. The roses on the wallpaper glowered down at them. Mrs Vane glanced at Lady Maud. That afternoon she herself had expressed regret for the death of Willa Rittenhouse, although in a roundabout way, and there had been a moment when it was possible to see how the horror around her was clawing at her soul. No longer; the armour was back in place. Freud would have a thing or two say about Lady Maud, she thought.

'Tell us about yourself, Mrs Vane,' Edith said finally. 'Where are you from?'

'I grew up in a small town called Edenbridge,' said Mrs

Vane. 'It's not far from here, actually. My father was a physician in general practice there. I had a fairly ordinary childhood, I suppose. After I finished school I moved to London and took a secretarial course, and then I went to work for an architect's practice. It was there that I met my husband.'

'Do you—' Edith began, and she checked herself.

'Go on,' said Mrs Vane.

'This is frightfully personal of me. Do you have children?'

'We were not so blessed,' said Mrs Vane.

Penelope reached over and patted her knee. 'You mustn't worry, you know.' She looked meaningfully at her mother. 'There's so much more to marriage than having children. The union of two souls, the happiness they bring to each other, that's what matters.'

Lady Maud said nothing. 'I should quite like to have children,' said Edith. She looked into the fire for a moment. 'Perhaps one day we shall get the chance, Geraint and I. Not soon, though. His work is all-important now, and a family would be a distraction.'

Penelope was curious. 'What does your husband do at the Admiralty?' she asked.

Edith smiled. 'You would have to ask him. He doesn't tell me, and I don't ask. All I know is that he works terribly long hours. Some days I barely see him.'

Something in the back of Mrs Vane's mind had begun to tick. 'That must be very lonely for you,' she said. 'Have you thought of taking a job yourself? There's no prejudice against married women working, not any more.'

'It is utterly unfitting for a married woman to work,' said Lady Maud, shuffling the cards. 'This is yet one more way in which this war is quite ruining society. God knows how we shall ever begin to repair the damage, once it is over.'

'Perhaps we won't,' said Penelope. 'Perhaps we shall have a new order, where women have more freedom and more rights. Perhaps we shall finally even get the chance to vote. Would that be such a bad thing?'

'Oh, Penelope, for pity's sake. You sound like a socialist.'

Colour rising, Penelope opened her mouth to reply, but Mrs Vane cut her off. 'I think Mr Price is quite fortunate to be posted to the Admiralty,' she said. 'It is a fascinating building. So much history under one roof.'

'The home of our superb Royal Navy,' Penelope said. She giggled, good humour quickly restored. 'Thanks to them, we *nearly* defeated the American rebels.'

'You must be so proud of coming second,' said Edith. 'I've never been to the Admiralty. I've begged Geraint to show me around, but he says there is nothing to see. According to him, he has a pokey little office that is freezing cold in winter and full of dead flies in summer. Not so romantic.' She looked at Penelope. 'I imagine your husband has a very grand office.'

A train whistle sounded in the distance. 'Not at all,' said Penelope. 'Nicky doesn't believe in spending money on himself. His office is positively spartan. Oh, but you should see his partner's offices in Saint Petersburg! We went there once, before the war. The boardroom has gold walls, would you believe it?'

'Hush,' said Lady Maud.

'Mother, I—'

'Hush!' Lady Maud sat stiff in her chair, looking up at the ceiling, her eyes wide. 'They're coming again.'

Thrum–thrum–thrum–thrum–thrum . . .

'There's more than one,' said Mrs Vane.

Lady Maud did not look as if she had heard. Her eyes were closed now, her hands clenched white on the card table in front of her. The skin of her face was stretched taut over its framework of bones. Penelope rose and ran across the room, throwing her arms around her mother and holding her close.

The train whistle sounded again, like the scream of a frightened animal. The sound of the engines grew louder, *thrum–thrum–thrum–thrum–thrum*. The door opened and Borden hurried into the room, looking at his wife. 'Maud, are you all right?'

'She will be,' Penelope said. 'Don't worry, Mummy. They'll be gone soon, I promise.'

The house began to vibrate; Mrs Vane's coffee cup rattled in its saucer. Some of the other men followed Borden into the drawing room. Colson was one of them, his face pale. 'Where is Geraint?' Edith asked.

THRUM–THRUM–THRUM–THRUM–THRUM.

Borden had to raise his voice to make himself heard. 'He went outside for some air, I think.'

'*Outside?*' Edith's voice rose to a squeak. 'He's out there now? Sir John, I beg you, fetch him back!'

THRUM–THRUM–THRUM–THRUM–THRUM.

Borden's hands clenched. 'I don't know where he went.'

'And it is dark,' said Makarian, looking at Colson and Ryder. 'One cannot expect the Royal Navy to navigate in the dark.'

The first zeppelin was directly overhead, passing, racing away towards Tonbridge. The second swept across the park, searchlights flashing as it probed for the railway line, and then it too was gone. But a third one was coming, and they heard the beat of its engines slowing. *THRUM. THRUM. THRUM.*

Gallagher came to stand beside Mrs Vane's chair, looking up. The others stood or sat, transfixed. They listened to the zeppelin moving past to the south, *THRUM. THRUM. THRUM,* turning over the woods, coming back again. 'They're circling the house,' whispered Mrs Vane.

'Reconnaissance,' Gallagher murmured.

Invisible in the night, the zeppelin hung over them. Searchlight beams stabbed downward, sweeping over the park and the lake, glowing brilliant behind the window drapes. 'My God!' said Fairbairn. 'Are they intending to land?'

Lady Maud fainted, collapsing onto the floor. Penelope crouched over her, shielding her with her body. Borden knelt beside them, looking up white-faced at the ceiling. The windows shuddered with vibration. Dust fell from the plaster, fine white flecks drifting in the lamplight.

The deep boom of a shotgun rattled the windows. A second shot followed a moment later. A pause of a few seconds and the shotgun fired both barrels again. The zeppelin was moving again now, the beat of its engine picking up, moving not towards Tonbridge after the others, but east away towards the coast. They heard the beat of its engines fading away, thrum–thrum–thrum–thrum–thrum, and finally silence fell.

A maidservant hurried in, herself pale and shaking, holding a bottle of smelling salts. After a moment Lady Maud revived and slowly sat up, Borden and Penelope supporting her. Gallagher watched them, his heart beating painfully in his chest.

The door slammed open and Maisie the gamekeeper's granddaughter ran into the room, wrapped in a tweed coat far too large for her with a shotgun broken over her arm. The open breech reeked of cordite. 'I shot at them!' she cried. 'Sir, I shot at them! I chased them off!'

'You young fool,' Borden said sharply. 'What were you doing out there?'

'Looking out for those poachers, sir! I was coming across the park and I saw the gasbags come, three of them, and one came right over the house. I gave it both barrels, *bam! bam!* and then again!'

'Those zeppelins carry machine guns, Maisie,' said Makarian, more gently. 'You could have been killed.'

'Yes, sir, but think how grand it would have been if I'd hit him! *Whoosh!* Oh, sir, I'd love to see one of them burn!'

Makarian smiled. 'It would make a pretty sight, I agree. You're a brave girl, Maisie. Now, go and find your pops. He'll be worried for you.'

'Yes, sir. Goodnight, sir, goodnight, my lady.' The girl curtseyed and hurried out of the room. Borden looked around. 'I shall see my wife to bed,' he said. 'I wish you good evening, ladies and gentlemen. Breakfast is at eight, with church to follow.'

Slowly, gently, Borden helped Lady Maud from the room. Penelope followed them. Price came in, wide-eyed, and Edith gave a small scream and hurled herself across the room, embracing him. 'Where have you been?' demanded Captain Ryder.

'I went out for some air,' Price said. 'I saw them coming and took shelter in the stables. What did that fool of a girl think she was doing?'

'Protecting us,' Makarian said. The words *unlike the Royal Navy* hung unspoken in the air.

Lansing shook his head. 'Where in hell is the Royal Flying Corps?'

'We will send word to Chiddingstone Causeway in the morning,' Makarian said. 'No point tonight, the pilots will all be getting drunk in the Station Tavern. We'll ask if some scouts can be sent down from Biggin Hill.' He paused. 'Something must be done. Twice in two days is very unusual for this time of the year, and if they should come again . . . I doubt if my mother-in-law's nerves can stand much more.'

'She has my sympathies,' Lansing said, somewhat unexpectedly. He took a deep breath. 'Well, the night is still young. Anyone fancy a game of billiards?'

PRICE AND EDITH retired. Colson, weary with strain, followed them. Lansing and Ryder went off to play billiards. Mrs Vane sat down at the table beside the window and began to finish Lady Maud's game of patience. Fairbairn sat too, staring into the fire. Gallagher watched him for a moment, and turned as Makarian tapped him on the shoulder. 'A word,' said the latter.

They walked out into the hall. 'What is it?' asked Gallagher.

'As we were leaving the library, Mr Tovey came up alongside me. He said he was interested to hear me talk about Armenia, and he knew some people who might be able to help me.'

'Did he say which people?'

'Some people in Russia. That's all he said.'

A suspicion which had been growing in Gallagher's mind suddenly hardened. 'Tovey is a transport officer in the Royal Navy. What has he to do with Russia?'

'I know.' Their eyes met. 'Curious, isn't it?' Makarian said.

'Did you take him up on the offer?'

'We have a saying in Armenia, Pat. Never buy a fish unless you first know the fisherman.'

Gallagher paused. 'You're negotiating with the Russians already, aren't you? The opposition, I mean. You'll provide money to help them overthrow the Tsar, they'll help you to create an independent Armenia.'

'Of course.'

'Who are you talking to? The Kadets?'

'Those fools? No, of course not. We're talking to the Bolsheviks, Pat. You must have guessed,' Makarian added.

'Don't tell your father-in-law. He regards the Bolsheviks as the spawn of the devil.'

'Perhaps they are. Perhaps we all are. But Russia has been blown wide open, Pat. Grigori Rasputin was a man of the people, and the aristocrats murdered him. The people will not forgive that. Revolution is coming, and I mean *real* revolution, not just some palace coup.'

'And Russia will be knocked out of the war,' Gallagher said slowly.

'Very probably. But there is nothing you or I can do about that, Pat. All we can do is make the best of the situation. I told you, I would make a pact with the devil himself if it will save Armenia.'

'Faustian bargains,' Gallagher said. 'That's what everyone is making these days. That thing about the fish. Is that really an old Armenian proverb?'

'No. But I learned long ago that dubious moral arguments are much more easily accepted when disguised as folk wisdom.' Makarian clapped him on the shoulder. 'I must see that Penelope is all right. Goodnight, Pat.'

BACK IN THE drawing room Gallagher stopped and looked down at Fairbairn. 'Have you seen Tovey?'

'Not since the zeppelins came. Perhaps he has gone to bed.' Fairbairn rose heavily to his feet. 'As shall I.'

'I want to talk to you,' Gallagher said.

'I'm sure you do. It can wait until morning.'

'Very well,' said Gallagher. 'If that is how you want to play it.'

Fairbairn departed without a word. Gallagher walked over to Mrs Vane, who was just finishing the game of patience. 'I thought you weren't fond of cards,' Gallagher said.

'I'm not. But I needed an occupation while I worked

something through.' She rubbed her bare arms, which were covered in goosebumps. 'Let's go to the music room.'

In the music room she sat down on the piano bench and began to play through the Brahms ballade again. The music came more easily this time, and there were only a few pauses. 'I have a theory about the stationery cupboard,' she said. 'Do you want to hear it?'

The music covered the sound of their voices. 'Of course,' Gallagher said.

'When you searched the room, did you find cracks on the left-hand wall?'

'Yes. There had once been a door there, but when I pushed on the wall, nothing moved.'

Mrs Vane's eyebrows rose. 'Remember when I said that the room had once been a servants' pantry? That's where servants prepared the wine and grog that the Lords of the Admiralty consumed while plotting world dominion. There would have been a service door between the pantry and the boardroom, but when the pantry was closed, the door was plastered over.'

'Go on,' Gallagher said.

'You'll recall too that I was in the boardroom not long ago, and saw a large sideboard on the wall adjoining the stationery cupboard. The sideboard covered whatever traces of the door might remain. I think it would be a fairly simple matter for someone to shift the sideboard, cut through the plaster with a fine saw and re-open the door. That would give our thief, the one who is stealing documents, a second door into the stationery cupboard. When he left the room, all he had to do was move the shelves to cover the door inside the stationery cupboard, close the door, pull the sideboard back into place on the boardroom side, and the door itself would be invisible. And the cupboard would be an excellent place to hide the stolen documents until they could be passed on to the Dreamer.'

Gallagher nodded. 'Where better to hide papers than with a lot of other paper?'

'Exactly,' said Mrs Vane. 'Of course, that only solves one problem. The boardroom is always kept locked too. So, we still have to work out how the killer got into the boardroom in the first place.'

Gallagher smiled a little. 'How are you going to do that?'

'Who? Me?'

'It's your idea,' Gallagher said. 'Run with it.'

She played another couple of bars. 'I am flattered that you should take me seriously,' she said finally.

'Jonquil Vane, you are intelligent, perceptive and intuitive. You have the makings of a very fine intelligence officer. Colonel Kell thinks so too. The only person who doesn't yet believe it is you.'

'I find it very hard to believe in myself,' she said quietly. 'As do you.'

The silence this time was longer. The music continued softly, her fingers light on the keys. 'I have no joy of this contract tonight,' Gallagher said finally. 'It is too rash, too unadvised, too sudden. Too like the lightning.'

The music stopped and she turned to him. 'Those are Juliet's words,' she said.

'Yes. I first heard them spoken by an actress named Roxanne Felix.'

'I've heard of her,' said Mrs Vane. 'She was killed, wasn't she?'

'Ten years ago. I could have prevented it, and I failed.'

'Will you tell me what happened? If you don't want to, I will understand.'

Gallagher spread his hands, examining his fingernails one by one. 'She was travelling to New York on board the *Lusitania*,' he said finally. 'I was in charge of the ship's security. She was murdered one night in her cabin, shot dead. I turned the ship upside down, looking for her killer, but I never found a suspect, or even a motive. It was the greatest failure of my professional career, and the greatest tragedy.'

A clock ticked in the silence. 'I'm sorry', she said finally.

'The whole thing was senseless,' Gallagher said. 'Literally, nothing at all made sense. Who would want to kill a beautiful young actress? And why? I don't know, I still don't know, and that is the hell of it. She was someone I knew well, someone I cared about very deeply, who I will never replace in my life, and I could not protect her. That tears at my soul.'

'Were you in love with her?' Mrs Vane asked quietly.

'It's more complicated than that,' said Gallagher.

'I thought it probably would be. You're not the sort of man who makes life easy for himself, are you?'

'I come by that naturally,' Gallagher said. 'And now, may we please change the subject?'

This is probably not the time or place for such a conversation, Mrs Vane thought. She dismissed the thought and plunged in. 'Very well. What happened between you and your mother?'

'My mother . . .' Gallagher sighed, and sat down. 'I should probably have told you this before, when we started to work together. My mother was a debutante, and expected to marry well. Instead, she met my father, an officer in the merchant navy and, in the eyes of her family, a completely unsuitable match. One thing led to another, and they went off to Gretna Green.'

'Ah,' said Mrs Vane.

'Her family found her and brought her back, and forced her to sign a divorce. To be honest, I don't think they had to push very hard, as I suspect she was already regretting her decision.

They found her a nice, understanding husband in the form of Sir John Borden, baronet, rising star in the Conservative Party, thoroughly sound chap. Everything worked out fine for her. The only problem was me. I was a living reminder of her reckless past, and she couldn't stand the sight of me. I was raised by a nanny, and at the earliest possible moment packed off to boarding school.'

Mrs Vane waited. 'I hated school,' Gallagher said. 'I ran away at every opportunity. Each time I managed to get a little further, and each time when I was brought back, the headmaster added a few more strokes of the cane. Eventually I got as far as Portsmouth, where I joined the Royal Marines as a boy bugler. When I was old enough, I enlisted as a rifleman.'

'Why did you leave the marines?'

'In 1900 we were sent to Peking, to relieve the siege of the foreign legations by the Boxers. When the fighting was over, my comrades in arms went wild, looting, killing civilians at random. One of my platoon, a man I had thought of as a good soldier, shot a woman in the back and left her to die in the street. As soon as I could, I handed in my uniform. I joined Special Branch for a while, but resigned again when something happened in Ireland that I couldn't stomach, and took a job with Cunard.'

'On the *Lusitania*.'

'Yes. That was where I met Roxanne. That was where she died. And now, all I have of her is at the bottom of the sea.'

'I'll tell you something you don't know,' she said after a moment. 'My mother was also on the *Lusitania*'s final voyage.'

She saw the shock in his face. 'No,' he said. 'I didn't know.'

'The ninth of May, 1915,' she said. 'At around eleven o'clock in the morning a telegram arrived from the War Office informing me that my husband had been killed at Cape Helles, on the first day of the battle of Gallipoli. Just over two hours later another telegram arrived from Cunard, saying that my mother's body had been recovered and identified. All I can remember is how paralysed I felt. I was like a fly trapped in amber.'

Gallagher looked down at his hands again. 'My God,' he said quietly. 'I spend so much time wallowing in my own misery that I forget the horrors other people have to live with. Jonquil, I am truly sorry.'

'There is no need to be sorry,' she said. 'My husband and my mother are both at peace. You, on the other hand, are not.'

'I wish I had your stoicism.'

'That's the second time someone has said that to me. I carry on living because I have no choice. Is that stoicism? I don't know, perhaps it is. All I know is that when my own time comes, I will go gladly.'

'Yes,' he said, still looking at his hands. 'Me too.'

The silence ran on for some time. The conversation had become much more deeply personal than either of them had intended, and both struggled to resolve it. In the end it was Mrs Vane who reached for the relative safety of the present. 'There's nothing in Price's file to suggest that he has done any-thing wrong,' she said. She paused. 'I hope that is true. I have become quite fond of his wife, and I should hate to do anything to hurt her.'

'Don't let sentiment cloud your judgement,' Gallagher said.

Mrs Vane rose to her feet and stood for a moment, looking down at him. 'Yes,' she said. 'I could say the same about you.'

14

'GOOD MORNING, YOU two,' Mrs Vane said brightly. 'My goodness, that wind is bitter, isn't it?'

Price and Edith were standing on the wisteria bridge, looking out across the fields towards the Medway. Mrs Vane, who had been walking purposefully around the lakeside path, stopped and joined them. The wind, though not strong, was full of cold moisture and sharp as the edge of a razor. Clouds hung low and ragged overhead, with no hint of the sun.

'We came out to get some fresh air,' said Edith. 'I think we got more than we bargained for.'

'I've seen worse,' Price said. 'Out in the North Sea in winter we had to chip ice off the guns, and use steam hoses to clear the decks.'

Mrs Vane smiled a little. 'Do you miss being at sea?'

'Very much so,' said Price. 'That's why I joined the navy in the first place, to go to sea. I love it. Even during the most dangerous storms there is something beautiful about the sea. Perhaps the danger is part of the attraction.'

I've never heard him more eloquent, thought Mrs Vane. *Perhaps he feels better in the mornings. Or perhaps his wife brings out the best in him.* Aloud she said, 'I've never been much of a sailor, but I've always felt I was missing something. Perhaps in the next life.'

'Do you believe in an afterlife?' Edith asked, almost eagerly.

'Why not? None of us knows for certain. Therefore it doesn't really matter what we believe.'

'I can't bring myself to believe it,' said Price. 'I reckon we all just return to the dust, we and all our works. Even civilization itself will crumble in time.'

Edith smiled. 'But new civilizations will arise from the ruins of the old. They always do.'

'I love your optimism,' Mrs Vane said. 'Come, this is simply too cold. Let us go in for breakfast.'

THE BREAKFAST ROOM was quiet. Nathalie Fairbairn did not appear, nor did Lady Maud. Tovey sat at one end of the table, eating kedgeree and talking to no one.

Lansing, carrying a plate loaded with devilled kidneys and bacon, sat down beside Tovey. 'Any luck with the Flying Corps, Sir John?' he asked.

'I sent a message to the aerodrome at Chiddingstone Causeway earlier this morning,' Borden said. 'There are no scouts available, but the commandant at Biggin Hill thinks he can spare a couple of B.E.12s. They will arrive some time next week.'

Lansing snorted. 'We'll be gone by then. Well, it looks like it's set to rain. Maybe they won't come back tonight.'

'Zeppelins can fly through rain,' said Ryder, buttering a piece of toast. 'They cope with it better than our scouts do. It's only high winds that are dangerous to them.'

'You know something about zeppelins?' Makarian enquired politely.

'I made a study of them when I was with the embassy in Berlin. I even befriended the commander of the zeppelin fleet, Kapitän Peter Strasser. He gave me a great deal of information that he certainly shouldn't have. I wrote a report for their lord-ships at the Admiralty, recommending that we develop our own fleet of airships. Unsurprisingly, I never heard another word.'

Colson looked at him. 'Now that you are in the naval plan-ning division, perhaps you can revive the idea,' he said cuttingly. 'Put it before your friend Admiral Jellicoe.'

Lansing chuckled. 'Is that sour grapes I hear, Commander? You miss out on a promotion at some point? Still, not to worry. You're a lot richer than Captain Ryder, that must count for something.'

'A gentleman doesn't talk about money, Lansing.'

'Ah, yes, that old chestnut,' Lansing said. 'They don't talk about it because they don't like thinking about where it comes from. In your family's case it came from women's undergar-ments, didn't it? That's where your old man made his money.'

Colson stiffened. 'Leave my family out of this.'

'What was the name of the firm?' Lansing asked. 'Colson's Corsets, that was it. The old boy made a mint, built himself a big house in Berkshire and married into an old family, all from manufacturing tit-squeezers.'

Penelope Makarian gasped. Edith, sitting beside her, put a hand over her mouth, her face shocked, her eyes hilarious. Sur-prisingly, it was Price who spoke first. 'You are a boor, Lansing,' he said. 'A boor and a cad. I am surprised that our host puts up with you.'

Borden had gone red. Gallagher watched the struggle in his face: wanting to rebuke Lansing on the one hand, know-ing that he desperately needed the oilman's good will on the other. Lansing raised one hand. 'All right, maybe I used some choice language, and I apologize. But I think I'm owed a little revenge. Commander Colson has been doing his best to under-cut me ever since I arrived in this country. He's trying to stop me investing in the Middle East because he wants his chums in Anglo-Persian to have the oilfields instead. Ain't that right, Commander?'

Colson said nothing. 'I'll take silence as assent,' Lansing said. 'I'll give you fair warning, Commander. Stop interfering with my plans. If you don't, I'll do you harm. You have my word on that.'

'I don't think this is suitable conversation for the breakfast table,' Borden said finally. 'Mr Lansing, if you and Commander Colson have a dispute, perhaps you could settle it in private.'

'There's no dispute,' Lansing said. 'There are facts, plain and simple. But out of deference to you, Sir John, I'll cease and desist. For now.'

The rest of the meal was consumed in silence.

At the end of breakfast, Gallagher rose and went up to his mother's room, and knocked at the door. Phoebe her maid, red-eyed and hollow-cheeked, admitted him without speaking.

Lady Maud was in her dressing room, fully dressed, pulling on a pair of gloves in preparation for going to church. A breakfast tray with an uneaten boiled egg sat on a table by the window. Grey light filled the park outside.

'I came to see how you are feeling,' Gallagher said.

'Thank you for your concern,' Lady Maud said. Her voice was calm, but her face was full of strain. 'I am fully recovered, as you see.'

The first time the zeppelins came she had apologized, unnecessarily, for being afraid. Now, she was denying that anything had happened. 'There is no shame in showing fear,' Gallagher said.

'We will not talk of this now,' said Lady Maud.

'Why not?' Gallagher demanded suddenly.

'Because it is not the right time.'

Their eyes met for a moment, his puzzled, hers challenging. 'Last night, Sir John explained to me the true nature of your work,' she said. 'I am sorry that you did not feel you could confide in me. I am sorry also that you have dragged Mrs Vane into your work. She deserves better.'

There was no point in trying to explain that Mrs Vane had volunteered. Gallagher bowed his head. 'I am glad to see you are well,' he said, and turned away to the door. Outside in the corridor he stopped, resting his forehead against the wall and fighting down his emotions. *I should not have come here*, he thought. *It only harms both of us.*

In the hall he found Fairbairn taking his overcoat down from its peg. 'We need to talk,' Gallagher said abruptly. 'Now.'

'I am about to go to church.'

'This won't take long.' Gallagher walked into the drawing room. Fairbairn followed him, nervously twirling the ends of his waxed moustache.

'I imagine you are in a difficult position,' Gallagher said. 'Lansing and Sir John are lobbying you to break the government's agreement with Anglo-Persian and hand over the oil concession, while Colson is pressing you to force the government to keep its promises.'

'You are mistaken,' Fairbairn said stiffly. 'There is no pressure at all. Commander Colson has his personal views, but he no longer has the support of his own board.'

Gallagher stared at him. 'Winston Churchill gets his way. The oilfields go to Lansing. Did the Foreign Secretary overrule you?'

'No,' Fairbairn said. 'I myself had a change of heart. I believe this is the right thing to do.'

Gallagher considered this. 'How is your wife this morning?' he asked.

'Much as she always is.'

'Tell me about her. I met her only a couple of times in Boston, and I don't know her well. I'd like to hear more.'

'About Nathalie?' Fairbairn was surprised. 'Why do you want to know about her? I thought you were going to question *me*.'

Gallagher ignored this. 'Where and when did you meet her?'

'London, in the summer of 1908. My family supported a school for poor children, and she was hired as a teacher there. I found her captivating.' Fairbairn paused, choosing his words. 'I was under some pressure from my family to marry, and she needed a husband.'

'Why?'

'The usual reason. She had been in a relationship with a real blackguard, some trades union organizer. A swine, like all communists. He got her with child and left her. She had just discovered she was pregnant when we met, and she needed a father for the child.'

Gallagher went still. 'What happened?' he asked quietly.

Fairbairn studied his hands for a moment. When he spoke, his rich voice was layered with sorrow. 'We named her Louisa. She contracted whooping cough when she was about a year old. She is buried in Brompton Cemetery, with a little white headstone. I visit her from time to time, when I can.'

And many knots unravelled by the road, but not the knot of human death and fate. 'I am very sorry,' Gallagher said after a moment.

'Yes. So am I. Things were all right between us, up until then. After the child died she went to pieces. Became very bitter, turned against the world. As you see her now.'

'What do you know about her background?'

'Not much. She didn't talk much about her childhood, but

I gather it was unhappy. Her father was a riveter who worked at John Brown's yard in Clydebank. Bolshevik through and through, a real agitator. He named Nathalie after one of the socialist leaders of the Paris Commune. Her mother was a teacher, I think.'

'Does Nathalie herself hold political views?' Gallagher asked.

'She flirted with socialism when she was younger, but the affair with the blackguard put paid to that. She has never professed any interest in politics, at least in my hearing.'

'Which I suppose could explain why she had no qualms about sleeping with the German ambassador. Except, she claims she didn't know who he was.'

Fairbairn examined his hands again. 'She knew who he was,' he said finally, and his rich voice was shaking a little. 'I begged her to stop. But . . . Nathalie has a destructive streak. If you know what I mean.'

'I do,' said Gallagher, 'but there's more to it than that, isn't there? The meeting with Bernstorff on your yacht, the *Chasseur*. You told me in Boston that it was an ambush, that you weren't expecting Bernstorff, but that's not true, is it? Nathalie helped to arrange the meeting. She and Sadie Lansing brought you all together: you, Bernstorff, Nabokov the Kadet leader, and Lansing.'

'Yes,' Fairbairn said. He looked directly at Gallagher. 'What do you want to know?'

'Were you acting on orders from London?'

'Unofficially, yes. We knew President Wilson was trying to persuade Germany to enter into peace talks, and Bernstorff was the conduit for messages between Wilson and Berlin. My task was to sound Bernstorff out and see how serious the Germans were about making peace. You know what it was like last summer, the Allies were losing a hell of a lot of men at the

Somme and Verdun, but so were the Germans. If we really could negotiate a peace with honour, why not?'

'And you enlisted Nathalie to help you pass messages to Bernstorff.'

'I didn't whore my wife out, if that is what you mean,' Fairbairn said sharply. 'She was already sleeping with him, so I asked if she would help. She was very willing. Unusually so, in fact.'

'You found this surprising,' said Gallagher.

'I did, yes.'

'And the meeting on the yacht? What was the purpose of that?'

'Nathalie said that Bernstorff was very much interested in talking to the British, and wanted to meet me. I thought this might be an opportunity to learn more, and arranged the party on the *Chasseur*. Unfortunately, Sadie Lansing showed up with her husband, and Bernstorff spent most of the time talking to Lansing instead. Apart from the handshake, we exchanged only a few words.'

Gallagher shook his head. 'That's not true. We have other photographs of the meeting, you know. Frank Warren stole them from his sister and sold them to a journalist. Now, tell me what you discussed with Bernstorff.'

Fairbairn stared at him. 'Frank sold the photographs?'

'He did.'

The other man's shoulders slumped a little. He stared at his hands. 'Bernstorff was arrogant,' he said finally. 'He said that Russia would collapse, America would not come to our aid, and Britain would be forced to sue for peace. I brought Nabokov in to try to convince Bernstorff that even if the Tsar was forced to abdicate, the Kadets and their allies would continue to prosecute the war. He was impressed by that argument, but said that even if the Kadets could take power, he doubted if they could hold it. Nabokov tried to convince him, but he said he had heard enough, and went off to talk to Lansing. The truth is, the Germans have never been serious about peace, but the Americans refuse to see it. They still think a negotiated peace is possible.'

Gallagher stood for a moment, studying Fairbairn, considering his words. 'Did you know Frank Warren had come to London?' he asked finally.

Fairbairn blinked. 'No, I didn't. What's he doing there?'

'Did he contact you?'

'No. We . . . didn't part on the best of terms. He went a little peculiar after his sister died. Became very moody, hard to get along with, and then one day he just disappeared. Is he still in London?'

'He is dead,' Gallagher said.

'*What?*' Fairbairn was shocked, his mouth open, his ruddy face turning pale except for red burning spots on his cheeks. 'When did it happen?'

'A few days ago.'

'Oh, Frank,' said Fairbairn, and the sorrow was back in his voice. 'Oh, dear God . . . I know things ended badly between us, but there was a time . . . Ah, God. It's too soon, Frank, too soon.

Alas, that spring should vanish with the rose,
That youth's sweet-scented manuscript should close,
The nightingale that in the branches sang,
Ah, whence, and whither flown again, who knows?

Oh, my boy, my boy. Why did it have to end like this?'

'You were close to him,' Gallagher said.

Fairbairn's eyes were wet. 'Isn't it obvious?'

'You just quoted from the *Rubaiyat of Omar Khayyam*.' Gallagher's voice was soft. 'May I ask why?'

'It was Frank's favourite poem. He carried a copy with him, everywhere he went. He wasn't just a wastrel, you know, he had a fine soul, loved poetry, music . . .' Fairbairn broke down, covering his face with his hands. His voice was a quiet howl of despair. 'Oh, Frank, my poor boy! My poor boy!'

Gallagher felt suddenly sick. 'I have to ask this,' he said. 'God knows I don't want to, but I must. Did you know Frank was also working for the Germans?'

Fairbairn lowered his hands. His whole body had gone limp, everything but his moustache; once, a pompous affectation, but now simply tragic. 'If I had ever suspected such a thing of Frank, I would have ceased all contact with him,' he said. He closed his eyes for a moment. 'God, this is a nightmare. I cannot believe it of Frank. Are you certain, Gallagher?'

'Yes,' said Gallagher. 'He was found with a highly secret document in his pocket, a telegram that we think he stole from the naval intelligence division. Do you know anything about this?'

'No,' Fairbairn said dully.

Gallagher coughed, covering his mouth. 'I am truly sorry, but there is one other thing I must ask you. That other line from the *Rubaiyat*, the hunter of the east. I asked you at Aquinnah if you knew why Sadie Lansing said you would know what it means.'

'I didn't know. I still don't. My God, I am beginning to question whether I actually know *anything*.' Fairbairn wiped his eyes. 'It feels like everything good in the world has gone.'

'"The hunter of the east" referred to you. Your boat was called the *Chasseur*, was she not? The hunter? I think Sadie Lansing and her colleagues were using a book code, probably based on the *Rubaiyat*. Hunter of the east was their code for you.'

'Why did they have a code for me?'

'I suspect the Germans were keeping you under surveillance, and passing messages about you.' Gallagher hesitated. 'I'm afraid it is entirely likely that Frank Warren was spying on you.'

'I had already worked that out. Forgive me, Gallagher, but I really need to be alone.'

Mrs Vane was standing in the hall when Gallagher emerged from the drawing room. She raised her eyebrows. Gallagher shook his head. 'God, I hate this job,' he said.

'I know. I'm sorry you had to do that.'

'Not half as sorry as I am. We pose as the forces of righteousness, don't we? We're on the side of good, standing against evil. Where in the laws of war does it say that we must harm the innocent to get what we want?' Gallagher paused. 'Don't worry, I'm not expecting you to answer that. I must go and meet Rintelen at the Rose and Crown. Are you off to church?'

Mrs Vane shook her head. 'I am about to feel a headache coming on. I shall remain behind.'

'Be careful,' Gallagher said.

She looked at him quietly. 'You too.'

SUNDAY, 4 FEBRUARY 1917

9.30 A.M.

A big black Daimler stood parked outside the Rose and Crown in Tonbridge. Gallagher recognized the man sitting behind the wheel and tapped on the window.

'Good morning, sir,' the driver said. 'They're waiting for you, as you asked.'

'Thank you. Is everything arranged for tonight?'

'Yes, sir. We'll be in position.'

Gallagher nodded. Entering the hotel, he climbed the stairs to Room 6. Two men stood outside the door, big men with guns bulging in the pockets of their overcoats; they nodded and saluted, and one of them opened the door for him. Inside the room were four men, two more British secret service agents and Agent Joe Flynn of the United States Secret Service, whom Gallagher had first met at Aquinnah. Flynn nodded in greeting.

The fourth man was tall with a long face and a receding hairline, dressed in a tweed suit with fraying cuffs and a shirt with no collar, seated in front of a small mahogany table. A cigarette smouldered in an ashtray in front of him. Dark, cautious eyes watched Gallagher enter and sit down opposite him.

'Good morning, Kapitän von Rintelen,' Gallagher said.

Franz von Rintelen, officer in the Nachrichten-Abteilung, the German naval intelligence service, picked up the cigarette and took a long drag, blowing out smoke. Gallagher coughed.

'You are in poor health?' Rintelen asked. His English was excellent, with a trace of an American accent.

'About the same,' said Gallagher.

'What a pity. I had hoped to see you in terminal decline.'

'There's still time,' Gallagher said. 'Are they treating you well at Donington?'

Rintelen ignored the question. 'Let us skip the preliminaries, shall we? Have you come to ask me more questions about the *Lusitania*?'

Gallagher shook his head. 'Today I want to talk about German spy rings in America. I know a fair amount already, but there are some details I need you to fill in.'

Rintelen took another drag on the cigarette. 'I have already told you everything I know.'

'Of course you haven't. You are a professional intelligence

officer, Herr Kapitän, and you were trained in how to deal with interrogation. Part of the strategy is, always hold something back. Keep your interrogators guessing, keep them coming back for more.'

'If I do tell you everything I know, you will hand me over to *him*.' Rintelen pointed towards Flynn, standing next to the wardrobe with his hands thrust into his pockets. 'The Americans want to extradite me, do they not? And uncomfortable though life at Donington prison camp is, I think I prefer it to the prospect of an American penitentiary.'

'People were killed in the Black Tom bombing,' Flynn said. His face was as impassive as ever. 'Somebody has to pay.'

'I do not know what you are talking about.'

Gallagher held up a hand. 'So long as you cooperate, I will not hand you over to the Americans. A colleague of yours known as der Träumer recruited a ring of agents in Boston, one of whom was Mrs Sadie Lansing. Her brother, Frank Warren, was another. Did you know about this ring?'

'I did. It was established before I arrived in America. My operations were conducted mostly in New York, but we collaborated with our Boston friends from time to time.'

'Was Mrs Nathalie Fairbairn also a member of this ring?'

Rintelen smiled a little. 'She did not work for us, no.'

'And Lily Sparrow?'

Rintelen reached for the cigarette again. Gallagher looked at Flynn. 'We can have him aboard the next ship for America, if you like.'

'Sounds good to me,' said Flynn.

Rintelen blew out more spoke. 'Lily Sparrow was a member of the ring,' he said. 'When der Träumer was reassigned, she became its leader. Our service does not often appoint women to positions of high rank, but she was an excellent agent. I respected her.'

'Tell me more about her.'

'Her family are German immigrants from the Schwarzwald. Their real name is Spatz, which translates as sparrow. Lily started using the English version of her name when the war broke out, to avoid attracting attention from the authorities. She was an agent for at least a year before the start of the war. I knew her as an idealist, a true believer in the Fatherland.'

Rintelen sounded like he himself did not believe in much of anything, Gallagher thought. He may have had ideals once, but prison camp had probably beaten them out of him. 'Would you say she is ruthless?' he asked.

'Ruthless does not begin to describe her. She will do anything, so long as she believes it is in the service of her country.'

'Why did Mrs Lansing and her brother agree to serve Germany?'

'Money. Mrs Lansing was rich, but her tastes outran her bank account. She was a good asset, too. She pulled off a considerable coup, bringing her husband to talk to Bernstorff and reach an agreement over the oil. Berlin was most pleased.'

'An agreement was concluded?'

'Oh, yes. Mr Lansing and his friends invested in the Baghdad railway, and our foreign office promised that the Ottoman government would hand over the oilfields to Germany. The concession would then go to Lansing.'

'What about Mrs Lansing's brother?' Gallagher asked.

'I thought he was a danger to us, and I told Lily to cut him loose, but she said he was too valuable. He had important connections in your diplomatic service.'

'Did you ever have any contact with a man named Paul

Vasiliev? He is British, but we think he is working with the Kadets.'

Rintelen stubbed out the cigarette and held out his hand. One of the secret service men took out a cigarette case and a lighter, lit a fresh cigarette and handed it to the captain. Rintelen took another long drag and blew a cloud of smoke towards the ceiling. 'I know of Vasiliev,' he said. 'I never had dealings with him, though. He left America before I arrived. You are correct, he was an agent of the Kadets, but at some point he jumped ship to the Bolsheviks.'

Suddenly, a few things started to make sense. 'Vasiliev was also Sadie Lansing's lover before the war. Were you aware of that?'

Rintelen shook his head. 'As I say, it was before my time.'

'Were you yourself in contact with the Bolsheviks in America?'

'Of course. We used them to stir up labour unrest in munitions factories and on the docks, both in America and in Russia. They were very effective.'

'Do you know the identity of der Träumer?' Gallagher asked.

'He is who he is,' Rintelen said enigmatically.

'Tell me his name, Herr Kapitän.'

Rintelen smiled. 'That is enough for one day. Come back another time if you want more.'

Gallagher stood up. 'A moment,' Rintelen said. 'I have a question for you. Are the British intercepting German wireless messages?'

'What makes you think that we might be?'

'I booked passage to Europe under a false name, disguised as a Swiss citizen, on a neutral ship, and yet your navy knew unerringly where to find the liner on which I was travelling. My orders from Germany were transmitted by wireless signal.

The only way you could have found me was by intercepting that signal and reading it.'

'Sorry to disappoint you,' Gallagher said. 'Our ships were looking for contraband cargo that might be destined for Germany. Finding you on board was a stroke of good fortune. For us, of course, not for you.'

'I don't believe you,' Rintelen said.

'Well, there you are,' Gallagher said. 'Thank you for your time, Herr Kapitän. Have a safe journey back to Donington. I don't imagine we shall meet again.'

Rintelen leaned back in his chair. 'I wouldn't be too sure of that,' he said.

'And why is that?'

'I will tell you one more thing,' said Rintelen. 'We have agents in the Royal Navy. The plan was put in motion at the start of the war. By now, they are probably deep inside the Admiralty. You see, I am not the only one who suspects you are trying to read our wireless messages, Herr Gallagher. Some of my fellow agents believe this too. You think you have been very clever in arresting me, but your own security has also been compromised. Think on that, and let me know if you wish to speak to me again.'

JOE FLYNN FOLLOWED Gallagher downstairs and out into the street. The car was still waiting at the kerb. 'You didn't press him about the Dreamer's identity,' Flynn said.

'I don't think he knows. It's not surprising. The Dreamer is obsessive about secrecy.'

'If it was me, I'd put thumbscrews on the son of a bitch. I'd have him singing like a nightingale.'

Gallagher smiled. 'And you wonder why he doesn't want to go back to America.'

'I want the Dreamer just as much as you do, Pat. I want him put out of business.'

'That's exactly what we're hoping to do. Have your people been able to find Lily Sparrow?'

'No luck yet. It turns out she's been gone for several months. According to the Boston cops, that art gallery where she worked got shut down for selling forged pictures. Lily left soon after that, telling her neighbours she was moving to New York. We'll keep looking.'

Flynn paused. 'I did what you asked,' he said. 'I put in one of my freelancers to stir the pot.'

'And the pot has been well and truly stirred. Frank Warren has turned up dead. Killed the same way as his sister.'

Flynn rarely registered emotion, but he was startled now. 'Warren? I didn't even know he was in the country.'

'Neither did we. God knows how he got here.'

'Low-lifes like him always find some way of crawling under the fence,' Flynn said. 'We'll try to trace his movements. What are you fellows going to do about that telegram?'

'Nothing, until we know more about what's going on. We thought Vasiliev was working for the Kadets, but it was hard to see what interest they would have in the telegram. But if he really is a Bolshevik agent, that changes things. When you see Colonel Kell, can you ask him to start a search for Vasiliev?'

Flynn nodded. 'The colonel asked me to pass on a couple of messages for you. You asked for a photo of Vasiliev, but they can't find one. There's nothing in any of the files.'

Gallagher sighed. 'Typical. What else?'

'A couple of days ago, you asked for information about one of your naval officers, a Lieutenant Charles Tovey.' Flynn rubbed his chin. 'They found Tovey in the river this morning, tangled up in a piece of rope at the foot of Charing Cross pier. His throat had been cut. The autopsy report suggests he's been dead for several days.'

'*God damn it!*' Gallagher slammed his fist into the palm of his other hand. 'He's been there all along! Right in front of my bloody eyes!'

'You still want a search for Vasiliev?' Flynn asked.

'No need,' Gallagher said grimly. 'I know exactly where he is.'

15

THE OTHERS HAD departed for church in Tudeley some time before: Borden, Penelope and Lady Maud in a dogcart, Colson, Ryder, the Prices and a silent Fairbairn on foot, all heavily muffled against the wind. The servants followed them. Nathalie Fairbairn remained in her room; Lansing and Makarian, neither of whom were church-goers, had taken guns and gone out to shoot. It had been agreed that, now that the police had searched the woods, it was safe to do so once more.

Once the house was quiet, Jonquil Vane went into the west wing and along the narrow passageway to the Prices' bedroom. The door was a little ajar. She pushed it open slowly, looking around. Everything was neat and tidy, as one might expect from a sailor and his wife. Carefully, she began to search the room. The wardrobe held a few suits and Price's evening jacket, a few very pretty gowns and some small clothes and stockings. A couple of bottles of scent stood on the dressing table, next to a woman's travelling case and a black leather Gladstone bag. Both were packed as if for departure.

She did all of the other things she had been trained to do, checking under the pillows and the mattress and under the bed, testing the floorboards. She found nothing. Turning back to the wardrobe, she checked the pockets of every garment. Again, there was nothing. She began to wonder if she was wrong. Perhaps the Prices were exactly what they seemed to be: a brave young officer who suffered from shell shock, and his pretty, bubbly wife. That they doted on each other was undeniable, but something about them rang false, like an out-of-tune key on a piano.

She turned to the fireplace. The grate was warm, a few coals glowing under a blanket of black ash. Someone had burned papers here, last night or early this morning. She picked up the fire tongs and prodded at the larger fragments of burnt paper, hoping something could be salvaged, but every piece dissolved into powder and fell among the coals.

She gazed again at the dressing table. The Gladstone bag was closed but not locked. Carefully, she lifted out the contents: a few more items of clothing, shirt collars and studs, something dark and hard that puzzled her at first until she pulled it out and saw that it was a wooden prosthetic hand. Of course, a person would need to have a spare . . . Beneath the hand was a silver case, not unlike a cigarette case but a bit larger. She pressed the stud on the front and the case opened with a little click. Inside, neatly lined up, were a silver and glass syringe with a long thin needle, a silk cord and a dozen vials of clear liquid. She studied these for a moment, and replaced everything in the bag as she had found it.

She was about to leave when the travelling case caught her eye. It was not large, but the leather base seemed unusually thick. Something whispered across the back of her neck. She opened it.

The case was full of more glass bottles, another hairbrush, jars of cosmetics. Wrapping a handkerchief around her fingers, she removed the contents. Around her the house was silent save for the wind hissing softly around the window.

She pressed her fingers down on the bottom of the travelling case, and was rewarded with another soft click. Lifting the bottom out, she found a thin compartment which contained three pieces of paper. One was a list of musicals currently on show in London's West End: *Pell-Mell, Vanity Fair, See-Saw, High Jinks*, with dates and times, all during the past three months. The second contained a series of phrases: *fire of spring, the lion and the lizard, tower of darkness, distant drum, the wild ass, dawn's left hand, hunter of the east, seventh gate, throne of Saturn*, each followed by a long series of very small printed numbers.

'Here is our book cipher,' Mrs Vane said softly. 'Or at least, part of it.'

The final item was a small white card. She turned it over and saw an eagle with spread wings bearing the Stars and Stripes, the seal of the United States government, and another badge with a five-pointed star. Underneath was a clear printed script:

THE BEARER OF THIS WARRANT IS
Agent 857
Mrs Edith Price
UNITED STATES SECRET SERVICE

'Well,' Mrs Vane said aloud, 'that changes things rather.'

She folded the papers carefully and replaced them in the bottom of the travelling case, pressing the base back into place. Quietly, she slipped out of the room, leaving the door ajar as she had found it. Walking down the corridor, she heard soft voices in Nathalie Fairbairn's room. One voice was Nathalie's; the other she could have sworn was Tovey, but they were speaking too quietly to be certain. Frowning, she went down to the music room to wait.

Sunday, 4 February 1917
10.48 a.m.

Nathalie Fairbairn propped herself up on one elbow, brushing her hair out of her eyes. 'Very nice,' she said, running her finger down the man's sweat-damp chest. 'This is what Sunday mornings should really be for. Not sitting in a damp church listening to dirges and superstitions.'

They were lying on the bed in Nathalie's room, listening to the cold wind whistle outside. Paul Vasiliev, the man posing as Charles Tovey, looked up at her. 'Do you really have no faith at all?'

'My mother did, once upon a time. My father beat it out of her.' She leaned over him, body rubbing against his, kissing his throat. 'Religion is the opium of the people, remember? We don't need it.'

Vasiliev was quiet for a moment. 'I'm worried, Nathalie,' he said.

'About what?' Her voice was sardonic. 'Your immortal soul?'

'Yes, if you want to know. I keep telling you, I'm not cut out for this.'

'That's because you were born with a silver spoon in your mouth. You've never known want or hardship. You've never gone hungry when the bosses cut your father's pay, or he had been beaten up by the police. Screw the afterlife. What happens here and now, that's where the pain is. That's why we have to keep up the fight.'

'I know, I know!' Vasiliev pushed her off and sat up abruptly. 'I'm sorry, Nathalie. I know I'm weak, but I really can't do this any longer. This is the end.'

Nathalie watched him. 'Seriously?' she said, a note of contempt in her voice.

'Yes, seriously. I've been squeezed from both sides for months now, and I can't take any more. If I'm caught, no one will bother with the police or a trial. They'll just shoot me on the spot. And I don't want to die.'

She sat up beside him, putting an arm around his bare shoulders. 'We're nearly at the end,' she said, her voice more conciliatory now. 'The telegram is here in the house, I'm certain of it. The cause demands this, Paul. And I need your help.'

'No, you don't. You're tough and resourceful, and you have a hard edge that I wish I had, but I don't. You'll find a way.'

Vasiliev stood up and reached for his clothes. Nathalie sprawled across the bed, watching him like a cat. 'That's it? You're really going, right now?'

'The others will be coming back from church any minute now, and I need to get away before they do. I'll walk into Tonbridge and pick up the car, and drive down to the coast. I'll wait for you there. That is, if . . .'

'All right,' she said calmly. 'I'll join you when I've finished here.'

'You will? You're certain?' The expression on his face was a mixture of apprehension and relief. 'God knows I wouldn't blame you if you didn't. I know I'm running out on you.'

'If you really are this fearful, you're a liability,' she said. 'I'm better off without you.' She smiled suddenly. 'Don't worry. You'll serve the cause in other ways.'

He looked worried again. 'You won't tell Ryder. Will you?'

She sat up at this. 'Do you think I'm a monster? Ryder is the enemy, Paul. Don't worry, I'll protect your secret.'

Vasiliev fastened his collar and pulled on his coat. 'You're being very good to me,' he said. 'More than I deserve.'

'I'm fond of you,' she said. 'And you're right. You probably don't deserve it.'

He bent and kissed her. 'Good luck. I'll be waiting for you.'

'You'd better be.' She watched Vasiliev go out, closing the door behind him, and her face hardened. She dressed quickly, calculating how long it would take him to reach the woods and how soon she could start after him without being spotted. She opened the drawer of the dressing table where she kept her revolver.

The drawer was empty.

Slowly, she closed the drawer again and sat down on the bed, staring at the wall and trying to think what this meant. In the house below, the front door opened and closed.

SUNDAY, 4 FEBRUARY 1917
11.07 A.M.

Jonquil Vane heard Gallagher's voice speaking to the footman. Walking through to the hall, she found him standing before the fire, warming his hands. 'I have news,' she said.

'So have I,' Gallagher said bleakly. 'You go first.'

In a few sentences she told him what she had found. Gallagher listened intently. 'The identification card,' he said at the end. 'Is it genuine?'

'Honestly, I have no idea. I have never seen an American Secret Service card. Don't forget, I've been in our service for less than a year.'

'It is possible,' Gallagher said. 'Flynn told me one of his agents was on hand, stirring the pot, as he put it. I wouldn't put it past him to send her into Hartlake Hall, to keep an eye on us.'

THE SPIES OF HARTLAKE HALL

'Wouldn't he tell you?'

Gallagher smiled without humour. 'Of course not, any more than we would tell him if the positions were reversed. We're a belligerent, they are neutral. It's entirely possible that Flynn sent in an agent because he wants to know more about the telegram himself. He's certainly interested in the Dreamer . . . What do you think about the list of theatrical performances? Meeting places, perhaps, or message drops?'

'One or the other,' Mrs Vane said. 'Who was she meeting, do you think? There was a long pause. 'What about Lansing?' she said suddenly. 'I'll bet *he* would like to know what's in the telegram.'

Gallagher's eyebrows rose. 'Lansing has given no sign that he is even aware of the telegram, but . . . the United States Secret Service reports to the Secretary of the Treasury, who just happens to be the son-in-law of Lansing's good friend President Wilson. So, yes. What you are suggesting is possible.'

Reaching for his handkerchief, he covered his mouth and coughed, long and hard. 'My apologies. That blasted wind. My own news, I'm afraid, is bleakly factual. Lieutenant Charles Tovey's body was pulled out of the Thames this morning.'

Her eyes widened. '*What?*'

'What, indeed. Tovey was killed so that Paul Vasiliev could steal his identity.'

'Vasiliev . . .' She shook her head, struggling to take it in. 'Do you think Captain Ryder knows about Tovey's killing?'

'Well,' said Gallagher. 'Once again, it will be interesting to find out, don't you think? Where is Vasiliev?'

'He went out a few minutes ago. He was in Nathalie Fairbairn's room for a long time, and then he came downstairs quite quickly and departed. He went down the road towards

Tonbridge . . .' Her eyes opened wide as she realized the implications. 'He's done a runner,' she said.

'If he has, he won't get far. Our people are on watch at the lodge, and they'll pick him up before he ever gets to town. We'll interrogate him, never fear, but right now the man who has some questions to answer is Captain Ryder.'

Sunday, 4 February 1917
11.15 a.m.

Watching from the windows of the library, Gallagher saw the church party return, the dogcart with its pony clip-clopping in harness, Ryder and Colson walking behind it and followed at a respectful distance by Platt the butler and the rest of the servants. There was no sign of the Prices, or Fairbairn. The servants peeled off to the kitchen entrance; the others entered through the front door and he heard them dispersing around the house. Someone began to play the piano in the music room, very well; that must be Makarian, returned from shooting. A shotgun banged in the distance; Lansing, still out in the woods.

The door opened and Captain Ryder entered the room, looking up in irritation at the thumping water pipes. Walking to a table at one end of the room, he picked up a copy of the *Sunday Times*. 'Gallagher. We missed you at church.'

'I had some business to attend to,' Gallagher said.

'Does this concern the investigation?'

It had begun to rain outside, and the windows were streaked with water. 'Yes,' Gallagher said. 'How well did you know Lieutenant Charles Tovey?'

Ryder turned abruptly. 'What do you mean, how well *did* I know him?'

'He's dead,' Gallagher said. His own voice was hard. 'Someone cut his throat.'

Carefully, Ryder laid down the newspaper. 'Ah,' he said slowly. 'That is unexpected . . . I am not sure what to say.'

'You could start by answering my question. How well did you know Tovey?'

'Middling well, I suppose. I spoke to him after a meeting with the director of naval ordnance, and he mentioned that he was planning to go away to the country this weekend and would be out of contact with the Admiralty. He was about the same height and build as Vasiliev, so I thought it would be easy for Vasiliev to impersonate him. And by good fortune, neither he nor Vasiliev had ever met Commander Colson.'

'Tell me exactly what happened,' Gallagher said.

'My orders from Admiral Jellicoe were that this should remain most secret but . . . yes, of course. You need to know. As I said earlier, I ordered Vasiliev to investigate the naval intelligence division for any signs of wrongdoing. He wasn't able to tell me very much at first, because Colson and his men are hot on security. Whatever they are concealing, they are doing it very well. Then I got wind of the telegram, the one from Zimmermann.'

'So you already knew about the telegram when I first mentioned it. Did Vasiliev tell you?'

'No,' Ryder said, 'that came from my American source. You remember, the one who told me about the bombers, the Gothas.'

'Very well. You ordered Vasiliev to find the telegram. Why?'

A sudden shower of rain splattered against the windows. 'Three reasons,' Ryder said. 'First of all, to determine whether it was genuine and not some sort of elaborate ruse by naval intelligence. Second, if it *was* genuine, to find out how they got hold of it. And third, to find out why they were keeping it secret.'

'Why not simply go to Admiral Hall and ask him?'

'Because we don't know whom we can trust!' Ryder snapped. 'I don't blame Blinker personally, of course not, he's a fine officer, but are his own staff telling him the truth? Or are men like Colson pulling the wool over his eyes? I don't like these methods, Gallagher, I detest being underhanded, but needs must! Do you understand?'

'Yes,' Gallagher said. 'Did you instruct Vasiliev to employ Frank Warren?'

'Of course not. I had never even heard of Warren.'

'Very well. What happened next?'

'Vasiliev was supposed to report to me as soon as he had found the telegram. When he failed to show up, I knew something had gone wrong. Early in the morning I went to Vasiliev's rooms and found him in a blue funk. He confessed to me that he didn't know how to open a safe, and so he had sent someone else in his stead, disguised as a navy officer. Unfortunately, his agent hadn't returned from the Admiralty. I was furious, I thought my entire plan had been ruined, and I hurried back to the Admiralty myself. There I learned that an officer's body had been discovered, and assumed it must be Vasiliev's agent. I realized there was an opportunity here, and as I said, I decided to use this as a chance to send Vasiliev underground.'

'You took one hell of a chance. What if Colson, or ourselves, had known Vasiliev and knew the body wasn't him?'

'As I told you, Vasiliev and Colson had never met. Given his service record, I also thought it unlikely that he had ever been interviewed by or involved with the secret service. The risks were present, but containable.'

'Why send Vasiliev underground?'

'To continue the investigation,' Ryder said sharply. 'I strongly believed, and I continue to believe, that someone at naval intelligence is in direct contact with their German counterparts. We know how successful the Nachrichten-Abteilung has been at setting up intelligence networks. I believe we are dealing with one of these networks right now, and in my view, the murder of this man Warren proves as much.'

Gallagher remembered Rintelen's words. 'You could be right,' he said. 'So, this deception is for Commander Colson's benefit. He is your principal suspect.'

Ryder looked briefly annoyed. 'That should surely be obvious by now.'

'I will have to ask Vasiliev to corroborate what you have said.'

Still irritated, Ryder moved towards the bell. 'I'll have the servants fetch him in now.'

Gallagher held up a hand. 'He went out for a walk earlier. We can talk to him when he returns. Can you think of any reason why the real Lieutenant Tovey was murdered? According to our files, he was quiet, reasonably efficient, had very few friends and kept himself to himself. There's no obvious reason why anyone would cut his throat and put him in the river.'

'Then he must have had secrets,' Ryder said. '*Someone* clearly wanted to kill him. You need to dig more deeply into his background.'

'We will,' Gallagher said. 'Let's get back to the telegram. What did your source in America tell you about it?'

'Only that its contents are explosive, so powerful that it could drag America into the war. If that is so, naval intelligence needs to disclose the contents at once, so we can pass them on to the Americans.'

'They don't know the contents, because the telegram hasn't been decrypted yet,' Gallagher said. 'Your American contacts may think they know what the message is, but they are guessing. Colson's people have the telegram, but they can't read it.'

'You said that before,' Ryder said sharply. 'I have to tell you that my source claims otherwise. My source was also quite certain that the telegram was intercepted by our wireless operators, but you claim it was acquired by other means. Who am I meant to believe?'

Gallagher looked around the room for a few moments, thinking. 'Very well,' he said. 'You have, finally, been straight with me, so I suppose I owe you some honesty in return. I am not saying you are wrong about Colson, by the way, you could very well be right. If you are, we really do have a bloody disaster on our hands. But so far as the telegram is concerned, you are reaching the right conclusions, but for the wrong reasons.'

'Explain,' Ryder said curtly.

Gallagher sighed. 'Our embassy in Washington has exaggerated our intelligence capabilities. They have done so for obvious reasons, to impress the Americans and show them how efficient we are. The truth is exactly as I told you yesterday. Our operators can hear German wireless chatter and pinpoint its source, but they can't decipher the German codes. It's like listening to a conversation in an unknown foreign language. We can hear them talking, but we can't understand a damned thing they are saying.'

'How do you know this?' Ryder demanded.

'Because I have already looked into this myself. I had a theory that some of our people had a hand in the sinking of the *Lusitania*, either by withholding information as you suggested, or perhaps even active collusion. There are, or were, people in government who would have been quite happy to see the ship go down and American lives lost, if this would change American public opinion and compel President Wilson to declare war. However, I found absolutely no evidence to support my theory. I can't explain the withholding of information about the U-boats, but I can confirm beyond doubt that we are not reading German messages. Not unless every single logbook since the start of the war has been doctored, and even then I would have seen evidence of the doctoring.'

'Very well,' Ryder said. 'Explain to me again how we acquired the telegram.'

'As I said, bribery, lies and theft. Our agents in Mexico City bribed an operator at the central telegraph office.'

'And you are certain that this telegram is genuine?'

'Good question,' Gallagher said. 'Zimmermann certainly *sent* a telegram to Mexico, and we *think* we have the text of it, but until it is decrypted, we can't be absolutely certain. For all we know, our telegram contains the ambassador's laundry list.'

Silence fell. 'So,' Ryder said abruptly. 'Where does this leave us?'

'Are you still satisfied that Vasiliev is loyal? That he wasn't working for anyone else?'

'To what are you referring?' Ryder asked. 'His affair with Sadie Lansing, or his connection to the Kadets?'

'Either, or both.'

'As I understand it, the Lansing affair ended when the war broke out. And given that the Kadets are likely to form the next government of Russia, and will therefore be our allies, I see no reason to question his loyalty. Do you?'

Gallagher thought back to the interview with Rintelen. *At*

some point he jumped ship to the Bolsheviks. A few more pieces fell into place.

'No,' he said. 'But I wanted to be sure.'

Sunday, 4 February 1917
11.34 a.m.

Outside, the rain continued. The smell of roasting beef drifted into the hall, accompanied by another odour which might have been poison gas but, from experience, was more likely to be over-boiled cabbage. Gallagher paced around the hall, waiting for Vasiliev to return. The Prices came in, Edith's face flushed with cold. 'We went for a lovely walk around the lake,' she said to Gallagher.

He forgot his anxiety for a moment and was briefly amused. 'A lovely walk? In this weather?'

'Oh, but walking in the rain is so romantic,' Edith said, beaming.

Gallagher smiled. He watched them go upstairs, his smile fading. As Jonquil Vane had said, Edith Price had always seemed too good to be true, and the news that she was an American agent went a long way towards explaining her presence at the house this weekend. He stood for a moment, irresolute, debating with himself about whether to confront her. The plans he had laid were delicate ones, and he did not want her interfering; but on the other hand, if Joe Flynn was running some scheme of his own . . . He needed Flynn onside, at least for the moment.

Fairbairn came in a few minutes later, shaking the water off his coat and hat and hanging them up. His face was heavy with unhappiness. 'Don't tell me you enjoy walking in the rain too,' Gallagher said.

'I remained in the church for a while after the service. I wanted some time for prayer and reflection.'

Warren had been a drunk, a thief and a spy, *but*, said Roxanne's voice, *who among us gets to choose whom we love? Did you choose? Did I?*

Gallagher studied him. 'You look exhausted,' he said. 'You should take some leave. Go to Tunbridge Wells, take the cure and get some rest.'

'It's too late for that,' Fairbairn said quietly. He walked through to the drawing room, and a few minutes later Gallagher heard the faint sound of a piano coming from the music room. It was Wagner, the 'Liebestod' from *Tristan and Isolde*, haunting and full of both beauty and sorrow.

Love and death, Gallagher thought. In his mind's eye he saw again the bodies in the streets of Peking, while gunfire crashed and rattled in the distance. More bodies, young men and boys, lying in pools of blood below a bullet-pocked wall in Ireland. The corpses in the water after *Lusitania* sank, bumping against his face. Roxanne, lifeless in the morgue, her skin cold to the touch. *Love and death.* He listened to the music for a long time, drowning quietly in his own memories while the rain continued to lash the windows and the wind keened around the house.

'SOMEONE HAS SEARCHED the room,' said Edith Price.

The scars on her husband's face were dull red in the dim light. 'How can you be certain?'

Edith emptied her travelling bag and lifted out the bottom. She held up the Secret Service identity card. 'This has been moved,' she said. 'So, they know.'

'I never understood why you didn't show that card to Gallagher in the first place,' Price said. 'It would have saved a lot of tiptoeing around.'

'I will show him, when the time is right,' said Edith. She pondered. 'It wasn't Gallagher who searched the room. He wouldn't make a mistake like putting the papers back in the wrong order. I wonder if it was Colson.'

'Why? What would he be looking for?'

'Trying to find out who we are, of course. Or more correctly, who I am. Colson is starting to get rattled, haven't you noticed? He thinks Ryder and Gallagher are closing in on him.'

Price pointed to the identity card. 'If Colson knows who you are, will he make an approach?'

'It will be interesting to see,' said Edith. 'It will depend on what game he is playing. And on who he really is.'

Price shifted his prosthetic hand a little, wincing. Edith watched him in concern. 'Are you in pain, darling?'

'Nothing I can't handle. Let me get this straight. Are you saying Colson might be der Träumer?'

'It's possible. He couldn't remove the telegram himself, not without arousing suspicion, but he could hire someone else. And we know he met Frank Warren.' Edith looked out at the grey fields and dark bare trees. 'Nearly midday,' she said. 'Not long to wait now.'

'What exactly are we waiting for?'

'You keep asking that, and I keep telling you, I don't know. All I have is the date and time. Nothing else.' She turned and put her arms around Price. 'I'm sorry, darling. I didn't mean to snap at you. Especially not at a time like this.'

He smiled down at her, caressing her hair. 'Don't worry. You can rely on me.'

Sunday, 4 February 1917
11.46 a.m.

Time passed. After a while Gallagher realized he could hear voices coming from the music room. One of them was Fairbairn's, suddenly raised in anger. Quietly, he walked into the drawing room and stopped near the door of the music room.

'I thought we had an arrangement,' Fairbairn was saying. 'I thought I could count on you, Nicholas. Now I find that you have gone behind my back! It's bad enough that you have stitched up a deal with that pig Lansing, but to find that you've also been talking to the Bolsheviks, and that you have dragged my wife into it! This is too much. I really thought we were friends.'

'Herbert, we are friends,' said Makarian. 'I admire you and respect you, you know that. But, as I have said many times, I will do anything to protect my people. I want to help the Armenians find a homeland, and I will give everything I have, including my entire fortune, to bring that about.'

'Everything?' Fairbairn said, and his voice was sharp. 'Including your wife's happiness?'

'Penelope will not be unhappy. She knows my mind on this. I do not keep secrets from her.'

There was a pause. 'No? There is nothing that you do not tell her?'

'I tell her what she wants to know, yes. If she does not wish to know, she does not ask.'

'That sounds like sophistry.'

'Perhaps it is. But you of all people do not have the right to criticize my marriage. Shall we talk about something else?'

'No,' Fairbairn said sharply. 'This is betrayal, Nicholas. You and I have finished talking. I do not think we shall see each other again.'

'If that is your wish.' The door opened and Makarian entered the drawing room. His eyes met Gallagher's for a moment, and he walked out into the hall. Gallagher followed him. 'What was that about?' he asked.

'Herbert is not happy with me. He is angry, which is understandable, but he will come around in time.'

'I didn't know you and he were friendly.'

Makarian smiled. 'We have known each other for some time. We share an interest in church brasses.'

Gallagher gazed at him. 'Be very careful, Nick,' he said. 'I may not show it, but I am fond of Penelope. If you hurt her, you will have me to reckon with.'

'Thank you for the warning,' Makarian said. 'And now, I invite you most cordially to mind your own business.'

'Who is your contact with the Bolsheviks? Vasiliev?'

'I do not know any Vasiliev.'

'Who, then?'

'Of course, this is the other reason why Herbert is upset,' Makarian said. 'My contact is a senior official in the Social Democratic Labour Party and a member of the Central Committee for Great Britain. I refer, of course, to his wife.'

Gallagher said nothing. Makarian smiled. 'Ah. I have surprised you.'

'Does Fairbairn know she is a Bolshevik?'

'Of course,' said Makarian. 'He has known all along.'

The front door of the house opened with a bang. Maisie the gamekeeper's granddaughter stood in the doorway, shotgun crooked over her arm, water dripping from the brim of her sou'wester. 'Sir, Pops says you need to come quick. There's another body been found in the woods. He says it's Mr Tovey, sir.'

16

GALLAGHER WALKED ACROSS the park through the rain, his mind dark with anger. *I should have spotted this*, he told himself. *I should have known that Vasiliev was being manipulated, and that he was in danger. I could have protected him, but I failed. How many times has this happened? How many more times?*

Soft as a whisper, Roxanne's voice spoke to him. *I never asked you to protect me. And neither of us could predict what happened. Stop blaming yourself.*

But he did blame himself, and he always would.

Maisie trotted beside him, shotgun over her shoulder. 'Do you think the gasbags will come back tonight, sir?' she asked.

'I don't know,' said Gallagher.

'I hope they do, sir. I'd love to have another crack. Pops says that when they catch fire, the crew sometimes jump out rather than burn to death. That would be a fine thing to watch, wouldn't it, sir?'

Gallagher glanced at her. 'They're human beings like us, Maisie. Some of those men will have families.'

'Oh, but they're Huns, sir! They kill babies, and crucify our soldiers, and they shot Nurse Cavell! I read all about it in the newspapers, sir.'

Gallagher was silent, wondering how one so young could

have learned to hate so thoroughly. But he had seen it before, of course. Some of the boys who had been shot at Victoria Barracks during his time in Ireland had been no older than Maisie.

Tompkins waited in the woods, shotgun in one hand and walking stick in the other, his overcoat dark with rainwater. The body huddled at the foot of an oak tree seemed curiously small. Gallagher looked down at Vasiliev's dead white face and was immediately reminded of Warren's body at the Admiralty. Ryder had been right, Warren and Vasiliev were not dissimilar in appearance. It was easy to see how the subterfuge had been managed.

There was none of the gory brutality of Willa Rittenhouse's death here; this had been a neat assassination. A single round hole in Vasiliev's overcoat, just over the heart, showed how he had died. There was blood around the bullet hole, and more had trickled from his mouth, although the rain was already washing it away. 'Was this how you found him?' Gallagher asked.

'Aye, sir,' said Tompkins. 'He was already dead. Hour or more, I reckon.'

'Did you hear a shot?'

'No, sir. Maisie and me was out in them woods on the far side of the park, looking out for foxes, and we only came back this way a few minutes ago. And, he was shot with one of them little pop-guns. Sound wouldn't have carried far in this weather.'

'How do you know?'

'Cuz I found the gun.' Tompkins motioned with his hand. 'Come and see, sir.'

A few yards away was a patch of bracken, brown and withered in the rain. The gun had been dropped in among the ferns, perhaps in haste. Gallagher picked it up by the barrel, avoiding the grips where any fingerprints might remain. It was a pocket revolver, .22 or perhaps .25 calibre; the stamp on the barrel said it was made by the F.D. Bliss company in New Haven, Connecticut. He turned the cylinder and saw at once that one of the chambers had been fired.

He put the revolver into his overcoat pocket. 'You've searched the area?' he asked.

'Aye, sir,' said Tompkins. 'There's a few footprints, but I can't tell if they're his or someone else's. Rain's making a right mess of everything.'

'All right. Keep watch on him, if you will.' Gallagher turned to Maisie, fidgeting like a spaniel beside him. 'Run to the lodge, please, Maisie. You'll find some policemen waiting there. Tell them what has happened.' The police already had their orders; they would wait until the secret service people arrived, and the plumbers would do the rest.

Maisie scudded away through the woods. Gallagher looked at Tompkins and started to speak about what Maisie had said earlier, about the zeppelins, but something stopped him. 'Is Maisie's father at the wars?' he asked.

'Aye.' Tompkins' lined face was unreadable. 'Got himself captured by the Turks at Kut last spring.'

'Have you heard from him?'

A minute shake of the head. 'Red Cross don't know where he is. We hear the Turks don't feed their prisoners none too well.'

'What about Maisie's mother?'

'Up at Gillingham, working in a shell factory. It's no place for a young girl. She's better with me.'

'Yes,' Gallagher said quietly. 'She is.'

He returned to the house to find Mrs Vane waiting in the hall. 'Makarian told me,' she said. 'What happened?'

'As you said, the damned fool tried to make a run for it,' Gallagher said grimly. 'Someone followed him and tracked him down. Who else didn't go to church?'

'Mr Lansing and Mr Makarian went shooting. Mrs Fairbairn remained at the house, as I said.'

Gallagher nodded. 'Find Nathalie Fairbairn, please, and tell her I need to see her. Bring her to the music room and make sure she stays there until I arrive.'

He walked through the house. Lady Maud was in the freezing drawing room, playing patience once more; she did not look up as he entered the room. Penelope Makarian and Edith Price were chatting by the fire, both with shawls wrapped tightly around their shoulders. Borden was in his study, a red dispatch box open on the desk in front of him, reading rapidly through a bound report and initialling each page as he finished it. He saw the look on Gallagher's face and stood up. 'What is it, Pat?' he asked.

'Does anyone in the house own a pocket revolver? A Bliss .22, or .25?'

'Your mother hates guns,' Borden said. 'I'm afraid I don't own a revolver. What is this about, Pat?'

'There's been another murder,' Gallagher said.

He went into the library, Borden following him. Lansing and Ryder were reading newspapers by the fire. 'Tovey has been shot,' Gallagher said.

Lansing lowered his newspaper. Ryder dropped his paper and stood up abruptly. 'Shot? Where?'

Gallagher faced him, looking into his eyes. 'Out in the woods,' he said. 'It seems a popular place for murder.'

'I'll be damned,' Lansing said. He too rose to his feet, more slowly. 'Is there any connection with Rittenhouse?'

'Almost certainly,' Gallagher said, still staring at Ryder. 'Did either of you bring a gun with you? Not your shotguns, but a pocket revolver.'

Ryder drew a short, sharp breath. 'I have my service revolver. What of it?'

Service revolvers were chambered for a .455 cartridge, far bigger than the weapon that killed Vasiliev. 'What about you, Mr Lansing?'

Lansing folded his newspaper. 'I have a Smith and Wesson .44 in my travelling bag. I don't hold with those little pocket pieces. But I know who does have one, though. Mrs Fairbairn.'

Gallagher looked at him. Was there a certain sound of satisfaction in Lansing's voice? 'Thank you,' he said. 'Captain Ryder, I'd appreciate a word.'

They walked out into the cold hall. Wind keened in the chimney, fluttering the pale flames on the fire. 'I haven't disclosed your deception,' Gallagher said. 'For the moment, everyone will continue to think that he was Tovey.'

'Thank you. I appreciate that.' Ryder rubbed his jaw. For once, some of his confidence had deserted him. 'I know how badly I have played this. Thank you for giving me a chance to salvage my career.'

'Is that the most important thing at the moment?'

Ryder accepted the rebuke. 'No, of course not. What do you need from me?'

'Now that Vasiliev is not here to give his own story, I need the absolute truth from you. Why did you bring him down here this weekend?'

'He was still searching for the telegram,' Ryder said quietly. 'I believe it is here in the house.'

'Oh? Why do you think that?'

'Someone, somehow, learned that Vasiliev had hired Warren to take the telegram, and killed him in order to stop him. I think we can agree on that, don't you? But whoever is protecting the secret of the telegram will have realized then that the Admiralty is not secure. If I were them, I would have taken the telegram away, and passed it to someone who would keep it secret. Have you searched Colson's room?'

'No,' said Gallagher. 'If Commander Colson is as subtle and clever as you are implying, he would hardly keep the telegram in his bedroom. And if your theory is right, he will probably have passed it on by now.'

'To whom, though? Who in this house is likely to be Colson's accomplice?'

'What does it matter?' Gallagher asked. 'If naval intelligence can't decode the telegram, then neither can the person who took it, and neither can you. The telegram on its own is of no use to anyone.'

Ryder shook his head. 'Regardless of what you say, Gallagher, I still think that naval intelligence *has* broken the German ciphers, and they know full well what is in that telegram, and probably many others as well. They have deceived you and the secret service just as they have deceived all the rest of us. One way or another, I intend to get to the bottom of this.'

'Why is this so important to you?' Gallagher asked.

Ryder stared at him in amazement. 'Do you need to ask? We are on a knife edge, Gallagher. The war is going against us on every front, and now the navy is being undermined from within. My family have a proud tradition of service in the navy going back centuries, and I will *not* let them down. I will not let the navy down. I want evidence that will break Colson and everyone associated with him, and expose the treachery within naval intelligence. Once that is done, we can rebuild the intelligence service and make it fit for purpose once more.'

'With you in command?'

'If Admiral Jellicoe so decrees it. I know I could do a better job than the current leadership.'

'Now that you have lost Vasiliev, what do you intend to do?' There was a pause. 'We should never have been running parallel investigations,' Ryder said finally. 'I should have cooperated with you from the beginning, but Admiral Jellicoe's orders . . . Anyway, that's by the by. Let us assume for a moment that I am right about two things: that the analysts in naval intelligence have succeeded in breaking the German codes, and that the Dreamer has discovered this and reported back to his masters in Germany.'

'Go on,' Gallagher said.

'I know something about the Nachrichten-Abteilung, not as much as you, obviously, but I crossed swords with them a few times in Berlin. Their field officers are daring and resourceful men, but their senior officers, at least the ones that I met, are hidebound and arrogant. They will want proof of what the Dreamer says. Do you agree?'

'Yes,' said Gallagher, 'but I would add that those senior officers have a point. If we *have* broken their codes, they will need to develop new ones, but writing a new cipher takes a long time. Equipping every ship with new codebooks and smuggling books out to their embassies abroad will take even longer. I can understand them wanting to make sure that the Dreamer isn't crying wolf, or that he has been duped by some clever forgeries.'

Ryder nodded. 'My hypothesis is that the Dreamer is here, with the original telegram and the decrypt. He is waiting for another agent to come and inspect them, perhaps even photograph the documents and take the evidence back to Germany.'

'Then the agent will be walking into a trap,' said Gallagher. 'Did you happen to notice the ink marks on Warren's shirt cuff, captain.'

'I can't say that I did.'

'There was a phrase of code from the book code the

Germans are using, *throne of Saturn*, and a date and time. Eight thirty p.m., today. We know something is going to happen then, but until now we didn't know what. But by this evening, the entire estate will be surrounded with police and secret service men.'

'If you arrest this agent, can you force him to reveal the Dreamer's identity?'

'We can be very persuasive,' Gallagher said. 'But you think you already know who the Dreamer is, don't you?'

'It must be Colson. Don't you agree?'

'It could well be Colson, but there are others who fit the bill as well. So, be careful, Captain. You are playing for high stakes here. If you are right, Colson will go to the gallows. But if you are wrong, your own career could be finished.'

'I understand,' Ryder said. 'That is a risk I am prepared to take.'

NATHALIE FAIRBAIRN WAS sitting on the piano bench, her lips compressed into a thin, bitter line. 'Am I under arrest?' she demanded as Gallagher entered the room.

Mrs Vane stood by the door, hands clasped gently in front of her. 'You have told her what happened?' Gallagher asked.

'I have. She knows that we know about Vasiliev.'

Gallagher turned to Nathalie Fairbairn, pulling the little revolver out of his pocket. 'Does this belong to you?'

Nathalie stared at it. 'Where did you find that?'

'In the undergrowth, not far from Vasiliev's body.' Gallagher put the gun back into his pocket. 'We seem to have a case of the biter bit,' he said. 'It was you who tried to implicate Lansing by putting that empty shotgun shell into his pocket, wasn't it? Now, someone has used your gun to kill Vasiliev, and dumped it by the body in order to frame you.'

'What makes you think I didn't kill him?' Nathalie demanded.

'Because Vasiliev was also a Bolshevik agent. You were working together, and you used Vasiliev to penetrate British naval intelligence and attempt to steal a highly secret telegram. That attempt failed, so now you are both here at Hartlake Hall, trying again. Why do you think the telegram is here?'

'I have no idea what you are talking about.'

'Do you deny that you are a Bolshevik? That you are a member of the Social Democratic Labour Party?'

'That's not a crime.'

'No, but acting as an agent for a foreign power is. And in wartime, it is punishable by death.'

She stared him down. 'Do you want me to betray my comrades? It'll never happen. I'm not a clipe.'

Her accent was slipping, her native Clydeside showing through. Gallagher studied her for a moment, one finger rubbing the scar on his temple. 'I don't give a damn about your comrades. All I want to know right now is who killed Vasiliev and why. Tell me, and we'll have an excuse for clemency.'

He paused, waiting for her reaction. None came. 'I'm offering you a chance to cheat the hangman, Mrs Fairbairn,' he said. 'If I were you, I'd take it.'

Her chin came up. 'I'm not afraid to die for the cause.'

'Neither was Vasiliev, and look where it got him.'

'Ah, now that's where you're wrong,' Nathalie said, and her voice went quiet for a moment. 'He was afraid, very afraid. That's why he tried to run away.'

'Afraid of whom?'

She looked down suddenly, and he saw the mask of composure finally beginning to slip. She too was afraid. 'The Dreamer,' she said, finally. 'And that's who killed him.'

Gallagher glanced at Mrs Vane. 'Go on,' he said.

Nathalie closed her eyes for a moment, and he watched her steady herself. *A story is coming*, he thought. *How much of it will be true? How many more layers of lies will we need to peel away?*

'I first met Paul at Aquinnah,' she said. 'At one of Sadie's parties. At first I thought he was just another effete public schoolboy, but we got to talking politics. He told me about his grandfather, and how he himself had met Nabokov and become involved with the Kadets, partly as a way of honouring the old man's memory. He was full of guff about Mother Russia, but I began to see possibilities in him.'

'You converted him to your cause.'

'It wasn't hard. He is quite impressionable. Bed helped too. Oh, yes, I knew he was Sadie's lover, but so what? Like I said, bedhopping is a favourite pastime on Cape Cod. Once Paul was fully committed, I asked him to gather information about his Kadet friends and I passed it back to the comrades in Russia. We hate the liberals even worse than the aristocrats, you see. The bourgeois are the real enemy. We'll have to break them before the revolution can succeed.'

'Spare me the rhetoric,' Gallagher said. 'When the war broke out, Vasiliev returned to England. Did you stay in touch with him?'

'No.' Her tone was deliberately hard, almost brutal. 'Why would I?'

'Vasiliev is dead, Mrs Fairbairn. Do you not feel anything for him?'

She looked straight at him. 'I cannae afford feelings. I've got a revolution to win.'

'You restarted your relationship with Vasiliev when you returned to England.'

'He learned I was back in London and came to see me,

hoping I would welcome him with open legs. I wasn't sure at first, but when he told me he was working at the Admiralty I started to grow interested again. I informed my comrades, who instructed me to keep him sweet and play him along. I did, but I could tell he was in some kind of trouble. Then last week, he told me about the Dreamer.'

'What did he say?'

'That Sadie had once tried to recruit him to work for the Germans. He had refused, or so he said. But back in England, he had been approached by agents of someone called the Dreamer, who knew about Sadie and also about his Bolshevik connections. They threatened to expose him to his superior officers, and blackmailed him into working for them. He agreed, the fool. Once you're on the hook, there's no way off it.'

'What did the Dreamer's agents ask him to do?'

'Steal papers from the Admiralty. More recently, there was a telegram that they were dead keen to get their hands on. He tried to steal it, but he bungled it. That's all he would tell me.'

'Continue,' Gallagher said, watching her face.

Nathalie leaned forward, resting her elbows on the piano lid. 'The Party is in the midst of some rather tricky negotiations at the moment,' she said. 'Revolution is coming in Russia. Our leader, Comrade Lenin, is in exile in Switzerland. We need him back in Russia, but to get there he needs German help. Do you see what I mean?'

Gallagher nodded. 'The Germans will allow Lenin free passage to Russia, and in exchange he will take Russia out of the war. But there's more to it than that.'

'Aye,' she said. The knuckles of her clasped hands were white, but otherwise she was calm. 'There's more to it than that. I'll tell you the rest when I see what deal is on the table.'

'We could beat it out of you,' Gallagher said.

There was a moment's pause, and she smiled again. 'No chance. I thrive on cruelty. It makes me stronger.'

'Did you know at the time that Sadie Lansing was a German spy?'

Nathalie shrugged. 'Looking back, it doesn't surprise me. At the time, I never really thought about it.'

'Where were you on the night that Sadie Lansing died?'

'In bed back in Boston. Don't ask me who with. I don't think I asked his name.'

'Thank you,' Gallagher said. 'Once again, Mrs Fairbairn, you have been most helpful.'

'I asked you earlier if I was under arrest. You didn't answer.'

'Let's say you are under house arrest. If you attempt to leave Hartlake Hall, you will be caught by our officers and brought back.'

Nathalie rose to her feet. 'Oh, I don't intend to set foot outside,' she said. 'I know what happens to those that do. If I'm going to be shot, I want it to be by a jealous wife. I'll be on my best behaviour, Mr Gallagher, you can count on that.'

THE DOOR CLOSED behind her with a soft click. Gallagher looked at Mrs Vane. 'What do you think?'

'It's a good story,' she said. 'Strong narrative line, believable characters. The plot felt a bit weak, though.'

'That's because there are bits of it missing,' Gallagher said. 'She knew damned well Sadie Lansing was an agent, and I reckon if we dig around enough, we'll find that she was already using Sadie as a conduit to the Germans last year. Setting up a plot like returning Lenin to Russia didn't happen overnight. As for Vasiliev, she wasn't taking orders from her comrades, she was giving them. She's the one in control.'

'And as she said, there's more to it than that,' said Mrs Vane.

'Much more. Germany and the Bolsheviks are already working together to stir up unrest in America. I doubt if they can really start a revolution there, but even the threat will be a further distraction for the American government and make them less likely to commit to Europe. Thanks to Mrs Fairbairn and her friends, we're looking at the worst possible case: American neutrality, and Russian collapse. If that happens, we are staring into the abyss.'

Gallagher drew a deep breath, looking at the clock on the wall. 'Which means that the course of the war and the fate of nations rests on that telegram. Let's hope we get this right, Mrs Vane. We won't get a second chance.'

FAIRBAIRN WAS IN the library, a newspaper on his lap, staring fixedly at the fire. Gallagher sat down opposite him. 'We need a word. It won't take long.'

'I am at your disposal,' Fairbairn said quietly.

Gallagher coughed, feeling the tension in his throat. 'Yours is a marriage of convenience,' he said. 'You and your wife went your own ways and lived largely separate lives.'

Fairbairn stiffened. 'What is this about?'

'There is nothing unusual about this,' Gallagher said. 'Plenty of couples do the same, and live their separate lives undisturbed. However, in this case, you are in charge of the Russia and Middle East desk at the Foreign Office, and your wife is a member of the central committee of the communist party – the Social Democratic Labour Party, to give them their full name – in Britain. And that presents a few problems.'

Fairbairn stood up. The points of his waxed moustache seemed to quiver with anger. 'This is outrageous,' he said.

'Mmm,' said Gallagher. 'That's one word for it. The question that will be on everyone's lips is, how much did you know about her activities?'

Fairbairn turned away towards the door. 'I don't have to listen to this.'

Gallagher rose to his feet. 'The hunter of the east,' he said.

He waited while the other man halted and turned slowly to face him once more. 'The hunter of the east,' Gallagher repeated. 'I was taken in by the reference to your boat, the *Chasseur*. The real hunter of the east was Nathalie, and you knew it. That's why Sadie Lansing suggested we ask you what it meant.'

Fairbairn stood rigid, arms at his sides. 'Yes,' he said after a long moment. 'I knew.'

'You berated Makarian for having dealings with the Bolsheviks, when you were already colluding with them yourself. What does that make you?'

'I know what it makes me.'

Gallagher regarded him. 'Or was this some sort of clever ploy on your part? Having a member of the Bolshevik leadership as an asset would have been a real feather in your cap, especially once you returned to the Foreign Office and took over responsibility for Russia. Did Nathalie agree to spy on her comrades for you, in exchange for you covering up for her?'

'No,' Fairbairn said quietly. 'Nathalie despises me and everything I stand for. To her, I am an effete bourgeois, a class that should be wiped from the face of the earth. She has said as much to my face.'

Gallagher coughed. 'Then why did you help her?'

'Out of pity,' Fairbairn said, and his rich voice was a well of darkness and loss. 'And by pitying her, I only made her hate me more.'

Sometime during the next twenty-four hours I am going to have to break a good man. Gallagher paused for a moment, fighting down a wave of bitter anger. 'You knew your wife was a Bolshevik agent, in contact with the Germans during a time of war. So, it follows that you also knew that both Sadie Lansing and Frank Warren were German agents.'

'I suspected that Sadie was, of course. I reported this to the embassy. That's why you and Flynn and Bielaski came to Aquinnah.'

'No, Fairbairn, you didn't just *suspect* Sadie was an agent, you *knew*. You knew because Frank Warren had told you, and confessed that he was also involved. You covered up for him. You told us you suspected Sadie, but not her brother. Why?'

Tears were starting at the corners of Fairbairn's eyes. 'I didn't know for certain at first,' he said finally. 'I only learned the full truth after Sadie was killed. Frank was terrified. He thought that whoever had killed Sadie would come for him next. He confessed everything to me and begged my protection. I promised I would help him.'

'Why?'

Fairbairn opened his eyes again and stared straight at Gallagher. 'Don't make me spell it out for you, Gallagher. Spare me that much, at least.'

'You had it in your power to blow an entire German spy ring wide open,' Gallagher said. 'We could have broken their cipher and taken Lily Sparrow. Through her we could have found the Dreamer, the most important German spymaster in the field since Rintelen was caught. We could also have disrupted the agreement between the Bolsheviks and the Germans, to return Lenin to Russia and to take Russia out of the war. Thanks to you, Fairbairn, our nation is now in deadly peril. You might want to reflect on that.'

Fairbairn wiped his eyes. 'What are you going to do with me?'

'Nothing, for the moment,' said Gallagher, and this time he

could not quite keep the anger out of his voice. 'But I advise you to end your association with Nicholas Makarian. Nothing good will come of that.'

'It is already ended,' Fairbairn said quietly.

COLSON WAS IN the billiards room, playing a moody solo game. Gallagher walked around the table and stood in front of him.

'Did you know Tovey's real identity?' he asked.

Colson's face was blank. 'What are you talking about?'

'The real Charles Tovey was murdered in London last week, probably on Wednesday morning, not long after Warren was killed. The man impersonating him was Ryder's staff officer, Paul Vasiliev.'

Colson said nothing. 'Ryder is coming for you,' Gallagher said. 'You still have one chance to save yourself. Tell me about your real relationship with Frank Warren.'

Still Colson remained silent. Gallagher turned on his heel and walked out of the room.

SUNDAY, 4 FEBRUARY 1917

1.04 P.M.

Quietly, the guests gathered in the dining room for lunch. Lady Maud entered and was seated by Makarian. Borden was absent, and Gallagher guessed he had gone out to the meet with the police; a conscientious man, he would want to do his duty as a landowner and ensure that both the killing of Vasiliev and the murder of Willa Rittenhouse were being properly investigated. Well, Gallagher thought, there was no harm in that; the police inspector he had spoken to yesterday evening had seemed reliable, and would tell Sir John what he needed to know and no more.

Neither Fairbairn nor his wife came down to lunch, which was unsurprising for different reasons. Colson sat in gloom, hunched over in his chair. Captain Ryder stood by the window, watching silver curtains of rain drift across the park before finally taking his seat just as Edith Price hurried in, murmuring an apology. Walking around the table to take his own place, Gallagher noticed she had changed into a rifle green skirt and blouse. The colour suited her fair complexion, and his mind drifted for a moment to painting.

Price rose and seated his wife, and Gallagher pulled up his own chair and sat down. He had no appetite, but he needed to keep an eye on the others. 'You are late,' his mother said. 'What detained you, Patrick?'

Overhead the water pipes where thumping like a drum. 'I had some business to attend to.'

'On a Sunday?' Lady Maud demanded.

'They don't stop the war for Sundays, Mother.'

'Don't be facetious, Patrick. I saw policemen in the park earlier. What has happened?'

Ryder and Colson were both watching him. Price sawed one-handed at his roast beef. 'It's Mr Tovey,' Gallagher said. 'He has met with an accident.'

'What sort of accident?'

Gallagher stared at the gravy congealing on his plate. Penelope came to his rescue. 'For heaven's sake, Mother, what difference does it make? The poor man is hurt, that's all. The rest of us should mind our own business.'

'What a good idea,' said Makarian. He too was looking at Gallagher. 'Minding one's own business, I mean. As usual, Penelope, darling, you speak excellent sense.'

Edith Price's eyes were wide. 'Oh, but that surely is too harsh,' she said. 'It is right that we should care about other people, and to be sympathetic to them when they are hurt. Surely I have read somewhere that to love our neighbour as we love ourselves is the perfection of human nature.'

Colson, who had been picking at his food, looked faintly surprised. 'Adam Smith,' he said. '*The Theory of Moral Sentiments*. I read it when I was studying law.'

'You were a lawyer, Commander?' asked Makarian.

'For a time, yes. Before I joined the navy.'

'So why did you give it up?' asked Lansing.

Colson thought for a moment. 'I enjoyed studying law,' he said, 'but I realized that I hated the practice of it. I found courtrooms tedious. The endless arguments, people in wigs droning on and on, and on. It bored me rigid. I joined the navy because I thought it would be a more active life. You were in the marines, Gallagher, you must know the feeling.'

'Yes,' said Gallagher. 'However, I found standing night watches on the deck of a battleship during typhoon season equally tedious.'

The water pipes were thumping harder than ever, like the drum section of a marching band. Edith Price smiled. 'I sense that the two of you have something in common. Neither of you has ever found a place where you feel you belong.'

Gallagher said nothing. 'I expect you are right,' Colson said after a while.

'I sympathize,' Makarian said. 'Indeed, I know something of what you feel. What about you, Captain Ryder? Does service life suit you?'

Ryder smiled too. 'The navy is bred into my bones. Cut me, and I bleed saltwater.'

Everyone laughed a little, except for Lady Maud. The mood

in the room lightened. 'What shall we do this afternoon?' asked Edith. 'The rain is letting up, and I am sure the clouds have lifted a little. Perhaps we could walk into Tonbridge? I should like to see the castle.'

Lansing snorted. 'One old pile of stones looks pretty much like another.'

'That's because you have no sense of history, Mr Lansing,' Edith scolded gently. 'Everything in this world has meaning, even the stones.'

Her husband looked up sharply. 'There's water coming through the ceiling,' he said. 'Lady Maud, I think you must have a burst pipe somewhere.'

Everyone else looked up too. A stain was spreading across the plaster ceiling, pale at first but quickly flushing to a rosy pink. They sat transfixed, watching as the stain reached the central rose and worked its way around the chandelier boss. Before anyone could move or react, red water began to drip in steady streams, falling onto the snow-white tablecloth below.

17

The bathroom door was locked, but Gallagher kicked it hard and the lock yielded at once. Price and Captain Ryder followed him into the room. All was dark; the bathroom window was firmly closed and the drapes pulled across. Water bubbled and gurgled and he could feel the steam on his face. He found the light switch and flicked it on.

The taps were still running, and the bath was overflowing with bloody water that poured across the floor. Herbert Fairbairn reclined in the bathtub, his head rolled back and his eyes closed. The steam had melted some of the wax in his moustache, and the tips drooped forlornly. Price switched off the taps and stood back, gazing at the dead man. His own face was a little pale, the scars flaming angry red, and Gallagher wondered what memories were running through his mind.

The room smelled of soap and blood and something else, sharp yet sweet at the same time. Ryder lifted Fairbairn's arms out of the water. The arteries of both wrists had been cut neatly through; the wounds were still leaking a little blood. Lowering the arms again, Ryder touched Fairbairn's neck, feeling for a pulse. He shook his head.

'Poor devil,' the captain said softly. 'What would make him do a thing like that?' He pointed to the bloody razor lying on the floor beside the tub. 'Will you need to finger-print that?'

'There's no need,' said Gallagher.

Ryder looked surprised, but he picked up the razor and began to wipe it clean with a towel. 'We need to clear this up,' Price said.

'Leave it to the servants,' said Ryder.

Price turned on him. 'Really? You're going to ask the poor bloody maidservants to clear up this mess? Is that how you do things when someone dies on your watch, Captain? Get some-one else to clean it up?'

Ryder started to speak, stopped, and made a gesture of apol-ogy. 'You're right, of course. Come along, Price, find some more towels and start mopping.'

Gallagher walked along the creaking corridor to Fairbairn's room. The door was unlocked. A single sheet of paper lay on the writing table by the window, a gold fountain pen beside it.

My career is finished, and my life is over. I never sought to do wrong, but I know that will not matter. I must atone for what I have done, and this is the best way. Frank, Nathalie: I cared for both of you.

Gallagher swallowed the sick taste in his throat and knocked on the door of Nathalie Fairbairn's room. After a moment she answered, and he entered the room and closed the door behind him. She was sitting by the window regardless of the cold, watching a train steam up the line towards Tonbridge.

'What do you want?' she asked without turning her head.

There was no point in soft-soaping this, he thought. 'Your husband is dead.'

There was a long pause. The train's whistle echoed dimly

across the park. It did not need much imagination to make it sound like a funeral dirge.

'What happened?' Nathalie asked.

Silently, Gallagher held out the note and watched her read it. Her face was as brittle and hard as ever, but inside he saw her crumple.

'That's Herbert, all over,' she said finally. 'Always trying to do the right thing. Always coming up just that little bit short.'

'That is harsh. He tried to protect you.'

'And what did it get him? A sad life and a lonely death. He should have turned us both in to the police.'

'But the result would have been the same,' Gallagher said. 'His career and reputation would have been destroyed.'

'You're right, of course. Bourgeois society never forgets or forgives. He could have just about withstood marrying a Bolshie, or having a homosexual relationship, but to do both at once would be unforgiveable . . . Frank at least gave him some sort of loyalty. I was unable to do even that.'

'There will be an inquest,' Gallagher said. 'You will have to give evidence.'

'I don't care. It's over for me too, you know. Now that I have been exposed, the Party will drop me like rotten fruit. But I did my bit. I helped to pave the way for the revolution, which is all I ever wanted.'

'All you ever wanted?' he asked quietly. 'Really?'

'All I ever dared hope for, then. Thank you for coming to tell me yourself. I appreciate that. You may be bourgeois yourself, but at least you have feelings.'

'Let me know if there is anything you need,' Gallagher said.

'I need nothing,' said Nathalie and she turned back towards the window, hiding her face so he could not see her tears.

*

By the time he returned to the bathroom, Ryder and Price had emptied the bathtub and lifted the body out, wrapping it in a sheet. Makarian came into the bathroom. 'The police are here, Pat. Sir John returned to the house a few minutes ago, and when he learned what had happened he sent for them.'

Gallagher cursed inwardly. 'I'll talk to them,' he said. 'Do the other guests know?'

'After that drama in the dining room, we had to say something. I told them that Mr Fairbairn had tragically taken his own life. What happened, Pat? Why did he do it?'

'It's a long story,' Gallagher said.

Makarian drew him out into the hallway, out of earshot of Price and Ryder. His eyes were hard and challenging. 'Tell me, Pat. I have a right to know.'

'Do you?'

After a moment Makarian lowered his eyes. 'A little common decency, Pat. That's all I ask.'

'I'll tell you this evening,' Gallagher said. 'Right now, I have work to do.'

He brushed past Makarian and went downstairs. Lady Maud was in the drawing room, pale as a ghost; Penelope stood protectively behind her. There was no sign of the other guests. Gallagher knelt beside his mother's chair and started to reach for her hand. She saw the gesture and moved her hand away.

'Are you all right?' he asked.

'I am perfectly well,' she said. Her voice creaked with shock. 'What a pity lunch was ruined. Cook had made an apple tart.'

'The food on the sideboard wasn't touched. I am sure we can have it for dinner.'

'We shall have a cold collation for dinner, as we always do on Sunday.'

Gallagher looked at Penelope, who shook her head slightly. 'You should rest,' he said to his mother.

'I am not in need of rest, Patrick. There are some policemen in the library, and Sir John says they wish to speak to you. Go to them.'

In the library Borden was talking to two uniformed constables and the young inspector with the empty sleeve. A secret service man was there too, standing unobtrusively to one side. Gallagher looked at the inspector. 'I thought I had made myself clear,' he said.

'You had, sir. But when Sir John requested we attend at the house, we could hardly refuse. And given the circumstances, the other guests might have thought it a bit odd if we did *not* attend.'

That made sense. Gallagher nodded. 'Very well. The official line is that Mr Fairbairn took his own life, so there is no need for you to conduct a detailed investigation or interview anyone else in the house. Sir John, will you make this clear to the guests?'

Borden looked worried, but he nodded too. Gallagher turned back to the inspector. 'Mr Fairbairn was a prominent official in the Foreign Office, so keep this quiet. If any of the papers get word, threaten them with a D-notice.'

'Yes, sir. Shall I inform the coroner?'

'We'll handle that, just as with Mr Tovey and Miss Rittenhouse. Our people will keep you informed. The body is in the bathroom upstairs. If you could remove it as discreetly as possible, I would be grateful.'

'I'll show you the way,' Borden said. The inspector and the two constables followed him out of the room. Gallagher turned to the secret service man. 'Get the body up to London and have an autopsy performed as soon as possible. Ask the doctors to look for signs of diethyl ether. I smelled it as soon as I entered the bathroom.'

'Of course, sir. What would you like me to tell Colonel Kell? He's expecting a full report this evening.'

'We've had two murders in two hours,' Gallagher said. 'At this rate, no one will be left alive by evening. Tell the colonel I'll report as soon as I can.'

'Very good, sir.' The man touched his cap and went out. Gallagher stood in the middle of the hall, thinking. Diethyl ether had a particularly pungent smell; the killer had put soap into the water to try to mask it, but not successfully. Somewhere there must be a bottle and the ether-soaked cloth pad that was used to knock Fairbairn out before his wrists were cut, and he wondered whether to search the house. *No point*, he told himself. *I already know how he was killed.*

Floorboards creaked and the inspector came downstairs, followed by the two policemen carrying the bundled body. Gallagher turned to the inspector. 'May I ask if you have heard the latest weather report?'

The inspector blinked in surprise. 'Er, yes, sir. A report came through from the Meteorological Office this morning. Wind still from the east but the rain easing and skies clearing towards evening.'

'Thank you. I'll leave you to carry on.'

After the police had gone Gallagher went back into the library and stood in silence, fists clenched, staring at the fire. Jonquil Vane came into the room a few moments later and stopped in front of him.

'Stop blaming yourself,' she said.

'How do you know that's what I'm doing?'

'Because it is what any civilized human being would do, were they in your shoes. You did what you had to do.'

'I don't *have* to do any of this. I could quit right now, and walk away.'

'Mmm,' she said. 'Like you did from the marines, and from Special Branch. But walking away won't change the past.'

He stared at her. 'Why are you doing this?'

'To bring you to your senses,' she said directly. 'We have just over six hours to go. And like you said, we'll only get one chance. You need to be on your game.'

'On my game? Yes, of course. How many more decent, well-intentioned public servants can I allow to be killed under my watch before the day is out? You want to be careful, Mrs Vane. You might be one of them.'

'I'll take my chances,' she said.

SUNDAY, 4 FEBRUARY 1917

2.14 P.M.

The door opened and Edith Price looked into the room. 'Am I interrupting?'

Gallagher's eyes met Mrs Vane's. 'Not at all,' he said.

'I am so sorry about Mr Fairbairn,' Edith said, closing the door behind her. 'Mr Gallagher, Mrs Vane, I think we need to talk.'

'Of course,' Mrs Vane said calmly. 'What do you wish to discuss?'

Edith held out the little white Secret Service card. 'My orders are to not reveal my identity to anyone. But I think we've rather moved beyond that, don't you?'

Gallagher took the card and read it. 'Do you report to Joe Flynn?'

Her eyelashes fluttered a little. 'Sorry,' Gallagher said. 'Stupid question.'

'My position, as I am sure you will realize, is a bit delicate. Rather like yourself last year at Aquinnah, I have no official standing here. You could arrest me and turf me out of the country if you want to, although I'd really rather you didn't. I love this country, and I intend to make it my home.'

'Does your husband know who you are?' asked Mrs Vane.

'He does,' said Edith. 'It was unfair to marry him without telling him. I've also told my own service that this is my last case. I intended to stop after we got married, but this case was too important to walk away from.'

'How much are you able to tell us?' asked Gallagher.

'We know about the telegram from Zimmermann, and we know the Dreamer and his associates are aware that you've intercepted it. We also know they are trying to infiltrate your naval intelligence service. So, the stakes are pretty high.'

'They are,' Gallagher agreed. 'How did you learn about the telegram?'

'Me personally? Willa Rittenhouse told me. Where *she* got the information, she wouldn't say, but she thought it was her patriotic duty to pass it on.'

In the back of Gallagher's mind, another piece of the puzzle fitted into its place. Mrs Vane stirred a little. 'Why is America interested?' she asked.

'A couple of reasons. First, according to Miss Rittenhouse, whatever is in that telegram is political dynamite. Our assumption is that the Germans are trying to stir up trouble in Mexico to distract America's attention away from Europe. Not for the first time,' she added. 'So, we'd really like to know the contents. Second, more generally, there are signs that the Dreamer is trying to re-establish his spy network in America. We'd like to take him out of the game.'

I want the Dreamer just as badly as you do, Pat, Joe Flynn had said. 'Why are you here at Hartlake Hall?' Gallagher asked.

'Willa Rittenhouse told me about the body at the Admiralty, and also about the gathering this weekend. We put two and two together, and assumed that the dead man might be one of the Dreamer's agents. We also worked out that you were setting some sort of trap for the Dreamer here, with the telegram as bait. Geraint's father knows Sir John – I mean, does everyone in Britain know everyone else? – so it was easy to wangle an invitation.'

'In answer to your question, all of the people who matter do know each other,' said Gallagher. 'I've noticed America is much the same. So, you came down here to offer assistance?'

For the first time, Edith looked uncomfortable. 'Not exactly. You weren't even supposed to know we were here. My chief is going to give me a hiding when he finds out that I've blown my cover. We came to find out as much as we could about the Dreamer and the telegram, and report back. But I'm sensing that you could use some help.'

'You're not wrong,' Gallagher said, struggling to hide the anger in his voice. 'You already seem to be well informed about this case. Does the phrase *throne of Saturn* mean anything to you?'

Her eyes widened a little. 'Yes, it's part of a book code the Dreamer's team are using. I'm assuming you already know about that?'

'We do,' said Mrs Vane. 'Have you been able to break the cipher?'

'Good Lord, no. For a start, I think there's at least nine different ciphers, each tied to a particular person. Ever since I acquired that list of code names, I've been trying to work out who each refers to. From the pattern of messages I intercepted, I'm pretty sure that *throne of Saturn* refers to an agent from Germany that the Dreamer is expecting. And *seventh gate* is someone in British naval intelligence, but I don't know who.'

'Are you certain of that?' asked Gallagher.

Edith spread her hands. 'Mr Gallagher, I'm not certain of *anything* right now. But that's my best guess.'

'Do you mind if I ask how you acquired the list of code names?'

'Frank Warren sold it to me,' she said. 'Bless his heart, he'd sell his grandmother for money to buy whisky. But I guess we shouldn't speak ill of the dead.'

'How did you intercept the messages?'

'A few weeks back, I discovered that they were using theatres as message drops. I managed to copy some of the shorter messages without getting caught.'

'Will you share them with us?'

Edith shook her head. 'Mr Gallagher, I said my chief would give me a hiding. If I shared those messages with you, he'd skin me alive with a rusty knife.' She looked sombre for a moment. 'This is starting to get messy,' she said. 'Truly, can I be of any assistance?'

'Are you certain?' Gallagher asked. 'I don't want to get you into any more trouble with your chief.'

'Things are due to come to a head at about eight thirty this evening, aren't they? Yes, I thought so. Frank Warren told me. O.K., I'm tearing up my orders. Tell me what you need me to do.'

'I'm worried that Mrs Fairbairn may be in danger,' Gallagher said. 'Especially now that her husband is dead. She has a great deal of information that can be useful to both yourselves and us, and we must keep her alive. Can you guard her? She's in her room at the moment, but I'd like her down in the public rooms where we can see her. Persuade her to come downstairs, if you can, and sit with her. If she refuses, tell her who you are and say you are acting on my orders. Are you armed?'

'No, but Geraint has his service revolver.'

'You might want to suggest he keeps it handy,' Gallagher said. 'Welcome on board, Mrs Price. We are relieved and delighted to have your help. I'll smooth things over with your service once this is all over.'

'No need,' she said cheerfully. 'I'm leaving the service when this is all over. After that, my only job will be to become the best Mrs Price in the world. I'll go and find Mrs Fairbairn.'

The door closed behind Edith. Mrs Vane looked at Gallagher, her eyebrows arched. 'Was that wise?' she asked.

'Oh, she'll keep Nathalie Fairbairn quite safe, we can be sure of that. For someone who can't tell us anything, she told us quite a lot, don't you think?'

'Perhaps it was an audition,' Mrs Vane suggested. 'Never mind the nice little housewife act, now that she has settled in Britain, maybe she's hoping for a job with us.'

Silence fell, broken only by the clock ticking on the mantelpiece. 'I apologize for my temper earlier,' Gallagher said finally.

'My dear man, you are angry and upset. If you weren't, you would not be human. I haven't been in this job for very long, but I'm beginning to understand the costs we all have to pay.'

'The costs,' Gallagher repeated. 'Sadie Lansing, Frank Warren, Willa Rittenhouse, Paul Vasiliev, Herbert Fairbairn have paid the costs. And it is not yet over.'

The fire popped. He stared towards it, eyes unseeing, listening to the shades in his mind and hearing Roxanne's voice like a distant murmur, *Is there no pity sitting in the clouds, that sees into the bottom of my grief?* And there was so much to grieve for, so many failed hopes, so many lost opportunities; so many dead, their numbers multiplying relentlessly with each passing day. *I'm tired of this world*, he thought. *I've had enough.*

He looked back at Mrs Vane. He saw her quiet face, her dark hair in its severe bun, the pain lines at the corners of her eyes. He thought about her husband dead at Gallipoli, her mother drowned on the *Lusitania*, and once again knew a moment of shame. *Why should my grief be more important than hers, or anyone else's? If she can live with her own horrors and carry on, then surely so can I.*

It took Mrs Vane some time to track down Lieutenant Price, but eventually she found him playing billiards with Commander Colson. A cigarette burned in an ashtray on a side table, sending little curls of smoke into the air. 'Very sensible of you both to come in here,' she said. 'I swear this is the warmest room in the house.'

Price was playing left-handed, resting the cue on his prosthetic right hand. 'I can't wait to return to London,' he said. 'You couldn't pay me enough to come back to this place.'

'I imagine we all feel the same. Especially after what happened to Mr Fairbairn and Mr Tovey, not to mention that poor lady on Saturday. Do you suppose this house has some sort of curse on it?'

'Of course it has a curse,' said Price, lining up a shot. 'God, that poor fellow Fairbairn. That's not a sight I'll forget in a hurry.'

He played a cannon, and Colson grunted in approval. He, at least, seemed unmoved by Fairbairn's death. 'You're bloody good at this, Price,' he said.

'The convalescent home where I recovered after Jutland had

a table,' Price said. 'I used to practise every day. The doctors said it was therapeutic.'

'I should imagine it was,' said Mrs Vane. 'Was that the home where you met Mrs Price?'

'Yes.' Price played another shot. 'It was a horrible time, but at least something good came out of it. Without Edie, I really don't know where I would be right now.'

Mrs Vane chose her moment. 'You told me the other night that you were thinking of leaving the navy. Are you still minded to do so?'

'Yes,' Price said briefly. 'As soon as possible.'

Colson took a drag on his cigarette. 'Sounds a bit drastic. Why don't you just put in for a transfer? See if you can get back on active service.'

'If they'd have me, I'd go back in a moment. Like I said to you this morning, Mrs Vane, I joined the navy to go to sea. But no captain wants a watchkeeping officer with one arm.'

'Nelson had one arm,' Mrs Vane pointed out.

Price snorted. 'Nelson wouldn't recognize today's navy. After Jutland, I reckon he must be turning in his grave.'

Colson tensed. 'What's that supposed to mean?'

'It means what it means, Commander. Fourteen ships sunk, battlecruisers blown to pieces in a moment, thousands of sailormen killed and wounded, and for what? Absolutely nothing, that's what. The German fleet still sits snug in its harbours, and all that pain and death gained us not a damned thing.'

'I'm not listening to this,' Colson said. He threw his cue down onto the baize, stubbed out his cigarette and walked out of the room, slamming the door behind him.

Price snorted with disgust. 'Pathetic,' he said. 'God help us all, if these are our leaders.'

'Forgive me,' said Mrs Vane, 'but I think he may have a point.

You loved the navy, so why leave it now? It's clear that working at the Admiralty isn't for you, but there must be other posts that would suit you. How does your wife feel about this?'

'Edie supports me.'

'You know about her own work, of course.'

Price tensed. 'Her work? You mean, nursing?'

'No, I mean her other work. She told us who she really is, Mr Price.' She smiled, attempting to keep the mood light. 'You're a very tolerant man. Not every husband would be willing to have a spy for a wife.'

'She's not a spy,' Price said, 'any more than you are. She's a Secret Service agent. And *you* don't seem to have a problem.'

'I'm a widow,' Mrs Vane said quietly. 'It's different for us.' She paused for a moment. 'I'm thinking about Nelson again. Did you know that after he was killed at Trafalgar his body was laid out in the Admiralty boardroom, the night before his funeral?'

Price shook his head. 'It wasn't the boardroom. It was the servants' pantry next door. I believe it's now a stationery store.'

'Oh, really? I didn't know that. What an odd coincidence. Did you hear about the body that was found there last week?'

'Yes. Bit surprising, that. I thought that cupboard was kept locked.'

'It is, but we found a second concealed door leading in from the boardroom. On the subject of locks, do you know who keeps the keys to the boardroom?'

Price shifted a little. 'The keys are in the custody of Sir Graham Greene, the permanent secretary to the Admiralty board. He keeps them locked in his desk.'

Mrs Vane was thoughtful. 'Well, I can't imagine Sir Graham tiptoeing around the Admiralty late at night murdering people in cupboards. Does anyone else know where the keys are kept?'

'I imagine most of his staff do,' said Price. 'Are you suggesting that one of us, one of the secretariat, killed that man?'

Mrs Vane looked impatient. 'Of course not. I meant, does anyone else in the Admiralty apart from yourselves know where those keys are? Would anyone from naval intelligence know, for example?'

'I doubt it,' said Price. 'We don't have any real contact with naval intelligence. No one does, except at the highest level. They keep themselves to themselves.'

Mrs Vane smiled a little. 'That's what the newspapers always say about murderers,' she said. 'Mr Price, I am sorry you are leaving the navy, but when I stop and think about it, I suppose I can understand why. You have been treated very badly.'

She was surprised to see him look almost grateful. 'Thank you,' he said. 'I am glad that someone understands.'

WALKING BACK TO the hall, Mrs Vane found Colson waiting for her. 'What was that about?' he demanded.

'Have you been listening at keyholes, Commander?'

'Answer my question.'

'You know perfectly well what that was about,' Mrs Vane said. 'You have a security breach in Room 40. We are trying to find out who is behind it.'

Colson stared at her. 'And you think it might be me.'

Mrs Vane was discovering that, despite the cold, the bad food and the succession of dead bodies, it was possible to enjoy her work. 'You have admitted that you recognized Frank Warren,' she said. 'You met him and you gave him money. Give me some good reasons to think that it *isn't* you.'

'Go to hell,' Colson said, and he took his overcoat down from its peg and went out. This time, at least, he refrained from slamming the door.

Nathalie Fairbairn was seated on the piano bench when Gallagher entered the music room, leafing through the book of sheet music. Edith Price sat in a chair on the far side of the room, watching her.

'How are you feeling?' Gallagher asked Nathalie.

'Still a little shocked, but coming to terms with it.' She paused. 'Herbert never intended to betray his country. He concealed what he knew about me, and Frank, because he was trying to protect us. His note said as much. Deep down, he was actually a good man, wasn't he?'

Today I shall have to break a good man. 'He was,' Gallagher said. 'He made mistakes, but his intentions were honest.'

'So are mine,' she said, and some of the flint returned to her voice. 'Not that I expect you to give me credit for that.'

Gallagher said nothing. Nathalie raised her head and looked at Gallagher. 'What do you want from me?' she asked.

'Did you know that Sadie Lansing was having her portrait painted?'

Nathalie looked startled; clearly, that was not the question she had been expecting. 'No . . . but it doesn't surprise me. Next to Sadie, Narcissus would have looked shy and retiring.'

'The painter was her friend Lily Sparrow, the one who worked in the art gallery. She was also a painter, quite a good one. She was there working on the portrait the afternoon before Sadie died.' Gallagher raised a hand, rubbing the scar on his temple. 'Subsequently, we discovered that her real name is Lily Spatz and that she was – and still is – an agent working for the Nachrichten-Abteilung, German naval intelligence. Before the war, at least, Lily herself reported to a senior agent called the Dreamer who had established the original spy ring.'

'Why are you telling me all of this?' Nathalie demanded.

'Did you ever hear Sadie mention that name? The Dreamer?'

'No.'

'But you knew she was a German agent,' Gallagher said gently.

Nathalie sat as if frozen. 'Yes,' she said finally.

Edith was listening intently. 'That's why you approached her in the first place, wasn't it?' Gallagher said. 'Your comrades instructed you to open up a channel to Count von Bernstorff, and Sadie was eager to help you. She also taught you how to use the book cipher. You were given your own sign and your own code, *hunter of the east.*' Gallagher glanced at Edith. 'Who was Sadie?'

'Sadie was *fire of spring*,' Nathalie said. 'I don't know any of the others. She was my only direct contact with the German operation. And to save you asking, I never met Lily Sparrow and I don't know who the Dreamer is.'

Gallagher nodded. 'Paul Vasiliev was a keen yachtsman, as was your husband. Fairbairn maintained he had never met Vasiliev. Is that true?'

Nathalie nodded. 'I had plenty of lovers, but I never rubbed Herbert's nose in it. I kept them out of his way. I have to say my heart was in my mouth when Paul told me he was coming to Hartlake Hall, but there's no way that he and Herbert could have recognized each other.'

'Tell me exactly what Vasiliev was doing at the Admiralty,' Gallagher said.

Nathalie sighed, staring down at the piano keys. 'When war broke out, the Party ordered Paul back to Britain, with instructions to join the navy. The plan all along was to insert him into naval intelligence, where he could gather information that would help us to craft our own strategy for revolution.'

'How did he get out of seagoing duties?'

'Our people gave him some pills to fake a heart condition. He applied for a transfer to naval intelligence, and with his language skills it was a racing certainty he would be accepted. Unfortunately, your side had discovered his Kadet connections and identified him as a security risk, so he was transferred over to naval planning pretty sharp. He was of no use to use to the Party there, so he became dormant. Until I returned to London, he thought we had forgotten all about him.'

'Then what happened?'

'Captain Ryder arrived at naval planning and started making noises about potential traitors in naval intelligence. Paul told me, and I saw our chance at once. I told him to volunteer his services to Ryder and offer to slip into naval intelligence and look around for evidence. While he was there, he could also copy or steal anything that might be helpful to us.'

'You said he was being blackmailed by the Dreamer,' Gallagher said. 'But that's not true, is it?'

'No.' For the first time, Nathalie was nervous. 'I'm sticking my head in the noose now,' she said. 'I'll tell you what happened, but I want your promise that I won't face the death penalty.'

Gallagher raised his eyebrows. 'I thought you were ready to die for the cause.'

'I am,' she said bluntly, 'but not just yet. I've risked everything for the revolution. I want to live to see it happen.'

'I'll do my best,' Gallagher said. 'Go on.'

There was no way back now, and Nathalie knew it. 'The Dreamer contacted me, using the book cipher. He offered to buy any documents we could steal, and promised good money. I agreed, and we set up a series of drops at London theatres. We didn't give him very much, a few transport returns, statistics on fuel consumption and so on. Anything important, we kept for ourselves.'

'Why?'

'Because knowledge is power,' she said. 'Hobbes said that, in *Leviathan*. Very clever man, Hobbes. The first man to expose the rot at the heart of the capitalist-feudal system . . . No, you're not interested, I can see it in your eyes. The Germans are useful to us because they can help us get what we want, but they're still the enemy.'

'What about the telegram?'

'Ryder told Paul about it, and asked him to find it. He wanted to know whether it was genuine or part of some plot being cooked up at naval intelligence. Paul was in a complete funk. The telegram was in a safe, but he had no idea how to get into it.'

Gallagher nodded. 'But Frank Warren had arrived in London, and was looking for money.'

'He said he was on the run from the law in America, and was desperate. We stashed him away in Paul's rooms so Herbert wouldn't find out – believe it or not, I did this to protect Herbert – and put together a plan. I altered one of Paul's uniforms so it would fit Frank, and Paul gave him his pass and helped him get into the Admiralty. It was quite easy, by the way, a lot easier than it should have been . . . Frank was supposed to burgle the safe around midnight, then come straight out and meet Paul, but he never returned. You know what happened after that.'

'And the next day?' Gallagher asked.

'Captain Ryder tracked Paul down and gave him orders to impersonate Tovey and come to Hartlake Hall. He had a theory, he said, that Commander Colson intended to pass the telegram to enemy agents, and that he would try to make the handover this weekend. I hadn't been intending to go, I detest country house weekends, but when Paul told me I decided to come too. The telegram was important, and I wanted it for our people. That's all there is.'

'Not quite,' said Gallagher. 'What happened to Willa Rittenhouse?'

Nathalie's face had gone pale. 'Paul killed her.'

'Why?'

'He thought she had recognized him out in the field. He managed to get close enough to hear part of your conversation, and realized she was planning to come back and meet you, so he went out to wait for her. To cover for him, I tried to throw the blame onto Lansing.'

'With whom you were also sleeping.'

'Lansing was a useful source of information,' Nathalie said. 'But he is also a capitalist bourgeois pig, and I cannot wait to see him hanging from a lamp post.'

'Yes,' Gallagher said. 'Quite. But is it not the case, Mrs Fairbairn, that you had met Willa Rittenhouse in America, and were worried that if she came to the house it would be *you* she would recognize? And that you knew Frank Warren had sold her information that might have implicated *you*? And that it was *you* that instructed Vasiliev to shoot her?'

There was a long silence. Gallagher bit back the urge to cough. 'You will be charged with treason and murder,' he said. 'You didn't kill Willa Rittenhouse yourself, but the principle of joint enterprise means you will be treated just as if you had pulled the trigger. I don't know what happened to turn a playboy like Vasiliev into the sort of monster who can shoot a defenceless woman in the chest with a shotgun, but you pointed him towards his target. For that alone, Mrs Fairbairn, there can be no forgiveness.'

'Forgiveness is a bourgeois emotion,' she said stonily. 'You promised to save my life.'

'I said I would do my best.' Gallagher pointed to Edith. 'Mrs Price will be your bodyguard for the moment, until you can be handed over to Special Branch. This is for your own protection as much as anything else.'

'Am I in danger?'

'The Dreamer murdered Sadie Lansing,' Gallagher said. 'He kills anyone who might be a danger to him. I'm sure that as a good communist you don't believe in God, but you might want to start praying anyway. It can't hurt.'

He nodded to Edith, and rose and left the room. Edith followed him out, closing the door behind her. 'Wow,' she said quietly. 'Why do you think she confessed so much?'

Gallagher coughed hard, clearing his throat. 'I don't know,' he said. 'Perhaps the deaths of her husband and her lover in short order have made her think about her own mortality. Has she said anything else to you?'

'She talked about her childhood a bit. Her father sounds like a real bastard. Drank, beat her and her mother, all the rest, but funnily enough, it was her father's example that led her to communism. Your people will execute her, won't they? Once they've wrung her dry, I mean.'

'I have no idea,' Gallagher said. 'What happens to her now is out of my control, and yours. Keep watching her. We don't have long to go, now.'

18

Lansing and Makarian faced each other in the billiards room. 'Fairbairn's death changes nothing,' said Nicholas Makarian. 'The Foreign Office will have no choice but to give you the oil concession. If they do baulk, I will use Sir John's influence, and Churchill's.'

Lansing studied the other man for a moment. 'You were friendly with Fairbairn,' he said. 'Personally, I couldn't stand the man, but I wouldn't wish that fate on anyone. Why do you think he killed himself?'

'His world was falling apart, and he broke. We all lose friends, Mr Lansing. This is war. It happens.'

Lansing grunted. 'All right. What about Colson?'

'His fellow directors will not support him. If they try to do so, the Foreign Office will intervene.'

Lansing nodded. 'And the Russians?'

'I had confirmation from the Bolsheviks yesterday. They have a price, obviously. They need money to fund their revolution in Russia. In exchange, they will recognize an independent Armenia, and will support your claim to the oilfields. If the British try to seize the oil wells by force, Russia will send troops to defend them.'

'Assuming the Bolsheviks take control of Russia,' Lansing said.

'They will. The liberals have no support among the people. They are tainted by association with the old regime. Mark my words, Mr Lansing. Vladimir Ilyich Lenin will be ruler of Russia before the year is out.'

'In that case, God help Russia,' Lansing said.

'What happens to Russia is not our concern. We concentrate on getting what we want. A free Armenia, and oil.'

Lansing smiled his unpleasant smile. 'So, you've got Russia lined up, and I have Germany in my pocket. From what you say, the British are ready to fall into line. No matter who loses the war, we win.' He held out his hand. 'You're a pretty sharp fellow, Makarian. It's been a pleasure doing business with you.'

The weather forecast had been correct: the clouds were parting, ragged scraps blown on a fitful east wind, and the sky was blue with twilight. Price stood in the drawing room, looking out at the park and the sodden meadows by the river, absently rubbing the scars on his face. 'It's Colson,' he said.

'How do you know?' asked Edith.

'Mrs Vane started asking me about the boardroom and the stationery cupboard, and Colson reacted badly. I think his nerves are going.'

'God, that's the last thing we need,' Edith said. 'I must go, I'm supposed to be standing guard over Mrs Fairbairn. Watch Colson closely. I don't trust these people, Geraint.'

'The only person in the world I trust is you,' said Price.

'You're sweet.' She kissed him softly on the lips. 'I must go.'

Captain Ryder and Commander Colson stood on the wisteria bridge at the far end of the lake, watching twilight fall over the water meadows. The headlamp of a train, an unwinking yellow eye, moved up the railway line. Stars sparkled in the gaps between the clouds. Behind them, the woods were ominous and black.

'I'm offering you a way out,' Ryder said.

Colson was silent for a moment. 'Way out of what?' he asked finally.

'Don't be coy, Colson, there isn't time. The net is closing in. Gallagher is certain that you are the Dreamer. It's only a matter of time until he gathers the evidence to prove it.'

'The Dreamer! Ryder, are you mad?'

'Perfectly sane,' Ryder said. 'Rather more than you, I suspect. I can only guess at what you suffered in France, and because of that you have my sympathy. I saw the same thing happen to my own father. That is why I am offering you a way out.'

Colson said nothing. 'Resign your commission and leave the service,' Ryder said. 'After that, get out of England as soon as possible, preferably to a neutral country. The weather is good in Mexico, I hear.'

Colson reached into his pocket and pulled out a silver case, extracted a cigarette, struck a match and lit it. The cigarette glowed into life, and he dropped the match into the dark water below. Ryder watched him. 'You're tired,' the captain said quietly. 'I understand that. You're ill and you're exhausted. God knows what kind of strain you have been under, all compounded by shell shock. But the end is coming now. I can hold off Gallagher and ensure you get away, but you have to give me something in return. You need to tell me the truth about naval intelligence.'

'Why should I tell you anything?' Colson asked. 'Oh, wait. I see it. You want the credit for exposing the spy. You want Admiral Jellicoe to dismiss Admiral Hall and put you in charge of the intelligence division.'

Ryder's voice was hard. 'I want to know why naval intelligence is failing to disclose information that could be vital to the war effort. Like the telegram, for instance. Zimmermann is hatching some scheme in Mexico, there's no doubt about that, and the Americans need to know what it is. Why are you sitting on the telegram?'

Colson turned on him. 'God damn it, Ryder, if you weren't my senior officer, I would smash your face in.'

'Which would achieve precisely nothing,' Ryder said calmly. 'You have two choices, Colson. You can explain to me, or you can explain to Gallagher. In your shoes, I know which I would prefer.'

The train passed, moving on towards Tonbridge as darkness fell over the fields. 'We gather a great deal of information,' Colson said. 'We don't release all of it because to do so would betray how the information was acquired. We need to protect our sources.'

'Is that what happened at Jutland? You failed to send the message about the German fleet because you wanted to protect your sources?'

'I sent the damned message, Ryder! I told Scapa Flow that the German fleet had left port! Someone at your end must have messed it up!'

'No one at Scapa Flow *messed it up*,' Ryder said. His voice was colder than ever. 'Who or what are these sources you refer to?'

Colson's voice cracked with strain. 'I'm not telling you anything, Ryder.'

'Don't be a fool, Colson. Take the chance you are offered. Give me something I can tell Admiral Jellicoe, and then you can have peace.'

'You and Jellicoe can both kiss my arse,' Colson said. He dropped his cigarette into the water, and turned and walked across the bridge and back over the park. The cigarette smoke faded on the wind, replaced by the deeper, more pungent aroma of a cigar. A few moments later James Lansing walked onto the bridge and came to stand beside Ryder.

'Did you hear all of that?' the captain asked.

'Every word,' said Lansing.

'This puts you in a difficult position, of course.'

'On the contrary,' Lansing said, puffing on the cigar. 'I'd say my position is crystal clear. I'm going to recommend to President Wilson that America remains neutral.'

Ryder held up a hand. 'Do nothing rash, I beg you. Britain and America have a shared destiny. You know that as well as I do.'

'Shared destiny? Christ, you British. You talk about your empire like you have a God-given right to it. Even if you somehow manage to scrape your way to winning the war, the way I see it, the British Empire is a house of cards just waiting for a good gust of wind to blow it down. And without the empire, where in hell are you? Just some dirty little island off the coast of Europe. History will forget you, Ryder, sooner than you think.'

'History forgets everyone, in the end,' Ryder said. 'Borden is desperate for the American alliance, and you have the whip hand. Use it. You'll get your oil concession, and more if you ask for it.'

Lansing drew on his cigar again. Another train passed, this one heading back down the line towards Dover, steaming to collect a fresh cargo of the maimed and the gassed. 'You said something to Colson about a telegram,' Lansing said. 'Is that the one from the German foreign minister? The top secret one that no one's supposed to know about?'

'The telegram purports to be from Zimmermann to Germany's ambassador in Mexico. If you want my advice, tell Borden that you want to see the telegram. Borden has friends in very high places. They can force Colson to divulge it.'

'Why should I do that?'

'Because if I'm right, Colson is suppressing that telegram to prevent your government from learning about it.' Ryder paused. 'Whatever secret Colson is concealing, President Wilson needs to know about it. America could be in grave danger.'

'America can handle itself.'

'Against an alliance of foreign powers determined to do you harm? Are you willing to take that chance, Mr Lansing? Talk to Borden.'

Lansing considered this. 'How do you know this telegram even exists? Or that it is genuine?'

'I believe it exists, as do quite a number of other people. Several have already been killed for it. But only Commander Colson knows the truth.'

'You as good as accused Colson of being a German agent.'

'I know. A fellow officer . . . It sickens me, but I had to do it. Time is passing and we need to put pressure on Colson, to force a confession. If Borden forces him to reveal the contents of the telegram, we can flush him out, and then set about cleaning up the intelligence service. And you will get vital intelligence about whatever the Germans are planning in Mexico. If you help me now, you will also be doing a great service for your president and your country.'

Lansing nodded slowly. 'All right. How do you want to play this?'

'We'll talk to Borden after dinner. I'll take control, you follow my lead.' Ryder turned and held out his hand. 'Thank you, Mr Lansing. You won't regret this, and neither will America.'

Sunday, 4 February 1917
4.43 p.m.

Tea was being served in the drawing room. Once again, war and death could not disturb the routine of the house; and, Gallagher thought, perhaps that was a good thing. In a time of chaos, routines gave people a sense of normalcy, a life raft that they could cling to. He remembered, briefly, the bodies rolling and bumping in the waves after *Lusitania* sank, and pushed the memory out of his mind.

The door to the music room was open and music rippled softly through, a pavane by Couperin played very expertly on the harpsichord. Ryder and Lansing were just coming into the drawing room, taking off their gloves and rubbing cold hands, accepting cups of tea from Hunton the footman. Nathalie Fairbairn, still pale, and Edith Price were seated in a corner, drinking tea and talking in low voices. Lady Maud sat staring at the fire, her husband standing beside her. Price sat by the window, leafing through a magazine that he did not appear to be reading. There was a darkness in the atmosphere, Gallagher thought. Was it the killings that had cast a pall over the room, or the thought that the zeppelins might return, or some more general foreboding? Perhaps it was all three.

There was no sign of Colson.

Mrs Vane handed Gallagher a cup of tea. 'Did you get what you wanted?' she asked.

'Some of it. And you?'

Mrs Vane told him about the conversation with Price, and Gallagher nodded. He pulled an envelope from his pocket and handed it to her. 'Here are the final instructions for our people.

They will be waiting at the gatehouse. Do you mind taking this out to them?'

'Of course not,' she said. 'I'm not afraid of the dark.'

Gallagher smiled a little. 'Perhaps you should be.'

Mrs Vane went out into the hall to fetch her coat. Gallagher drank his tea, set the cup down on a side table and walked into the music room, closing the door behind him.

As before, he stood for a moment listening to Makarian play, unwilling to break the spell. Music reminded him of Roxanne, and the evenings they had spent listening to the great musicians of their age. She had introduced him to some of them, people like Amy Beach and Teresa Carreño, and in those gentle days before the war they had become friends. He remembered, too, standing in the salon of the *Lusitania* listening to a white-haired Spanish professor play the music of Albéniz like he had been touched by the hand of God.

Makarian spoke, his fingers still moving over the keyboard. 'Is Commander Colson planning to leave us, do you think?'

'Why do you ask?'

'Because his chauffeur is in the stables, tuning the engine of that Silver Ghost. I wish he would do it somewhere else. The noise of the engine is frightening the horses.'

'I'll send someone to have a word with him,' Gallagher said.

Makarian continued playing. Gallagher did not move. 'Do you have nothing better to do than watch me play, Pat?' the other man asked.

'As it happens, no, I don't,' Gallagher said. 'I am studying you, you see.'

'And what is it about me that fascinates you?'

'I am puzzled. I cannot understand how a successful businessman and gifted musician can also be such a blethering idiot.'

'If you are referring to Fairbairn—'

'I am not referring to Fairbairn. I am referring to the political plots you have managed to get yourself involved in. How much have you promised, Nick? And to how many people?'

Makarian was still playing. 'I have done what I had to do,' he said.

'Does Penelope know about your schemes?'

'I told you. Penelope knows as much as she wants to know.'

That was not an answer, Gallagher thought. 'Your partner in Saint Petersburg, Litzov. Did you know that he was present when Rasputin was killed?'

'What are you talking about?'

Gallagher pulled a postcard out of his pocket and laid it on the top of the harpsichord. 'We found this in Vasiliev's rooms. *R. is respected, M.I. was there.* R is Rasputin, and as you know, to be respected is Russian slang for a killing or an assassination. M.I. is Maxim Ivanovich Litzov, your partner and friend.'

Makarian stopped playing and sat back, folding his arms across his chest. 'Yes,' he said. 'I knew Maxim was there.'

'What the hell was he playing at? Rasputin's killing will turn the Russian people against the nobility. Civil war is a certainty.'

'Of course,' Makarian said. 'And the Bolsheviks will win, and establish their dictatorship of the proletariat. It is all ordained.'

Gallagher stared hard at the other man. 'Wait a moment. Are you telling me Litzov *set up* Rasputin's assassination?'

'Certainly he did. He is well known in the city, a leading figure in the financial community. The nobles and Rasputin both trusted him, and believed he was on their side. He planned the rendezvous with Rasputin, and Prince Yusupov and the others did the killing. In Russia, the fuze is now lit. Revolution is inevitable.'

'How does that benefit you, Nick?'

'The Bolsheviks will support a free Armenia, and provide troops to defend it if necessary.'

'In exchange for what?'

'Money. Lots and lots of money, from Maxim and myself.'

'Litzov has an office with gold wallpaper, but the Bolsheviks are willing to work with him?'

'Of course. Even Bolsheviks like money, Pat, and Lenin's government will need plenty of it. Maxim and I are prepared to work with them.'

'I see,' Gallagher said. 'Now, tell me about the private deal you have struck with Lansing.'

'If I do not, what will you do? Tell Penelope about myself and Fairbairn? But you have no idea what really passed between us, do you? A Platonic friendship? A harmless flirtation? Penelope will not care about those.'

'No,' Gallagher said. 'But Maud will.'

Makarian's face showed his anger. 'You can be a real shit, Pat, do you know that?'

'There are three possible outcomes in the Middle East,' Gallagher said. 'One is that the Allies win the war and Britain takes control of the oilfields. The second is that the Germans win the war and receive the oilfields from their allies the Ottoman Turks. The third is that no matter who wins, neither side is strong enough to establish control and the Bolsheviks will step in and seize the oil. You and Lansing are making deals with all three sides, Britain, Germany and the Bolsheviks.'

Makarian froze. 'I have made no deal with Germany.'

'No, but Lansing has. Didn't he tell you?'

He watched Makarian's face as the other man considered his options. 'Yes,' Makarian said finally. 'He told me. I admire his determination.'

'His determination!'

'Lansing wants the oilfields,' Makarian said. 'As you said, no matter which way the fortunes of war happen to turn, he will get them. Lansing always gets what he wants, and so long as I can ride his coat tails, so will I.'

'You really are an absolute bloody fool,' Gallagher said. 'Don't you realize this is about much more than oil? Lansing is betraying us! Even as we speak, Winston Churchill and your father-in-law are preparing to hand over the oil concession to Lansing in hopes that he will use his influence with President Wilson. Once he has the concession in his hands, Lansing will publicly declare his support for the war, but secretly he will advise Wilson to remain neutral. He is screwing us, Nick, and he will screw you too, if you let him.'

'And who is to say the British government will not?' said Makarian. 'Thank you, but I will take my chances with Lansing.'

When Gallagher spoke again, his voice was cold. 'I am sorry, Nick. But *when* we win the war, this will be remembered. The oilfields will go to Anglo-Persian, and you and Lansing will be frozen out.'

Makarian leaned forward. 'You really don't understand, do you? One way or another, Lansing will get the oil. You see, we really have thought of everything.'

'Have you?' said Gallagher. 'When I was serving in China, someone told me about an ancient sage named Sun Tzu. He said something quite interesting, I think. If you know neither yourself nor the enemy, you will lose every time. If you know the enemy but don't know yourself, the odds are about fifty-fifty. If you know both the enemy and yourself, you need not fear the result of a hundred battles.'

'What has this to do with me?' demanded Makarian.

'You know the enemy, that much is clear by the careful plans you have laid. But how well do you know yourself?'

SUNDAY, 4 FEBRUARY 1917
5.19 P.M.

'You are late,' said Lady Maud. 'There is no more tea, but there may still be some sandwiches.'

The drawing room was quiet now. Borden stood by the fire; Price was still pretending to read his magazine. In the music room, Makarian had resumed playing, and the soft precise notes of the harpsichord sounded gently in the air.

Gallagher looked at the fire, which was starting to die. He resisted the temptation to go to the log basket. 'I am not hungry,' he said. 'I am sorry that there has been so much disruption this weekend. By tomorrow morning we will all be gone, and hopefully your life will go back to normal.'

Lady Maud ignored this. The shock she had felt after Fairbairn's death had worn off; either that, or it had been damped down hard and suppressed. 'Where is your friend Mrs Vane? She also did not appear for tea.'

'She had some errands to run,' Gallagher said.

'In the dark?' demanded Lady Maud. 'On a Sunday?'

Gallagher smiled a little. 'She's a busy woman.' He paused. 'You should be kinder to Penelope.'

His mother's dark eyes bored into his face. The skin of her face was like parchment. 'I don't believe I asked for your opinion,' she said.

'I am giving it, nevertheless. You have made your feelings towards me very clear over the years, and now you have cut your ties with Alice. Penelope is the only one of your children that is not alienated from you. You need her.'

'My relationship with my daughters is none of your business.'

'Actually, it is. Like it or not, I am part of this family and I am fond of both Penelope and Alice. I can't help Alice, I wish I could, but she is beyond reach now. As for Penelope, difficult times lie ahead. She will need her mother.'

'I assume that you are referring to her husband. What has he done now?'

'His intentions are honest, but he has overreached himself. Trouble is coming.'

Her voice was full of iron. 'I learned a harsh lesson early in life. Marriage is not a game or a sport, or a thing to be done on a whim. It is time that Penelope learned this also. Makarian is from rotten stock. If his business fails, which I assume is what you mean, I will strongly encourage her to divorce him and start again. This time, she might find a husband who can give her children.'

There was silence for a while. 'That is the most cold-blooded thing I have ever heard you say,' Gallagher said.

'I do not require your approval, Patrick.'

'If it comes to a choice between you and Nicholas, Penelope will choose her husband.'

'Then she is a fool,' said Lady Maud.

Gallagher felt his anger rising. 'So that is it? You will drive them both away, just as you drove me away? Is this how you want it, Mother? Ending your days, bitter and alone?'

Her eyes met his. 'What do you think I am now?' she said. 'If you will forgive me, I must change for dinner.'

Lady Maud rose and walked a little stiffly out of the room. Gallagher turned to his stepfather standing by the fire. 'I assume you heard all of that.'

'Yes,' Borden said. He looked more exhausted than ever. 'What Nicholas is doing is highly unethical, but it is also quix-otic. I am not sure whether I disapprove of him, or admire him.

A little of both, perhaps . . . For Penelope's sake, I will do what I can to protect him.'

'Try to separate him from Lansing,' Gallagher said. 'What about yourself? Has Lansing demanded the oil concession?'

'Yes. He finally stopped waiting for me to offer it, and demanded it openly this afternoon. If I don't agree, he will walk away. I find the man utterly noxious, but what am I to do?'

'Resist,' Gallagher said, 'but keep him in play. We need him for the endgame.' He hesitated for a moment. 'Will you forgive me if I ask a personal question?'

'Of course.'

'Your marriage. Is it in difficulties?'

Borden ran a hand over his eyes. 'I don't really know what that means,' he said finally. 'Our marriage is like the rest of us, Pat. It endures.'

SUNDAY, 4 FEBRUARY 1917
5.43 P.M.

The house was silent, apart from the monotonous thump of the water pipes. Gallagher sat alone in the dark drawing room, staring at the fire and listening to the night outside. Wind hissed gently around the house. Yet another train whistle sounded, mournful and long, followed by the distant rattle of steel wheels.

After a moment he reached into his coat pocket and took out the folded letter, the one he had carried with him everywhere since the day the *Lusitania* sank. The paper was fraying now, the ink beginning to fade. He knew the words by heart, but he read them anyway. *Know that the bearer of this letter is protected, and is acting upon my full authority . . . The outcome of the war and the fate of nations are at stake.*

More than a hundred Americans had died when the *Lusitania* was torpedoed, and everyone had expected that America would immediately declare war on Germany. But nothing had happened. Whatever Winston Churchill had hoped for when he wrote that letter, whatever he had been prepared to gamble, it had not succeeded.

So now, here we are, Gallagher thought. One last throw of the dice before bankruptcy and starvation, the U-boats and zeppelins and bombers force us to our knees. One way or another, in three hours' time it would be done. *But let there be no more killing*, he thought. *Enough people have died.*

In answer, Roxanne's voice spoke from far away. *This bloody knife shall play the umpire* . . . She was right, of course. He could control some of the events that were to come, but not all of them.

The door opened and he looked up to see Penelope standing in the doorway. Her usually cheerful face was firmly set. 'I hear you have had a fight with Mother,' she said. 'Was it about me?'

'Yes.'

'Stay out of it, Pat. This is none of your affair. I can look after myself.'

'I'm sure you can. Strangely, my concern was for her, not you. If she drives you away, she will have lost the last of her children.'

'That is her problem, not mine,' Penelope said vigorously. 'Why should I be the one to stay home? Why isn't Alice here? I've played Martha to her Mary for too long, Pat. Not any more.'

'Aren't you being rather selfish?' Gallagher asked.

'Really, Pat? *I'm* the selfish one? How often do you show up, hmm? How often do you visit her?'

'It's different. She doesn't want me here.'

'How would you know what she wants? You barely speak to her!'

'For God's sake, Penelope! Don't you think I haven't tried? Over and over again down through the years, I have made the first approach and always been rebuffed. Do you know, she will tell me nothing about my father? *I don't even know his name!*'

They stared at each other for a long moment, and then her shoulders slumped. 'I'm sorry, Pat,' she said softly. 'I know she treats you badly.'

'She treats herself badly. I'm trying to stop her doing it to you as well.'

'It may be too late,' Penelope said.

'When the war ends, if an Armenian state is established, I assume Nick will go there. Will you go with him?'

She stared at him as if he had two heads. 'He's my husband! Of course I will go with him. Nicky needs me, and I shall support him to the end.'

'The end?' Gallagher said. 'Do you realize what the end might be?'

'I am not a child,' Penelope said, and she walked out of the room.

COMMANDER COLSON CAME in a moment later. His face was pale and he looked cold. 'Where have you been?' Gallagher asked.

'I went for a walk,' Colson said, moving towards the fire. 'I needed to think.'

'About what?' Gallagher asked after a moment.

Colson stared at the fire a long time. 'I'm going to resign my commission,' he said finally. 'I'll tell Blinker as soon as I get back to London.'

'Resign your commission, in a time of war? Do you really think anyone will accept?'

'I can't do this any more, Gallagher. No one trusts me, not Ryder, not Blinker, not you. For God's sake, you put Mrs Vane into the intelligence division to spy on me! Well, I hope you're bloody satisfied with the result, because I've had enough. I'm getting out.'

'Wait until after dinner,' Gallagher said. 'Then we will talk.'

The engine of a car could be heard, idling in the carriage drive outside. Colson shook his head. 'I'm leaving, right now. My driver is waiting. I'll send for my bags when I get back to London. I just wanted to say one thing to you before I go.'

He paused, swallowing.

'Go on,' Gallagher said.

'You asked about Warren. You were right, I haven't told the truth about him. That was not the first time we had met. Before the war I employed him to do some work for me, in America.'

Gallagher rose to his feet. 'Let me save you the trouble,' he said. 'You were with the Anglo-Persian delegation negotiating an alliance with Standard Oil. You and your fellow directors wanted to know what Standard Oil's negotiating position was, and you hit on the idea of conducting a little espionage. You hired Warren to burgle their offices and crack their safe.'

'It was a lunatic idea,' Colson said. He swallowed again. 'We'd been there for a couple of months and the negotiations had stalled. The others insisted that spying on the Americans was our best chance of coming out on top. So, I made some discreet enquiries at our embassy, and one of our attachés introduced me to Warren. Said he'd used him before, for some cloak-and-dagger work.'

Gallagher sighed. 'Dear God,' he said. 'The British embassy

was employing a German spy to do their intelligence work. No wonder Lansing thinks we are incompetent. What happened?'

'Warren bungled it. He found the papers we wanted and got away without getting caught, but he left so many tracks that the Standard Oil people knew immediately what had happened. They complained to the embassy, and the ambassador hauled us in and tore us off a strip. We had to take the next ship home.'

'Why are you telling me this?'

'To set the record straight,' Colson said. 'I knew Warren, yes, but I didn't hire him to steal the Zimmermann telegram and I certainly didn't kill him. And now, I am going.'

'You should stay here,' Gallagher said.

'You can't stop me.' Colson turned and walked back into the hall. Gallagher followed him. From outside came a gentle clash of metal as the car's clutch engaged, and engine noise picked up. Tyres crunched on gravel as the car drove away. Colson stopped in astonishment, staring in the direction of the retreating sound.

Geraint Price stood in front of the door. 'Going somewhere, Commander?'

'Get out of my way,' Colson said, still looking after the car.

Price raised his prosthetic hand. 'It's a bit rude to leave now, don't you think? Without even saying goodbye to your host, and the other guests?'

The door opened before Colson could speak and Mrs Vane came in, her cheeks flushed with cold. 'Ah, there you are, Commander. I'm afraid we've commandeered your car. We needed to send an urgent message to London. I'm sorry for the inconvenience, but there was no other choice.'

Colson stared at her. Gallagher moved forward. 'Don't think of trying to go on foot, Commander,' he said quietly. 'The park and house are surrounded. Anyone who does try to leave will be stopped.'

Colson turned, still wordless, and walked upstairs. They heard the door to his room bang shut. Price stared after him for a moment before going into the drawing room, taking a seat where he could watch the hall through the open door. Mrs Vane looked at Gallagher. 'Our people will stop the car at the gatehouse, and hold the driver until morning.'

'Everything else is in place?'

'All is set. Why did Colson decide to do a runner?'

'He is feeling the pressure,' Gallagher said. He felt suddenly tired. 'By his own admission, his nerves are going.'

There was a little pause. 'I ought to say something harsh at this point,' said Mrs Vane. 'But actually, I feel rather sorry for him.' She looked at Gallagher. 'Don't worry, I'm not going soft.'

'I didn't for a moment think you were.' Gallagher coughed, feeling a sudden stab of pain in his throat. 'You have done extremely well. I shall be submitting a glowing report about you to Colonel Kell.'

'Thank you.' The clock struck the half hour, chimes echoing in the hall. 'The bird of time has but a little way to fly,' said Mrs Vane.

'And the bird is on the wing,' said Gallagher. 'So, let's do what we British do best.'

'We change for dinner?' asked Mrs Vane.

Gallagher smiled a little. 'You're learning,' he said.

19

As was the usual custom, the servants had been given Sunday evening free, although they had been warned not to leave the house. That did not make it much of a night off, Mrs Vane thought; stuck out here at Hartlake Hall, there was nothing to do except listen to the wind in the trees and the whistle and rattle of the trains.

Smoothing out the wrinkles in her black evening gown, she followed Gallagher into the gloomy dining room. A white sheet had been pinned up to cover the blood-stained ceiling until it dried and could be repainted, adding to the general air of ghostliness. Borden and Lady Maud were already there, along with Makarian and his wife. Penelope's usual effervescence was gone and her mouth was set in a grim line.

Before they retired the servants had set out dinner on the sideboard: cold ham and cold roast beef, lobsters, a selection of dismal salads, a dry Victoria sponge and blackcurrant fool. Makarian opened bottles of wine and began filling glasses. Ryder and Lansing entered the room, followed by the Prices and Nathalie Fairbairn. Nathalie was pale and silent. The brittle façade was collapsing now, and the eyes of a frightened child looked out of her face.

Her comrades would not help her, Gallagher thought. She

was right, they would drop her immediately now that she was of no more use to them. Communists were, in his experience, even more misogynistic than the bourgeoisie. Nathalie Fairbairn had been a strong and successful woman in their midst, and they would be only too happy to throw her to the wolves.

Everyone was quiet apart from Lansing, who walked to the sideboard and began noisily filling his plate. Ryder looked around. 'Where is Commander Colson?'

'I believe he is in his room,' Price said.

'I'll fetch him,' said Mrs Vane. 'Perhaps he fell asleep, and didn't hear the bell.'

She went upstairs and knocked at Colson's door. Ominously, there was no answer. She knocked again and this time, to her relief, Colson opened the door. He looked, she thought, like death. His face was pale, and his usually immaculate evening dress was creased and rumpled. The room behind him was full of cigarette smoke.

'What do you want?' he demanded.

'It's time for dinner,' Mrs Vane said.

'I'm not coming to dinner. Please give my apologies to her ladyship and Sir John.'

'You really should come down,' Mrs Vane said.

Colson stared at her with red-rimmed eyes. 'This is some sort of trap.'

'This entire house is a trap,' said Mrs Vane. 'Haven't you realized that by now?'

'Damn you and Gallagher both! And damn Ryder, too. If you have an accusation against me, make it now.'

'All in good time,' said Mrs Vane. 'You won't improve matters by starving yourself. Come and eat.'

*

337

In the dining room Mrs Vane took a small plate of ham and something that resembled a Waldorf salad and took a seat next to Price. Colson, after a few moments of hesitation, took some food as well and sat down alone, an empty chair on either side of him; the chairs that Vasiliev and Fairbairn would have occupied.

Lansing was noisily cracking lobster shells. 'At last, some decent grub,' he said. 'Not as good as New England lobsters, but what can you do?'

'We try our best,' Borden said heavily.

'I have to agree with Mr Lansing,' said Ryder. 'New England lobsters are the best in the world. Our ambassador in Washington had an arrangement with the fishermen, and used to charter a boat to bring lobsters down from Maine. But if we think about crabs, now, that's a different matter. A Dungeness crab is a dish fit for a king.'

'They're in short supply since the war began,' said Makarian. 'Too many minefields for the crabbers to get out.'

'Ah, not if you know where to look,' Ryder said. 'I remember when I was with the Dover patrol. Whenever our destroyers went out on sortie, they used to drop pots just outside the minefields, and pick them up when they returned. Some of the destroyer skippers even made bets with each other about how many crabs they would bring home.' Ryder chuckled a little. 'Halcyon days,' he said.

'At least, for the ships and crews that did come back,' Price said.

'It's war, Price. You of all people should know that not everyone comes back. Let the men have their fun while they can.'

Price laid down his fork. 'Oh, I'm all for fun, sir,' he said. 'But those destroyers on the Dover patrol go out time after time with no intelligence of where the Germans are, what strength they are, or any other damned thing that might matter. Every night, they sail into ambushes. That, sir, is not *fun*.'

'I never said it was,' Ryder said calmly. 'Price, you really are becoming rather boring on this subject.'

Price persisted. 'You said that I of all people should know. What I *know*, sir, is that when we went out from Scapa Flow to fight the Germans at Jutland, we were blind. We had no idea where the German fleet was.'

Colson laid down his own fork. 'Christ, not this again.'

Lady Maud's face was a grim mask. Borden intervened, sounding more tired than ever. 'Gentlemen, if you please. Can we find some other subject of conversation while the ladies are present?'

'I was talking about shellfish,' Ryder said mildly. 'Perhaps the other gentlemen would care to give us their views on winkles?'

'Do not tease us, Captain,' said Penelope Makarian, and unusually, her voice had a little edge to it. She looked at her mother, her eyes bright with challenge. 'My father is right. Let us talk about something else entirely. The prospects of freedom for Armenia, perhaps?'

A train whistle sounded in the distance. 'We will not speak of Armenia,' Lady Maud said forcefully. 'We will not speak of Jutland, or the war, or anything else that reminds us of the horror around us. If you cannot find a civilized topic of conversation, then I would prefer that we finish our dinner in silence.'

Several minutes passed before Edith looked around the table. 'There's a new musical opening at Daly's Theatre next week,' she said. 'It's called *Maid of the Mountains*. They say that José Collins has some wonderful songs. Does anyone fancy going to see it?'

7.02 P.M.

No one, apart from Lansing, had much appetite. No one had mentioned Fairbairn's name; equally, no one had forgotten the grisly scene at lunch. Even Edith Price had finally learned that one did not speak of the dead.

The women rose after a while and moved into the drawing room. Borden fetched a decanter of port; Lansing walked to the sideboard and filled a tumbler to the brim with whisky and water, and trimmed and lit a cigar. Gallagher helped himself to a small glass of port and passed the decanter, and sat back, watching.

'This evening will be our last chance to talk, Mr Lansing,' Borden said.

Lansing blew out smoke. 'Do we have anything to talk about?'

'You have insisted several times over the past few days that we cannot win the war. I would still like to persuade you that we can. Perhaps these other gentlemen can help me.'

'Oh, we can win the war,' Ryder said. 'But not, I am afraid, without American assistance.' He looked at Colson. 'Do you wish to disagree, Commander?'

Colson said nothing. 'I will venture an argument,' Makarian said. 'If America will not join you, then you need to persuade Russia. A new government will be in power in Saint Petersburg within weeks. Give them incentives to stay in the fight. If you do, those fifty German divisions will stay in the east, and the Allies will still have a fighting chance.'

Ryder shook his head. 'The Russian army is collapsing as we speak. Their army is rotten with Bolshevism.'

'Then speak with the Bolsheviks,' Makarian said.

Borden stared at him. 'Have you gone mad?'

'On the contrary, it is the only sensible course of action. The soldiers support the Bolsheviks, yes, but they are still soldiers. They will fight if their leaders tell them to, and their leaders will fight if we make it worth their while.'

Ryder was still looking at Colson. 'What do you think, Commander? Should we be talking to the Bolsheviks?'

Colson stared at his port glass. Gallagher could almost see his mind at work, analysing the question, wondering what answer would cause the ground to give way under his feet. 'Of course not,' he said finally. 'The Bolsheviks have designs on the Middle East, we all know that. If we help them into power, we can kiss goodbye to the oilfields.'

'And your family fortune goes down the drain,' Ryder said, nodding. 'Has it ever occurred to you, Colson, that to an outsider, your actions could be construed as putting personal interest over the needs of your country?'

'What are you insinuating?' Colson demanded.

'You know damned well what I am insinuating.'

Borden slapped his hand on the table. 'Gentlemen, *please*. Can we return to the subject at hand?'

Another train whistle; another, in the long chain of macabre monotony. The velvet window drapes stirred in the draught. Lansing pushed his chair back and walked to the sideboard, refilling his glass. 'Not here,' he said. 'The fire is dying, and it's too damned cold. Let's go into the drawing room, and then we'll talk.'

7.17 P.M.

In the drawing room the women were playing cards in silence, Mrs Vane and Lady Maud partnering Edith and Penelope, sitting at the card table by the window despite the cold. Nathalie Fairbairn sat alone, staring at the wall.

Makarian picked up the silver coffee pot. 'Cold,' he said. 'I'll fetch some more from the kitchen.'

'Don't bother,' said Borden. He faced Lansing, his face lined and tired, his eyes burning with frustration. 'Let's have this out once and for all. What do you intend to tell President Wilson?'

'That depends,' Lansing said. 'Are you willing to give me the oil concession?'

'I have told you before, Lansing. That concession is not within my gift.'

Lansing glanced at the women playing cards, who were pretending not to listen. 'Out of respect for the ladies, I won't call that what we all know it is,' he said. 'Something that comes out of a horse, that you might spread on the rose beds. Anglo-Persian Oil owns that concession, and Anglo-Persian Oil is part-owned by the British government, of which you are an important member. All you have to do is send word to your friend Churchill. That concession will be in my hands by morning.'

The others were silent, watching. Gallagher watched them in turn: Ryder, relaxed with his hands behind his back; Colson sitting in a chair, tense and fuming; Makarian absolutely still; Price inscrutable, but glancing towards his wife from time to time.

'And if I do not?' said Borden.

'Then it's all over,' Lansing said. 'I will tell Woodrow that I do not recommend an alliance. Come to that, I'm not even sure we should be supporting you as we are, providing arms and ammunition and artillery shells. Why are we doing that? This ain't our fight. We should stand back and let events take their course, and make a deal with whoever comes out on top.'

'A deal for what?' asked Borden.

Lansing smiled, his teeth gleaming in the firelight. 'World domination, *of course*. That's what this is all about, isn't it? I'm talking about where American influence should be directed, and where American power should be exerted. If we join the losing side, our influence and power will be diminished. We can't afford that. There's too much at stake.'

'But if you join forces with us, we won't lose,' said Ryder.

'Sure. Like the old Spartan said. *If.* And in this case, it's a damned big *if.*'

The captain stirred a little. 'Why do you think we are losing the war?'

Lansing was still looking at Borden. 'You don't know? All right, I'll tell you. You've got this great big navy, but it's ineffective against U-boats. Your army is barely holding on. Your Flying Corps can't even protect the capital against those gasbags. And on top of that, you've been torpedoed below the waterline.'

Colson's fists clenched in his lap. 'What do you mean?' Borden said.

'Your intelligence service is a joke. There are spies inside the Admiralty, telling the Germans everything you do. I hear someone stole a top-secret telegram from your naval intelligence chief's own safe, for God's sake. How can you expect to stop the Germans on the battlefield when you can't even keep them out of your own headquarters?'

'How do you know about the telegram?' Colson demanded.

'From the sounds of things, pretty much everybody knows about it. Even that woman, the journalist, she knew about it.'

Gallagher cleared his throat. 'You saw her, Mr Lansing? May I ask when?'

Lansing turned on him. 'See? Here's another one of your *top* secret agents, asking all the right questions about a week too late. I saw her in London. She told me she was going to publish an article defaming me, and I told her to publish and be damned. She warned me to be careful, because the Admiralty had a telegram that was going to bring America into the war, and if that happened and my German connections were exposed, my life would become pretty difficult. I thanked her for her concern and kicked her out.'

Captain Ryder's eyes had narrowed. 'My God,' he said quietly. 'This is even worse than we imagined. If the press know about the telegram and start publishing articles, there will be merry hell to pay.'

The women had stopped playing cards. Mrs Vane rose to her feet and went to stand by the door. Gallagher saw the goosebumps on her arms. She deserves a decoration, he thought. The Polar Medal, perhaps.

'You are correct, Mr Lansing,' Ryder continued. 'We've known about the existence of a German agent in the Admiralty for some time.'

Lansing was incredulous. 'You *know* about him? And you've done nothing to stop him?'

'We are investigating,' Ryder said.

Lansing rose to his feet. 'You're investigating! Well, that's just bully. God damn, I've had enough of this. Sir John, I know it's late, but I'll thank you to harness up a carriage and tell one of your servants to take me into Tonbridge for the night. I'll put up at the Rose and Crown. I'm not staying here for another damned minute.'

Borden took a step forward. 'Lansing, wait. Let Captain Ryder explain.'

Colson looked like he wanted to be sick. Lansing hesitated, but after a moment he nodded. 'Make it good,' he said.

'Carry on, Captain,' Borden said, and there was a seldom-heard tone of real authority in his voice. 'But before you begin, everyone in the room should know that what Captain Ryder is about to say is covered by the Official Secrets Act. That means it must not be repeated outside of this room. That includes you, ladies.'

'We understand,' said Edith Price.

Borden nodded. 'The floor is yours, Captain,' he said.

7.33 P.M.

Ryder walked to the fireplace and turned to face the room. Colson looked towards Mrs Vane standing by the door, and looked away again. Around them, the red roses on the wallpaper looked like severed heads, lying in pools of blood at the foot of the guillotine.

'I first became aware that something was wrong when I was in command of our naval base in Ireland,' Ryder said. 'Messages not being passed, poor intelligence about German intentions and so on. It could have been simple incompetence, of course, but as time passed the instances became so frequent and so egregious – and in some cases, the consequences so tragic – that I began to wonder. After the debacle at Jutland, my suspicions began to harden. I shared them with my commanding officer, Admiral Jellicoe, and he agreed with me.'

'Why didn't you do something?' demanded Lansing.

'We did,' said Ryder. 'As soon as Admiral Jellicoe was ensconced at the Admiralty as First Sea Lord, he sent for me. He charged me, in strictest secrecy, to investigate and find out whether this really was just incompetence on the part of naval intelligence, or whether enemy agents were at work. One of the first things I discovered was the theft of documents, not just from intelligence but other divisions in the Admiralty as well.

The documents, I discovered, were being sold to a German agent. We didn't know this agent's name, only his code name, the Dreamer.

'In accordance with Admiral Jellicoe's orders, I began to investigate further. At first I made only slow progress, but things came to a head last week when someone tried to steal the telegram. The thief, Mr Lansing, was your brother-in-law, Frank Warren.'

Lansing stabbed a finger at Ryder. 'Are you suggesting *I* had something to do with it?'

Ryder let the question hang in the air, unanswered. 'Warren was hired by someone in naval intelligence to steal the telegram and pass it on to a foreign agent. This intelligence officer couldn't remove the telegram himself, not without falling under suspicion, so he brought in Warren. Only something went wrong, and Warren was killed.'

'Good riddance,' Lansing said. 'So, the telegram *is* real?'

'It is very real,' Ryder said, 'and for the moment it is still in our possession, but I have no doubt that another attempt will be made to steal it, very soon. Fortunately, Mr Gallagher and his colleagues from the secret service are vigilant, so I am confident that the attempt will fail. But the problem of the Dreamer remains.'

'What is in this telegram?' asked Makarian. 'Why is it so important?'

Ryder looked straight at Gallagher. 'We believe it contains details of a German plot against America,' he said.

Lansing turned towards Borden. 'I demand to see that telegram,' he said. 'If there is any threat to America, I need to inform Washington immediately.'

Ryder held up a hand. 'We'll come back to the telegram in

a moment,' he said. 'First, there is something else we need to discuss. It is time to expose the identity of the Dreamer.'

There was a moment of silence. One of the logs on the fire was greener than the others and it began to hiss and pop, oozing little droplets of pitch. Colson watched Ryder with eyes full of hate. *He knows what's coming*, Gallagher thought. *Of course he does; whatever else Colson might be, he is not stupid.*

'It was 1912, wasn't it, Colson?' Ryder said. His tone was almost conversational. 'When you visited America with your colleagues from Anglo-Persian Oil, and hired Frank Warren to burgle a safe. Things didn't go terribly well, but you found Warren to be useful. He helped you to recruit his sister, Lansing's wife, and you began passing information about American industry, especially the oil industry, back to Germany.

'You handed over control of the spy ring you had established, and returned to England, and began setting up another network here. You were sidelined for a while in 1914 when you served in France, but once back in England and recovered from your breakdown – how real was that, I wonder? – you used your connections to get a post in the Admiralty, right at the centre of our intelligence operation. You had access to all of our secrets.'

In the corner, Nathalie Fairbairn sat absolutely still; Gallagher could not even see her breathing.

'This is ridiculous,' Colson said. His voice was a little unsteady. 'I didn't even know Vasiliev.'

'Who was on watch at the Admiralty every time there was a major failure of intelligence?' Ryder demanded. 'Who failed to pass the message about the German fleet to my office at Scapa Flow? Who was on watch the night Warren tried to steal the telegram? And who pretended not to recognize Warren, even though you had employed him many times? It was *you*, Colson. *You* have undermined us at every turn, thwarting our naval strategy, betraying our secrets, sabotaging our desperately needed alliance with America, putting innocent lives at risk. You have betrayed the navy and you have betrayed your country. Gallagher, it is time we drew this to an end. Please place Commander Colson under arrest.'

Gallagher coughed. 'I'd like to,' he said, clearing his throat. 'But unfortunately, Captain, although your deductions make perfect sense, we're going to need more evidence than this. Commander Colson has powerful connections, remember, in business and government, even the royal family. We can't just lock him up on suspicion.'

Lansing shook his head in disgust. 'So, you're going to do nothing. Spies and crooks at the heart of the Admiralty and you're going to let them get away with it.'

Gallagher held up a hand. 'Hold on, Mr Lansing. It's not that simple.'

'Then make it simple!' Lansing snapped. 'I'm a simple man and I like simple things. Tell me in plain English what the hell is going on. And tell me what is in that telegram!'

Gallagher looked at Borden. 'Perhaps I may be permitted to have the floor,' he said.

7.38 P.M.

'Part of the problem has been that Captain Ryder and I have been conducting parallel investigations,' Gallagher said. 'We only realized this quite recently. It would have been useful if we had known earlier, as we could have worked together. However, that is so often the nature of intelligence work.'

Lansing shook his head. 'More incompetence,' he said. 'Is this going to take long, Gallagher?'

Gallagher glanced at the clock. 'Not too long,' he said. 'We have also been on the trail of the Dreamer. Last year, we and the Americans working together identified Mr Lansing's estranged wife as a potential member of the Dreamer's operation and began to interrogate her. Mrs Lansing was then killed by the head of the spy ring, a woman called Lily Sparrow. She later fled the country, as did Frank Warren.'

For once, Lansing looked genuinely shocked. 'Wait a minute. The cops told me my wife died of an accidental over-dose of heroin. They said it couldn't have been murder, there was no way in or out of the room except through a locked door.'

'No door is ever truly locked,' Gallagher said. 'Anyone can get through one, if they have enough skill and determination. Lily Sparrow was painting your wife's portrait the afternoon before she died. She departed in the afternoon, but accord-ing to our reconstruction of events, she secretly returned to the house and concealed herself until Mrs Lansing returned to her bedroom. Lily Sparrow incapacitated Mrs Lansing with diethyl ether, administered the overdose and removed a number of photographs which would have identified herself. She sprayed the room with eau de violette to mask the smell of the ether – not entirely successfully – and left the room, leaving the key in the lock on the inside of the door. Once outside, she used an implement such as a nail file or a hairpin, inserting it into the lock to turn the key and lock the door. Her only mistake was to leave a smudge of paint on the key. Apart from Mrs Lansing herself, she was the only person likely to have handled the key.'

'That's hardly sufficient evidence,' Ryder said.

'Lily was interviewed by the police after Mrs Lansing's death, but at that point they had no cause to suspect her. Later, after she disappeared, a more thorough search of her lodgings was made. A pair of leather gloves was found, also smudged with the same white paint that was found on the key. I agree, Captain Ryder, that is not enough to hang her, but there is more to come. Did Lily Sparrow's name come up in your own inquiry?'

Ryder shook his head. 'I knew nothing of the events around Mrs Lansing's death. I didn't even know there was a connection with this affair until now. Mr Lansing, this must be dreadful news for you. I am truly sorry.'

'Don't be,' Lansing said. 'I didn't care for the woman.' He finished his drink, walked to the sideboard and poured another. Ryder looked at Gallagher, his face and voice impatient. 'Where is all of this leading, Gallagher?'

'You'll see in a moment.' Gallagher turned to Edith Price. 'Mrs Price, I would like to call upon you, if I may. I hope you don't mind explaining your real identity, but you did say this would be your last case.'

Edith nodded and rose to her feet, coming forward and holding up her warrant card. 'I am Edith Price,' she said. 'I am an agent of the United States Secret Service.'

'Kindly tell us your connection with this case,' Gallagher said.

'Our agency was called in after Mrs Lansing's murder,' Edith said. 'Unfortunately, Lily Sparrow had disappeared by the time we began to suspect her. We traced her as far as New York City, but by the time we'd gotten that far, she had already sailed for England. I was sent to London to see if we could discover her whereabouts. Needless to say, she is wanted in America on charges of murder and espionage.'

'And have you had any luck in finding her?' Gallagher asked.

'Not so far. She may have gone dormant, or she may be trying to get away to Germany.' Edith paused. 'We hadn't considered Commander Colson as a suspect until now. But if you want more information about Commander Colson's activities in

America before the war, I am sure we can help. As you know, we want to put the Dreamer out of action just as much as you do.'

'Thank you,' Gallagher said. 'But I think we have the situation in hand.' He reached over and took the identity card out of her hand, tore it in half and threw it on the fire.

7.48 P.M.

Price reached into his pocket. 'No!' Gallagher said sharply.

Price pulled out his revolver. Penelope screamed. Faster than thought, Nicholas Makarian struck Price with two powerful blows, left hand chopping down hard onto Price's wrist, right fist connecting with his jaw. The revolver fell to the carpet with a thud; Price reeled, half-stunned, and collapsed into a chair.

Edith bolted towards the door. Mrs Vane stood still, waiting for her. Edith raised her arm to strike, and Mrs Vane seized her by the wrist and spun the younger woman around, twisting her arm up behind her back until she gasped with pain.

Gallagher had a brief glimpse of his mother sitting frozen in her chair, watching as her carefully constructed world of civility and good manners collapsed. He looked at Makarian, who had picked up Price's revolver and was standing over him. 'Well done,' Gallagher said.

'I told you. I come from a nation of warriors.'

'So do I,' said Mrs Vane, and she shoved Edith hard, throwing her down onto the floor and standing with one foot on her midriff. 'Will you do the introductions, Mr Gallagher?'

'Certainly,' said Gallagher, looking down at Edith. 'Everyone, allow me to introduce Lily Sparrow, also known as Lily Spatz. Artist, forger and one of Germany's most trusted agents for many years. You will be much missed in Berlin, I think.'

351

Ryder, for once, looked startled. 'Good God! *She* was working with the Dreamer?'

'Well?' said Gallagher. 'Were you?'

Edith was pale. 'Promise me one thing,' she said. 'Tell me you won't hurt Geraint.'

'Never mind hurting *him*,' said Makarian, rubbing his hand. 'Damn it, I think I've broken a finger.'

Penelope hurried to him and examined his hand, touching it gently. 'Geraint doesn't know about the Dreamer,' Edith said. 'He thinks I'm an American agent, and he'll be devastated when he learns the truth. Surely that is punishment enough.'

'It is very sweet of you to try to protect him,' Mrs Vane said calmly. 'However, you are lying through your teeth. Mr Price is also a German agent, recruited by yourself.'

'In fact, she did tell some of the truth,' Gallagher said. 'The best liars always do. The American Secret Service really was on her trail, and she fled to England to get away. On instructions from the Dreamer she forged the identity card, an easy task for a talented artist, and made up a story about being an agent. The story would only last until we checked with the Americans, of course, but she only needed a few hours until she and her husband could get away to Germany.'

'Germany?' Borden said blankly. 'From *here*? How?'

'Good question,' Gallagher said. 'We don't know how, but we know it was all arranged. They were due to leave in about half an hour. Frank Warren thought he was going with them, as it happens. He didn't know that the Prices and the Dreamer had already planned to kill him.'

Behind them Price lunged out of his seat, grabbing for the gun in Makarian's hand, but he was groggy and too slow. Makarian stepped back out of reach. Price seized Penelope's arm, trying to pull her in front of him to use her as a shield. Penelope screamed again, struggling to get away, and Makarian raised the revolver and shot Price in the forehead. The crash of the gunshot in the confined space of the drawing room reverberated like the blow of a hammer. Price collapsed and fell to the floor, blood pouring from his shattered head.

20

Penelope sagged into a chair, half conscious. Makarian knelt beside her, laying down the gun, pulling out a handkerchief and tenderly wiping the splattered blood from the side of her face. Some of the blood was her own, leaking from her ear. Borden stooped over her too, touching her shoulder, his voice shaking. 'Penelope? Darling girl, are you all right?'

'She can't hear you,' Makarian said. 'She has a perforated eardrum. The gun was only a few feet from her head when I fired.'

'She could have been killed,' Borden whispered.

'I did what I had to do,' said Makarian. He looked at Gallagher. 'I have just killed a man. Do you wish to arrest me?'

Lady Maud sat immobile in her chair by the window, her face like a death mask. 'Don't be ridiculous,' said Ryder. 'It was clearly self-defence.'

'Let me go,' said Edith, and the pain in her voice was raw as an electric shock. 'Let me go to him.'

Mrs Vane looked at Gallagher, who nodded. She stepped back and Edith struggled up. Her face was white. She tried to stand but her knees gave way, and she crawled slowly across the floor to where Price lay on the carpet. Kneeling beside him, she embraced him with her head resting on his chest, oblivious to the blood staining her dinner gown and her fair hair. Her voice whispered softly, just on the edge of hearing. 'Spring will come one day, Geraint. It will come, my darling. I gave you my promise.'

Makarian snorted. 'The spy weeps. Listen to the sound of the crocodile tears.'

The door flung open and Platt the butler stood in the doorway, wide-eyed; Hunton the footman was behind him. 'Sir!' the butler gasped. 'My lady! We heard a shot.'

'There has been an accident,' said Borden. He looked down at the blood-soaked carpet. 'I'm sorry to ask you to do this, Platt, but we need to remove the body. The carpet is already ruined. Roll him up in that, if you please, and take him away. When you have done that, send for the police.'

'Not the police,' Gallagher said. 'Not yet. We'll send for them when we're done.' He bent down and, not without compassion, touched Edith on the shoulder. 'Come away,' he said. 'There is nothing that you can do.'

Edith did not move. 'You did your duty,' Gallagher said. 'But it is over now. Come away.'

Slowly Edith sat up, and Gallagher helped her up and into a chair and handed her his handkerchief so she could wipe her face. Her eyes were wide and staring with shock and pain. Her grief was undeniable, Gallagher thought, perhaps the only genuine thing about her. Perhaps it was fortunate that, for her, it would not last for long.

He waited while the two servants rolled up the body in the carpet and dragged it away. Neither seemed very perturbed, but Gallagher recalled that both men had been in the army in South Africa; they had probably seen much worse. Makarian knelt, holding Penelope close to his chest, Borden standing protectively over them. Ryder and Lansing stood motionless in front of the fireplace.

'You're probably wondering what that was all about,' Gallagher said.

Lansing had lost some of his ebullience. He pointed at Edith. 'Am I to understand that this woman killed my wife?'

'Yes,' Gallagher said. 'Between them, she and her husband have left quite a trail of death. The next to die was Frank Warren. To some extent, Warren was the architect of his own downfall. He arrived in London desperately needing money, and began hitting up all of his old acquaintances, including Commander Colson, Mrs Fairbairn and Lily Sparrow, or Mrs Price as she now was. Mrs Fairbairn and Vasiliev hired him to burgle Admiral Hall's safe, but being Warren, he tried to play both sides against the middle and informed Mrs Price, thinking German intelligence might be willing to take him on again. Am I right so far?' he asked Edith.

Edith nodded, mute.

'I suspect he may have paid more than one visit to your house, perhaps when you were out', Gallagher said. 'He found your coded messages and deciphered one of them, *Throne of Saturn 2030 2417*.' Gallagher paused. 'As a matter of interest, Mrs Price, how did he manage to do that?'

Edith looked down at her hands. 'Frank knew all of the ciphers because he devised them. It was his idea to use the *Rubaiyat* because it was his favourite book. Frank Warren was unreliable and degenerate, but he had a genius for designing things. Including codes.'

Gallagher nodded. 'You and your husband planned his murder. Price intercepted Warren in the Admiralty, enticed him into the stationery cupboard, killed him and left the syringe behind to make it look like suicide in a locked room. I have to admit it took us a while to work out how it was done. The final clue came when Mrs Vane discovered a syringe and vials of morphine in Price's bags. Price used morphine as a painkiller, but it also made a very handy murder weapon. Then earlier today, Price stole Mrs Fairbairn's revolver, followed Vasiliev into the woods and shot him. Soon after, Mrs Price killed Herbert Fairbairn in the bathtub. Another day of this, and the mice would have had the house to themselves.'

Nathalie Fairbairn spoke with an effort. 'Herbert took his own life,' she said.

Gallagher shook his head. 'Lily Spatz has a talent for artistry in more ways than one. Among other things, she is adept at making murder look like suicide. She killed both Sadie Lansing and Fairbairn by first drugging them with ether and then injecting the former with heroin and cutting the latter's wrists. She also used the same trick of turning the key in the lock from the outside with a nail file or something similar.'

'Why?' asked Borden.

'Why kill them? Because they knew too much about the Dreamer's operation. Sadie Lansing was under suspicion and would have cracked under further interrogation. Vasiliev had panicked and was trying to run away. If the police had caught him, and they would have done so, he too would probably have confessed everything. Warren was unreliable, to say the least; he was already selling secrets, and he would probably have confessed to his own role for twenty quid and a bottle of whisky. Fairbairn . . . Poor Fairbairn. He tried to do his duty to everyone, and got caught in the middle. It's hard to say how much he actually knew, or had guessed, or how much his wife and Frank Warren had told him. But the Dreamer couldn't take a chance, and so Fairbairn had to die.'

Ryder frowned. 'There was no attempt to make Vasiliev's death look like suicide. I wonder why not?'

'There was no time,' Gallagher said. 'The Prices were already planning to kill Vasiliev, but he tried to forestall them by making a run for it. Price tracked him down before he could get away. I suspect that Price must have slipped out of the church service early, or perhaps he didn't go at all.'

'I didn't see him there,' said Borden. 'I still don't understand. Killing so many people is a desperate step. What did the Dreamer want?'

'He wanted the Zimmermann telegram,' Gallagher said. 'Or more precisely, he wanted to know how we obtained the telegram and whether we could read it. Are we able to intercept German wireless messages? And more importantly, have we broken their codes? The Dreamer was ordered to find out.'

Colson rose slowly to his feet. Gallagher looked at him, willing him to be silent.

'So where did this telegram come from?' Lansing demanded.

'We sent word to our agents in Mexico City to secure a copy of the telegram at all costs. They tried several times to break into the German embassy, without success. Then, they got lucky. They learned of an Englishman living in Mexico City who had been accused of forging banknotes and was about to be executed. Our people also discovered that this man had a friend who worked in the central telegraph office. We intervened with the authorities and got the Englishman released, on condition that he would act as a go-between with his friend. Money changed hands, and the friend procured a copy of the telegram and passed it over to us.'

He looked at Lansing. 'You said you wanted to see the telegram. Mrs Vane?'

'No!' Colson said sharply. 'Gallagher, you can't do this! It's against orders!'

'Sorry, Commander,' Gallagher said. 'This is the only way.' He nodded to Mrs Vane, who opened her reticule and handed a piece of paper to Lansing. The oilman unfolded it, frowning.

'One-three-oh,' he said aloud. 'One-three-oh-four-two. One-three-four-oh-one. Eight-five-oh-one. One-one-five . . . This is just a series of numbers. What is this?'

8.17 P.M.

Colson stared, his mouth open. Gallagher ignored him. 'What is this?' Lansing repeated.

'Well, that's just it,' Gallagher said. 'We don't know for certain. We *think* this is the telegram that Zimmermann sent to the ambassador. But as I said earlier to Captain Ryder, this could be the ambassador's laundry list for all we know. We can't decipher it.'

Lansing's eyes narrowed. 'And this is the famous telegram that is going to catapult America into the war? The one that suggests Germany is conspiring with Mexico against us? What a cock-and-bull story! You just *happened* to find a telegram you can't even read, but you think it is vital to the security of the USA. You just *happened* to find a crook who was able to bribe his way into the telegraph office and buy a sheet of paper covered in numbers? You bloody British. How many god-damned times have you tried stunts like this before, conjuring up shadows and bogeymen, trying to stampede us into *your* war?'

Colson took a step forward. Gallagher held up a hand. Lansing crumpled the telegram and threw it on the fire. 'This is a swindle,' he said. 'A cheat. A fraud.' He turned to Borden.

'This has the stink of your friend Churchill about it. Cook up an imaginary Mexican–German plot against America in order to buffalo us into declaring war on Germany. My God, how crude! Somebody told me Churchill was a subtle man. Not by this account.'

'This plot did not come from Churchill,' Borden said. He hesitated. 'Or if it did, I knew nothing about it.'

'Of course it didn't come from Churchill,' Gallagher said. 'It came from me.'

Everyone was watching him; even Penelope had roused a little and was sitting forward. Edith Price was suddenly tense, dark bloodstains like shadows on her face and hair.

'You?' Lansing said blankly.

The telegram form caught fire, burning quickly away to crumbling black ash. 'You can rest easy on one count, Mr Lansing,' Gallagher said. 'We did not fabricate this plot for your benefit, or to compel America to join the war. As I said, once the Germans became aware of a potential security breach, they ordered the Dreamer to find out what was happening. This was our way of smoking him out into the open.'

Borden nodded slowly. 'Of course. If the Germans thought we might be reading their signals, they would have to take action. But why would they not just change their codes?'

'Devising new codes and distributing the codebooks is expensive and takes a long time,' said Gallagher. 'They needed to be certain before taking such a drastic step.'

He paused, once again fighting back the urge to cough. 'I could rehearse all of the evidence,' he said. 'I could talk about each suspect, and why they might or might not be guilty. But I'm tired, and I can't be bothered. The game is over now, Captain Ryder. This is the end of the road.'

8.25 p.m.
Five minutes remaining

Even before Gallagher had finished speaking, Ryder had pulled a revolver from his pocket. Makarian reached down for the gun he had taken from Price, and Ryder raised the revolver and pointed it at Makarian's head. 'No,' he commanded.

Makarian hesitated. 'No, Makarian,' Ryder said. 'I admire your spirit, but it will do you no good. Push the gun across the floor to me. Carefully.'

'Do as he says,' commanded Borden.

Makarian pushed the revolver with his foot and it slid across the polished wood floor to Ryder, who picked it up and put it into his pocket. Edith Price stared at Ryder with wide eyes. 'You,' she said quietly, in a voice full of wonder. 'You are the Dreamer.'

Makarian looked at her with contempt. 'Did you really not know?'

'No one knew,' Edith said. 'We never met the Dreamer. We communicated only through message drops, using the book code.'

Colson's fists clenched. 'Do you deny this accusation, Ryder?'

'I no longer need to,' said Ryder, 'If you listen very carefully, ladies and gentlemen, you will hear my transport, coming to pick me up and take me away to Germany.'

Everyone fell silent. There it was, faint in the distance, a murmur in the air.

Thrum–thrum–thrum–thrum–thrum . . .

Ryder spoke again, reciting.

'Up from Earth's centre, through the seventh gate
I rose, and on the throne of Saturn sate,
And many knots unravelled by the road;
But not the knot of human death and fate.

'You are hearing the throne of Saturn,' Ryder said. 'The zeppelins, or more specifically Kapitän Peter Strasser, commander of the German airship force. Peter insisted on coming personally to collect me. What a good friend he is.'

'Gallagher!' Colson's voice was a scream of panic. 'Stop him, for God's sake!'

Gallagher threw up his hands. 'What do you want me to do, Commander? We've sealed off the estate on the ground, but we never imagined anyone would try to leave by air. And even if we did, there's nothing we can do! We have no aeroplanes that can challenge the zeppelins, remember?'

Ryder smiled. The gun was steady in his hand. 'Your thinking is too conventional, Gallagher,' he said. 'You should have learned to anticipate the unexpected. Now, it is too late. We shall win the war because the Germans are better equipped, better trained, better led and above all more intelligent than the Allies. I'm not surprised you can't break their codes; the German mind is naturally attuned to mathematical genius. Think of Kepler, Leibniz, Gauss. The obvious superiority of the Germans to all other races is one of the reasons why I decided to join them.'

'One of the reasons?' asked Gallagher.

'I assume you know the other. The callous and disgraceful way my father was treated by the authorities after his mental breakdown during the Crimean War. I spent years looking for a way to pay the Royal Navy back, and when I was posted to Berlin, I found it. The Nachrichten-Abteilung welcomed me with open arms, and made me one of their own.'

'You treacherous bastard,' said Colson. His face had gone pale and he was staring at the ceiling, listening to the approaching engines.

'Please,' said Ryder. 'Accept the situation, Commander. There is nothing you can do, not now.'

Thrum–thrum–thrum–thrum–thrum. Two zeppelins, Gallagher thought. One would be the ship that had reconnoitred the park the previous evening, looking for a landing place. It would set down while the second cruised overhead on top cover, keeping watch for British scouts. 'What happens now?' asked Borden.

'I shall walk out, board the airship and sail away. You will not try to stop me.' He reached into his pocket and pulled out a set of keys. 'You will have observed that I have taken the keys to the gun room, which is locked. Your servants really should keep their keys more safely.'

Lady Maud rose to her feet. 'The Germans are going to land?' she asked, her voice shaking. 'Here?'

'I fear so, my lady,' said Ryder. He bowed a little, the gun never wavering. 'My apologies for any inconvenience.'

'*No!*' said Lady Maud in an agonized whisper. She staggered a little, putting out an arm to steady herself. 'Not here! They can't come *here!*'

'Mother, get down to the cellar!' Gallagher said sharply. 'Penelope, go with her.' He looked at Colson, whose hands had begun to shake. 'You too, Commander. Go! There is nothing more to be done here!'

Colson rose, head bowed a little, and ushered the two women out of the room. Maud leaned on Penelope's arm, gasping with panic. Penelope turned in the doorway, her eyes meeting Makarian's for a moment, and Gallagher saw the fear in her face. Then they were gone.

363

THRUM–THRUM–THRUM–THRUM–THRUM.
Once again, searchlights flashed like white lightning through the drapes. 'Why all the drama?' asked Borden. 'Why not just slip away, disappear? And why accuse Commander Colson?'

Ryder looked at his watch. 'I accused Colson partly to distract attention from myself,' he said. 'And there was always the hope of also sowing a little discord in your intelligence service. As well as learning the truth about the telegram, I had some final points to negotiate with our Bolshevik friends before we send Vladimir Lenin back to Russia. Mrs Fairbairn and her friends – including you, Makarian – have been very useful fools. I also hoped to convince Mr Lansing to use his influence to keep America neutral. Our plans for Russia and America are maturing very nicely, something for which I can claim at least partial credit.'

'You will not succeed,' Borden said quietly.

THRUM–THRUM–THRUM–THRUM–THRUM.

The windows rattled with vibration. 'History will be the judge,' Ryder said, raising his voice a little to make himself heard. 'Now, if you will forgive me, I must depart. The thanks of the Kaiser, promotion to the rank of admiral and a rather fine house in Oranienburg await me.'

'Wait a moment.' Gallagher pointed at Edith Price, who had risen to her feet. 'She's your agent. Aren't you taking her with you?'

Ryder surveyed Edith. 'Take her with me? I have no further need for her. Hang her, and bury her with her husband.'

Edith's voice was shaking. 'I gave everything for the Fatherland!'

'Not quite, not yet,' Ryder said. 'But you will very soon, I am sure. Mr Gallagher and his friends will see to that. Ladies and gentlemen, it is time to go.'

8.30 p.m.
Time.

Ryder backed towards the drawing room door, still covering the group with his gun. He stepped through into the hall, closing the door behind him. They heard him turn the key in the lock. A moment later the front door opened and closed. Gallagher turned off the electric lights and opened the drapes to look out into the park.

A monster was descending from the night sky. Six hundred feet long, its mighty hull several times the height of the house, thundering with engines, huge and bristling with menace, it swam down through the darkness and halted on the far side of the lake. The engine noise abated a little and the zeppelin sank down until the gondola slung beneath the hull was only about fifty feet above the ground. A powerful searchlight blazed out again, playing across the front of the house. Shading his eyes against the glare, Gallagher watched Ryder walk across the park towards the airship. A door in the side of the gondola opened and a man leaned out, unrolling a rope ladder and waving to Ryder. The captain raised his hand in salute and walked on.

Out of the sky another searchlight beam stabbed downwards: the second zeppelin, cruising on guard. The searchlight swept around the park, probing for an ambush. Gallagher thought of his own men waiting in the woods, and prayed that they would obey orders.

From nearby, someone shouted. Gallagher turned to see Tompkins the gamekeeper run out from behind the stables, shotgun in hand. '*Stop!*' Gallagher screamed, but if the keeper heard, he gave no sign. He raised his gun.

The bow of the gondola spat tongues of flame. Gallagher

heard a sound like a pneumatic drill, and the hard thud of bullets smacking into the stables. Tompkins dropped his shotgun and collapsed to the ground.

Another sound, a scream this time, and to Gallagher's horror Maisie ran out and stood over her grandfather's body. '*Burn, you bastards!*' she yelled at the zeppelin, and fired both barrels in quick succession, breaking open the breech to reload. Another series of flashes came from high overhead, sparkling and glittering where the second zeppelin cruised invisible. Bullets thudded into the earth around Maisie, kicking up fountains of mud and grass, and the girl fell beside Tompkins and did not move.

'Jesus Christ!' Gallagher shouted. He ran to the drawing room door and kicked it frantically, but the heavy oak did not budge. Running back to the window, he picked up the card table by its legs and swung it hard. The glass shattered. Gallagher climbed through the broken pane, ignoring the sounds of tearing cloth as glass splinters caught on his evening coat, and ran towards Tompkins and Maisie. The zeppelin lifted off, engines throbbing as it climbed up to meet its consort. By the time Gallagher reached the bodies both airships had disappeared into the night, rising away towards the east.

21

ALL WAS QUIET for a while, and then the cars began to arrive. Gallagher stood and watched them, his hands dark with blood, his mind numb.

A secret service officer approached him. 'We've taken Mrs Fairbairn and Mrs Price into custody, sir.'

'Good.' He heard his own voice speaking, but it sounded like it came from far away. 'Take them back to London and hold them securely.'

'Yes, sir.'

Both women would be interrogated, of course; probably not gently. Nathalie Fairbairn could probably bargain for her life. For Edith, there was no hope.

Someone else walked up, a square-built man in a long coat with a fedora hat tilted back on his head. 'Well?' said Joe Flynn. 'Did he get away?'

'He did.'

'Do you think it worked?'

'We'll know in a few days. If the Germans keep using the same ciphers, we're in the clear. If not, then I've just destroyed two years of hard work.'

Flynn nodded. 'Lansing keeps trying to leave. You'd better come and talk to him.' He glanced at Gallagher's hands. 'You might want to get cleaned up first.'

Gallagher sighed. 'Ask Mrs Vane to help you pacify Lansing. She won't like it, but she'll do it. I shall wash my hands and join you in a moment.'

Borden stood in the centre of the drawing room. He looked exhausted. 'Tompkins and Maisie,' he said. 'How bad is it?'

'I'm sorry,' Gallagher said quietly. 'Tompkins is dead. A bullet creased Maisie's skull and she is concussed, but she should make a full recovery in time.'

Borden bowed his head. 'The girl was lucky,' said Colson, not quite able to keep the tremor out of his voice. 'Of course, shooting downwards in the dark is never easy.'

Lansing and Makarian were there too, attended by Flynn and Mrs Vane. The latter wore a thick shawl over her shoulders. Lady Maud and Penelope had both been put to bed, the former with a sleeping draught.

A blanket had been hung over the broken window, but the cold wind still permeated the room, even though the fire had been heaped up high. Lansing had a fresh glass of whisky in his hand. 'Once again,' he said. 'What the hell is going on?'

Gallagher coughed, covering his mouth. There were still dried flecks of blood under his fingernails. 'Actually, this was quite a simple plot to expose a German agent,' he said. 'Unfortunately, three unexpected things complicated it, and very nearly derailed it. First, Paul Vasiliev turned out to be a Bolshevik, which we were not expecting. Second, Frank Warren was a loose cannon, which we should have expected. And third, Nick Makarian decided to play at politics, which was not unexpected but was certainly unhelpful.'

Makarian was silent. 'A wise man said something to me earlier this week,' Gallagher said. 'Ryder alluded to it, too. There are only two questions that matter right now: will America enter the war, and will Russia leave it? Everything that has happened in the past few days hinges on the answers to those two questions.'

'But it goes back further than this week, I think,' said Borden.

'Of course. This has been part of Germany's grand strategy all along: keep America neutral and knock Russia out of the war. To that end, Count von Bernstorff in America was directed to hold out the promise of peace negotiations to President Wilson, while at the same time supporting the Russian opposition to overthrow the Tsar. We knew Bernstorff was in contact with the Kadets in America. We didn't know until recently that he was also intriguing with Lenin's Bolsheviks.'

'I could have told you that,' said Makarian.

'Thank you, Nick. One day, we must have a conversation about why you didn't.'

Makarian fell silent again. 'Ryder established the Boston spy ring while he was posted in America, probably on Bernstorff's orders,' Gallagher said. 'When he returned to Britain he handed it over to Lily Sparrow, or Edith Price, or whatever we want to call her. After Lily fled to Britain, Ryder brought her back into the fold and helped her to recruit Price. I suspect that when we investigate, we will find that Ryder used his influence to get Price posted to the secretariat of the Board of the Admiralty, where he had access to useful information.'

'And the keys to the Admiralty boardroom,' Mrs Vane said.

'Why did Price betray his country?' Borden asked quietly.

Gallagher sighed. 'Take your pick. He was shell-shocked and badly injured, and he was bitter over the fact that he had not been recognized or rewarded for bringing his ship home from Jutland. Like Captain Ryder, he was looking for revenge. I suspect Edith didn't have to try very hard to recruit him.'

'But why did she marry him?' asked Colson.

'Because she was in love with him,' said Mrs Vane. 'They were obviously devoted to each other. Even spies and murderers have emotions, Commander.'

There was a moment of silence before Gallagher continued. 'The Dreamer had been suspicious for some time that we were intercepting German wireless transmissions. Thanks to the patronage of Admiral Jellicoe, Ryder was able to wangle a posting to the Admiralty for himself. He immediately started probing naval intelligence, and invented spurious orders from Jellicoe to investigate a security breach. As I said, the plot was simple. If we weren't able to intercept messages and break German codes, all was well. If we were, and thus had foreknowledge of the plots they were hatching in America and Russia, the Dreamer needed to let Berlin know so that they could change the codes.'

'So, we set a trap for him,' Mrs Vane said. 'I was sent into naval intelligence, with Admiral Hall's consent, to keep watch. When the telegram was intercepted, we planted a rumour about its existence and waited to see who would respond.'

Gallagher nodded. 'We knew that if the rumour was traced back to us, the Dreamer would smell a rat, so I asked Agent Flynn for help.'

Flynn nodded too. 'One of my freelancers dropped a hint that she knew about the telegram, and made sure it got to the right ears. Unfortunately she got killed a few days later. Too bad.'

'I'm sorry,' Gallagher said. 'I didn't know at the time that Willa Rittenhouse was one of yours. I wish you had told me.'

'We're the Secret Service,' Flynn said, his face registering no expression. 'If we tell people everything, we're no longer secret.'

'However, things then started to become complicated,' Mrs Vane said. 'Ryder sent Vasiliev into naval intelligence to find the telegram, but he didn't know that Vasiliev was a Bolshevik and was trying to steal the telegram for his own people. When he discovered this weekend who Vasiliev was really working for, he gave orders to have him killed.'

'Yes,' said Gallagher. 'Then came the second complication, when Vasiliev decided on his own initiative to hire Frank Warren to burgle the safe in naval intelligence. Warren was desperate for money, and tried to play off everyone involved in the plot against each other. The Dreamer realized that Warren was dangerous, and ordered the Prices to get rid of him. Price intercepted Warren, let them both into the boardroom using the keys he had stolen from Sir Graham Greene's desk, and took Warren through the old serving hatch and into the stationery cupboard, where he killed him. He emptied Warren's pockets to conceal his identity, then wedged the main door to the stationery cupboard from the inside, retreated into the boardroom, closed the serving hatch and pushed the sideboard in front of it and went out, locking the boardroom door behind him. On the Dreamer's orders, he left the telegram behind, partly as a way of muddying the waters.'

'The Dreamer didn't need to steal the telegram,' said Mrs Vane. 'He already knew its contents. He just needed to confirm that we had a copy. From there, his chief interest was in how we had acquired it and whether we could read it. That's all he needed to know.'

'And where do I come in?' Makarian asked.

'Your plan for an Armenian homeland was well meaning, but you also muddied the waters. By intriguing with the British government through Fairbairn, the Germans through Mr Lansing, and the Bolsheviks through Mrs Fairbairn all at the same time, you created a scene where everyone seemed to be scheming with everyone. You didn't just create one red herring; you released a bloody great shoal of them.'

Makarian started to speak, but Borden raised a hand. 'No, Nicholas,' he said. 'There will be time to discuss this later. Carry on, please, Pat.'

'After the discovery of Warren's body, Ryder realized that the secret service was on his trail,' Gallagher said. 'He activated his escape plan. We knew the Dreamer would be trying to get out of the country. His most likely method of escape was by air, and Hartlake Hall is close to the railway line that the zeppelins use to navigate their way to London. The nearby aerodrome had no machines capable of attacking the zeppelins, so a landing could be made safely. We used Sir John's good offices to arrange the shooting party. I already knew that he had invited Mr Lansing for the weekend, but I hadn't anticipated that Captain Ryder would ensure that the Prices and Vasiliev were invited as well. The subsequent mayhem was not part of the scheme.'

'Ryder was still trying to find the secret, right to the end,' Mrs Vane said. 'Still unaware of Vasiliev's real loyalties, Ryder ordered him to impersonate Charles Tovey, and arranged for Tovey to be killed. We suspect that when Tovey's murder is more fully investigated, we will find that Price killed him and disposed of his body. Vasiliev, as Tovey, then wrote to Sir John and asked for a meeting, while Price persuaded his father to get him an invitation to the shooting party. This is hypothesis, of course, but I'm sure it can be easily proved.'

'Wait a moment,' Borden said. 'Edith said she didn't know Ryder was the Dreamer. How did Ryder give orders to her and Price?'

'Edith told the truth about one thing,' Gallagher said. 'In London they used a series of message drops at West End theatres. We found a list of them in Edith's possession. Here at Hartlake Hall, they wrote coded messages in the book of music on the piano.' He paused for a moment, thinking. 'I suspect Edith was the one in contact with Germany.' he continued. 'She received the message about the throne of Saturn, indicating when the zeppelins would arrive. Once the meeting at Hartlake Hall was arranged, she presumably sent a message in reply, giving the location. We'll need to find out how she was communicating, but her interrogators will take care of that.'

There was a short silence. 'Warren's carelessness was Edith's undoing,' Gallagher went on. 'He found the decoded message and wrote the date on his shirt cuff, possibly because he was intending to escape too. She then wrote the same message in the music book for Ryder to see.'

'Wasn't that risky?' asked Colson. 'Anyone might have seen the messages.'

'Not if messages were rubbed out,' Gallagher said. 'And even if an outsider did spot the marks, they would assume someone was doodling, as Mr Lansing did. We owe you thanks, by the way, Mr Lansing. Had you not spotted those marks, we would not have known what to look for. But from that moment on, we knew the Dreamer was at Hartlake Hall.'

'But you failed, Gallagher,' Lansing said sharply. 'You lost. The Dreamer got away.'

'The Dreamer got away,' Gallagher repeated. 'And that was the plan all along.'

Silence fell in the room. 'You planned to let the most important German agent in Britain escape scot-free?' Makarian said finally.

'Yes,' said Gallagher. 'As we speak, the zeppelin carrying Captain Ryder is crossing the English Channel, on its way back to its base at Düsseldorf. By tomorrow Ryder will be in Berlin, reporting to the German high command that although we have a copy of Zimmerman's telegram, we cannot decipher it. He will also confirm that we are not able to read German wireless messages, meaning the Germans should feel safe to carry on using the same codes and ciphers.'

'So that telegram you showed me was a fake,' Lansing said. 'No,' said Gallagher. 'It was real.'

There was a moment of silence. 'Earlier, Sir John invoked the Official Secrets Act,' Gallagher said. 'It applies to everyone in this room, including you, Mr Lansing. The truth is that naval intelligence experts in an office called Room 40 have been intercepting and decoding virtually every wireless message the German army, navy and diplomatic service have sent since the beginning of the war. We know what their intentions are, often before their own commanders in the field know. That is why the secret of Room 40 has been so closely guarded. Commander Colson, your conduct has not been above reproach. But you have kept that secret closely and well, and you are to be commended for that.'

Colson looked down at his hands. His confidence was still in rags, Gallagher saw. *We will have to do something about that . . .*

'So what does this telegram actually say?' demanded Lansing.

Gallagher turned to Colson. 'Commander? Do I have your permission?'

Colson hesitated. 'This is important, sir,' Mrs Vane said. 'I will be answerable to Admiral Hall.'

'Do whatever you want,' Colson said heavily.

Mrs Vane drew another piece of paper from her reticule and handed it to Lansing. 'Read it aloud, please,' she said.

We intend to begin unrestricted submarine warfare on the first of February. We shall endeavour in spite of this to keep the United States of America neutral. In the event of this not suc‑ceeding, we make Mexico a proposal of alliance on the following basis: make war together, make peace together, generous financial support and an understanding on our part that Mexico is to reconquer the lost territory in Texas, New Mexico and Arizona. The settlement in detail is left to you. You will inform the President of Mexico of the above most secretly as soon as the outbreak of war with the United States of America is certain, and add the suggestion that he should, on his own initiative, invite Japan to immediate adherence and at the same time mediate between Japan and ourselves. Please call the president's attention to the fact that the ruthless employment of our submarines now offers the prospect of compelling England in a few months to make peace.

Zimmermann

The others waited. Lansing looked up. 'God Almighty,' he said, and his voice was almost soft. 'I've seen oil well blowouts that were less inflammatory than this. Germany, urging two foreign powers to attack us, to invade and conquer parts of the United States? This is a provocation to war.'

'If nothing else, America owes our codebreakers a great debt,' Borden said. 'The attacks from Mexico and Japan would have come out of the blue. You would have repelled the invaders, of course, but the damage from these surprise attacks would have been terrible. But now, Mr Lansing, you are forewarned. You can strengthen your borders and make it clear that you are ready to fight. Both nations will probably back down.'

Lansing looked at the telegram again. 'Mexico is no threat to us. Hell, the ranchers in Texas and Arizona probably have more and better guns than the entire Mexican army. But Japan, now. That's something else. You're right, Sir John, if they launched a surprise attack on Hawai'i, or California . . . God damn it. I just want to know if this is real, and not something cooked up by your intelligence people.'

'It is real,' Gallagher said. 'We'll provide evidence, never fear.'

'What if I don't believe the evidence? What if I decide to ignore this?'

'If you do, in a few days' time we will release the text of the telegram to the American newspapers. The result will be a firestorm of outrage and anti-German sentiment, more powerful even than the one that followed the sinking of the *Lusitania*, and President Wilson will be unable to resist going to war. You will gain nothing. On the other hand, if you give this telegram to the president and advise him it is genuine, we will look kindly on your request for the oil concessions. Some of them, anyway. I reckon you and Anglo-Persian can learn to get along.'

Lansing and Colson stared at each other. Neither looked happy. 'All right,' Lansing said abruptly. 'I need time to think. I'll let you know my decision in the morning.'

He drained his glass and walked out of the room. Some of the tension in the atmosphere went with him. Borden closed his eyes for a moment, rubbing his temples. Colson looked at Gallagher, his gaze both curious and nervous. 'When did you realize it was Ryder and not me?' he asked.

The sudden release of tension scratched at Gallagher's throat, and he coughed. 'Ryder gave himself away on Saturday night, actually. He told me that his secret investigation into the naval intelligence division had been ordered by Admiral Jellicoe. I knew that was untrue.'

Borden opened his eyes again. 'How did you know?'

'Ryder was quite correct that Jellicoe was unhappy about the failure of intelligence at Jutland, and he had ordered an investigation, but not by the Admiralty. He contacted Colonel Kell at the secret service and asked for my services. I have been reporting to his lordship for the past three months.'

'And I knew nothing about it,' Colson said. The lack of trust was bitter in his throat. 'Why did he ask for you especially?'

Gallagher thought about Peitsang and the Chinese shrapnel humming around him, and Jellicoe's blood on his coat. He heard again the medic's voice, *You needn't have bothered, mate . . .*

'It's a long story,' he said.

Silence fell again. 'Do you think Lansing will give the telegram to President Wilson?' asked Makarian.

'He will,' Gallagher said. 'For one thing, he knows that *we* know about his deal with Germany. If America does go to war and we leak word of it to the American newspapers – which we absolutely would do – Lansing will become, as the Americans say, public enemy number one. For his own self-preservation, he will go along with us.'

'Which is a pity, on one level,' said Mrs Vane. 'I'm not sure I approve of Mr Lansing being preserved.'

'So,' Borden said. 'We've won.'

'Have we?' said Gallagher. He looked around the little group. 'Oh, we'll win the war, now. The Americans will come in numbers, and even if Russia collapses, we'll have enough strength to beat Germany down. We can break the German Empire to our will. But in the end, what will we have gained, do you think? When the day of victory comes, what will we really have won?'

22

Delighted by the success of the Dreamer operation and the arrest of two dangerous agents, Colonel Kell had dug into the secret service purse and dispatched a car to bring Gallagher and Mrs Vane back to London. It waited outside now, next to Commander Colson's Rolls-Royce. Lansing had departed early, taking a carriage to the railway station. He had, he said, urgent business in London.

The farewells did not take long. Penelope, one ear full of cotton wool, put her arm around Gallagher's neck. 'Look after yourself,' she said.

'You too,' Gallagher said. 'Will you carry on with the Red Cross?'

She glanced at her father. '*Of course,*' she murmured behind her hand. 'It's the least I can do. I'll be watching my fellow volunteers a little more carefully, though. My goodness, Edith of all people!'

'Trust your friends,' Gallagher said. 'Leave *dis*trusting people to me. It's my job.'

She laughed and kissed his cheek. Makarian shook his hand. 'This episode has made me reassess myself,' he said, and he sounded almost subdued. 'I am cutting my ties with Lansing. And I shall stop dabbling in politics and stick to commerce.'

'Don't give up on your dream, Nick.'

'Never. But no more Faustian bargains.'

Borden stood by the foot of the stairs. Gallagher glanced upwards. 'Is Mother awake?'

'She is, but she is still in bed.'

'Will she see me?'

'Of course.'

Gallagher hesitated. 'I am so sorry about Tompkins,' he said.

'So am I.' Borden's face showed his pain. 'You mustn't worry about Maisie. We will take care of her.'

'I know you will.'

Borden nodded again. Gallagher drew a deep breath and started up the stairs.

His mother was propped up against the pillows of her big bed, a plain woollen bedjacket draped over her shoulders. A breakfast tray was placed on a side table. She had taken a cup of tea, but had not touched her food. 'You have come to say farewell,' she said.

'I have. And also to apologize for everything. I know how painful this weekend has been for you.'

'As I understand it, you were doing your duty,' Lady Maud said. 'There is, therefore, no need to apologize.'

Silence fell. Gallagher stood looking down at the bed. 'I don't want to end like this,' he said.

'What are you hoping for, Patrick? Some sort of resolution?'

'No. Acknowledgement, perhaps. Of who I am, and where I come from.'

'I have always been aware of who you are,' his mother said. 'That has never been in doubt.'

'Is there anything that can be done? Anything that can break down this wall between us?'

'Why do you want to break it down?' asked Lady Maud. 'Why, after all of this time, does it suddenly matter?'

Silence. Gallagher became aware of how tired he was. 'Farewell, Mother,' he said finally, and he bent to kiss her cheek, but saw how she drew back from him. He nodded a little, straightened, and left the room.

Back downstairs, Borden waited alone in the hall. 'Mrs Vane is in the car,' he said. 'I'd like a quick word with you before you go.'

'What about?'

'That letter from Churchill. What are you going to do with it?'

Gallagher sighed. 'Nothing,' he said. 'The moment has passed.'

'The moment?'

'Let me set your mind at rest,' Gallagher said. 'I do not believe that Churchill directed the sinking of the *Lusitania* or even expressed a wish that she should sink, but I would very much like to know why that letter ended up in the hands of a German agent. However, as I say, the moment has passed. America is about to enter the war, and I must do nothing to upset the balance. If I start to investigate further, and if Lansing and his friends should hear even a rumour that Britain might have somehow had a hand in the loss of the *Lusitania*, all trust between our two nations would be shattered. The Americans would remain neutral, and we would lose the war.'

'But you will never know the answer to your question,' Borden said seriously.

'It happens in intelligence work,' Gallagher said. 'We're not Sherlock Holmes. We don't solve every case.' He held out his hand. 'Goodbye, John. Thank you for everything.'

GALLAGHER STEPPED INTO the back seat of the waiting car and sat down beside Mrs Vane. The driver closed the door and took his seat behind the wheel, and started the engine. The car purred slowly through the woods, past the gamekeeper's cottage silent and dark, and the lodge where the secret service men were packing up to depart. They saluted Gallagher as the car passed.

They drove through Tonbridge and over the Medway, crossing the damp meadows beyond. The car's engine took on a deeper note as it began to climb up over the South Downs towards Sevenoaks. 'We did it,' Mrs Vane said finally.

'We think we did it. We won't know for certain for a couple of days.'

'I am sorry about Mr Fairbairn. Of all the people who died, he is the one who feels the most like a victim.'

'He tried to do the right thing by everyone else,' Gallagher said. 'But in the end, he forgot to do the right thing by himself. That seldom ends well.'

'You are speaking from experience,' she said. It was a statement, not a question.

You are too kind, Roxanne had said to him once. *You want to help all the lame ducks, stand up for the waifs and strays, like me. That will only bring you hurt.*

I don't mind being hurt, he had replied. *Not if I am fighting for a good cause.*

She had shaken her head. *There is enough hurt in the world already, Pat. Don't go looking for more. Take care of yourself first.*

It was good advice, he knew. He realized he ought to get around to taking it one day.

Beside him, Mrs Vane spoke again. 'I joined the service because I hoped it would take me out of myself,' she said reflectively. 'It did, for a while. So long as the case lasted I had something to distract me, something to concentrate on. Something to live for, if that is not too dramatic.'

'And now that it is over, what do you feel?' Gallagher asked.

'I feel . . . empty. I thought I would experience a sense of relief, even elation, but all I have is a terrible sense of let-down. Like it is all over, and I have nothing left to do.'

'That often happens at the end of a case,' Gallagher said. 'You ride the tension, living on your nerves, until you reach a resolution. Then comes the reaction. All you can do is wait it out, and hope another case comes along soon.'

'You've been through this,' Mrs Vane said after a moment. 'When does it end? The deadness inside, this sensation that the world is dark, and it will never be light again. The line of empty days stretching out in front of me, like a high road to nowhere. When does that feeling go away?'

'When it does, I will let you know,' Gallagher said.

The car purred on. Leafless trees waved like skeletons beside the road. Spring would come again, but at the moment it seemed very far away.

> The moving finger writes; and, having writ,
> Moves on: nor all thy piety nor wit
> Shall lure it back to cancel half a line,
> Nor all thy tears wash out a word of it.

Historical Note

ONE OF THE best kept secrets of the First World War was Room 40, the codebreaking operation run by British naval intelligence in the heart of the Admiralty building in Whitehall. Outside of the intelligence division, only a few very senior navy officers were aware of its existence.

Within a few days of the outbreak of war, the British had cut the underwater telegraph cables connecting Germany with its overseas embassies, forcing the German government to rely on wireless signals. These could be intercepted, as could communications between Germany naval headquarters and ships at sea, but the Germans had developed very sophisticated ciphers which were widely considered to be unbreakable. Even Winston Churchill, then First Lord of the Admiralty (the civilian head of the navy, as opposed to the First Sea Lord, who was a serving navy officer), doubted if the ciphers could ever be broken.

However, thanks to a combination of good luck – several German codebooks were captured early in the war – and hard work by a dedicated team of amateur codebreakers, the ciphers were broken. From then until the end of the war, the codebreakers in the office known as Room 40 were able to intercept and read virtually every wireless message sent from and to the German government and high command. But the naval intelligence officers faced the same dilemma as their later counterparts at Bletchley Park in the Second World War: if they revealed all of the information they received, the German government would realize that telegrams were being intercepted and change the codes. A priceless source of intelligence would be lost.

To protect their source, therefore, Room 40 sometimes held back information from the rest of the navy and the British government. The two examples we cited here – the failure to warn about German submarines in the *Lusitania*'s path, and the delay in informing Admiral Jellicoe that the German fleet was at sea, leading to a missed opportunity to trap the entire German fleet and destroy it – were almost certainly not caused by deliberate withholding; both are more likely to have been mistakes or miscommunication. But they contributed to a suspicion in the rest of the Admiralty that naval intelligence was holding back vitally needed information. Jellicoe in particular was openly critical of naval intelligence after the battle of Jutland, and is said to have lost faith in the division's abilities.

THE YEAR 1917

At the outset of 1917, the prospects for the allied powers looked bleak. Both France and Britain had suffered appalling casualties the previous year during the battles of Verdun and the Somme. The French army was on the point of collapse, and in April 1917, elements of forty-nine French divisions mutinied or refused orders to attack German positions. Britain was running out of money. At the end of January, the German government declared the resumption of unrestricted submarine warfare – suspended after the sinking of the *Lusitania* in 1915 – promising to sink all ships carrying supplies to British ports and raising the spectre of starvation.

For Britain, much depended on those key questions, whether Russia would collapse and whether America would abandon its neutrality and enter the war. The German government was quite aware of this, and did its best to influence events in its favour. Especially after the death of Rasputin, the Russian people lost confidence in Tsar Nicholas II, who was forced to abdicate six weeks after the events of this book. Power passed into the hands of the Constitutional Democrats (Kadets) and their allies, but they were weak and disunited. (One of the leaders of the Kadets, Vladimir Dmitrievich Nabokov, was the father of the later novelist, Vladimir Nabokov.) The German government offered the Bolshevik leader Vladimir Ilyich Lenin free passage to Russia from his place of exile in Switzerland, the equivalent of tossing a hand grenade into the room. In Russia, the centre could not hold, and in November 1917 Lenin seized power and took Russia out of the war, freeing up approximately fifty German divisions to reinforce the Western Front. The next step was to attempt to force America to remain neutral.

THE ZIMMERMANN TELEGRAM

On the 17 January 1917 the codebreakers at Room 40 received a wireless intercept of a telegram from Arthur Zimmermann, the German foreign minister in Berlin, to Heinrich von Eckhardt, German ambassador in Mexico. (The telegram was actually sent to Johann von Bernstorff, the ambassador in the United States, who believed he had a secure wireless signal that the British could not intercept; Bernstorff was asked to relay the signal to Eckhardt.)

Even before they had finished decoding the message, the codebreakers realized the telegram was political dynamite. Eckhardt was instructed to urge the Mexican government to attack the United States should the latter take steps towards going to war with Germany. The German government would provide full assistance, and Zimmermann also urged the Mexicans to form an alliance with Japan.

This was not necessarily a bad idea, provided it could be kept secret. A surprise attack by Mexico on America's southern border would distract the Americans and prevent them from lending full assistance to Britain and France. If Japan – rapidly emerging as America's chief rival for influence in the Pacific – could be persuaded to join in, so much the better. However, Zimmermann's gamble failed on three counts. First, the Mexican army knew it could never stand up to the much better armed Americans, and categorically refused to take action. Second, despite a lot of secret German lobbying, the Japanese government showed no interest (Japan was nominally on the Allied side during the First World War but played only a limited role; the German government tried several times to persuade Japan to switch sides). And third, the interception of the telegram at Room 40 meant that the element of surprise had been lost.

The head of naval intelligence, Rear-Admiral William Hall – known in the navy as Blinker – now faced a dilemma. Making the telegram public would lead to outrage in America and would probably lead to America declaring war on Germany. However, the Germans would also know that Room 40 was breaking German codes. Hall agonized for some time before finally coming up with a plan. The telegram was shown secretly to senior American diplomats, while a cover story was concocted claiming that the telegram had been stolen from the central telegraph office in Mexico City. President Wilson of the USA was informed of the contents of the telegraph, but continued to believe that he could negotiate a peace between Germany and the Allies. Eventually the telegram was leaked to the American newspapers, and the resulting wave of public outrage forced Wilson to back down and declare war.

Astonishingly, while the German government did suspect that its codes were being broken, it did nothing about this. Zimmermann even sent a second telegram a month or so later, warning that the diplomatic code might have been broken, but he sent it in the same code as the original telegram!

Inadvertently, Zimmermann's telegram changed the course of the war. Despite Russia's collapse, the American infusion of manpower, weapons and money was enough to ultimately break the German army. In November 1918, twenty-one months after the telegram was sent, German and Allied negotiators met near Compiègne to sign an armistice, bringing the war to an end.

PAUL RAMSAY'S BOOK *Before Bletchley Park: the Codebreakers of the First World War* devotes a good deal of time to the interception and decoding of the Zimmermann telegram, as does David Ramsay's biography of Admiral Hall, *'Blinker' Hall: Spymaster*. Barbara Tuchman's *The Zimmermann Telegram* was the first book to treat the subject in detail; the work is older and some details are out of date, but the book is highly readable and a good introduction to the subject. A view of espionage from the other side can be found in *The Dark Invader*, the autobiography of Captain Franz von Rintelen, the German naval intelligence officer who appears in Chapter 14. Rintelen is a highly unreliable narrator, but the book gives a perspective that we don't always see.

Jutland: The Unfinished Battle by Nick Jellicoe – grandson of Admiral Jellicoe – gives a useful account of the bitter infighting within the Royal Navy including the run-up to the battle, while Catherine Merridale's *Lenin on the Train* details the political machinations in the run-up to Lenin's return to Russia and the downfall of Tsar Nicholas II. This was a bleak time in European history, and our own book perhaps mirrors some of that bleakness; that, and the darkness in our own souls as we planned this work. To paraphrase the *Rubaiyat of Omar Khayyam*, no amount of tears can wash out the words.

Acknowledgements

Particular thanks must go to Alex Saunders, publishing director at Pan Macmillan, who saw the potential for this series and was a huge support during the writing of both this book and its predecessor. Alex, you have been a great source of ideas and a tower of strength, and we shall miss you.

Thanks too to Jon Wood, our agent at RCW, who has believed in us from the beginning and offered his own wisdom and experience. These books would not have been written without you.

At Pan Macmillan we were able to get the band back together, and as well as Alex it was a real pleasure to work again with editorial manager Rebecca Needes, as patient and good-humoured as ever, and copy-editor Fraser Crichton, whose detailed knowledge of the geography of Glasgow and ability to distinguish Schumann from Schubert saved us from a couple of egregious errors. Another fabulous cover illustration was again provided by James Weston Lewis and Kieryn Tyler has once again done a great job on cover design. Thanks also to Lorraine Green for her diligent proofreading. Of course, any errors that remain are our responsibility.

Further thanks go to Simon Robinson, who checked the details of the shooting chapter, and the Leigh and District Historical Society, which long ago commissioned Morgen to write a history of the parish during the Second World War which led to a further interest in the airfield at Chiddingstone Causeway. Thanks too to old friends from West Kent, where we lived for twelve years, who taught us so much about the area and its landscape and history.

RLG, 23 February 2025

DEATH ON THE LUSITANIA

**Discover the immersive WWI historical
novel set aboard the ill-fated ocean liner.**

Welcome on board the **Lusitania***'s final voyage* . . .

New York, 1915. RMS *Lusitania*, one of the world's most
luxurious ocean liners, departs for war-torn Europe. Among
those on board is Patrick Gallagher, a civil servant in His
Majesty's government tasked with escorting a British
diplomat back to England.

When a fellow passenger is believed to have shot himself in
his cabin, Gallagher is asked by the captain to investigate
the scene – but one crucial detail doesn't fit. The man's
body was discovered in a locked cabin with the key inside
and no gun to be found. Was it really suicide? Or murder?

Gallagher believes one of the passengers is a deadly
killer – one who could strike again at any moment. And all
the while, the ship sails on towards Europe, where enemy
submarines patrol dark waters . . .

OUT NOW